Other Sides of Silence

Other Sides
of
Silence

NEW FICTION FROM
PLOUGHSHARES

Edited by DeWitt Henry

Faber and Faber

BOSTON · LONDON

Published in the United States by Faber and Faber, Inc.,
50 Cross Street, Winchester, MA 01890.

A CIP record for this book is available from the Library of Congress.

ISBN 0-571-19811-2

Cover design by Julie Ann Markfield

Printed in the United States of America

Contents

Acknowledgments

The following works are reprinted by permission of the publishers and authors.

"Rose" © 1986 by Andre Dubus. Reprinted from *Last Worthless Evening* by Andre Dubus. Published by David R. Godine, Publisher. English edition published by Picador.

"In a Father's Place" © 1990 by Christopher Tilghman. Reprinted from *In a Father's Place* by Christopher Tilghman. Published by Farrar, Straus & Giroux.

"The History of Rodney" © 1989 by Rick Bass.

"The Palace" © 1988 by Maura Stanton. Reprinted from *The Country I Come From* by Maura Stanton. Published by Milkweed Editions.

"The Body Politic" © 1992 by Theodore Weesner. Reprinted from *Children's Hearts* by Theodore Weesner. Published by Summit Books.

"The Time-to-Teach-Jane-Eyre-Again Blues" © 1987 by Linda Bamber.

"Displacement" © 1991 by David Wong Louie. Reprinted from *Pangs of Love* by David Wong Louie. Published by Alfred A. Knopf, Inc.

"What Happened to Red Deer" © 1990 by Wayne Johnson. Reprinted from *The Snake Game* by Wayne Johnson. Published by Alfred A. Knopf, Inc.

Introduction

ORIGINALLY the editorial idea of *Ploughshares,* in practice now for two decades, was to explore and encourage the diverse directions of a new literary generation. The founding editors were poets and fiction writers with significantly varying literary backgrounds, aspirations, and viewpoints; their differences resulted in spirited disagreements, which, to the positive, voiced a shared passion about writing and reading. We hoped in some way with *Ploughshares,* editorially, to dramatize that collective passion and to awaken and encourage a kindred passion in our readers.

From our beginning, then, in 1971, we had a different writer edit each issue and sought to counterpoint tastes and interests in a lively, ongoing discussion concerning "what mattered" in contemporary writing.

This is our third book-length retrospective so far, drawing short fiction, in this case, from fourteen issues published since 1984, and celebrating the achievement of their coordinating editors, each with his or her own editorial vision.

Justin Kaplan and Anne Bernays, for instance, co-edited a special issue where they explored "the interrelationship or overlap of autobiography, biography, and fiction," and asked contributors to "think of the three genres as forming a triangle," with the work being sought falling within its area. Ethan Canin's "Pitch Memory" and Marjorie Waters's "Still Life" are reprinted from their issue.

Leonard Michaels entitled his issue *What's a Story,* and focused on "the transformational drama" of metaphor as the essence of stories; "the best story I know that contains all I've been trying to say," Michaels wrote, referring to selections in his issue that ranged from traditional fiction to scholarly essays, "is Kafka's: 'A cage went in search of a bird.' " Phillip Lopate's "Against Joie de Vivre" and Sue Miller's "What Ernest Says" were two of his most controversial selections.

James Alan McPherson, in correspondence with me as we co-edited what we came to think of as our "maximalism" issue in 1985, wrote: "I have to confront the influence of minimalist fiction in my classes at Iowa . . ̇. this fiction deemphasizes character and emotional depth and gives the reader only a transitory mood. My bias is towards 'traditional' fiction . . . but the problem, it seems to me, is larger than its expression in contemporary fiction. There is such a deep current of personal frustration in the country, such deep frustrations, that minimalist writers can justify not touching deep emotions. People are willing to identify with the generalized tension that is undefined. This is a dangerous mood—the stylization of tension—because it confirms for readers things that remain undefined." From that issue Andre Dubus's long story, "Rose," written in creative response to Conrad's "Heart of Darkness," set our standard; also from the issue, I include here stories by Gina Berriault, Maura Stanton, and Tess Gallagher.

Madeline DeFrees and Tess Gallagher wrote of Ann Beattie's "Honey" and other fiction in their issue that "there will be an instant of recognition when the reader sees him- or herself given back by the mirror that alternately comforts and warns."

Maxine Kumin wrote that "I like fiction that has the thickness of authenticity to it. I want to experience a frisson of identification with characters who are to some degree obsessed." She commented on Joyce Carol Oates's "Geese" that "we have all stood at lakeside feeding these tame creatures, but this time, the atmosphere is suffused with violence."

George Garret set out to edit a *Fiction Discoveries* issue by inviting established writers to nominate some new writers and to introduce their stories with brief notes. Garrett observes: "Note how the women, writing in several kinds of voices, are writing with grace and ease and a new kind of candor about the deeper feelings of sexuality, of pregnancy, of love and birth and death . . . our writing has finally begun to reflect and represent the wide diversity of American society . . . we are in the midst of an explosion of ethnic American literature . . . these beginning writers . . . are free and open to all kinds of methods, really to all the ways of telling stories and to every kind of story we know about." David Wong Louie's "Displacement" is reprinted from this issue.

James Carroll edited an issue on *The Virtue of Writing* and contributed an important essay of that title as his introduction, where he argued that the very material of fiction forces us "to face the question of moral meaning," yet warns, when it comes to judging fiction, "Whose virtue? Whose morality? Whose notions both of good behavior and of the ultimate human good? The Pope's? The Ayatollah's? Oliver North's? Ian Paisley's?" He went on: "The ploughshare is the sharpened blade of the plow, the thing that cuts the furrow. But it is also, in our culture, a moral symbol. The founders of this magazine made a moral and a political statement when they chose its name, and it is that aspect of the meaning of *Ploughshares* that this issue emphasizes. It is dedicated to the idea that writing is a morally serious enterprise; and more than that, that fiction inevitably involves us in a mode of thinking which is, at its core, thinking about morality. In an age where every other mode of thinking about morality is debased, this characteristic of fiction is its great virtue. . . . Fiction writers live in the realm of what is wrong with the world—with their own worlds—not what is right with it. . . . There is never a moral failing of which they accuse others that they have not first—because this is way the invention of fiction works—accused themselves. . . . Their work is nothing but cutting through the surface, as with that ploughshare, then going down." Stories by Christopher Tilghman and Theodore Weesner are reprinted here from Carroll's issue.

With the help of Associate Fiction Editor Don Lee, I was privileged to co-edit with James Alan McPherson again an issue on *Confronting Racial Difference,* where the challenge was for writers of different ethnic backgrounds to pay mutual regard. McPherson wrote in the issue: "There is much work that all Americans have to do to revitalize our country's spiritual life, to reclaim from the clutches of the domain of law those heartfelt assumptions that are our own. But there is a tremendous amount of work that African Americans have to do to reclaim, perhaps for the entire society, the momentum of the movement toward greater spiritual civility that was the lifework of Dr. Martin King." My own hope, for confronting both my own racism and that of my society, lay partly in the "true teaching" of such fictions as Carol

Roh-Spaulding's, Louis Berney's, and Alberto Alvaro Ríos's, included here from that issue.

Most recently, in introducing the fiction in our *Twentieth Anniversary Issue,* I wrote of "affirmations in the irreal." I found, rather than sought, stories in which the realities brought to mind were discomfiting and "irreal." In some there would be a longing for normality, with normality conceived of as the functional family, say, then despaired of like paradise lost, with wit, with anger, with bafflement, with regret. Other stories, however, passed from longing into deeper human recognitions, where the source of affirmation was, in words attributed to Mark Van Doren, "the courage to go to the depths of yourself and tell your story." From this issue, I include here Joy Williams's "Craving."

In making these selections for this particular occasion, I am choosing among many possible "bests," but I have attempted both to follow the tradition of tastes and standards described above, and to present a collection with its own integrity. I have also tried to include as many writers as possible who were not represented in the earlier *Ploughshares Reader* (in fact, Dubus, Berriault, Dybek, and Miller proved irresistible, regardless). I am pleased to note that since originally appearing in *Ploughshares,* many of these "bests" have already been reprinted in the annual prize collections as well as in collections or a novel by the author: Tilghman, Dubus, Gallagher, Oates, Beattie, Miller, Johnson, Lopate, Canin, Louie, Bass, Roh-Spaulding, Berney, so far, and may the other be so blessed in the near future. I have included outstanding long stories, as well as stories that reflect our consistent interest in ethnicity, pluralism, and moral and social conscience. I have included stories, such as Lopate's, Bamber's and Waters's, that challenge our ordinary definitions of story.

I offer these "bests" as writing that attempts to confront contemporary experience at the deepest levels. Also as stories that attain definitiveness, that make some final say about something that matters. I take George Eliot's phrase as the title for this collection, and for my epigraph the famous passage in *Middlemarch* from which it comes: "If we had keen vision and feeling of all ordinary human life, it would be like hearing the grass grow and the squirrel's heart beat, and we should die of the roar which lies on the other side of silence." These are writers with keen vision and feeling as well as the strength of mind and spirit to confront the "other side of silence." My joy in these stories is in their appetite for life, and in the variety of subject, theme, setting, style, culture: the sense of open doors, of sudden new departures, the principle of life as renewal, resilience, as surprise, always unsettling, always wonderful.

I also celebrate the sheer glory, fluency, and vigor of the short story form, very likely to prove to be the medium of choice and genius during these closing years of the century. To the question whether there is a masterpiece of our times, an age-shaping and reflecting canon of a master artist, I would probably answer no, so far, but contrary to conservative observers such as John W. Aldridge (see his essay on contemporary fiction, "The New American Assembly-Line Fiction"), I do see in the aggregate, in the work I read as an editor, and I hope in the wholeness of the work presented here, a claim for our times to pride and greatness.

We are partners, I believe, in the making of a literature. Writers, editors, and readers. I hope that spirit pervades in these pages.

DeWitt Henry

Other Sides of Silence

Rose

Andre Dubus

In memory of Barbara Loden

SOMETIMES, WHEN I see people like Rose, I imagine them as babies, as young children. I suppose many of us do. We search the aging skin of the face, the unhappy eyes and mouth. Of course I can never imagine their fat little faces at the breast, or their cheeks flushed and eyes brightened from play. I do not think of them beyond the age of five or six, when they are sent to kindergartens, to school. There, beyond the shadows of their families and neighborhood friends, they enter the world a second time, their eyes blinking in the light of it. They will be loved or liked or disliked, even hated; some will be ignored, others singled out for daily abuse that, with a few adult exceptions, only children have the energy and heart to inflict. Some will be corrupted, many without knowing it, save for that cooling quiver of conscience when they cheat, when they lie to save themselves, when out of fear they side with bullies or teachers, and so forsake loyalty to a friend. Soon they are small men and women, with adult sins and virtues, and by the age of thirteen some have our vices too.

There are also those unforgivable children who never suffer at all: from the first grade on, they are good at schoolwork, at play and sports, and always they are befriended, and are the leaders of the class. Their teachers love them, and because they are humble and warm, their classmates love them too, or at least respect them, and are not envious because they assume these children will excel at whatever they

3

touch, and have long accepted this truth. They come from all manner of families, from poor and illiterate to wealthy and what passes for literate in America, and no one knows why they are not only athletic and attractive but intelligent too. This is an injustice, and some of us pause for a few moments in our middle-aged lives to remember the pain of childhood, and then we intensely dislike these people we applauded and courted, and we hope some crack of mediocrity we could not see with our young eyes has widened and split open their lives, the homecoming queen's radiance sallowed by tranquilized bitterness, the quarterback fat at forty wheezing up a flight of stairs, and all of them living in the same small town or city neighborhood, laboring at vacuous work that turns their memories to those halcyon days when the classrooms and halls, the playgrounds and gymnasiums and dance floors were theirs: the last places that so obediently, even lovingly, welcomed the weight of their flesh, and its displacement of air. Then, with a smile, we rid ourselves of that evil wish, let it pass from our bodies to dissipate like smoke in the air around us, and freed from the distraction of blaming some classmate's excellence for our childhood pain, we focus on the boy or girl we were, the small body we occupied, watch it growing through the summers and school years, and we see that, save for some strength gained here, some weaknesses there, we are the same person we first knew as ourselves; or the one memory allows us to see, to think we know.

People like Rose make me imagine them in those few years their memories will never disclose, except through hearsay: *I was born in Austin. We lived in a garage apartment. When I was two we moved to Tuscaloosa* . . . Sometimes when she is drinking at the bar, and I am standing some distance from her and watch without her noticing, I see her as a baby, on the second or third floor of a tenement, in one of the Massachusetts towns along the Merrimack River. She would not notice, even if she turned and looked at my face; she would know me, she would speak to me, but she would not know I had been watching. Her face, sober or drunk or on the way to it, looks constantly watched, even spoken to, by her own soul. Or by something it has spawned, something that lives always with her, hovering near her face. I see her in a tenement because I cannot imagine her coming from any but a poor family, though I sense this notion comes from my boyhood, from something I learned about America, and that belief has hardened inside me, a stone I cannot dissolve. Snobbishness is too simple a word for it. I have never had much money. Nor do I want it. No: it's an old belief, once a philosophy which I've now outgrown: no one born to a white family with adequate money could end as Rose has.

I know it's not true. I am fifty-one years old, yet I cannot feel I am growing older because I keep repeating the awakening experiences of a child: I watch and I listen, I write in my journal, and each year I discover, with the awe of my boyhood, a part of the human spirit I had perhaps imagined, but had never seen nor heard. When I was a boy, many of these discoveries thrilled me. Once in school the teacher told us of the men who volunteered to help find the cause of yellow fever. This was in the Panama Canal Zone. Some of these men lived in the room where victims of yellow fever had died; they lay on the beds, on sheets with dried black vomit, breathed and slept there. Others sat in a room with mosquitoes and gave their skin to those bites we simply curse and slap, and they waited through the itching and more bites, and then waited to die, in their agony leaving sheets like the ones that spared their comrades living in the room of the dead. This story, with its heroism, its infinite possibilities for human action, delighted me with the pure music of hope. I am afraid now to research it, for I may find that the men were convicts awaiting execution, or some other persons whose lives were so limited by stronger outside forces, that the risk of death to save others could not have, for them, the clarity of a choice made with courage, and in sacrifice, but could be only a weary nod of assent to yet another fated occurrence in their lives. But their story cheered me then, and I shall cling to that. Don't you remember? When first you saw or heard or read about men and women who, in the face of some defiant circumstance, fought against themselves and won, and so achieved love, honor, courage?

I was in the Marine Corps for three years, a lieutenant during a time in our country when there was no war but all the healthy young men had to serve in the armed forces anyway. Many of us, who went to college, sought commissions so our service would be easier, we would have more money, and we could marry our girlfriends; in those days, a young man had to provide a roof and all that goes under it before he could make love with his girl; of course there was lovemaking in cars, but the ring and the roof waited somewhere beyond the windshield.

Those of us who chose the Marines went to Quantico, Virginia, for two six-week training sessions in separate summers during college; we were commissioned at graduation from college, and went back to Quantico for eight months of Officers' Basic School; only then would they set us free among the troops, and into the wise care of our platoon sergeants. During the summer training, which was called Platoon Leaders' Class, sergeants led us, harrassed us, and taught us. They also tried to make some of us quit. I'm certain that when they first lined us up and looked at us, their professional eyes saw the ones who would not complete the course: saw in a young boy's stiffened shoulders and staring and blinking eyes the flaw—too much fear, lack of confidence, who knows—that would, in a few weeks, possess him. Just as, on the first day of school, the bully sees his victim and eyes him like a cat whose prey has wandered too far from safety; it is not the boy's puny body that draws the bully, but the way the boy's spirit occupies his small chest, his thin arms.

Soon the sergeants left alone the stronger among us, and focused their energy on breaking the ones they believed would break, and ought to break now, rather than later, in that future war they probably did not want but never forgot. In another platoon, that first summer, a boy from Dartmouth completed the course, though in six weeks his crew-cut black hair turned grey. The boy in our platoon was from the University of Chicago, and he should not have come to Quantico. He was physically weak. The sergeants liked the smaller among us, those with short lean bodies. They called them feather merchants, told them You little guys are always tough, and issued them the Browning Automatic Rifle for marches and field exercises, because it weighed twenty pounds and had a cumbersome bulk to it as well: there was no way you could comfortably carry it. But the boy from Chicago was short and thin and weak, and they despised him. Our platoon sergeant was a staff sergeant, his assistant a buck sergeant, and from the first day they worked on making the boy quit. We all knew he would fail the course; we waited only to see whether he would quit and go home before they sent him. He did not quit. He endured five weeks before the company commander summoned him to his office; he was not there long; he came into the squad bay where we lived and changed to civilian clothes, packed the suitcase and seabag, and was gone. In those five weeks he had dropped out of conditioning marches, forcing himself up hills in the Virginia heat, carrying seventy pounds of gear—probably half his weight—until he collapsed on the trail to the sound of shouted derision from our sergeants, whom I doubt he heard.

When he came to Quantico he could not chin himself, nor do ten push-ups. By the time he left he could chin himself five quivering times, his back and shoulders jerking, and he could do twenty push-ups before his shoulders and chest rose while his small flat belly stayed on the ground. I do not remember his name, but I remember those numbers: five and twenty. The sergeants humiliated him daily, gave him long and colorful ass-chewings, but their true weapon was his own body, and they put it to use. They ran him till he fell, then ran him again: a sergeant running alongside the boy, around and around the hot blacktop parade ground. They sent him up and down the rope on the obstacle course. He never climbed it, but they sent him as far up as he could go, perhaps halfway, perhaps less, and when he froze then worked his way down, they sent him up again. That's the phrase: *as far up as he could go.*

He should not have come to Virginia. What was he thinking? Why didn't he get himself in shape during the school year, while he waited in Chicago for what he must have known would be the physical trial of his life? I understand now why the sergeants despised him, this weak college boy who wanted to be one of their officers. Most nights they went out drinking, and once or twice a week came into our squad bay, drunk at three in the morning, to turn on the lights, shout us out of our bunks, and we stood at attention and listened to their cheerful abuse. Three hours later, when we fell out for morning chow, they waited for us: lean and tanned and immaculate in their tailored and starched dungarees, and spit-shined boots. And the boy could only go so far up the rope, up the series of hills we climbed, up toward the chinning bar, up the walls and angled poles of the obstacle course, up from the grass by the strength of his arms as the rest of us reached fifty, seventy, finally a hundred push-ups.

But in truth he could, and that is the reason for this anecdote while I contemplate Rose. One night in our fifth week the boy walked in his sleep. Every night we had fire watch: one of us walked for four hours through the barracks, the three squad bays that each housed a platoon, to alert us of fire. We heard the story the next day, whispered, muttered, or spoken out of the boy's hearing, in the chow hall, during the ten-minute break on a march. The fire watch was a boy from the University of Alabama, a football player whose southern accent enriched his story, heightened his surprise, his awe. He came into our squad bay at three-thirty in the morning, looked up and down the rows of bunks, and was about to leave when he heard someone speak. The voice frightened him. He had never heard, except in movies, a voice so pitched by desperation, and so eerie in its insistence. He moved toward it. Behind our bunks, against both walls, were our wall lockers. The voice came from that space between the bunks and lockers, where there was room to stand and dress, and to prepare your locker for inspection. The Alabama boy stepped between the bunks and lockers and moved toward the figure he saw now: someone squatted before a locker, white shorts and white tee shirt in the darkness. Then he heard what the voice was saying: *I can't find it. I can't find it.* He closed the distance between them, squatted, touched the boy's shoulder, and whispered: *Hey, what you looking for?* Then he saw it was the boy from Chicago. He spoke his name, but the boy bent lower and looked under his wall locker. That was when the Alabama boy saw that he was not truly looking: his eyes were shut, the lids in the repose of sleep, while the boy's head shook from side to side, in a short slow arc of exasperation. *I can't find it,* he said. He was kneeling before the wall locker, bending forward to look under it for—what? any of the several small things the sergeants demanded we care for and have with our gear: extra shoelaces, a web strap from a haversack, a metal button for dungarees, any of these things that became for us as precious as talismans. Still on his knees, the boy straightened his back, gripped the bottom of the wall locker, and lifted it from the floor, six inches or more above it, and held it there as he tried to lower his head to look under it. The locker was steel, perhaps six feet tall, and filled with his clothes, boots, and shoes, and on its top rested his packed haversack and helmet. No one in the platoon could have lifted it while kneeling, using only his arms. Most of us could have bear-hugged it up from the floor, even held it there. *Gawd damn,* the fire watch said, rising from his squat; *Gawd damn, lemmee help you with it,* and he held its sides; it was tottering, but still raised. Gently he lowered it, against the boy's resistance, then crouched again and, whispering to him, *like to a baby,* he told us, he said: *All rot now. It'll be all rot now. We'll fin' that damn thing in the mawnin';* as he tried to ease the boy's fingers from the bottom edge of the locker. Finally he pried them, one or two at a time. He pulled the boy to his feet, and with an arm around his waist, led him to his bunk. It was a lower bunk. He eased the boy downward to sit on it, then lifted his legs, covered him with the sheet, and sat beside him. He rested a hand on the boy's chest, and spoke soothingly to him as he struggled, trying to rise. Finally the boy lay still, his hands holding the top of the sheet near his chest.

We never told him. He went home believing his body had failed; he was the only failure in our platoon, and the only one in the company who failed because he lacked physical strength and endurance. I've often wondered about him: did he ever learn what he could truly do? Has he ever absolved himself of his failure? His was another of the inspiring stories of my youth. Not *his* story so much as the story of his body. I had heard or read much of the human spirit, indomitable against suffering and death. But this was a story of a pair of thin arms, and narrow shoulders, and weak legs: freed from whatever consciousness did to them, they had lifted an unwieldy weight they could not have moved while the boy's mind was awake. It is a mystery I still do not understand.

Now, more often than not, my discoveries are bad ones and if they inspire me at all, it is only to try to understand the unhappiness and often evil in the way we live. A friend of mine, a doctor, told me never again to believe that only the poor and uneducated and usually drunk beat their children; or parents who are insane, who hear voices commanding them to their cruelty. He has seen children, sons and daughters of doctors, bruised, their small bones broken, and he knows that the children are repeating their parents' lies: they fell down the stairs, they slipped and struck a table. He can do nothing for them but heal their injuries. The poor are frightened by authority, he said, and they will open their doors to a social worker. A doctor will not. And I have heard stories from young people, college students who come to the bar during the school year. They are rich, or their parents are, and they have about them those characteristics I associate with the rich: they look healthy, as though the power of money had a genetic influence on their very flesh; beneath their laughter and constant talk there lies always a certain poise, not sophistication, but confidence in life and their places in it. Perhaps it comes from the knowledge that they will never be stranded in a bus station with two dollars. But probably its source is more intangible: the ambience they grew up in: that strange paradox of being from birth removed, insulated, from most of the world, and its agony of survival that is, for most of us, a day-to-day life; while, at the same time, these young rich children are exposed through travel and—some of them—culture, to more of the world than most of us will ever see.

Years ago, when the students first found Timmy's and made it their regular drinking place, I did not like them, because their lives were so distant from those of the working men who patronize the bar. Then some of them started talking to me, in pairs, or a lone boy or girl, drinking near my spot at the bar's corner. I began enjoying their warmth, their general cheer, and often I bought them drinks, and always they bought mine in return. They called me by my first name, and each new class knows me, as they know Timmy's, before they see either of us. When they were alone, or with a close friend, they talked to me about themselves, revealed beneath that underlying poise deep confusion, and abiding pain their faces belied. So I learned of the cruelties of some of the rich: of children beaten, girls fondled by fathers who were never drunk and certainly did not smoke, healthy men who were either crazy or evil beneath their suits and briefcases, and their punctuality and calm confidence that crossed the line into arrogance. I learned of neglect: children reared by live-in nurses, by housekeepers who cooked; children in summer camps and boarding schools, and I saw the selfishness that wealth allows, a selfishness beyond greed, a desire to have children yet give them nothing, or very little, of oneself. I know one boy, an only child, whose mother left home when he was ten. She no longer wanted to be a mother; she entered the world of business in a city across the country from him, and he saw her for a week-end once a year. His father worked hard at making more money, and the boy left notes on the door of his father's den, asking for a time to see him. An appointment. The father answered with notes on the boy's door, and they met. Then the boy came to college here. He is very serious, very polite, and I have never seen him with a girl, or another boy, and I have never seen him smile.

So I have no reason to imagine Rose on that old stained carpet with places of it worn thin, nearly to the floor; Rose crawling among the legs of older sisters and brothers, looking up at the great and burdened height of her parents, their capacity, their will, to love long beaten or drained from them by what they had to do to keep a dwelling with food in it, and heat in it, and warm and cool clothes for their children. I have only guessed at this part of her history. There is one reason, though: Rose's face is bereft of education, of thought. It is the face of a survivor walking away from a terrible car accident: without memory or conjecture, only shock, and the surprise of knowing that she is indeed alive. I think of her body as shapeless: beneath the large and sagging curve of her breasts, she has such sparse curvature of hips and waist that she appears to be an elongated lump beneath her loose dresses in summer, her old wool overcoat in winter. At the bar she does not remove her coat; but she unbuttons it and pushes it back from her breasts, and takes the blue scarf from her head, shakes her greying brown hair, and lets the scarf hang from her neck.

She appeared in our town last summer. We saw her on the streets, or slowly walking across the bridge over the Merrimack River. Then she found Timmy's and, with money from whatever source, became a regular, along with the rest of us. Sometimes, if someone drank beside her, she spoke. If no one drank next to her, she drank alone. Always screwdrivers. Then we started talking about her and, with that ear for news that impresses me still about small communities, either towns or city neighborhoods, some of us told stories about her. Rumors: she had been in prison, or her husband, or someone else in the family had. She had children but lost them. Someone had heard of a murder: perhaps she killed her husband, or one of the children did, or he or Rose or both killed a child. There was talk of a fire. And so we talked for months, into the fall then early winter, when our leaves are gone, the reds and golds and yellows, and the trees are bare and grey, the evergreens dark green, and beyond their conical green we have lovely early sunsets. When the sky is grey, the earth is washed with it, and the evergreens look black. Then the ponds freeze and snow comes silently one night, and we wake to a white earth. It was during an early snowstorm when one of us said that Rose worked in a leather factory in town, had been there since she appeared last summer. He knew someone who worked there and saw her. He knew nothing else.

On a night in January, while a light and pleasant snow dusted the tops of cars, and the shoulders and hats and scarves of people coming into Timmy's, Rose told me her story. I do not know whether, afterward, she was glad or relieved; neither of us has mentioned it since; nor have our eyes, as we greet each other, sometimes chat. And one night I was without money, or enough of it, and she said *I owe you,* and bought the drinks. But that night in January she was in the state when people finally must talk. She was drunk too, or close enough to it, but I know her need to talk was there before vodka released her. I won't try to record our conversation. It was interrupted by one or both of us going to the bathroom, or ordering drinks (I insisted on paying for them all, and after the third round she simply thanked me, and patted my hand); interrupted by people leaning between us for drinks to bring back to booths, by people who came to speak to me, happy people oblivious of Rose, men or women or students who stepped to my side and began talking with that alcoholic lack of manners or awareness of intruding that, in a neighborhood bar, is not impolite but a part of the fabric of conversation. Interrupted too by the radio behind the bar, the speakers at both ends of the room, the loud rock music from an FM station in Boston.

It was a Friday, so the bar closed at two instead of one; we started talking at eleven. Gradually, before that, Rose had pushed her way down the bar toward my corner. I had watched her move to the right to make room for a couple, again to allow a man to squeeze in beside her, and again for some college girls, then the two men to my left went home, and when someone else wedged his arms and shoulders between the standing drinkers at the bar, she stepped to her right again and we faced each other across the corner. We talked about the bartender (we liked him), the crowd (we liked them: loud, but generally peaceful) and she said she always felt safe at Timmy's because everybody knew everybody else, and they didn't allow trouble in here.

"I can't stand fighting bars," she said. "Those young punks that have to hit somebody."

We talked about the weather, the seasons. She liked fall. The factory was too hot in summer. So was her apartment. She had bought a large fan, and it was so loud you could hear it from outside, and it blew dust from the floor, ashes from ash trays. She liked winter, the snow, and the way the cold made her feel more alive; but she was afraid of it too: she was getting old, and did not want to be one of those people who slipped on ice and broke a hip.

"The old bones," she said. "They don't mend like young ones."

"You're no older than I am."

"Oh yes I am. And you'd better watch your step too. On that ice," and she nodded at the large front window behind me.

"That's snow," I said. "A light, dry snow."

She smiled at me, her face affectionate, and coquettish with some shared secret, as though we were talking in symbols. Then she finished her drink and I tried to get Steve's attention. He is a large man, and was mixing drinks at the other end of the bar. He did not look our way, so finally I called his name: my voice loud enough to be heard, but softened with courtesy to a tenor. Off and on, through the years, I have tended bar, and I am sensitive about the matter of ordering from a bartender who is making several drinks and, from the people directly in front of him, hearing requests for more. He heard me and glanced at us and I raised two fingers; he nodded. When I looked at Rose again she was gazing down into her glass, as though studying the yellow-filmed ice.

"I worry about fires in winter," she said, still looking down. "Sometimes every night."

"When you're going to sleep? You worry about a fire?"

She looked at me.

"Nearly every night."

"What kind of heat does your building have?"

"Oil furnace."

"Is something wrong with it?"

"No."

"Then—" Steve is very fast; he put my beer and her screwdriver before us, and I paid him; he spun, strode to the cash register, jabbed it, slapped in my ten, and was back with the change. I pushed a dollar toward him, he thanked me, and was gone, repeating an order from the other end of the bar, and a rock group sang above the crowd, a ceiling of sound over the shouts, the laughter, and the crescendo of juxtaposed conversations.

"Then why are you worried?" I said. "Were you in a fire? As a child?"

"I was. Not in winter. And I sure wasn't no child. But you hear them. The sirens. All the time in winter."

"Wood stoves," I said. "Faulty chimneys."

"They remind me. The sirens. Sometimes it isn't even the sirens. I try not to think about them. But sometimes it's like they think about me. They do. You know what I mean?"

"The sirens?"

"*No.*" She grabbed my wrist and squeezed it, hard as a man might; I had not known the strength of her hands. "The flames," she said.

"The flames?"

"I'm not doing anything. Or I'm at work, packing boxes. With leather. Or I'm going to sleep. Or right now, just then, we were talking about winter. I try not to think about them. But here they come, and I can see them. I feel them. Little flames. Big ones. Then—"

She released my wrist, swallowed from her glass, and her face changed: a quick recognition of something forgotten. She patted my hand.

"Thanks for the drink."

"I have money tonight."

"Good. Some night you won't, and I will. You'll drink on me."

"Fine."

"Unless you slip on that ice," nodding her head toward the window, the gentle snow, her eyes brightening again with that shared mystery, their luster near anger, not at me but at what we shared.

"Then what?" I said.

"What?"

"When you see them. When you feel the fire."

"My kids."

"No."

"Three kids."

"No, Rose."

"Two were upstairs. We lived on the third floor."

"Please: no stories like that tonight."

She patted my hand, as though in thanks for a drink, and said: "Did you lose a child?"

"Yes."

"In a fire?"

"A car."

"You poor man. Don't cry."

And with her tough thumbs she wiped the beginning of my tears from beneath my eyes, then standing on tiptoe she kissed my cheek, her lips dry, her cheek as it brushed mine feeling no softer than my own, save for her absence of whiskers.

"Mine got out," she said. "I got them out."

I breathed deeply and swallowed beer and wiped my eyes but she had dried them.

"And it's the only thing I ever did. In my whole fucking life. The only thing I ever did that was worth a shit."

"Come on. Nobody's like that."

"No?"

"I hope nobody is."

I looked at the clock on the opposite wall; it was near the speaker that tilted downward, like those mirrors in stores, so cashiers can watch people between shelves. From the speaker came a loud electric guitar, repeating a series of chords, then two or more frenetic saxophones blowing their hoarse tones at the heads of the drinkers, like an indoor storm without rain. On that clock the time was two minutes till midnight, so I knew it was eleven thirty-eight; at Timmy's they keep the clock twenty minutes fast. This allows them time to give last call and still get the patrons out by closing. Rose was talking. Sometimes I watched her; sometimes I looked away, when I could do that and still hear. For when I listened while watching faces I knew, hearing some of their voices, I did not see everything she told me: I saw, but my vision was dulled, given distance, by watching bearded Steve work, or the blonde student Ande laughing over the mouth of her beer bottle, or old grey-haired Lou, retired as a factory foreman, drinking his shots and drafts, and smoking Camels; or the young owner Timmy, in his mid-thirties, wearing a leather jacket and leaning on the far corner of the bar, drinking club soda and watching the hockey game that was silent under the sounds of rock.

But most of the time, because of the noise, I had to look at her eyes or mouth to hear; and when I did that, I saw everything, without the distractions of sounds and faces and bodies, nor even the softening of distance, of time: I saw the two little girls, and the little boy, their pallid terrified faces; I saw their father's big arm and hand arcing down in a slap; in a blow with his fist closed; I saw the five year old boy, the oldest, flung through the air, across the room, to strike the wall and drop screaming to the couch against it. Toward the end, nearly his only sounds were screams; he virtually stopped talking, and lived as a frightened yet recalcitrant prisoner. And in Rose's eyes I saw the embers of death, as if the dying of her spirit had not come with a final yielding sigh, but in a blaze of recognition.

It was long ago, in a Massachusetts town on the Merrimack River. Her husband was a big man, with strongly muscled arms, and the solid rounded belly of a man who drinks much beer at night and works hard, with his body, five days a week. He was handsome too. His face was always reddish-brown from his outdoor work, his hair was thick and black, and curls of it topped his forehead, and when he wore his cap on the back of his head, the visor rested on his curls. He had a thick but narrow moustache, and on Friday and Saturday nights, when they went out to drink and dance, he dressed in brightly colored pants and shirts that his legs and torso and arms filled. His name was Jim Cormier, his grandfather Jacques came from Quebec as a young man, and his father was Jacques Cormier too, and by Jim's generation the last name was pronounced *Cormeer,* and he was James. Jim was a construction worker, but his physical strength and endurance were unequally complemented by his mind, his spirit, whatever that element is that draws the attention of other men. He was best at the simplest work, and would never be a foreman, or tradesman. Other men, when he worked with them, baffled him. He did not have the touch: could not be entrusted to delegate work, to plan, to oversee, and to handle men. Bricks and mortars and trowels and chalk lines baffled him too, as did planes and levels; yet, when he drank at home every night—they seldom went out after the children arrived—he talked about learning to operate heavy equipment.

Rose did not tell me all this at first. She told me the end, the final night, and only in the last forty minutes or so, when I questioned her, did she go farther back, to the beginning. Where I start her story, so I can try to understand how two young people married, with the hope of love, in those days before pandemic divorce even the certainty of love, and within six years, when they were still young, still in their twenties, their home had become a horror for their children, for Rose, and yes: for Jim. A place where a boy of five, and girls of four and three, woke, lived, and slept in isolation from the light of a child's life: the curiosity, the questions about birds, appliances, squirrels and trees and snow and rain, and the first heart-quickening of love for another child, not a sister or brother, but the boy or girl in a sandbox, or on a tricycle at the house down the street. They lived always in darkness, deprived even of childhood fears of ghosts in the shadowed corners of the rooms where they slept, of dreams of vicious and carnivorous monsters. Their young memories and their present consciousness were the tall broad man and his reddening face that shouted and hissed, and his large hands. Rose must have had no place at all, or very little, in their dreams and their wary and apprehensive minds when they were awake. Unless as a wish: I imagine them in their beds, in the moments before sleep, seeing, hoping for Rose to take them in her arms, carry them one by one to the car while the giant slept drunkenly in the bed she shared with him, Rose putting their toys and clothes in the car's trunk, and driving with them far away to a place—What place could they imagine? What place not circumscribed by their apartment's walls whose very colors and hanging pictures and calendar were for them the dark grey of fear and pain? Certainly, too, in those moments before sleep, they must have wished their father gone. Simply gone. The boy must have thought of, wished for, Jim's death. The younger girls, four and three, only that he vanish, leaving no trace of himself in their home, in their hearts, not even guilt. Simply to vanish.

Rose was a silent partner. If there is damnation, and a place for the damned, it must be a quiet place, where spirits turn away from each other and stand in solitude and gaze haplessly at eternity. For it must be crowded with the passive: those people whose presence in life was a paradox; for, while occupying space and moving through it and making sounds in it they were obviously present, while in truth they were not: they witnessed evil and lifted neither an arm nor a voice to stop it, as they witnessed joy, and neither sang nor clapped their hands. But so often we understand them too easily, tolerate them too much: they have universality, so we forgive the man who watches injustice, a drowning, a murder, because he reminds us of ourselves, and we share with him the loyal bond of cowardice, whether once or a hundred times we have turned away from another's suffering to save ourselves: our jobs, our public selves, our bones and flesh. And these people are so easy to pity. We know fear as early as we know love, and fear is always with us. I have friends my own age who still cannot say what they believe, except in the most intimate company. Condemning the actively evil man is a simple matter; though we tend not only to forgive but cheer him if he robs banks or Brink's, and outwits authority: those unfortunate policemen, minions whose uniforms and badges and revolvers are, for many of us, a distorted symbol of what we fear: not a fascist state but a Power, a God, who knows all our truths, believes none of our lies, and with that absolute knowledge will both judge, and exact punishment. For we see to it that no one absolutely knows us, so at times the passing blue figure of a policeman walking his beat can stir in us our fear of discovery. We like to see them made into dupes by the outlaw.

But if the outlaw rapes, tortures, gratuitously kills, or if he makes children suffer, we hate him with a purity we seldom feel: our hatred has no roots in prejudice, or self-righteousness, but in horror. He has done something we would never do, something we could not do even if we wished it; our bodies would not obey, would not tear the dress, or lift and swing the axe, pull the trigger, throw the screaming child across the room. So I hate Jim Cormier, and cannot understand him; cannot with my imagination cross the distance between myself and him, enter his soul and know how it felt to live even five minutes of his life. And I forgive Rose, but as I write I resist that compassion, or perhaps merely empathy, and force myself to think instead of the three children, and Rose living there, knowing what she knew. She was young.

She is Irish: a Callahan till marriage, and she and Jim were Catholics. Devout Catholics, she told me. By that, she did not mean they strived to live in imitation of Christ. She meant they did not practice artificial birth control, but rhythm, and after their third year of marriage they had three children. They left the church then. That is, they stopped attending Sunday Mass and receiving Communion. Do you see? I am not a Catholic, but even I know that they were never truly members of that faith, and so could not have left it. There is too much history, too much philosophy involved, for the matter of faith to rest finally and solely on the use of contraceptives. That was long ago, and now my Catholic friends tell me the priests no longer concern themselves with birth control. But we must live in our own time; Thomas More died for an issue that would have no meaning today. Rose and Jim, though, were not Thomas Mores. They could not see a single act as a renunciation or affirmation of a belief, a way of life. No. They had neither a religion nor a philosophy; like most people I know their philosophies were simply their accumulated reactions to their daily circumstance, their lives as they lived them from one hour to the next. They were not driven, guided, by either passionate belief, nor strong resolve. And for that I pity them both, as I pity the others who move through life like scraps of paper in the wind.

With contraception they had what they believed were two years of freedom. There had been a time when all three of their children wore diapers, and only the boy could walk, and with him holding her coat or pants, moving so slowly beside her, Rose went daily to the laundromat, pushing two strollers, gripping a paper grocery bag of soiled diapers, with a clean bag folded in her purse. Clorox rested beneath one stroller, a box of soap beneath the other. While she waited for the diapers to wash, the boy walked among the machines, touched them, watched them, and watched the other women who waited. The oldest girl crawled about on the floor. The baby slept in Rose's lap, or nursed in those days when mothers did not expose their breasts, and Rose covered the infant's head, and her breast, with her unbuttoned shirt. The children became hungry, or tired, or restless, and they fussed, and cried, as Rose called to the boy to leave the woman alone, to stop playing with the ash tray, the soap, and she put the diapers in the dryer. And each day she felt that the other women, even those with babies, with crawling and barely walking children, with two or three children, and one pregnant with a third, had about them some grace, some calm, that kept their voices soft, their gestures tender; she watched them with shame, and a deep dislike of herself, but no envy, as if she had tried out for a dance company and on the first day had entered a room of slender professionals in leotards, dancing like cats, while she clumsily moved her heavy body clad in grey sweat clothes. Most of the time she changed the diaper of at least one of the children, and dropped it in the bag, the beginning of tomorrow's load. If the baby slept in her stroller, and the oldest girl and the boy played on the floor, Rose folded the diapers on the table in the laundromat, talking and smoking with the other women. But that was rare: the chance that all three small children could at the same time be peaceful and without need, and so give her peace. Imagine: three of them with bladders and bowels, thirst, hunger, fatigue, and none of them synchronized. Most days she put the hot unfolded diapers in the clean bag, and hurried home.

Finally she cried at dinner one night for a washing machine and a dryer, and Jim stared at her, not with anger, or impatience, and not refusal either: but with the resigned look of a man who knew he could neither refuse it nor pay for it. It was the washing machine; he would buy it with monthly payments, and when he had done that, he would get the dryer. He sank posts in the earth and nailed boards across their tops and stretched clotheslines between them. He said in rain or freezing cold she would have to hang the wet diapers over the backs of chairs. It was all he could do. Until he could get her a dryer. And when he came home on those days of rain or cold, he looked surprised, as if rain and cold in New England were as foreign to him as the diapers that seemed to occupy the house. He removed them from the rod for the shower curtain, and when he had cleaned his work from his body, he hung them again. He took them from the arms and back of his chair and lay them on top of others, on a chair, or the edges of the kitchen table. Then he sat in the chair whose purpose he had restored; he drank beer and gazed at the drying diapers, as if they were not cotton at all, but the whitest of white shades of the dead, come to haunt him, to assault him, an inch at a time, a foot, until they won, surrounded him where he stood in some corner of the bedroom, the bathroom, in the last place in his home that was his. His *querençia:* his cool or blood-smelling sand, the only spot in the bull ring where he wanted to stand and defend, to lower his head and wait.

He struck the boy first, before contraception, and the freedom and new life it promised, as money does. Rose was in the kitchen, chopping onions, now and then turning her face to wipe, with the back of her wrist, the tears from her eyes. The youngest girl was asleep; the older one crawled between and around Rose's legs. The boy was three. She had nearly finished the onions and could put them in the skillet and stop crying, when she heard the slap, and knew what it was in that instant before the boy cried: a different cry: in it she heard not only startled fear, but a new sound: a wail of betrayal, of pain from the heart.

Wiping her hands on her apron, she went quickly to the living room, into that long and loudening cry, as if the boy, with each moment of deeper recognition, raised his voice until it howled. He stood in front of his seated father. Before she reached him, he looked at her, as though without hearing footsteps or seeing her from the corner of his blurred wet vision, he knew she was there. She was his mother. Yet when he turned his face to her, it was not with appeal: above his small reddened cheeks he looked into her eyes; and in his, as tears ran from them, was that look whose sound she had heard in the kitchen. Betrayal. Accusing her of it, and without anger, but dismay. In her heart she felt something fall between herself and her son, like a glass wall, or a space that spanned only a few paces, yet was infinite, and she could never cross it again. Now his voice had attained the howl, and though his cheeks were wet, his eyes were dry now; or anyway tearless, for they looked wet and bright as pools that could reflect her face. The baby was awake, crying in her crib. Rose looked from her son's eyes to her husband's. They were dark, and simpler than the boy's: in them she saw only the ebb of his fury: anger, and a resolve to preserve and defend it.

"I told him not to," he said.

"Not to what?"

"Climbing on my legs. Look." He pointed to a dark wet spot on the carpet. "He spilled the beer."

She stared at the spot. She could not take her eyes from it. The baby was crying and the muscles of her legs tried to move toward that sound. Then she realized her son was silent. She felt him watching her, and she would not look at him.

"It's nothing to cry about," Jim said.

"You *slapped* him."

"Not *him*. You."

"Me? That's onions."

She wiped her hands on her apron, brushed her eyes with the back of her wrist.

"Jesus," she said. She looked at her son. She had to look away from those eyes. Then she saw the oldest girl: she had come to the doorway, and was standing on the threshold, her thumb in her mouth; above her small closed fist and nose, her frightened eyes stared, and she looked as though she were trying not to cry. But, if she was, there could be only one reason for a child so young: she was afraid for her voice to leave her, to enter the room, where now Rose could feel her children's fear as tangibly as a cold draft blown through a cracked window pane. Her legs, her hips, strained toward the baby's cry for food, a dry diaper, for whatever acts of love they need when they wake, and even more when they wake before they are ready, when screams smash the shell of their sleep. "Jesus," she said, and hurried out of the room where the pain in her son's heart had pierced her own, and her little girl's fearful silence pierced it again; or slashed it, for she felt as she bent over the crib that she was no longer whole, that her height and breadth and depth were in pieces that somehow held together, did not separate and drop to the floor, through it, into the earth itself.

"I should have hit him with the skillet," she said to me, so many years later, after she had told me the end and I had drawn from her the beginning, in the last half hour of talk. She could not hit him that night. With the heavy iron skillet, with its hot oil waiting for the onions. For by then something had flowed away from Rose, something of her spirit simply wafting willy-nilly out of her body, out of the apartment, and it never came back, not even with the diaphragm. Perhaps it began to leave her at the laundromat, or in bed at night, at the long day's end not too tired for lust, for rutting, but too tired for an evening of desire that began with dinner and crested and fell and crested again through the hours as they lay close and naked in bed, from early in the night until finally they slept. On the car seat of courtship she had dreamed of this, and in the first year of marriage she lived the dream: joined him in the shower and made love with him, still damp, before they went to the dinner kept warm on the stove, then back to the bed's tossed sheets to lie in the dark, smoking, talking, touching, and they made love again; and, later, again, until they could only lie side by side waiting for their breathing to slow, before they slept. Now at the tired ends of days they took release from each other, and she anxiously slept, waiting for a baby to cry.

Or perhaps it left her between the shelves of a supermarket. His pay day was Thursday, and by then the refrigerator and cupboard were nearly empty. She shopped on Friday. Unless a neighbor could watch the children, Rose shopped at night, when Jim was home; they ate early and she hurried to the store to shop before it closed. Later, months after he slapped the boy, she believed his rage had started then, alone in the house with them, changing the baby and putting her in the crib while the other girl and boy spat and flung food from their highchairs where she had left them, in her race with time to fill a cart with food Jim could afford: she looked at the price of everything she took from a shelf. She did not believe, later, that he struck them on those nights. But there must have been rage, the frightening voice of it; for he was tired, and confused, and overwhelmed by three small people with wills of their own, and no control over the needs of their bodies and their spirits. Certainly he must have yelled; maybe he squeezed an arm, or slapped a rump. When she returned with the groceries, the apartment was quiet: the children slept, and he sat in the kitchen, with the light out, drinking beer. A light from the living room behind him and around a corner showed her his silhouette: large and silent, a cigarette glowing at his mouth, a beer bottle rising to it. Then he would turn on the light and put down his beer and walk past her, to the old car, to carry in the rest of the groceries.

When finally two of the children could walk, Rose went to the supermarket during the day, the boy and girl walking beside her, behind her, away from her voice whose desperate pitch embarrassed her, as though its sound were a sign to the other women with children that she was incompetent, unworthy to be numbered among them. The boy and girl took from shelves cookies, crackers, cereal boxes, cans of vegetables and fruit, sometimes to play with them, but at other times to bring to her, where holding the cart they pulled themselves up on the balls of their feet and dropped in the box, or the can. Still she scolded them, jerked the can or box from the cart, brought it back to its proper place; and when she did this, her heart sank as though pulled by a sigh deeper into her body. For she saw. She saw that when the children played with these things whose colors or shapes drew them, so they wanted to sit on the floor and hold or turn in their hands the box or can, they were simply being children whom she could patiently teach, if patience were still an element in her spirit. And that when they brought things to her, to put into the cart, repeating the motions of their mother, they were joining, without fully knowing it, the struggle of the family, and without knowing the struggle that was their parents' lives. Their hearts, though, must have expected praise; or at least an affectionate voice, a gentle hand, to show that their mother did not need what they had brought her. If only there were time: one extra hour of grocery shopping to spend in this gentle instruction. Or if she had strength to steal the hour anyway, despite the wet and tired and staring baby in the cart. But she could not: she scolded, and jerked from the cart or their hands the things they had brought, and the boy became quiet, the girl sucked her thumb and held Rose's pants as the four of them moved with the cart between the long shelves. The baby fussed, with that unceasing low cry that was not truly crying: only the wordless sounds of fatigue. Rose recognized it, understood it, for by now she had learned the awful lesson of fatigue, which as a young girl she had never felt. She knew that it was worse than the flu, whose enforced rest at least left you the capacity to care for someone else, to mutter words of love; but that, healthy, you could be so tired that all you wanted was to lie down, alone, shut off from everyone. And you would snap at your husband, or your children, if they entered the room, probed the solace of your complete surrender to silence and the mattress that seductively held your body. So she understood the baby's helpless sounds for *I want to lie in my crib and put my thumb in my mouth and hold Raggedy Ann's dirty old apron and sleep.* The apron was long removed from the doll, and the baby would not sleep without its presence in her hand. Rose understood this, but could not soothe the baby. She could not have soothed her anyway; only sleep could. But Rose could not try, with hugs, with petting, with her softened voice. She was young.

Perhaps her knowledge of her own failures dulled her ears and eyes to Jim after he first struck the boy, and on that night lost for the rest of his life any paternal control he may have exerted in the past over his hands, finally his fists. Because more and more now he spanked them: with a chill Rose tried to deny, a resonant quiver up through her body, she remembered that her parents had spanked her too. That all, or probably all, parents spanked their children. And usually it was the father, the man of the house, the authority and judge, and enforcer of rules and discipline the children would need when they reached their teens. But now, too, he held them by the shoulders, and shook their small bodies, the children sometimes wailing, sometimes frighteningly silent, until it seemed their heads would fly across the room then roll to rest on the floor, while he shook a body whose neck had snapped in two like a dried branch. He slapped their faces, and sometimes he punched the boy, who was four then five, with his fist. They were not bad children; not disobedient; certainly they were not loud. When Jim yelled and shook them, or slapped or punched, they had done no more than they had in the supermarket, where her voice, her snatching from their hands, betrayed her to the other women. So maybe that kept her silent.

But there was more: she could no longer feel love, or what she had believed it to be. On the few nights when she and Jim could afford both a sitter and a night club, they did not dance. They sat drinking, their talk desultory: about household chores, about Jim's work, pushing wheelbarrows, swinging a sledgehammer, thrusting a spade into the earth or a pile of gravel or sand. They listened to the music, watched the band, even drummed their fingers on the table dampened by the bottoms of their glasses they emptied like thirsty people drinking water; but they thirsted for a time they had lost. Or not even that: for respite from their time now, and their knowledge that, from one day to the next, year after year, their lives would not change. Each day would be like the one they had lived before last night's sleep; and tomorrow was a certain and already draining repetition of today. They did not decide to sit rather than dance. They simply did not dance. They sat and drank and watched the band and the dancing couples, as if their reason for dancing had been stolen from them while their eyes had been jointly focused on something else.

She could no longer feel love. She ate too much and smoked too much and drank too much coffee, so all day she felt either lethargic from eating or stimulated by coffee and cigarettes, and she could not recall her body as it had once been, only a few years ago, when she was dating Jim, and had played softball and volleyball, had danced, and had run into the ocean to swim beyond the breakers. The ocean was a half-hour away from her home, yet she had not seen it in six years. Rather than love, she felt that she and Jim only worked together, exhausted, toward a nebulous end, as if they were digging a large hole, wide as a house, deeper than a well. Side by side they dug, and threw the dirt up and out of the hole, pausing now and then to look at each other, to wait while their breathing slowed, and to feel in those kindred moments something of why they labored, of why they had begun it so long ago—not in years, not long at all—with their dancing and love-making and finally marriage: to pause and look at each other's flushed and sweating faces with as much love as they could feel before they commenced again to dig deeper, away from the light above them.

On a summer night in that last year, Jim threw the boy across the living room. Rose was washing the dishes after dinner. Jim was watching television, and the boy, five now, was playing on the floor between Jim and the set. He was on the floor with his sisters and wooden blocks and toy cars and trucks. He seldom spoke directly to his father anymore; seldom spoke at all to anyone but his sisters. The girls were too young, or hopeful, or were still in love. They spoke to Jim, sat on his lap, hugged his legs, and when he hugged them, lifted them in the air, talked with affection and laughter, their faces showed a happiness without memory. And when he yelled at them, or shook or spanked them, or slapped their faces, their memory failed them again, and they were startled, frightened, and Rose could sense their spirits weeping beneath the sounds of their crying. But they kept turning to him, with open arms, and believing faces.

"Little flowers," she said to me. "They were like little flowers in the sun. They never could remember the frost."

Not the boy, though. But that night his game with his sisters absorbed him, and for a short while—nearly an hour—he was a child in a home. He forgot. Several times his father told him and the girls to be quiet or play in another room. Then for a while, a long while for playing children, they were quiet: perhaps five minutes, perhaps ten. Each time their voices rose, Jim's command for quiet was abrupt, and each time it was louder. At the kitchen sink Rose's muscles tensed, told her it was coming, and she must go to the living room now, take the children and their blocks and cars and trucks to the boy's bedroom. But she breathed deeply and rubbed a dish with a sponge. When she finished, she would go down to the basement of the apartment building, descend past the two floors of families and single people whose only sounds were music from radios, voices from television, and sometimes children loudly playing and once in a while a quarrel between a husband and wife. She would go into the damp basement and take the clothes from the washing machine, put them in the dryer that now Jim was paying for with monthly installments. Then she heard his voice again, and was certain it was coming, but could not follow the urging of her muscles. She sponged another dish. Then her hands came out of the dish water with a glass: it had been a jelly jar, humanly smiling animals were on it, and flowers, and her children liked to drink from it, looked for it first when they were thirsty, and only if it was dirty in the sink would they settle for an ordinary glass for their water, their juice, or Kool-Aid or milk. She washed it slowly, and was for those moments removed; she was oblivious of the living room, the children's voices rising again to the peak that would bring either Jim's voice or his body from his chair. Her hands moved gently on the glass. She could have been washing one of her babies. Her heart had long ago ceased its signals to her; it lay dormant in despair beyond sorrow; standing at the sink, in a silence of her own making, lightly rubbing the glass with the sponge, and her fingers and palms, she did not know she was crying until the tears reached her lips, salted her tongue.

With their wooden blocks, the children were building a village, and a bridge leading out of it to the country: the open spaces of the living room carpet, and the chairs and couch that were distant mountains. More adept with his hands, and more absorbed too in the work, the boy often stood to adjust a block on a roof, or the bridge. Each time he stood between his father and the television screen, heard the quick command, and moved out of the way. They had no slanted blocks, so the bridge had to end with two sheer walls; the boy wanted to build ramps at either end, for the cars and trucks to use, and he had only rectangles and squares to work with. He stood to look down at the bridge. His father spoke. He heard the voice, but a few seconds passed before it penetrated his concentration, and spread through him. It was too late. What he heard next were not words, or a roar, but a sustained guttural cry, a sound that could be either anguish or rage. Then his father's hands were on him: on him and squeezing his left thigh and left bicep so tightly that he opened his mouth to cry out in pain. But he did not. For then he was above his father's head, above the floor and his sisters, high above the room itself and near the ceiling he glimpsed; and he felt his father's grip and weight shifting and saw the wall across the room, the wall above the couch, so that when finally he made a sound it was of terror, and it came from him in a high scream he heard as he hurtled across the room, seeing always the wall, and hearing his scream, as though his flight were prolonged by the horror of what he saw and heard. Then he struck it. He heard that, and the bone in his right forearm snap, and he fell to the couch. Now he cried with pain, staring at the swollen flesh where the bone tried to protrude, staring with astonishment and grief at this part of his body. Nothing in his body had ever broken before. He touched the flesh, the bone beneath it. He was crying as, in his memory, he had never cried before, and he not only did not try to stop, as he always had, with pride, with anger; but he wanted to cry this deeply, his body shuddering with it, doubling at his waist with it, until he attained oblivion, invisibility, death. Somehow he knew his childhood had ended. In his pain, he felt relief too: now on this couch his life would end.

He saw through tears but more strongly felt his sisters standing before him, touching him, crying. Then he heard his mother. She was screaming. And in rage. At his father. He had never heard her do that, but still her scream did not come to him as a saving trumpet. He did not want to live to see revenge. Not even victory. Then he heard his father slap her. Through his crying he listened then for her silence. But her voice grew, its volume filled the world. Still he felt nothing of hope, of vengeance; he had left that world, and lived now for what he hoped and believed would be only a very short time. He was beginning to feel the pain in his head and back and shoulders, his elbows and neck. He knew he would only have to linger a while in this pain, until his heart left him, as though disgorged by tears, and went wherever hearts went. A sister's hand held his, and he squeezed it.

When he was above his father's head, the boy had not seen Rose. But she was there, behind Jim, behind the lifted boy, and she had cried out too, and moved: as Jim regained his balance from throwing the boy, she turned him, her hand jerking his shoulder, and when she could see his face she pounded it with her fists. She was yelling, and the yell was words, but she did not know what they were. She hit him until he pushed her back, hard, so she nearly fell. She looked at his face, the cheeks reddened by her blows, saw a trickle of blood from his lower lip, and charged it: swinging at the blood, the lip. He slapped her so hard that she was sitting on the floor, with no memory of falling, and holding and shaking her stunned and buzzing head. She stood, yelling words again that she could not hear, as if their utterance had been so long coming, from whatever depth in her, that her mind could not even record them as they rushed through her lips. She went past Jim, pushing his belly, and he fell backward into his chair. She paused to look at that. Her breath was deep and fast, and he sat glaring, his breathing hard too, and she neither knew nor cared whether he had desisted or was preparing himself for more. At the bottom of her vision, she saw his beer bottle on the floor beside the chair. She snatched it up, by its neck, beer hissing onto her arm and breast, and in one motion she turned away from Jim and flung the bottle smashing through the television screen. He was up and yelling behind her, but she was crouched over the boy.

She felt again what she felt in the kitchen, in the silence she had made for herself while she bathed the glass. Behind and above her was the sound of Jim's fury; yet she stroked the boy's face: his forehead, the tears beneath his eyes; she touched the girls too, their hair, their wet faces; and she heard her voice: soft and soothing, so soft and soothing that she even believed the peace it promised. Then she saw, beneath the boy's hand, the swollen flesh; gently she lifted his hand, then was on her feet. She stood into Jim's presence again: his voice behind her, the feel of his large body inches from her back. Then he gripped her hair, at the back of her head, and she shook her head but still he held on.

"His *arm's* broken."

She ran from him, felt hair pulling from her scalp, heard it, and ran to her bedroom for her purse but not a blanket, not from the bed where she slept with Jim; for that she went to the boy's, and pulled his thin summer blanket from his bed, and ran back to the living room. Where she stopped. Jim stood at the couch, not looking at the boy, or the girls, but at the doorway where now she stood holding the blanket. He was waiting for her.

"You crazy fucking bitch."

"What?"

"The fucking TV. Who's going to buy one? You? You fucking cunt. You've never had a fucking job in your life."

It was madness. She was looking at madness, and it calmed her. She had nothing to say to it. She went to the couch, opening the blanket to wrap around the boy.

"It's the only fucking peace I've *got.*"

She heard him, but it was like overhearing someone else, in another apartment, another life. She crouched and was working the blanket under the boy's body when a fist knocked loudly on the door. She did not pause, or look up. More knocking, then a voice in the hall: "Hey! Everybody all right in there?"

"Get the fuck away from my door."

"You tell me everybody's all right."

"Get the fuck *away.*"

"I want to hear the woman. And the kid."

"You want me to throw you down the fucking stairs?"

"I'm calling the cops."

"Fuck you."

She had the boy in her arms now. He was crying still, and as she carried him past Jim, she kissed his cheeks, his eyes. Then Jim was beside her. He opened the door, swung it back for them. She did not realize until weeks later that he was frightened. His voice was low: "Tell them he fell."

She did not answer. She went out and down the stairs, past apartments; in one of them someone was phoning the police. At the bottom of the stairs she stopped short of the door, to shift the boy's weight in her arms, to free a hand for the knob. Then an old woman stepped out of her apartment, into the hall, and said: "I'll get it."

An old woman with white hair and a face that knew everything, not only tonight, but the years before this too, yet the face was neither stern nor kind; it looked at Rose with some tolerant recognition of evil, of madness, of despair, like a warrior who has seen and done too much to condemn, or even try to judge; can only nod in assent at what he sees. The woman opened the door and held it, and Rose went out, across the small lawn to the car parked on the road. There were only two other cars at the curb; then she remembered that it was Saturday, and had been hot, and before noon she had heard most of the tenants, separately leaving for beaches or picnic grounds. They would be driving home now, or stopping to eat. The sun had just set, but most windows of the tenements on the street were dark. She stopped at the passenger door, started to shift the weeping boy's weight, then the old woman was beside her, trying the door, asking for the key. Rose's purse hung from her wrist. The woman's hands went into it, moved in there, came out with the ring of keys, held them up toward the streetlight, and found the one for the car. She opened the door, and Rose leaned in and lay the boy on the front seat. She turned to thank the woman but she was already at the front door of the building, a square back and short body topped by hair like cotton.

Rose gently closed the car door, holding it, making certain it did not touch the boy before she pushed it into place. She ran to the driver's side, and got in, and put the key in the ignition slot. But she could not turn it. She sat in the boy's crying, poised in the moment of action the car had become. But she could not start it.

"Jimmy," she said. "Jimmy, listen. Just hang on. I'll be right back. I can't leave the girls. Do you hear me?"

His face, profiled on the seat, nodded.

"I've got to get them."

She pushed open the door, left the car, closed the door, the keys in her hand, not out of habit this time; no, she clung to them as she might to a tiny weapon, her last chance to be saved. She was running to the building when she saw the flames at her windows, a flare of them where an instant before there had been only lamplight. Her legs now, her body, were weightless as the wind. She heard the girls screaming. Then the door opened and Jim ran out of it, collided with her, and she fell on her back as he stumbled and side-stepped and tried to regain balance and speed and go around her. Her left hand grabbed his left ankle. Then she turned with his pulling, his weight, and on her stomach now, she held his ankle with her right hand too, and pulled it back and up. He fell. She dived onto his back, saw and smelled the gasoline can in his hand, and in her mind she saw him going down to the basement for it, and back up the stairs. She twisted it away from his fingers on the handle, and kneeled with his back between her legs, and as he lifted his head and shoulders and tried to stand, she raised the can high with both hands and brought it down, leaning with it, into it, as it struck his skull. For a moment he was still, his face in the grass. Then he began to struggle again, and said into the earth: "Over now. All over."

She hit him three more times, the sounds hollow, metallic. Then he was still, save for the rise and fall of his back. Beneath his other hand she saw his car keys. She scooped them from the grass and stood and threw them across the lawn, whirling now into the screams of the girls, and windows of fire. She ran up the stairs. The white-haired woman was on the second-floor landing. Rose passed her, felt her following, and the others: she did not know how many, nor who they were. She only heard them behind her. No one passed her. She was at the door, trying to turn the knob, while her left arm and hand pressed hot wood.

"I called the fire department," a man said, behind her in the hall.

"So did we," a woman said.

Rose was calling to the girls to open the door.

"They can't," another man said. "That's where the fire is." Then he said: "Fuck this," and pulled her away from the door where she was turning the knob back and forth and calling through the wood to the screams from the rear of the apartment, their bedroom. She was about to spring back to the door but stopped: the man faced it then stepped away. She knew his name, or had known it; she could not say it. He lived on the second floor; it was his wife who had said *So did we.* He stepped twice toward the door, then kicked, his leg horizontal, the bottom of his shoe striking the door, and it swung open, through the flames that filled the threshold and climbed the doorjambs. The man leaped backward, his forearms covering his face, while Rose yelled to the girls: We're coming, we're coming. The man lowered his head and sprinted forward. Or it would have been a sprint. Certainly he believed that, believed he would run through fire to the girls and get them out. But in his third stride his legs stopped, so suddenly and autonomously that he nearly fell forward into the fire. Then he backed up.

"They'll have a net," he said. He was panting. "We'll get them to jump. We'll get them to a window, and get them to jump.

A man behind Rose was holding her. She had not known it till now.

Nor did she know she had been straining forward. The man tightly held her biceps. He was talking to her and now she heard that too, and was also aware that people were moving away, slowly but away, down the hall toward the stairs. He was saying: "You can't. All you'll do is get yourself killed."

Then she was out of his hands, as though his fingers were those of a child, and with her breath held and her arms shielding her face, and her head down, she was in motion, through the flames and into the burning living room. She did not feel the fire, but even as she ran through the living room, dodging flames, running through them, she knew that very soon she would. It meant no more to her than knowing that she was getting wet in a sudden rain. The girls were standing on the older one's bed, at the far side of the room, holding each other, screaming, and watching their door and the hall beyond it where the fire would come. She filled the door, their vision, then was at the bed and they were crying: Mommy! Mommy! She did not speak. She did not touch them either. She pulled the blanket from under them, and they fell onto the bed. Running again she grabbed the blanket from the younger girl's bed, and went into the hall where there was smoke but not fire yet, and across it to the bathroom where she turned on the shower and held the blankets under the spray. They soaked heavily in her hands. She held her breath leaving the bathroom and exhaled in the girls' room. They were standing again, holding each other. Now she spoke to them. Again, as when she had crouched with them in front of Jimmy, her voice somehow came softly from her. It was unhurried, calm, soothing: she could have been helping them put on snowsuits. They stopped screaming, even crying; they only sniffled and gasped, as she wound a blanket around each of them, covering their feet and heads too, then lifted them, pressing one to each breast. Then she stopped talking, stopped telling them that very soon, before they even knew it, they would be safe outside. She turned and ran through smoke in the hall, and into the living room. She did not try to dodge flames: if they were in front of her, she spun and ran backward through them, hugging the girls against each other, so nothing of their bodies would protrude past her back, her sides; then spun and ran forward again, fearful of an image that entered her mind though in an instant she expelled it: that she would fall with them, into fire. She ran backward through the door, and her back hit the wall. She bounced off it; there was fire in the hall now, moving at her ankles, and she ran, leaping, and when she reached the stairs she smelled the scorched blankets that steamed around the girls in her arms. She smelled her burned hair, sensed that it was burning still, crackling flames on her head. It could wait. She could wait. She was running down the stairs, and the fire was behind her, above her, and she felt she could run with her girls all night. Then she was on the lawn, and arms took the girls, and a man wrestled her to the ground and rolled with her, rolled over and over on the grass. When she stood someone was telling her an ambulance would—But she picked up her girls, unwrapped now, and looked at their faces: pale with terror, with shock, yes; but no burns. She carried them to the car. *"No,"* she heard. It was a man's voice, but one she did not know. Not for a few moments, as she lay the girls side by side on the back seat. Then she knew it was Jim. She was startled, as though she had not seen him for ten years. She ran around the car, got behind the wheel, reached over Jimmy who was silent now, and she thought unconscious until she saw his eyes staring at the dashboard, his teeth gritting against his pain. Leaning over his face, she pushed down the latch on his side. Then she locked her door. It was a two-door car and they were safe now and they were going to the hospital. She started the engine.

Jim was at her window, a raging face, but a desperate one too, as though standing outside he was locked in a room without air. Then he was motion, on her left, to her front and he stood at the middle of the car, slapped his hands onto the hood, and pushed. He bulged: his arms and chest and reddened face. With all his strength he pushed, and she felt the car rock backward. She turned on the headlights. The car rocked forward as he eased his pushing, and drew breath. Then he pushed again, leaning, so all she could see of him were his face, his shoulders, his arms. The car rocked back and stopped. She pushed the accelerator pedal to the floor, waited two or three seconds in which she either did not breathe or held what breath she had, and watched his face above the sound of the racing engine. Then, in one quick motion, she lifted her foot from the clutch pedal. He was gone as she felt the bumper and grill leap through his resistance. She stopped and looked in the rear view mirror; she saw the backs of the girls' heads, their long hair; they were kneeling on the seat, looking quietly out the back window. He lay on his back. Rose turned her wheels to the right, as though to back into a parking space, shifted to reverse, and this time without racing the engine, she slowly drove. She did not look through the rear window; she looked straight ahead, at the street, the tenements, the darkening sky. Only the rear tires rolled over him, then struck the curb. She straightened the front wheels and drove forward again. The car bumped over him. She stopped, shifted gears, and backed up; the bump, then the tires hitting the curb. She was still driving back and forth over his body, while beyond her closed windows people shouted or stared, when the sirens broke the summer sky: the higher wail of the police called by the neighbor, and the lower and louder one of the fire engine.

She was in the hospital, and by the time she got out, her three brothers and two sisters had found money for bail. Her parents were dead. Waiting for the trial, she lived with a married sister; there were children in the house, and Rose shied away from them. Her court-appointed lawyer called it justifiable homicide, and the jury agreed. Long before the trial, before she even left the hospital, she had lost the children. The last time she saw them was that night in the car, when finally she took them away: the boy lying on the front seat, his left cheek resting on it as he stared. He did not move while she drove back and forth over his father. She still does not know whether he knew then, or learned it from his sisters. And the two girls kneeling, their breasts leaning on the back of the seat, watching their father appear, then vanish as a bump beneath them. They all went to the same foster home. She did not know where it was.

"Thanks for the drinks," she said, and patted my hand. "Next time you're broke, let me know."

"I will."

She adjusted the blue scarf over her hair, knotted it under her face, buttoned her coat and put on her gloves. She stepped away from the bar, and walked around and between people. I ordered a beer, and watched her go out the door. I paid and tipped Steve, then left the bottle and glass with my coat and hat on the bar, and moved through the crowd. I stepped outside and watched her, a half-block away now. She was walking carefully in the lightly falling snow, her head down, watching the sidewalk, and I remembered her eyes when she talked about slipping on ice. But what had she been sharing with me? Age? Death? I don't think so. I believe it was the unexpected: chance, and its indiscriminate testing of our bodies, our wills, our spirits. She was walking toward the bridge over the Merrimack. It is a long bridge, and crossing it in that open air she would be cold. I was shivering. She was at the bridge now, her silhouette diminishing as she walked on it. I watched until she disappeared.

I had asked her if she had tried to find her children, had tried an appeal to get them back. She did not deserve them, she said. And after the testimony of her neighbors, she knew she had little hope anyway. She should have hit him with the skillet, she said; the first time he slapped the boy. I said nothing. As I have written, we have talked often since then, but we do not mention her history, and she does not ask for mine, though I know she guesses some of it. All of this is blurred; nothing stands out with purity. By talking to social workers, her neighbors condemned her to lose her children; talking in the courtroom they helped save her from conviction.

I imagine again those men long ago, sitting among mosquitoes in a room, or sleeping on the fouled sheets. Certainly each of them hoped that it was not the mosquito biting his arm, or the bed he slept on, that would end his life. So he hoped for the men in the other room to die. Unless he hoped that it was neither sheets nor mosquitoes, but then he would be hoping for the experiment to fail, for yellow fever to flourish. And he had volunteered to stop it. Perhaps though, among those men, there was one, or even more, who hoped that he alone would die, and his death would be a discovery for all.

The boy from Chicago and Rose were volunteers too. I hope that by now the man from Chicago has succeeded at something—love, work—that has allowed him to outgrow the shame of failure. I have often imagined him returning home a week early that summer, to a mother, to a father; and having to watch his father's face as the boy told him he had failed because he was weak. A trifling incident in a whole lifetime, you may say. Not true. It could have changed him forever, his life with other men, with women, with daughters, and especially sons. We like to believe that in this last half of the century, we know and are untouched by everything; yet it takes only a very small jolt, at the right time, to knock us off balance for the rest of our lives. Maybe—and I hope so—the boy learned what his body and will could do: some occurrence he did not have time to consider, something that made him act before he knew he was in action.

Like Rose. Who volunteered to marry; even, to a degree, to practice rhythm, for her Catholic beliefs were not strong and deep, else she could not have so easily turned away from them after the third child, or even early in that pregnancy. So the life she chose slowly turned on her, pressed against her from all sides, invisible, motionless, but with the force of wind she could not breast. She stood at the sink, holding the children's glass. But *then* — and now finally I know why I write this, and what does stand out with purity: she reentered motherhood, and the unity we all must gain against human suffering. This is why I did not answer, at the bar, when she told me she did not deserve the children. For I believe she did, and does. She redeemed herself, with action, and with less than thirty minutes of it. But she could not see that, and still cannot. She sees herself in the laundromat, the supermarket, listlessly drunk in a night club where only her fingers on the table moved to the music. I see her young and strong and swift, wrapping the soaked blankets around her little girls, and hugging them to her, and running and spinning and running through the living room, on that summer night when she was touched and blessed by flames.

In a Father's Place

Christopher Tilghman

DAN HAD FALLEN asleep waiting for Nick and this Patty Keith, fallen deep into the lapping rhythm of a muggy Chesapeake evening, and when he heard the slam of car doors the sound came first from a dream. In the hushed amber light of the foyer Dan offered Nick a dazed and disoriented father's hug. Crickets seemed to have come in with them out of the silken night, the trill of crickets and honeysuckle pollen sharp as ammonia. Dan finally asked about the trip down, and Nick answered that the heat in New York had forced whole families onto mattresses in the streets. It looked like New Delhi, he said. Then they turned to meet Patty. She stood there in her Bermuda shorts and shirt, her brown hair in a bun, smelling of sweat and powder, and looking impatient. She fixed Dan in her eyes as she shook his hand, and she said, I'm so glad to meet *you*. Maybe she was just talking about the father of her boyfriend, and maybe no new lover ever walked into fair ground in this house, but Dan could not help thinking Patty meant the steward of this family's ground, the signer of the will.

"Nick has told me so much about this place," she said. Her look ran up the winding Georgian staircase, counted off the low, wide doorways, took note of a single ball-and-claw leg visible in the dining room, and rested on the highboy.

"Yes," said Dan. "It's marvelous." He could claim no personal credit for what Patty saw, no collector's eye, not even a decorator's hand.

Rachel had arrived from Wilmington earlier in the evening, and she appeared on the landing in her nightgown. She looked especially large up there after Dan had taken in Patty's compact, tight features; Rachel was a big girl, once a lacrosse defenseman. "Hey, honey," she yelled. There had been no other greeting for her younger brother since they were teenagers. Nick returned a rather subdued hello. Tired, thought Dan, he's tired from the trip and he's got this girl to think about. Rachel came down the stairs; Patty took her hand with the awkwardness young women often show when shaking hands with other young women, or was it, Dan wondered as he watched these children meet in the breathless hall, a kind of guardedness?

Dan said, "You'll be on the third floor." He remembered his own father standing in this very place, saying these same words to polite tired girls; he remembered the underarms and collar of his father's starched shirt, yellowed and brushed with salt. But it was different now: when Dan offered the third floor — and he had done so for some years now — he meant that Rachel or Nick could arrange themselves and their dates in the three bedrooms however they wished.

"The third floor?" said Patty. "Isn't your room on the second floor looking out on the water?" She appealed to Nick with her eyes.

"Actually, Dad . . . " he said.

Dan was still not alert enough to handle conversation, especially with this response that came from a place outside family tradition. "Of course," he said after a long pause. "Wherever you feel comfortable." She wants a room with a view, that's all, he cautioned himself. They had moved deeper into the hall, into a mildewed stillness that smelled of English linen and straw mats. They listened to the grandfather clock on the landing sounding eleven in an unhurried bass.

Dan turned to Patty. "It just means you'll have to share a bathroom with Ray, and she'll fight you to the last drop on earth."

But Patty did not respond to this attempt at charm, and fortunately did not notice Rachel's skeptical look. It was an old joke, or, at least, old for them. Dan remained standing in the hall, slowly recovering from his dense, inflamed sleep as Nick and Patty took their things to the room. Patty seemed pleased, in the end, with the arrangements, and after Dan had said good night and retired to his room, he heard them touring the house, stopping at the portrait of Edward, the reputed family ghost, and admiring the letters from General Washington in gratitude for service to the cause. Theirs wasn't a family of influence anymore, not even of social standing to those few who cared, but the artifacts in the house bracketed whole epochs in American history with plenty of years and generations left over. He heard Patty saying *wow* in her low but quite clear-timbred voice. Then he heard the door openings and closings, the run of toilets, a brief, muffled conversation in the hall, and then a calm that returned the house to its creaks and groans, to sounds either real or imagined, a cry across the fields, the thud of a plastic trash can outside being knocked over by raccoons, the pulse of the tree toads, the hollow splash of rockfish and rays still feeding in the sleepless waters of the bay.

A few years ago Dan had taken to saying that Rachel and Nick were his best friends, and even if he saw Nick rarely these days, he hoped it was largely the truth. He'd married young enough never to learn the art of adult friendship, and then Helen had died young enough for it to seem fate, though it was just a hit-and-run on the main street of Easton. Lucille Jackson had raised the kids. Since Helen died there had been three or four women in his life, depending on whether he counted the first, women he'd known all his life who had become free again one by one, girls he'd grown up with and had then discovered as he masturbated in his teens, or who had appeared with their young husbands at lawn parties in sheer cotton sundresses that heedlessly brushed those young thighs, or who now sat alone and distracted on bleachers in a biting fall wind and watched their sons play football. At some point Dan realized if you stayed in a small town all your life, you could end up making love with every woman you had ever known and truly desired. Sheila Frederick had been there year after year in his dreams, at the lawn parties and football games almost, it seemed to Dan later, as if she were stalking him through time. When they finally came together Dan stepped freely into the fulfillment of his teenage fantasies, and then stood by almost helplessly as she ripped a jagged hole eight years wide out of the heart of his life. There had been one more woman since then, but it was almost as if he had lost his will, if not his lust; the first time he brought her to the house she asked him where he kept the soup bowls, and in that moment he could barely withstand the fatigue, the unbearable temptation to throw it all in, that this innocent question caused him.

He undressed in the heat and turned the fan to hit him squarely on the bed. The air it brought into the room was damp but no cooler, the fecund heat of greenhouses. He felt soft and pasty, flesh that had lost its tone, more spent than tired. He tried to remember if he had put a fan in Nick's room, knowing that Nick would not look for one but would blame him in the morning for the oversight; Rachel, in a similar place, would simply barge in and steal his. Dan knew better than to compare the two of them, and during adolescence boys and girls were incomparable anyway. But they were adults now, three years apart in their mid-twenties, and noticing their differences was something he did all the time. Rachel welcomed being judged among men; and her lovers, like the current Henry, were invariably cheerful, willing bores. This tough, assertive Patty Keith with those distrustful sharp eyes, there was something of Nick's other girls there, spiky, nursing some kind of damage, expecting fear. Patty would do better in the morning. They always did. As he fell asleep finally, he was drifting back into history and memory and it was not Patty Keith, and not even Helen meeting his father, but generations of young Eastern Shore women he saw, coming to this house to meet and be married, the ones who were pretty and eager for sex, the ones who were silent, the ones the parents loved much too soon and the ones who broke their children's hearts.

In the morning Dan and Rachel ate breakfast together in the dining room, under the scrutiny of cousin Oswald, who had last threatened his sinful parishioners in 1681. The portraitist had caught a thoroughly unpleasant scowl, a look the family had often compared to Lucille on off days. She had prepared a full meal with eggs, fried green tomatoes, and grits, a service reserved as a reward when they were all in the house. When Nick and the new girl did not come down, Lucille cleared their places so roughly that Dan was afraid she would chip the china.

"I'm done with mothering," she said, when Dan asked if she wasn't curious to meet Patty.

Dan and Rachel looked at each other and held their breath.

"I got six of my own to think about," she said. And then, as she had done for years, a kind of rebuke when Nick and Rachel were fighting or generally disobeying her iron commands, she listed their names in a single word. "LonFredMaryHennyTykeDerek."

"And you'd have six more if you could, besides Nick and me," said Rachel.

"And you better get started, *Miss* Rachel," she said.

"How about a walk," said Dan quickly.

August weather had settled in like a member of the family, part of the week's plans. The thick haze lowered a scorching dust onto the trees and fields, a blanched air that made the open pastures pitiless for the Holsteins, each of them solitary in the heat except for the white specks of cowbirds perched on their withers. Dan was following Rachel down a narrow alley of brittle, dried-out box bushes. She was wearing a short Mexican shift and her legs looked just as solid now as they did as she cut upfield in her Princeton tunic. He would not imagine calling her manly, because hers was a big female form in the most classic sense, but he could understand that colleagues and clients, predominantly men, would find her unthreatening. She gave off no impression that she was prone to periodic weaknesses; they could count on her stamina, which, the older he got, Dan recognized as the single key to business. Nick was slight and not very athletic, just like Helen.

"So what do you think?" she asked over her shoulder.

"If you're talking about Patty I'm not going to answer. I don't think anything."

She gave him an uncompromising shrug.

They came out of the box bush on the lower lawn at the edge of the water and fanned out to stand side by side. "The truth is," said Dan, "what I'm thinking about these days is Nick. I think I've made a hash of Nick."

"That's ridiculous." She stooped to pick a four-leaf clover out of an expanse of grass; she could do the same with arrowheads on the beach. They stood silently for a moment looking at the sailboat resting slack on its mooring. It was a heavy boat, a nineteen-foot fiberglass sloop with a high bow, which Dan had bought after a winter's deliberation, balancing safety and speed the way a father must. When it arrived Nick hadn't even bothered to be polite. He wanted a "racing machine," something slender and unforgiving and not another "beamy scow." He was maybe ten at the time, old enough to know he could charm or hurt anytime he chose. Rachel didn't care much one way or the other—life was all horses for her—and Dan was so disappointed and angry with them both that he went behind the toolshed and wept.

"It's not. I really don't communicate with him at all. I don't even know what his book is about. Do you?"

"Well, I guess what it's really about is you. Not really you, but a father, and this place."

"Just what I was afraid of," said Dan.

"I don't think any of it will hurt your feelings, at least not the pieces I've read."

"Stop being so reassuring. A kiss-and-tell is not my idea of family fun." But Dan was already primed to be hurt. He'd been to a cocktail party recently where a woman he hardly knew forced him to read a letter from her daughter. It was a kind of retold family history, shaped by contempt, a letter filled with the word "never." This woman was not alone. It seemed so many of the people he knew were just now learning that their children would never forgive things, momentary failures of affection and pride, mistakes made in the barren ground between trying to keep hands off and the sin of intruding too much, things that seemed so trivial compared to a parent's embracing love. And even at the time Dan had never been sure what kind of father Nick wanted, what kind of man Nick needed in his life. Instead, Dan remembered confusion, such as the telephone calls he made when he still traveled, before Helen died. Rachel came to the phone terse and quick—she really was a kind of disagreeable girl, but so easy to read. Nick never had the gift of summarizing; his earnest tales of friends and school went on and on, until Dan, tired, sitting in a hotel room in Chicago, could not help but drop his coaxing, nurturing tone and urge him to wrap it up. Too often, in those few short years, calls with Nick ended with the agreement that they'd talk about it more when he got home, which they rarely did.

"But that's really my point," said Dan after Rachel found nothing truly reassuring to say. "This has been going on for quite a while. I'm losing him. Maybe since your mother died, for all I know."

"Oh, give him time."

"He's changed. You can't deny that. He's lost the joy."

"No one wants to go through life grinning for everyone. It's like being a greeter in Atlantic City."

"I don't think he would have come at all this week if you weren't here." It felt good to say these things, even if he knew Rachel was about to tell him to stop feeling sorry for himself.

But Rachel cleared her throat, just the way her mother did when she had something important to say. "See," she said, "that's the thing. I've been waiting to tell you. I've got a job offer from a firm in Seattle, and I think I'm going to take it."

Dan stopped dead; the locusts were buzzing overhead like taut wires through the treetops. "What?"

"It's really a better job for me. It's general corporate practice, not just contracts."

"But you'll have to start all over again," he whined. "I'd really hate to see you go so far away."

"Well, that's the tough part."

Dan nodded, still standing in his footsteps. "I keep thinking, 'She can't do this, she's a girl.' I'm sorry."

He forced himself to resume walking, and then to continue the conversation with the right kinds of questions—the new firm, how many attorneys, prospects for making partner—the questions of a father who has taught his children to live their own lives. They didn't touch on why she wanted to go to Seattle; three thousand miles seemed its own reason for the move, to be taken well or badly, just like Nick's novel. Dan pictured Seattle as a wholesome and athletic place, as if the business community all left work on Fridays in canoes across Puget Sound. It sounded right for Rachel. They kept walking up toward the stable, and Dan hung back while Rachel went in for a peek at a loved, but now empty, place. When she came back she stood before him and gave him a long hug.

"I'm sorry, but you'll have to humor the old guy," he said.

She did her best; Dan and Lucille had raised a kind woman. But there was nothing further to say and they continued the wide arc along the hayfield fences heavy with honeysuckle, and back out onto the white road paved with oyster shells. They approached the house from the land side, past the old toolsheds and outbuildings, and Dan suddenly remembered the time, Rachel was ten, when they were taking down storm windows and she had insisted on carrying them around for storage in the chicken coop. He was up on the ladder and heard a shattering of glass, and jumped from too high to find her covered in blood. Dr. Stout pulled the shards from her head without permanent damage or visible scar before turning to Dan's ankle, which was broken. Helen was furious. But the next time Dan saw Dr. Stout was in the emergency room at Easton Hospital, and they were both covered with Helen's blood, and she was dead.

Patty and Nick had come down while they were gone, and Dan found her alone on the screened porch that had been once, and was still called, the "summer kitchen." It was open on three sides, separated from the old smokehouse on the far end by a small, open space where Raymond, Lucille's old uncle, used to slaughter chickens and ducks. The yellow brick floor was hollowed by cooks' feet where the chimney and hearth had been; Dan could imagine the heat even in this broad, airy place. Patty was sitting on a wicker chair with her legs curled under her, wearing a men's strap undershirt and blue jogging shorts. She was reading a book, held so high that he could not fail to notice that it was by Jacques Derrida, a writer of some sort whose name Dan had begun to notice in the Sunday *New York Times*. Perhaps she had really not heard his approach, because she put the book down sharply when he called a good morning.

"Actually we've been up for hours," she said.

"Ah. Where's Nick?"

"He's working," she said with a protective edge on it.

Again, all Dan could find to say was "Ah." She smiled obscurely — her smiles, he observed, seemed to be directed inward — and he stood for a few more seconds before asking her if she would like anything from the kitchen. There was no question in his mind now: he was going to have to work with this one.

Rachel had just broken her news to Lucille, and the wiry, brusque lady who was "done mothering" at breakfast was crying soundlessly into a paper towel.

"I don't know what it is about you children, moving so far away," she said finally. Dan knew at least one of her sons had moved to Salisbury, and she had daughters who had married and were gone even farther.

"We've gotten by, by ourselves," said Dan.

"But that was just for schooling, for training," she answered; training, if Dan understood her right, for coming back and assuming their proper places in the family tethers. She was leaning against the sink, a vantage point on her terrain, like Dan's desk chair in his Queensville office, the places where both of them were putting in their allotted time. Rachel was sitting at the kitchen table and she stayed there, much as she might have liked to come closer to Lucille and reach out to her.

Dan went back to the summer kitchen and sat beside the girl. "You'll have to excuse us. Rachel's just dropped a bit of a bombshell and we're all a little shaky."

"You mean about her moving to Seattle."

"Well, yes. That's right." He waited for her to offer some kind of vague sympathies, but she did not; it was asking too much of a young person to understand how much this news hurt.

"So," he said finally, "I hope you're comfortable here."

At this she brightened noticeably and put her book face-down on the table. "It's a museum! Nick was going to set up his computer on that pie crust table. Can you imagine?"

Dan could picture it well and he supposed it would be no worse than the time Nick had ascended the highboy, climbing from pull to pull, leaving deep sneaker scuffs on the mahogany burl as he struggled for purchase. But she was right, of course, and she had known enough to notice and identify a pie crust table. "You know antiques, then?"

Yes, she said, her mother was a corporate art consultant and her father, as long as Dan had asked, was a doctor who lived on the West Coast. She mentioned a few more pieces of furniture that caught her eye.

"My mother thinks Chippendales and Queen Anne have peaked, maybe for a long time."

"I wouldn't know," said Dan.

"But the graveyard!" she exclaimed at the end.

Dan was relieved that she had finally listed something of no monetary value, peak or valley, something that couldn't be sold by her mother to Exxon. "As they say in town," he answered, "when most people die they go to heaven; if you're a Williams you just walk across the lawn."

"That's funny."

"I guess," he said. It was all of it crap, he reflected, if he became the generation that lost its children. He'd be just as dead now as later.

"They're the essential past."

Essential past? Whatever could she mean, with her Derrida at her side, her antiques? "I'm not sure I understand what you mean, but to tell you the truth," he said, "I often think the greatest gift I could bestow on the kids is to bulldoze the place and relieve them of the burden."

"I think that's something for the two of them to decide."

"I suppose coming to terms with all this is what Nick is up to in his novel." The girl had begun to annoy him terribly and he could not resist this statement, even as he regretted opening himself to her answer.

"Oh," she said coyly, "I wouldn't say 'coming to terms.' No, I think just looking at it more reflexively. He's trying to deconstruct this family."

"Deconstruct? You mean destroy?" he said quickly, trying not to sound genuinely alarmed.

Patty gave him a patronizing look. "No. It's a critical term. It's very complicated."

Fortunately Nick walked in on this last line. It was Dan's first chance to get a look at him and he saw the full enthusiasm—and the smug satisfaction—of one who has worked a long morning while others took aimless walks. Nick was gangly, he would always be even if he gained weight, but surprisingly quick. As unathletic as he was, he had been the kind of kid who could master inconsequential games of dexterity; he once hit a pong paddle ball a thousand times without missing, and could balance on a teeter-totter until he quit out of boredom. All his gestures, even his expressions, came on like compressed air. And while Dan had to work not to speculate on what part of himself had been "deconstructed" today, this tall, pacing, energetic man was the boy he treasured in his heart.

"The Squire has been surveying the grounds?" said Nick.

"Someone has to work for a living," said Dan, quickly worrying that Nick might miss the irony.

"I was wondering what you called it," he answered.

Patty watched this exchange with a confused look. Any kind of humor, even very bad humor, seemed utterly to escape her. "Did you finish the chapter?" she asked.

"No, but I broke through. I'm just a scene away. Maybe two."

"Well," she said with a deliberate pause, "wasn't that what you said yesterday?"

Good God, thought Dan, the girl wants to marry a published novelist, a novelist with antiques. He said quickly, "But it seems you had a great"—too much accent on the great—"a really very productive morning of work."

Nick's face darkened slightly, as fine a change as a razor cut. "It's kind of a crucial chapter. It has to be right."

"Were you tired?" she asked.

"No. It's just slow, that's all."

During this conversation Rachel had shouted down that lunch was ready, and Dan hung back for the kids to go first, and he repeated this short conversation to himself. It was not such a large moment, he reflected, but nervous-making just the same, and during lunch Nick sat quietly while Patty filled the air with questions, questions about the family, about Lord Baltimore and the Calverts. They took turns answering her questions, but finally it fell back to Nick to unlace the strands of the family, to place ancestors prominently at the Battle of Yorktown. He looked now and again to Dan for confirmation, and Dan knew how he felt reciting these facts that, even if true, could only sound like family puffery. Dan wanted to do better by his son and did try to engage himself back into the conversation, but by the time Lucille had cleared the plates he felt full of despair, gummy with some kind of sadness for all of them, for himself, for Rachel now off to Seattle in a place where maybe no one would marry her, for Nick with this girl, for Lucille so much older than she looked, and hiding, Dan knew it, her husband's bad health from everyone.

Patty ended the meal by offering flatteries all around the table, including compliments to Lucille that sent her back to the kitchen angrily—but loud enough only for Dan's practiced ear—mimicking the girl's awkward phrase, "So pleasant to have eaten such a good lunch." As they left the table finally, Dan announced he had to spend the afternoon in his office. At this point, he wasn't sure what he would less rather do. He changed quickly and left for town with the three of them discussing the afternoon on the summer kitchen, and he could hear Rachel laboring for every word.

He was so distracted as he drove to town that he nearly ran the single stoplight. Driving mistakes, of any kind, went right to his living memory; once he slightly rear-ended a car on Route 301, and he bolted to the bushes and threw up in front of the kids, in front of a very startled carload of hunters. He crawled to Lawyer's Row and came in the door pale enough for Mrs. McCready—it had always been *Mrs.* McCready—to comment on the heat and ask him if his car air conditioner was working properly. His client was waiting for him, Bobbie Perlee, one of those heavy, fleshy teenagers in Gimme caps and net football jerseys, with greasy long hair. The smell of frying oil and cigarettes filled his office. Whenever he had thought of Rachel joining his practice, he had reminded himself that she would spend her time with clients like this one, court-appointed, Bobbie Perlee in trouble with the law again, assaulting his friend Aldene McSwain with a broken fishing pole. McSwain could lose the eye yet. But Dan couldn't blame a thousand Perlees on anyone but himself; he had made the choice to practice in Queensville when it became clear that the kids needed him closer to home and not working late night after night across the Bay in Washington. If she had lived, Helen would have insisted anyway.

"What do you have to say this time, Bobbie?"

Bobbie responded with the round twangy O's of the Eastern Shore, a sound that for so long had spelled ignorance to Dan, living here on a parallel track. He said nothing in response to Bobbie's description of the events; he didn't really hear them. Bobbie Perlee pawed his fat feet into Dan's worn-out Persian rug. For a moment it all seemed so accidental to Dan; sitting in this office with the likes of Bobbie Perlee seemed both frighteningly new and endlessly rehearsed. He could only barely remember the time when escape from the Eastern Shore

gave meaning and guided everything he did. It was there when he refused to play with the Baileys and Pacas, children of family and history
like himself. It was there when he refused to go to the "University,"
which, in the case of Maryland gentry, meant the University of Pennsylvania. It was there even the night he first made love, because it was
with his childhood playmate, Molly Tobin. They had escaped north
side by side for college, and came together out of loneliness, and went
to bed as if breaking her hymen would shatter the last ring that circled
them both on these monotonous farmlands and tepid waters.

But he'd come back anyway when his father was dying, and
brought Helen with him, a Jew and a Midwesterner who came with
a sense of discovery, a fresh eye on the landscape. Helen had given the
land back to Dan, and Sheila Frederick had chained him to it, coming
back out of his youth like a lost bookend, with a phone call saying *I
don't look the same, you know,* and because none of them did — it had been
thirty years — it meant she was still pretty. She lived in a bright new
rivershore condo in Chestertown. She was still pretty, but now when
she relaxed, her mouth settled into a tight line of bitterness. Their last
night, two years ago, after a year of fighting, she told Dan she worried
about his aloneness, not his loneliness which was, she said, her problem and a female one at that, but his aloneness as he rattled around that
huge house day after day, with no company but that harsh and unforgiving Lucille. From her, this talk and prediction of a solitary life was
a threat; to Dan, at that moment, anyway, being alone was perfect
freedom.

Dan finally waved Perlee out of his office without anything further
said. These lugs, he could move them around like furniture and they'd
never ask why. Dan looked out his office window onto the Queen
Anne's County courthouse park, a crosshatching of herringbone brick
pathways shaded under the broad leaves of the tulip trees. At the center gathering of the walks was a statue of Queen Anne that had been
rededicated by Princess Anne herself. She was only a girl at the time
but could have told that wildly enthusiastic crowd a thing or two
about history, if they'd chosen to listen. Dan had done well by his children, if today was any indication. They were free not because they had
to be, but because they wanted to be. Rachel won a job offer from three
thousand miles away because she was that good. My God, how would
he bear it when she was gone? And Nick was reaching adulthood with
a passion, on the wings of some crazy notion about literary decon-
struction that, who knew? could well be what they all needed to hear

and understand. So, in many ways, his thoughts ended with this sad girl, this Patty Keith, who seemed the single part of his life that didn't have to be, yet it was she who had been tugging him into depression and ruminations on the bondages of family and place all afternoon.

On the way home he stopped at Mitchell Brothers Liquors, a large windowless block building with a sign on the side made of a giant *S* that formed the first letter of "Spirits, Subs, and Shells." The shells, of course, were the kind you put into shotguns and deer rifles. The Mitchells were clients of his and were very possibly the richest family in town. He bought a large bottle of Soave and at the last minute added a jug of Beefeaters, which was unusual enough for Doris Mitchell to ask if he was having a party. He answered that Nick was home with a girlfriend that looked like trouble, and he was planning to drink the gin himself.

The summer kitchen was empty when he stepped out, gin and tonic in hand. A shower and a first drink had helped. He might have hoped for the three of them, now fully relaxed, to be there trading stories, but instead they came out one by one, and everyone was carrying something to read. He supposed Patty was judging him for staring out at the trees and water, no obscure Eastern European novel in his hand. Nick was uncommunicative, sullen really, this sullenness in the place of the sparkling joy he used to bring into the house. Dinner passed quickly. Afterwards, Patty insisted that Nick take her to the dock and show her the stars and the lights of Kent Island the way, she said firmly, he *promised* he would. Rachel and Dan turned in before they got back and Dan read *Newsweek* absently until the last of the doors had closed, and he slipped out of his room for one of his house checks, the changing of the guard from the mortals of evening and the ghosts of the mid-watch. He was coming back to his room when he heard a cry from Nick's room. In shame and panic he realized immediately that they were making love, but before he could flee he heard her say, "No. No." It wasn't that she was being forced, he could tell that immediately; instead, there was a harshness to it that, even as a father is repelled at the idea of listening to his son have sex, forced Dan to remain there. He had not taken a breath, had not shifted his weight off the ball of his left foot; if anyone had come to the door he would not have been able to move. There was more shuffling from inside, a creak as they repositioned in the old sleigh bed. "*That's* right," said Patty finally, "Like *that*. Like that." Her voice, at least, was softer now, clouded by the dreaminess of approaching orgasm. "Like that," she breathed one last time, and came with a thrust. But from Nick, this whole time, there had not been a word, not a grunt or a sound, so silent he was that he might not have been there at all.

"I think she's a witch," said Rachel. They were on their post-breakfast walk again, this time both of them digging in their heels in purposeful strides.

Dan let out a disgusted and fearful sigh.

"No. I mean it. I think she's using witchcraft on him."

"If you'll forgive the statement, it's cuntcraft if it's anything."

"That's pretty, Dad" she said. They had already reached the water and were turning into the mowed field. "But I'm telling you, it's spooky."

All night Dan had pictured Patty coming, her legs tight around Nick's body, her thin lips clenched pale, and her white teeth dripping blood.

"She controls him. She tells him what to do," said Rachel. "If this were Salem she'd be hanging as we speak."

They had now walked along the hayfield fence line through the brown grass, and said nothing more as they turned for the house, its lime-brushed brick soft and golden in the early morning sun.

"It won't last. He'll get over her," he said.

"Yes, but the older you are, the longer it takes to grow out of things, wouldn't you say?"

Dan nodded; Rachel, as usual, was quite right about that. It had taken him six months to figure out that Sheila Frederick was one of the worst mistakes of his life, and another seven years to do something about it. It would not have been so bad if it weren't for the kids. He could admit and confess almost everything in his life except for the fact that he had known, for years, how much they hated her. They hated her so much that when it was over, Nick didn't even bother to comment except to tell Dan he'd seen her twice slipping family teaspoons into her purse.

They skirted the graveyard and without discussion bypassed the house for another tour. As they went by Dan glanced over his shoulder, and there she was, Derrida in hand, a small voracious lump that had taken over a corner of the summer kitchen. He looked up at the open window where Nick was working.

"I think I'd better marry Henry," said Rachel.

"He's a very nice guy. You know how fond of him I am," said Dan.

"Nice, but not very interesting. Is that what you mean?"

"Not at all. But as long as you put it this way, I think this Patty Keith is interesting."

"So what are we going to do about Miss Patty?" asked Rachel.

"Well, nothing. What can we do? Nick's already mad at me; I'm not going to give him reason to hate me by butting into his relationships."

"But someday Nick's going to wake up, maybe not for a year, or ten years, and he'll realize he's just given over years of his life to that witch, and then isn't he going to wonder where his sister and father were all that time?"

"It doesn't work that way. Believe me. You don't blame your mistakes in love on others."

Rachel turned to look at him fully with just the slightest narrowing of focus. It was an expression any lawyer, from the first client meeting to the last summary to the jury, had to possess. "Are you talking about Mrs. Frederick?" she said finally.

"I suppose I am. I'm not saying others don't blame you for the mistakes you make in love." Without any trouble, without even a search in his memory, Dan could list several things Sheila had made him do that the kids should never, ever forgive. What leads us to live our lives with people like that?

"No one blames you for her. The cunt."

Dan was certain that Rachel had never before in her whole life used that word. He laughed, and so did Rachel, and he put his arm on her shoulder for a few steps.

She said finally, with an air of summary, "I really think you're making a mistake. I believe she's programming him. I mean it. I think she's dangerous to him and to us. It happens to people a lot more resilient and less sensitive than Nick."

"We'll see." They walked for a few more minutes, in air that was so still that the motion of their steps felt like relief. Again Rachel was right; he was a less sensitive man than his son but he had been equally powerless to resist the eight years he had spent with Sheila. Dan couldn't answer for his own life, much less Nick's, so they completed their dejected morning walk and climbed the brick steps to the back portico. As they reached the landing, he took his daughter in his arms again and said, "God, Rachel, I'm going to miss you."

When they came back Patty was in the kitchen talking to Lucille. From the sound of it she had been probing for details about Nick as a boy, which could have been a lovely scene if it hadn't been Patty, eyes sharp, brain calculating every monosyllabic response, as if, in the middle of it, she might take issue with Lucille and start correcting her memories. It's not the girl's fault, thought Dan; it's just a look, the way her face moves, something physical. There was no way for Patty to succeed with Lucille; no girl of Nick's could have done better. It's not Patty's fault, Dan said to himself; she's trying to be nice but she just doesn't have any manners; her parents haven't given her any grace. He said this to himself again later in the morning when she poked her head into his study and asked if his collection of miniature books was valuable. Mother obviously did not deal in miniatures although, Dan supposed, she would be eager to sell Audubons to IBM. Dan answered back truthfully that he didn't know, some of his books may be valuable, as a complete collection it could be of interest to someone. She took this information back with her to the summer kitchen. Dan watched her walk down the hall, a short sweatshirt that exposed the hollow of her back and a pair of those tight jersey pants that made her young body look solid as a brick.

Dan did not see Nick come down, did not hear whether he had finished his chapter and whether that was enough for Patty. At lunch Rachel noted that the Orioles were playing a day game, and Dan had to remind himself again that except for sailing, the athlete in the family was the girl, that she'd been not only older but much more physical than her brother. He remembered how he and Helen had despaired about Nick, a clinger, quick to burst into tears at the first furrowing of disapproval; how Dan had many times caught a tone from the voices in the school playground right across the street from his office, and how he had often stopped to figure out if it was Nick's wail he heard, or just the high-pitched squeals of the girls, or the screech of tires on some distant street. And how curious it was that with this softness also came irrepressible energy, the force of the family, as if he saved every idea and every flight of joy for Dan and Rachel. Yet it had been years now that Nick had turned it on for him.

For once, Patty seemed content to sit at the sidelines, while Rachel and Nick continued with the Orioles. Name the four twenty-game winners in 1971, said Rachel, and Nick, of course, could manage only the obvious one, Jim Palmer. Rachel's manners—they were Lucille's doing as much as his, Dan reminded himself—compelled her to ask Patty if she could do any better; Patty made a disgusted look and went back to her crab salad. At that point Dan saw the chance he had been waiting for, and he turned to Nick and told him he had to go see a client's boat—a Hinckley—that was rammed by a drunk at Chestertown mooring. "Come on along and we'll catch up," he said offhandedly. He looked straight into Nick's eyes and would not allow him to glance toward Patty.

"Hey, great," said Nick after the slightest pause. "How about later in the afternoon?"

"Nope. Got to go at low tide. The boat sank." His tone was jocular, the right tone for cornering his son before Patty could move, before she started to break into the conversation with her "Wait a minute" and her "I don't understand." Rachel moved fast as well and quickly suggested, in a similar tone, that they, in the meantime, would go see the Wye Oak, the natural wonder of the Eastern Shore. "We can buy T-shirts," said Rachel.

"But . . . "

A few minutes later Dan and Nick were on the road in Dan's large Buick. There was considerable distance between them on the seat. "I hope Patty doesn't mind me stealing you like this," Dan said finally.

Nick could not hide his discomfort, but he waved it all off.

"Women," said Dan.

Nick let out a small laugh. He was sitting with his body turned slightly toward the door, gazing out at the familiar sights, the long chicken sheds of McCready's Perdue operation, the rustic buildings of the 4-H park under the cool shade of tall loblolly pines.

"So how's it going? The novel."

Good, he said. He'd finished his chapter.

"You know," said Dan, working to something he'd planned to say, "I'm interested to read it anytime you're ready to show it. I won't mention it again, just so long as you know. I can't wait to see what it's about."

"Oh," said Nick, "it's not really *about* anything, not a plot, anyway. I'm more interested in process. It's kind of part of a critical methodology."

Dan wanted to ask what in the world that meant, but could not. "Patty seems interested. I'm sure that's helpful."

"Patty's energy," Nick said, finally turning straight on the seat, "is behind every word."

"She certainly is a forceful girl." Dan realized his heart was pounding, and that it was breaking as he watched Nick come to life at the mention of her name.

"She tore the English department at Columbia *apart*." He laughed at some private memory that Dan really did not want to hear. "I know she's not for everyone, but I've never known anyone who takes less shit in her life."

And I love her, he was saying. I'm in love with her because she doesn't take shit from anyone. Not like you, Dan heard him think, who is living out his life a prisoner of family history. Not like you who let Mrs. Frederick lock me out the night I ran away from my finals in freshman year. Dan supposed the list was endless.

And at this impasse something could well have ended for him and Nick. It would not come as a break, a quarrel, but it would also not come unexpectedly or undeserved. In the end, thought Dan, being Nick's father didn't mean he and his son couldn't grow apart; didn't mean a biological accident gave him any power over the situation. It meant only that it would hurt more. He could not imagine grieving over friends he once loved with all his heart and now never saw. The Hellmans, how he had loved them, and where in the world were they now? But Nick, even if he never spoke to him again, even if this Patty Keith took him away to some isolation of spirit, Dan would know where he was and feel the pain.

"So why so glum, Dad?" said Nick, a voice very far away from the place where Dan was lost in thought.

"What?"

"I mean, we're going to see a wreck, a Hinckley, for Christ's sake, and you're acting like you owned it yourself."

They were crossing the long bridge over the Chester, lined, as always, with market fishermen sitting beside plastic pails of bait and tending three or four poles apiece. Twenty years ago they'd all been black, now mostly white, but there had not been too much other change in this seventeenth-century town; Dan had never known how to take this place, old families jostling to the last brick even as they washed and sloshed their way down Washington Street on rivers of gin. But it was a lovely town, rising off the river on the backsides of gracious houses, brick and slate with sleeping porches resting out over the tulip trees in a line of brilliant white slats. Dan looked ahead at this pleasant scene while Nick craned his neck out to the moorings.

"Oh yes," he said. "There's a mast at a rather peculiar angle."

The boat was a mess, lying on its side on a sandbar in a confused struggle of lines, a tremendous fibrous gash opening an almost indecent view of the forward berths. Nick rowed them out in a dinghy no one knew who owned; he was full of cheer, free, no matter what, on the water. The brown sand bar came up under them at the edge of the mooring like a slowly breaching whale. As they came alongside, Nick jumped out and waded over to the boat, peered his head through the jagged scar, and then started hooting with laughter.

"What is it?" said Dan.

Nick backed his head out of the hull. "Porn videos. God, there must be fifty of them scattered over the deck."

Dan quickly flashed a picture of his rather proper Philadelphia client, who could have no idea that his most secret compartment had been burst in the crash.

"Jesus," said Nick. "Here's one that is actually called *Nick My Dick.* It's all-male."

"Stop it. It's none of your business," said Dan, but he could not help beaming widely as he said this, and together they plowed the long way back through the moorings, making loud and obnoxious comments about most of the boats they passed. Dan doubted any of these tasteless, coarse stinkpots, all of the new ones featuring a dreadful palette of purples and plums, contained a secret library to compare with the elegant white Hinckley's. After they returned the boat they strolled up Washington Street to the court square and stopped for an ice cream at one of the several new "quality" establishments that had begun to spring up here. Dan hoped, prayed, only that Sheila Frederick, who lived here, would not choose this moment to walk by, but if she did she would simply ignore him anyway, which would not be a bad thing for Nick to see.

But it was all bound by the return, as if Nick were on furlough. And it was certain to be bad, Dan could sense it by now as they turned through the gates back to the farm. This time, when they re-entered the summer kitchen, the Derrida remained raised. As far as Dan could tell she had made little headway in this book, but she stuck to it through Nick's stray, probing comments about their trip. For the first time she struck Dan as funny, touchingly adolescent, with her tight little frown and this pout that she seemed helpless, like a twelve-year-old, to control. No, she had *not* gone to see the Wye Oak. No, she did not wish for any iced tea.

This is how it went for the rest of the day and into the evening. She's in quite a snit, said Rachel when they passed in the front hall, both of them pretending not to be tiptoeing out of range of the summer kitchen, which had seemed to grow large and overpowering around that hard nub of rage. Nick also circled, spending some of the time reading alongside the girl, some of the time upstairs writing a whole new chapter, perhaps a whole new volume, as penance. It was Lucille's day off, and normally eating at the kitchen table gave the family leave to loosen up, a kind of relief from the strictures of life. Patty sat but did not eat, just made sure that everyone understood, as Nick might have said, that she wouldn't take this shit. Dan could not imagine what she was telling herself, how she had reconstructed the events of the afternoon to give her sufficient reason for all this. In the silence, everything in the kitchen, the pots and pans, the appliances and spices, seemed to close in, all this unnecessary clutter. The pork chops tasted like sand; the back of the chair cut into his spine. He tried to picture how she might describe this to friends, if she had any. He could not guess which one of them had earned the highest place in this madness, but he knew which one of them would pay. He'd seen it in couples all his life, these cycles of offense and punishment, had lived the worst of it himself with Sheila Frederick. When she finally left the table, and Nick followed a few minutes later—he gave a kind of shrug but his face was blank—Rachel tried to make a slight joke of it. "We are displeased," she said.

"No. This is tragic," said Dan. "She's mad."

They cleaned the dishes, and after Rachel kissed him good night he went out into the darkness of the summer kitchen. The air, so motionless all week, was still calm but was beginning to come alive; he could hear the muffled clang of the bell buoy a mile into the river. A break in the heat was coming; the wild life that never stopped encroaching on this Chesapeake life always knew about the weather in advance, and the voices became shortened and sharp. The squirrels' movements through the trees or across the lawns became quick dashes from cover to cover; the beasts and beings were ready, even to a lone firefly, whose brief flashes gave only a staccato edginess to a darkening night. Dan felt old; he was tired. For a moment or two his unspoken words addressed the spirits of the house—they too never stopped encroaching—but he stopped abruptly because he knew, had known since a boy, that if he let them in he would never again be free of them. He wondered if Helen would be among them. He waited long enough, deep into this skittish night, for everyone to be asleep; he could not stand the thought of hearing a single sound from Nick's room. But when he finally did turn in he could not keep from hesitating for a moment at the door, much as he and Helen used to when the children were infants, and they needed only the sound of a moist breath to know all was well.

Under the door he saw that the light was on, and through it he heard the low mumble of a monotone. It was her, and it was just a steady drone, a break now and again, a slightly higher inflection once or twice. It was a sheet of words, sentences, if they were written, that would swallow whole paragraphs, and though Dan wanted to think this unemotional tone meant her anger was spent, he knew immediately that this girl was abusing his son. She was interrogating him without questions; she was damning him without accusations, just this litany, an endless rosary of rage. It could well have been going on for hours, words from her mad depths replacing Nick's, supplanting his thoughts. He could make out no phrases except, once, for a distinct "What we're discussing here . . . " that was simply a pause in the process as she forced him to accept not only her questions, but her answers as well. He did not know how long he stood there; he was waiting, he realized after a time, for the sound of Nick's voice, because as Dan swayed tired back and forth in the hall, he could imagine anything, even that she had killed him and was now incoherently continuing the battle over his body. When finally the voice of his son did appear, it was just two words. "Christ, Patty." There was only one way to read these two names: he was begging, pleading, praying for her to stop. And then the drone began again.

He closed his bedroom door carefully behind him, and sat by his bay window in an old wingback that had been Helen's sewing chair. Her dark mahogany sewing table was empty now, the orderly rows of needles and spooled threads scattered over the years. The wide windows beckoned him. He could feel no breezes on his sweating forehead and neck, but the air was flavored now with manure, milk, gasoline and rotting silage, a single essence of the farm that was seeping in from the northwest on the feet of change. He stared out into the dark for a long time before he undressed, and was still half-awake when the first blades of moving air began to slice through the humidity. He was nodding off, when later, on his pillow, he heard the crustacean leaves of the magnolias and beeches begin to clatter in the wind.

The house was awakened by the steady blow, an extravagance of air and energy after these placid weeks of a hot August. Dan could hear excited yips from the kitchen as if the children were teenagers once again; he thought, after what he had heard and the hallucinations that plagued him all night long, that he was dreaming an especially cruel vision of a family now lost. But he went down to the kitchen and they were all there: Rachel, as usual grumpy and slow-moving in the morning and today looking matronly and heavy in her long unornamented nightgown; Patty, standing on the other side by the refrigerator with a curiously unsure look; Lucille at her most abrupt, wry best; and Nick, wearing nothing but his bathing suit, pacing back and forth, filled with the joy and energy only a few hours ago Dan had given up as lost forever.

"A real wind," he said. "A goddamn hurricane."

"Shut your mouth with that," said Lucille happily.

"We're going to sail all the way to the *bridge*," he continued, and poked Rachel in the side with a long wooden spoon until she snarled at him.

"I've got to wash my hair," said Rachel.

"Fuck your hair."

Lucille grabbed her own wooden spoon and began to move toward him, and he backed off toward Patty, who was maybe tired out from her efforts the night before, or maybe just so baffled by this unseen Nick that even she could not intrude. Nick picked her up by the waist and spun her around. She was in her short nightgown and when Nick grabbed her he hiked it over her underpants; even as Dan helplessly noticed how sexy her body was, he recoiled at the thought of Nick touching it. With mounting enthusiasm, Dan watched this nervy move and wondered whether it would work on her, but she struggled to get down and was clearly furious as she caught her footing.

"I agree with Rachel," she said. It was probably, Dan realized, the first time she'd ever used Rachel's name.

Nick persisted. "Wind like this happens once a year. It might blow out."

"It could be flat calm again by lunch," said Dan.

She turned quickly on Dan as if he hadn't the slightest right to give an opinion, to speak at all. "I *understand*," she whined. "I just think this is a good chance for him to get work done."

It was "him," Dan noticed. He waited for Nick's next move and almost shouted with triumph when it came.

"Fuck work." As he said this, a quite large honey locust branch cracked off the tree outside the window and fell to a thud through a rustle of leaves.

Patty screwed her face into a new kind of scowl—she had more frowns, thought Dan, and scowls and pouts than any person he ever met—and announced, "Well I'm not going. I'm going to get *something* done."

"Derrida?" said Dan. He was still giddy with relief.

She glared.

"Oh, come on, sweetie," Nick coaxed. "You won't believe what sailing in wind like this is like." He tried cajoling in other ways, promises of unbroken hours of work, a chance to see the place from the water; he even made public reference to the fight of the day before when he told her a sail would "clear the air after that awful night." He could be worn down by this, Dan knew; he could still lose. But earlier in the conversation Rachel had slipped out and now, with a crash of the door that was probably calculated and intentional, she came back into the kitchen in her bathing suit—she really should watch her weight, Dan couldn't avoid thinking—and that was all the encouragement Nick needed.

Dan walked down to the water with them and sat on the dock as they rigged the boat. The Dacron sails snapped in slicing folds; the boom clanked on the deck like a road sign flattened to the pavement in a gale. "Is it too much?" he called out. Of course it was; under normal circumstances he would be arguing strenuously that it was dangerous. They all knew it was too much. Nick called back something, but he was downwind and the sound was ripped away as soon as he opened his mouth. They cast off and in a second had been blown a hundred feet up the creek. They struggled quickly to haul in the sails; Rachel was on the tiller and Dan wished she wasn't because she was nowhere near the sailor Nick was; she would have been better on the sheets where her brute strength could count. But she let the boat fall off carefully and surely, and all of a sudden the wind caught the sails with a hollow, dense thud, and as they powered past the dock upwind toward the mouth of the creek, Dan heard Nick yell, full voice and full of joy, "Holy shit!"

When he got back to the house she was in her place in the summer kitchen. How tired he was of her presence, of feeling her out there. All the time—it was maybe nothing more than a family joke, but it was true—she had been sitting in his chair. Nick may have told her, or she may have even sensed it. He walked through the house and was met, as he expected, as he had hoped, with an angry, hostile stare.

"You don't approve of water sports, I gather?" he said, ending curiously on a slightly British high point.

She fixed him in her gimlet eyes; this was the master of the Columbia English Department.

"Not interested?" he asked again.

"As a matter of fact, I don't approve of very much around here."

"I'm sorry for that," he said. He still held open the possibility that the conversation could be friendly, but he would not lead it in that direction. "It hasn't seemed to have gone well for you."

"There's nothing wrong with *me*."

"Ah ha."

"I think you're all in a fantasy."

Dan made a show of looking around at the walls, the cane and wicker furniture, and ended by rapping his knuckles on the solid table. He shrugged. "People from the outside seem to make a lot more of this than we do," he said.

She leaned slightly forward; this was the master of his son. "It's not for me to say, but when you read Nick's novel you'll know where *he* stands."

The words exploded from him. "How dare you bring Nick's novel into this."

"Why do you think he wanted to come here, anyway?"

"Patty," said Dan, almost frightened by the rage that was now fevering his muscles, "when it comes to families, I really think you should let people speak for themselves. I think you should reconsider this conversation."

"You have attacked me. You have been sarcastic to me. I have nothing to apologize for." She made a slight show of returning to her book.

"Tell me something. What are your plans? What are your plans for Nick?"

"Nick makes his own plans."

It was not a statement of fact; it was a threat, a show of her larger power over him. "And you? What are your plans?"

"I'm going to live my own life and I'm not going to pretend that all this family shit comes to anything."

"Whose family? Yours or Nick's?"

"You mean do I plan to marry Nick? So I can get my hands on this?" She mimicked his earlier gesture. "I suppose that's why from the second, the very second I walked in, you have disapproved of me. Well, don't worry"—she said this with a patronizing tone, addressing a child, a pet—"the only thing I care about around here is Nick and . . . " She cut herself off.

"And what?"

"And his work. Not that it matters to you."

"Oh, cut the crap about his work. You want his soul, you little Nazi, you want any soul you can get your hands on."

She pounded the table with her small fist. "What we're talking about here . . . " she shouted, and Dan's body recoiled with this phrase, "is the shit you have handed out, and I'll cite chapter and verse, and—"

"Patty, Patty." He interrupted her with difficulty. "Stop this."

"I have some power, you know."

"Patty, I think it would be better for everyone if you left. Right now."

"What?"

"You heard me."

"You would throw me out?" She did, finally, seem quite stunned. "And just what do you think Nick's going to do when he gets back?"

"I don't know. But I will not tolerate you in my house for another minute."

She slammed her feet down on the brick floor and jumped up almost as if she planned to attack him, to take a swing at him. "Okay. I will. I'm not going to take this shit."

She marched through the kitchen, and a moment or two later he heard a door slam. He moved from his seat to his own chair; suddenly the view seemed right again, the pecan lined up with blue spruce by the water, and the corner of the smokehouse opened onto a hay land that had, from this vantage, always reminded him of the fields of Flanders. A few minutes later he heard a heavy suitcase being dragged over the yellow pine staircase, the steel feet striking like golf spikes into the Georgian treads. He heard a mumble as she came to the kitchen to say something tactical to Lucille, perhaps to give her a note for Nick or to play the part of the tearful girl unfairly accused. He heard the trunk of her car open and he pictured her hefting her large bag, packed with dresses and shortee nightgowns and diaphragms and makeup, over the lip of her BMW, and then she was off, coming into view at the last minute in a flash of red.

Dan heard Lucille's light step, and then saw her face peer out onto the summer kitchen. As many times as Dan had tried to make her change, she never liked to come into a room to say something, but would stand in the doorway and make everyone crane their necks to see her.

"Mister Dan?"

"Lucille, *please* come out."

She took two steps. "You're in a mess of trouble now."

He held his arms up. "What could I do?"

"You just gotta make sure you're picking a fight with the right woman."

Dan looked away as she said this, and hung his head slightly as if he expected her to say plenty more. But when he glanced back up she was smiling, such a rare and precious event.

"I got six of my own to worry about," she said. The wind was singing through the screens in a single, sustained high note. "But I do hope to the good Lord that those babies are okay out in this storm."

Dan stayed on the summer kitchen all morning. The winds weren't going to die down this time—he knew that the moment he woke up—it was a storm with some power to it and it would bring rain later in the day. He ate lunch in his study, and around two went down to the dock. The water was black and the wind was slicing the wave tops into fine spray. No one should be out in this, and not his two children. He pictured them, taking turns at the tiller as the boat pounded on the bottoms and broke through the peaks in a shattering of foam. He wasn't worried yet; he'd selected that big boat for days like this. It would swamp before it would capsize and they could run for a sandy shore any time they wanted. The winds would send them back to this side; he'd sailed more than one submerged hulk home as a boy, and he'd left a boat or two on the beach and hiked home through the fields. This was the soul of the Chesapeake country, never far from land on the water, the water always meeting the land, always in flux. You could always run from one to the other. The water was there, in the end, with Sheila, because he had triumphed over her, had fought battles for months in telephone calls that lasted for hours and evenings drowned in her liquors, until one morning he had awakened and listened to the songs from the water and realized that he was free.

He lowered his legs over the dock planking and sat looking out into the bay. From this spot, he had watched the loblolly pines on Carpenter's Island fall one by one across the low bank into the irresistible tides. When the last of the pines had gone the island itself was next, and it sank finally out of sight during the hurricanes of the Fifties. Across the creek Mr. McHugh's house stood empty, blindfolded by shutters. What was to become of the place now that the old man's will had scattered it among nieces and nephews? What was to happen to his own family ground if Rachel went to Seattle for good and Nick . . . and Nick left this afternoon never to come back?

Dan tried to think again of what he would say to Nick, what his expression should be as they closed upon the mooring, what his first words should cover. But the wind that had already brought change brushed him clean of all that and left him naked, a man. He could not help the rising tide of joy that was coming to him. He was astonished by what had happened to him. By his life. By the work he had done, the wills, the clients, all of them so distant that he couldn't remember ever knowing them at all. By the wife he had loved and lost on the main street of Easton, and by the women who had since then come in and out of life, leaving marks and changes he'd never even bothered to notice. By the children he fathered and raised, those children looking out from photographs over mounds of Christmas wrappings and up from the water's edge, smiles undarkened even by their mother's death. By his mistakes and triumphs, from the slap of a doctor's hand to the last bored spadeful of earth. It was all his, it all accumulated back toward him, toward his body, part of a journey back through the flesh to the seed where it started, and would end.

The History of Rodney

Rick Bass

IT RAINS IN Rodney, in the winter. But we have history; even for Mississippi, we have that. There's a sweet olive tree that grows all the way up to the third story, where Elizabeth's sun porch is. Butterflies swarm in the front yard, in the summers, drunk on the smell of the tree; but in the winter, it rains. The other people in the town of Rodney are the daughters, sons and grandchildren of slaves. They own Rodney now.

This old house I am renting costs fifty dollars a month. Electricity sizzles and arcs from the fuse box on the back porch, spills out and tumbles to the ground in little bouncing blue sparks. The house has thirty-five rooms, some of which are rotting—one has a tree growing up through the floor—and the ceilings are all high, though not as high as the trees outside.

Here in the ghost town of Rodney there is a pig, a murderer, that lives under my house, and she has killed several dogs. The pig had twenty piglets this winter, and like the bad toughs in a western, they own the town. When we hear or see them coming, we run, to get out of the street. We could kill them, shoot them down on the center of the dusty lane that used to be a street, but we don't: we're waiting for them to fatten up on their mother's milk.

We're waiting for Preacher to come back, too. He's Daisy's boyfriend, and he's been gone for forty years.

Loose peafowl scream in the night, back in the trees, and it is like the jungle. The river that used to run past Rodney—the Mississippi— shifted course exactly one hundred years ago, and isn't here anymore.

It happened overnight: the bend downstream, the earthen bulge of an oxbow, broke somewhere, sometime in the night, breaking like a human's heart, and the water rushed through. Instead of making its slow, lazy descent through the swamp—northern water, coming down from Minnesota—it pressed, like sex, and broke through.

I've been reading about Rodney, in the old newspapers, and talking to Daisy, who lives across the street, and also, I've been sitting under the sweet olive tree trying to imagine it—and I'm sure that in the morning, after it happened, the townspeople blinked and gaped, because there was only a wide sea of mud.

There were boats full of cotton, stranded in the mud. Rodney was the second largest port in the South, second only to New Orleans—and there were fish dying in the mud, and alligators and snakes wriggling out there, and the townspeople stood on the docks and waited around for a day or two, for a rain to come and fill the big river back up—but when the fish began to smell—a great muddy flat place, covered with dead fish; the river had been almost a mile wide—then they had to pack up, and hike into the hills, into the bluffs and jungles above the river, to escape the disease and stench.

When the mud had dried and grown over with beautiful grass, tall grass, they moved back. Some of the men tracked the river, hunting it as if it were a wounded animal, and they found it seven miles away, flowing big and strong, as wide as it had ever been. It was flowing like a person's life, like a woman in love with something. It had just shifted.

Sixteen thousand people lived in Rodney, before and during the Civil War; now there are only about a dozen of us.

Daisy says they only put you away in Whitfield for forty years, for being a chicken-chaser. That was what the social workers saw, on their visit: Preacher chasing chickens down the street, like a crazy man. He was just doing it for fun—he might have been a *little* hungry, says Daisy, but mostly for fun—but they took him away.

Daisy says she's been keeping track on her calendars—and there are old ones tacked over every wall in her house, beginning with the year they hauled Preacher away—and that forty years will be up this fall, and that she's expecting he'll be back after that, that he'll be coming back any day.

Daisy didn't see the river leave, but her mother did. Daisy says that some of the pigs are Union soldiers, that the townspeople barricaded the soldiers in the Presbyterian church one Sunday, boarded all the doors up, and then Daisy's mother turned them all into pigs.

The mother pig is the size of a small Volkswagen; her babies are the color and shape of footballs. They grunt and snort like a stable of horses, at night, beneath Elizabeth's and my house.

Across the street, Daisy has a TV antenna, rising a hundred and fifty feet into the air, up above the trees. Daisy can cure thrash, or tuberculosis, or snakebite, or ulcers, or anything, as long as it does not affect someone she loves. She's powerless, over that part; she's told me so. She cooks sometimes for Elizabeth and me; we buy the food, and give her some money, and she cooks. Sometimes Elizabeth isn't hungry— she'll be lying on the bed up in the sun room, wearing just her underpants and sunglasses, reading a book—and so I'll go over to Daisy's by myself.

We live so far from civilization: the mail comes only once a week, from Natchez. The mailman is frightened of the pigs. Sometimes they chase his jeep, like dogs, up the steep hill, up the gravel road, back out of town. Their squeals of rage are a high, mad sound, but they run out of breath easily.

Daisy never gets mail, and we let her come over and read ours.

"This used to be a big town," she said, the first time she came over to meet us, to introduce herself, and to read our mail. She gestured out to the cotton field behind her house. "A port town. The river used to lay right out there."

"Why did it leave?" Elizabeth asked.

Daisy shook her head, and wouldn't answer.

"Will you take us to the river?" I asked. "Will you show it to us?"

Daisy shook her head again. "Nope," she said, drawing circles in the dust with her toe. "You got to be in *love* to see the river," she said, looking at me, and then at Elizabeth.

"Oh, but we are!" Elizabeth cried, looking at me and taking my arm. "That's why we're here!"

"Well," said Daisy. "Maybe."

Daisy likes to tell us about Preacher; she talks about him all the time. He was twenty; she was nineteen. There was an old Confederate gunboat out in the middle of the cotton field—it's since rusted away to nothing, and the remains have been buried beneath years and years of slime-mud, from winters' floods, springs' hard rains—but the boat was still in fair shape then, and they lived on it, Preacher and Daisy, out in the middle of this field—the field that's still out there, rich and growing green with cotton, hazy in the fall—and they slept in the captain's quarters, on a striped old mattress with no sheets, and they rubbed vanilla on their bodies to keep the bugs from biting, she said.

There were breezes. There were skeletons in some of the other rooms, and skeletons all around the boat, out in the field, sailors that had drowned when the ship burned and sank, a cannon hole in the bow—but they were old skeletons, a Confederate gunboat, and no more harmful than, say, an old cow's skull, or a horse's.

Daisy and Preacher made love, she said, all the time: in the day, in the blazing afternoon out on the deck, in the middle of the field—the boat half-buried in the field, even then, as if sinking, back into time, back into the earth—and then wild at night, all night, with coal oil lamps burning all around the ship's perimeter, and cries so loud, said Daisy, cries from the boat, that birds roosting down in the swamp took flight into the darkness, confused, circling over the field then and coming back. . . .

"We weren't going to do anything," said Daisy. "All we were going to do was live out on that boat and make love mostly all day. He wasn't hurtin' anybody. We had a garden, and we went fishing. We rode our horses down to the river and had a real boat down there, a little canoe. We went out on the river in it one day and he caught a porpoise. It had come all the way up from the Gulf after a rainstorm, and was confused by the fresh water. It pulled us all over the river for a whole afternoon."

A whole afternoon. I can see the porpoise leaping; I can see Daisy, young, with no wrinkles, and a straw hat. I can see Preacher leaning forward, battling the big fish.

"It got away," said Daisy, "it broke the line." She was sitting on the porch, shelling peas from the garden, remembering. "Oh, we both cried," she said. "Oh, we wanted that fish."

Lazy skies; streaks of red in the west, streaks of blood, of war: this place has a history, it has skeletons, violence, but we are living here quietly, smoothing it over, making it tame again, carefully; it is like walking on ice. Sometimes I imagine I can hear echoes: noises and sounds from a long, long time ago.

"This place is not on the map, right?" Elizabeth will ask. It's a game we play. We're frightened of cities, of other people.

"It might as well not even exist," I'll tell her.

She seems reassured.

The seasons mix and swirl. Except for the rains, and the hard stifling brutality of August, it can be easy to confuse the seasons. Sometimes wild turkeys gobble and fan in the dust in the street, courting: their lusty gobbles awakening us at daylight, a watery, rushing sound; that means it is April, and the floodwaters will not be coming back. But the other seasons get mixed up. The years do, too.

I'm glad Elizabeth and I have found this place. We have not done well in other places: cities. We can't understand them. Everything seems like it is over so fast, in a city: minutes, hours, days, lives . . .

Daisy keeps her yard very neat, cuts it with the push mower weekly, and has tulips and roses lining the edges of it. She's got two little beagle pups, also, and they roll and wrestle in the front yard and on her porch. Daisy gives church services in the abandoned Mt. Zion Baptist Church—it used to be on the shores of the river—now it just looks out at cotton field—and sometimes we go. She's good.

Daisy's sister, Maggie, lives in the old ghost town of Rodney, too. She says that she used to have a crush on Preacher; and that when Preacher was a little boy, he used to sleep curled up in a blanket, in a big empty cardboard box, at the top of a long playground slide in the front of the church. The slide is still there, beneath some pecan trees. It's a magnificent slide, such as you find in big city parks, tall and steep and glittering, shiny with use. It's got a little cabin—a booth—at the top, and that's where he used to sleep, says Maggie.

He didn't have any parents. It kept the rain off. Sometimes the two girls would sit up there with him and play cards. They'd take turns sliding down in the box then. They'd watch the white chickens walk past; walking down the dusty street, clucking.

"Maybe he always wanted one for a pet," Maggie says, trying to figure it out.

Forty years!

All for maybe what was just a mistake. Maybe he just wanted one for a pet.

The mother pig catches dogs. She lures them into the swamp. She runs down the center of what used to be Main Street in a funny, high-backed sort of hobbling, as if wounded, with all the little runt pigs running ahead of her, protected—the foolish dogs following, chasing it, slavering at the thought of fresh and easy meat.

Then the pig reaches the woods, and disappears into the heavy leafiness and undergrowth—the dog, or dogs, follow—and then we hear the squalls and yelps of the dog, or dogs, being killed.

Though we've also seen the sow kill dogs in the center of the street, in the middle of the day. She just tramples them, much as a horse would. I'd say she weighs about six or seven hundred pounds, and maybe more. Elizabeth and I carry a rifle when we go for our walks, an old seven-millimeter Mauser slung over Elizabeth's shoulder on a sling, a relic from the First World War, which we never saw, and which never affected Rodney. But if that pig were to charge us one night, the pig would rue that there had been a war. Elizabeth is a crack shot.

"Are the pigs really cursed people?" Elizabeth asks one evening. We're over on Daisy's porch. Maggie is shelling peas. Fireflies are blinking, floating out in the field as if searching for something with lanterns.

"Oh my, yes," says Maggie. "That big one is a general."

"I want to see the river," says Elizabeth, for about the hundredth time, and Daisy and Maggie laugh.

Daisy leans forward and jabs Elizabeth's leg, laughing. "How you know there even *is* a river?" she asks. "How you know we're not foolin' you?"

"I can smell it," Elizabeth says. She places her hand over her heart and closes her eyes. There's a breeze stirring dry leaves out in the road, a breeze stirring Elizabeth's hair, up on the porch, and she keeps her hand over her heart. "I can *feel* it," she says.

No one's laughing, now. We're thinking about the river: about how once it ran right through our town, through the very heart of it, and how we could have had our chance to see it then, had we been around.

For these old people—Daisy, Maggie, Preacher, and the others—to still be hanging on, to still be waiting around to see it again—well, it must have been quite a sight, quite a feeling.

Elizabeth and I put fireflies in empty mayonnaise jars, screw the lids on tightly and punch holes in the tops, and decorate our porch with them at night; or we'll line the bed with them, and then laugh as we love, with their soft blinking green bellies going on and off like soft, harmless firecrackers, or as if they are applauding. It's almost as if we have become Preacher and Daisy. The firefly bottle-lights around us must be like what the coal-oil lamps looked like, lining the sides of their old boat out in the field. Sometimes we shout, too, out into the night.

The bed; it's one of the best things we've ever done, buying it for this old house. It's huge, a four-poster, and looks as if it came straight off the set from *The Bride of Frankenstein*. It has the lace canopy, and is sturdy enough to handle our shaking. We have to climb a set of wooden steps to get into it, and sleeping in it is like going off on some final voyage, each night, so deep is our slumber, so quiet are the woods around us, and what is left of the town.

The last thing I do before we fall into that exhausted, peaceful sleep is to get up and go over to the window and empty the groggy, oxygen-deprived fireflies into the fresh night air: I shake all the bottles, to make sure I get them all out.

They float feebly down into the bushes, blinking wanly; wounded paratroopers, being released back into their real world, the one they own and know. If you keep them in a bottle too long, they will die. They won't blink anymore.

Elizabeth loves to read. She has books stacked on all the shelves of her sun room, up on the third floor, books stacked in one corner all the way to the ceiling. Sometimes I take iced tea up to her, in a pitcher, with lemons and sugar. I don't go in with it; I just peek through the keyhole. She wears a white dress, with lace, in the sun room, when she's reading, if it's not too hot. Her hair's dark, but there by the window, it looks washed in the light, like someone entirely different. It's scary, and intriguing. I knock on the door, to let her know the iced tea is out there, whenever she feels like getting it. Then I hurry down the steps.

After a while, I hear the click of the old door opening, up there, and the sound of her picking up the tray and carrying it in to her table; shutting the door with the back of her foot, I imagine — and she goes back to reading, holding the book with one hand, and fanning herself with a little cardboard fan with the other, still reading. Reading about make-believe people, and other people, other lives!

I'll sit out on the front steps and picture her drinking the tea, and imagine that I can taste its sweetness; the coolness, and refreshment of it.

I sweat too, in the summer, even down below the sweet olive tree, sitting on the steps, but not like she does, in the oven of her upstairs room. There's no air conditioner, no ceiling fan, and late in the afternoon each day, when she takes the white lacy dress off, it is soaking wet, and we rinse it in the sink, and hang it on the porch to dry in the night breezes.

It smells of sweet olive, the next morning, when she puts it on.

Time is standing still. We are digging in and holding our own, and we are making time stand still.

"We were going to have a baby," says Daisy. "We were just about ready to start, when they took him away. We were going to start that week, so that the baby would be born in the summer."

The slow summer. The time when nothing moves forward, when everything pauses, and then stops. It's a good idea.

In August, the cotton is picked. Men come from all over this part of the state. Trucks drive out into the fields. The men pick by hand. They do not leave much behind. It's like a circus. White horses stand out in the cotton, and watch; red tractor-trailers, and blue sky, and then, behind all of it, the trees, and behind that, the river, which we cannot see, but have been told is there.

Leaves clutter the street. They're brown and dried up, curled, and the street is covered with them, like a carpet. You can hear the pigs rustling in them at night, snuffling for acorns. You can hear Daisy, in the daytime, walking through them.

Then the men are gone, almost all of the cotton is gone, and there are leaves on the roofs of the houses, leaves in our yards. Daisy rakes.

The sweet olive doesn't lose its leaves, but the other trees do.

Maggie and Daisy burn their leaves continuously, in wire baskets out by the side of the old road.

Something about the fall makes us want to go to Daisy's church services. They last about thirty minutes, and mostly she just reads Bible verses, coming straight from her mind, sometimes making a few up, but they all sound right. Then she sings for a while. She's got a good voice.

Sometimes it makes us sad. We sing, too. In the early fall, when everything is changing, the air takes on a stillness, and we feel like singing to liven things up.

It feels real lonely.

They're old slave songs, that Daisy sings, and mostly you just hum, and sway. You can close your eyes. You can forget about leaving the town of Rodney.

The owl calls at night, up in the attic. He's big. There's a hole in the ceiling, and we can hear him scrabbling through it, around ten or eleven o'clock each night.

The full moon pokes through the trees, booms through our many dusty windows and lights the rooms. We hear him scrabble out to the banister, and then with a grunt he launches himself, and we hear the flapping of wings, initially, and then silence: he makes no sound, as he flies.

He flies all through the house—third floor, second floor, first—looking for mice. He screams when he spots one. He nearly always catches them.

We've hidden in the corner, in the big kitchen, and have watched. We've seen it happen. Elizabeth was frightened, at first, but she isn't now.

The longer we live down here, the less frightened she is of anything. She is growing braver with age, as if it is a thing that she will be needing more of.

Elizabeth and I want to build something that won't go away. We're not sure how to go about it, but some nights, we go running naked in the moonlight, out in the field. There are these old white plugs, nag horses, that roam loose in the cotton fields, and we ride them some nights. We ride across the field, toward where we think the river is—riding through the fog, and through the blinkings of fireflies—but when we get down into the swamp, we get turned around, lost, and are frightened; and we have to turn back.

Daisy's standing out on her porch sometimes, when we come galloping back.

"You can't go to it!" she says, laughing in the night. "It's got to come to you!"

She's waiting for Preacher. No cards. No letters. The air hangs still in the fall, after the cotton men leave. The days do not budge.

Afternoons, in the fall, we go pick up pecans in front of the old church. We fix grilled cheeses for supper. Some nights, we share a bottle of wine.

We sit on the porch in the frayed wicker swing, and watch the moon, and can hear Maggie down the street, humming, hoeing weeds in her garden.

The days go by. I think that we will have just exactly enough time to build what Elizabeth and I want to build—to make a thing that will last, and will not leave.

One night I can't sleep. Elizabeth isn't in bed, when I awaken. I look all through the house for her; a slight, illogical panic that grows, with each empty room.

The moon is out; everything is bathed in hard silver. She is sitting out on the back porch, in her white dress, barefooted, with her feet hanging over the edge, swinging them. Out in the yard, the pigs are feeding in the moonlight: the huge mother and the little ones, small dirigibles now, all around her. There's a wind blowing, from the south. I can taste the salt in it from the coast; it is warm. Elizabeth has a book in her lap; she's reading by the light of the moon.

A dog barks, a long way off, and I feel that I should not be watching. So I climb back up the stairs, and get into the big bed, and try to sleep.

But I want to hold on to something!

Luther—an old blind man, who lived down the street, and whom we hardly ever saw—has passed on. Elizabeth and I are the only ones with backs strong enough to dig the grave; we bury him in the old cemetery on the bluff. There are gravestones from the 1850s. Gravestones from the war, too, with the letters "C.S.A." on the stone. Some of the people buried there were named Emancipation, while they were alive—it was a common name then. It's soft, rich earth.

We dig the hole without much trouble. I had to build a coffin out of old lumber.

Daisy says words, as we fill the hole back up. That rain of earth; shovels of it, covering the box, with him in it. Sometimes in the spring, and in the fall too, rattlesnakes come out of the cane and lie on the gravestones, for their warmth. No one ever goes up to the cemetery, because of the snakes.

The river used to be visible, below the cemetery. Probably one day again it will be.

A few years ago, one of Daisy's half-sisters died, and they buried her up here. It was the first time anyone had been up to the cemetery in a long time—it was all grown over with brambles and vines, and weedy—and there was the skeleton of a deer, impaled upon the iron spikes of the fence that surrounds the graveyard. Dogs, or something, had been chasing it, and it had tried to leap over the high fence, and had gotten caught. There were only bones left. It's still up there, too high for anyone to reach.

The skull seems to be opening its mouth in a scream.

We pile stones over the mound of fresh earth, to keep the pigs from rooting. One time they dragged a man back down into town, after he had been buried. They were fighting over him, dragging him around on the street and grunting.

Mostly, I just want to start over. I'd like one more chance. I feel so old, some days!

Daisy has a cream, a salve, made from some sort of root, which she smears over her eyelids at night. It's supposed to help her fading vision; maybe even bring it back, I don't know.

Whenever she comes over to read our own sparse mail, she mostly just holds it, and runs her hands over it, and doesn't really look at the words. Instead, I think she just imagines what each letter is saying: what history lies behind it, what chain of circumstances.

Daisy and Preacher used to ride horses up onto the bluff overlooking Rodney, riding through the trees, and would then get off their horses and climb up in one of the tallest trees so that they could see the river. They'd sit up there on a branch, says Daisy, and have a picnic, eat sandwiches and feel the river breezes, and feel the tree swaying, and they would just watch the faraway river for the longest time.

Then they would climb down and ride through the woods some more, looking for old battle things—old rusted rifles, bayonets, canteens, and the like. They would sell these things to the museum in Jackson for a dollar each, boxing them up for the mailman, tying them shut with twine, and sending them C.O.D., and there was always enough money to get by on.

Daisy and Preacher would ride their horses down off the bluff and out across the field, out toward the river, after that, and they would go swimming at night; or sometimes they would just sit on the sand-bar and watch the stars, and listen to the river sounds. Sometimes a barge would go by. In the night, in the dark, its silhouette would look like a huge gunboat.

There were wild grapes that grew along the riverbank, tart purple Mustang grapes, cool in the night, and they would pick and eat those, as they watched the river.

They took him away when he was twenty; they took him away when she was just nineteen.

"It can go just like that," Daisy says, snapping her fingers. "It can go that fast."

The pigs are growing fat for slaughter. Autumn, coming on again, and they're not piglets, anymore: they are pigs. One morning a shot awakens us, and we sit up in bed and look out the window.

Daisy is straddling one of the pigs, and is gutting it with a great bladed knife, a knife from a hundred years ago. She pulls the entrails from the pig's stomach, and feeds them to her pups. The other pigs have run off into the woods, but they will be back. It's a cool morning, almost cold, and steam is rising from the pig's open chest.

Later in the afternoon, there's the good smell of fresh meat cooking.

Maggie shoots a pig at dusk, for herself, and two of the old men back down on the other side of town get theirs, the next day.

"I don't want any," Elizabeth says one afternoon, after she's slid down the banister. Her eyes are magic, she's shivering and holding herself, dancing up and down, goose-pimply; she's very happy to be so young.

"I feel as if it will *jinx* me," she says. "I mean, those pigs lived under our *house*."

The smell of pork, of bacon, hangs heavy in the town, like the blue haze from cannon fire.

Coyotes, at night, and the peafowl, screaming. Pecans underfoot. A full moon. The gleam of night cotton. We ride around on an old white plug, out in the cotton field. The cotton is ready to be picked. It is a field of warm, blossoming snow, bursting with white, up to our ankles, even when we sit on the horse.

The men will be coming soon to pick the cotton again. It has been four years, since we've been down here, in the town of Rodney.

"I'm happy," Elizabeth says, and squeezes my arms, sitting behind me on the old horse, and she taps the horse's ribs with her heels. The smell of woodsmoke, and overhead, the slight, nasal, far-off cries of geese, going south. The horse plods along in the dust.

Daisy will be starting her church services again, and once more we'll be going. I'm glad that Elizabeth's happy, living down here in the swamp, in such a little one-horse shell of an ex-town. We'll hold hands, and carry our Bible, and walk slowly down the road to Daisy's church. There will be a few slow, lazy fireflies, in the beginning of dusk. We'll go in and sit on the bench, and listen to Daisy rant and howl.

Then the songs and moans will start. The ones about being slaves. I'll shut my eyes and sway, and try not to think of other places.

And then this is what Elizabeth might say: "You'd better love me," she might say — an order, an ultimatum. But she'll be teasing, playing; she'll know that's all we can do, down here.

There'll still be geese, outside, overhead, and a night wind, and stars — noises and feelings about leaving, about moving on — but I think that we can sing louder, and it'll be all right.

We'll not be able to hear them, if we sing loudly enough.

The air will be stuffy and warm, in the little church, and for a moment, we might feel dizzy, lightheaded — but the songs are what's important, what matters. The songs about being slaves.

There aren't any words. You just close your eyes, and sway.

Maybe Preacher is not coming, and maybe the river is not coming back, either. But I do not say these things to Daisy. She sits out on the porch and waits for him. She remembers when she was our age, and in love with him. She remembers all the things they did; so much time, they had, all that time.

She puts bread crumbs out in the middle of the road, stakes white chickens out in the yard for him, in case he comes in the night. All she really has left is memory, but Elizabeth and I, we are still young, and we live in the old house across the street from her, and we try to learn from her.

The days go by. I think that we will have just exactly enough time to build what Elizabeth and I want to build — to make a thing that will last, and will not leave.

The Palace

Maura Stanton

AFTER THE WEDDING, I rode to the reception in a shiny black car. I sat in the back seat between two other bridesmaids. I was sixteen and lightheaded with excitement. I had come up to Chicago on the train to be in my aunt's wedding. I wore a long satin dress, with an overskirt of yellow chiffon. It was pinned in the back to make it fit in the bust. My high heels were made of clear vinyl, through which I could see my toes, and I wore puckered nylon gloves which ran all the way to my elbows.

"What a beautiful ceremony," said the short bridesmaid on my left, whose name was Karen.

"Everything was so lovely," said the tall bridesmaid on my right, whose name I had never quite caught.

"That's the kind of wedding we all want." Karen sighed. She glanced at me. "Your orchid is crooked, sweetheart."

I adjusted the smooth petals on my shoulder. I had never seen an orchid before this afternoon, and I was surprised that it had no smell.

"Where did you say you were from?" the tall bridesmaid asked me in a voice that was sweeter and higher than normal. Because I was younger, and a stranger, the bridesmaids all talked to me differently than they talked to each other.

"Peoria," I said. "But we're moving to Minnesota this summer."

"Oh, how nice," said the tall bridesmaid.

"Isn't that the land of ten thousand lakes?" Karen laughed. "You know, I've never been north of Milwaukee."

"Did someone say Milwaukee?" The groomsman in a black tuxedo, who was driving, glanced back at us. "Best city in the country. That's where I'm from."

The two bridesmaids laughed, as if they thought he had told a joke. I leaned forward. It was a sunny March day. I could see the grey turrets of the Lakeshore Palace Hotel in the distance, and high against the sky the red-roofed cupola where I had always wanted to climb. I had been taken inside the hotel once by my grandparents when I was eight or nine, but all I could remember was drinking a limeade at the marble counter in the hotel's drugstore.

"I'll park in the garage," the groomsman said. "I'll let you girls off at the front entrance."

"It's quicker to go in the back," said Karen.

"Oh, let's go in the front," said the tall bridesmaid. "I love walking through the lobby."

We drove under the green-striped canopy, and stopped at the bottom of a monumental staircase. Bellboys in red uniforms were running up and down the stairs. Our door was opened for us, and we stumbled out. The marble steps were slick under my high heels, and I held on to the brass railing. There were three sets of revolving doors at the top of the staircase, and I twirled through the one in the middle. I paused on the other side. I tilted my head back, looking up at the three tiers of balconies. The lobby was dim and bright at the same time. There were slender columns of rose-colored marble, oriental carpets, leather chairs arranged in intimate groupings, and crystal chandeliers. I had never seen anything so beautiful. I wanted to walk slowly around, touching the little cherry tables and the lion's-head finials on the backs of antique chairs, but the other bridesmaids were moving swiftly toward the row of elevators. They entered one going down, and I almost lost my shoes as I hurried after them. The blond elevator boy closed the doors with a flourish. He pushed his buttons, then stood staring at the floor, whistling softly, never once looking at any of us.

The elevator door opened onto a long, brightly lit corridor. I was a little disappointed. The floor was only speckled gold tile and the ceiling low. We went into a large, windowless room where rows of tables with folding chairs had been set up for the wedding reception. My aunt and her new husband had already arrived, and were posing for the photographer in front of an enormous cake, covered with silver roses. My aunt's lace veil had been thrown back from her face, and her cheeks were pink. Her dress was covered with little seed pearls which glittered under the bright lights.

"Oh, don't you look beautiful," my grandfather said when he caught sight of me. He put his arm around me. "Come take our picture," he called to one of my uncles, who had a camera around his neck. I smiled and blinked into the flash. My grandfather looked exceptionally handsome in his tuxedo; his pale grey hair was still thick and wavy. He had his picture taken with three of the other bridesmaids, and then with my grandmother, whose new pink suit could not hide her painfully hunched shoulders.

I stood at the very end of the reception line while the guests arrived. The room filled quickly. I met cousins I never knew I had, from Gary, Indiana, or visiting from Ireland. Sometimes they asked about my father or told me how pretty I looked in my bridesmaid dress. Two nuns in huge headdresses admired my little hat of yellow organdy petals. I nodded and smiled at everyone. Finally I shook hands with an old priest, who suddenly leaned forward and hugged me.

"I bet you don't remember me," he said jovially. "I'm your great uncle Pat."

"Oh, Father Pat," I said.

"I haven't seen you since you were twelve," he said, stepping back to look at me with his sharp blue eyes. He resembled my grandfather except that his skin was smooth and unwrinkled, and his voice had a more pronounced lilt to it.

"How are you?" I asked nervously.

"Fine, fine. And how's your pretty mother? I hear she's pregnant again."

"Yes," I said. "The baby's due any day now."

"And how many will that make?"

"Nine," I said.

"And isn't your father here? Did he drive you up?"

I shook my head. "He had to work: I came up on the train by myself."

"Well, well," he said, moving away. "It won't be long before you'll be a bride yourself, will it?"

Finally the bridal party was able to sit down. Waiters in white jackets began pouring the champagne. I held my breath until they had filled my glass to the brim like everyone else's. I lifted it to my lips for the first toast, and it was as wonderful as I had expected. I drank the whole glass.

"Well, you're Irish all right," said Karen, who was sitting beside me at the end of the bridal party table.

"What do you mean?" I asked.

She pointed at my empty glass. Her own was still almost full. "I bet you're not even dizzy, are you?"

"No," I said. "I'd like some more."

She laughed. "So would the groom, but they're only letting him have one glass for the toast."

"Why only one?" I asked innocently.

"Never mind," she said, putting a piece of wedding cake in her mouth.

I ate my chicken salad, and had another glass of champagne. The musicians arrived, with their accordians, fiddles and flutes, and began to play something that sounded vaguely like the *Blue Danube Waltz.* The bride and the groom danced cheek to cheek while everyone applauded. Then they sat down and the Irish music began. Some of the guests clapped and others began singing "Who threw the overalls in Mrs. Murphy's chowder?" in gay voices. The waiters were still bringing champagne, but there were bottles of whiskey on some of the tables now, too. I saw Father Pat pour himself a shot.

"Do you think I could go walk around the hotel?" I asked Karen.

"Sure," she said. "They're going to push the tables back for dancing. We'll be here for hours."

I took the elevator back up to the lobby. Now I had time to notice the little shaded red lamps on the tables, and the distinguished men in suits sitting here and there, reading newspapers. The front desk was a long, mahogany counter, with heavy, carved pillars, and I told myself that someday, when I grew up, I would check in here as a guest. I walked down a wide corridor, where gold lamps hung on the paneled walls, to the restaurant. I stood outside the French doors, half-hidden by potted palms, looking in at the glittering tables where I would sit some evening in the future. There were silver ice buckets or small silver coffee pots on all the tables, and the diners—there were not very many at this hour—brought their forks or wine glasses slowly to their mouths, as if they were doing so underwater. The women had bare arms like swimmers, and their hands moved in undulating gestures when they talked.

I went up a wide, thickly carpeted staircase to the first balcony. I heard exquisite music, and walked towards it. I came to some felt covered doors, one of which was propped open with a chair. A tall, gangly bellboy stood just outside, his face strained with attention. He seemed to be leaning in towards the music. I looked past him into the room. A string quartet was performing on a low platform in front of a small audience of men in tuxedos and women in evening gowns. I held my breath and listened. I had never heard music like this before. It was clear and exhilarating.

"What is it?" I whispered to the bellboy, who did not seem to hear me at first.

"Beethoven," he answered in a moment, speaking from the corner of his mouth. "It's the *Grosse Fuge*."

Just then a bald man in a white jacket got up from his chair and darted to the door. The bellboy backed away, coughing.

"Do you have a ticket, Miss?" the man asked me in a sharp voice.

"No," I said, stepping back with the bellboy. My face burned with embarrassment.

With one swift movement, the bald man removed the chair from the door and pulled it shut behind him. I could no longer hear the music.

"Dirty bastard!" The bellboy kicked the carpet as he walked away. His voice was choked.

I took a deep breath, then went up to the second balcony. I stopped to look at some large, dark paintings in heavy gilt frames. Some were portraits of dour-looking men, but others were huge historical canvases. It was hard to make them out in the dim light. I was left with an impression of twisted male torsos and chariot wheels. I had just paused to study the marble statue of a woman in a toga, when I felt someone behind me.

I turned my head, and caught a glimpse of a thin, jet-haired man in a rumpled sport shirt. His closeness made me uncomfortable, and I moved rapidly away. I went back down the two flights of stairs to the lobby, and decided to see if I could find a way up to the cupola.

I waited for an elevator, watching the numbers above the doors light up as the cars passed from floor to floor. When the first elevator going up arrived, I told the elevator boy the number of the top floor.

"I suppose you're going to a party in one of the penthouses," he said as he pulled the inner grate shut. "That's a real pretty dress." He smiled at me cheerfully. He had a bad complexion and a crew cut. His scalp showed in white patches above his ears.

"No," I said. "I'm at a wedding reception downstairs. But I want to go up to that cupola. Do you know how to get there?"

"Sure. You're going to the right floor. There's a fire door in the middle of the hall. Just take the stairs. But watch out for the wind. Boy, is it windy up there!"

"Do you like working here?" I asked as the elevator jolted and rose. I pressed my hand against my stomach.

"It's great," the boy said. "You meet all kinds of people at the Palace. Celebrities, too. I rode with Cary Grant once. It's too bad they're tearing the place down."

"Tearing it down?"

"The land must be worth a million a square inch. They're going to put up apartments." The elevator stopped and he opened the door. "There you are. Maybe I'll catch you on the way down."

"Thanks," I said.

The fire door was right where he said it was. I could feel the wind in the stairwell, and as I climbed up the spiral stairs to the level of the open windows in the cupola, it made a whistling noise. At first, I could hardly open my eyes in the face of it. My hair was whipped back from my forehead. But then I grew used to its steady push against my body.

The lake was dazzling. No real sea could have pleased me better just then. The plane of the water seemed to tilt upwards towards a vaporous blue horizon, and across it ran foaming waves which broke on the rocks below me with stolid turbulence.

Then my eye caught the glint of the setting sun on the glass fronts of apartment buildings along Lake Shore Drive. I felt a pang. I would never see this view when I grew up—when the future came, this hotel would not exist. I ran my palm along the rough stone window ledge. It occurred to me for the first time that the other solid objects with which I had furnished my future would soon not exist—my home, my high school, and even my friends would all evaporate this summer when my family moved, and I could not begin to imagine what might replace them.

After a few minutes, I think I began to be self-conscious about my sadness. I told myself that I was grown up, that this was the way you felt as an adult. I threw my head back, and looked up at some soft hazy clouds that were gathering as the sun dropped. I tried to hum the scrap of Beethoven I had heard downstairs, but the melody eluded me. I could only faintly recall its effect on me.

I went slowly back down the spiral stairs, trying not to stumble in my wobbly heels. As I reached the fire door, I heard a grunt. In the corner of the stairwell stood the jet-haired man I had seen up on the second balcony. As I stared at him, startled and immediately uneasy, he fumbled with his pants and opened his fly.

"Here, Miss," he said softly, grinning at me.

I gasped, and ran past him. It took me a few moments to get the firedoor open, for in my panic I kept pushing against it instead of pulling it open.

"You want it, don't you, Miss?" the man said, coming closer to me. "You'd like to put it in your mouth, wouldn't you, Miss?"

I pulled the door open at last. I ran down the hall towards the elevator. I saw one open and waiting and I knew I had to reach it before the doors closed, or I would be trapped. My right shoe came off, but just at that moment the elevator boy, who was not the same one who had brought me up, reached out to close his door.

"Wait!" I called, abandoning my shoe.

He held the door open for me. I hopped awkwardly into the elevator with one stockinged foot. Before I had time to catch my breath and ask him to wait until I got my shoe, he had put his elevator in motion. He had a sullen face and bitter, twisted lips, so I did not speak to him. I leaned against the back wall, fighting tears and hysteria. "Be calm, be calm," I told myself over and over like a litany.

"Where to?" the elevator boy asked in a harsh voice.

"The basement," I said.

He shrugged, and pushed a button.

We shot down so quickly that I felt sick to my stomach. When the door opened, I stepped out immediately. I found myself in a gloomy area with rough stone walls, and I realized that I was in a real basement that must be below the level of the reception room. I heard the elevator door shut behind me, and I knew at once that the elevator boy had been maliciously literal when he let me off down here. I decided to find a stairway up, rather than call him back.

I took off my other shoe. I walked between bins that were piled almost ceiling-high with coal, and came to a huge furnace. The door of the furnace was open, and the flames shot up wildly. A man in overalls, covered with coal dust, was heaving coal inside with an iron shovel.

I was afraid to let him see me, and hurried past him. I went up three wide steps into another part of the basement, which was noisy with the roar of washing machines. The floor was wet and soapy, for some of the machines were overflowing. Three black women in white cotton smocks were pulling sheets out of the large commercial dryers that lined one wall. The next room was loud with the clank of ironing machines. Here there were about a dozen exhausted-looking women, some black and some white, feeding sheets through the big rollers. The women were plastered with sweat, and their shoulders seemed permanently hunched. A few of them glanced up at me when I passed, but their faces remained blank and expressionless.

I found a stairway up at last. I had to stop in a restroom to take off my stockings and wash my feet, which were covered with soap and coal dust. I flinched when I looked at myself in the mirror. My eyes, staring back at me, seemed furtive, and there was an unpleasant thinness about my lips. I tried not to think about the jet-haired man, but his ugly image was imprinted on my brain as if I had deliberately taken a photograph.

I could hear the Irish music coming down the hall. It struck me as tinny and garish. The reception room was so hazy with cigarette smoke when I entered that I coughed and gasped. Everything in the room was blurry and the smoke drifted in waves. My aunt was smoking in her satin gown, and her face looked grey and drawn. Her new husband was scratching under his collar. My uncle had drunk too much, and his embarrassing laugh rang through the room. I sat down beside Karen, and noticed the sharp, envious expression of her face as she talked to my aunt. Across the room, the groom's sisters were whispering together in the corner, and I knew by the shape of their mouths that they were saying nasty things.

I looked around me with surprise. I seemed to have X-ray vision. The martyred expression on my grandmother's face was carefully studied. My grandfather, as he hopped about in his tuxedo, doing some kind of jig with a cousin from Ireland, was vain and self-centered. Everyone I looked at was pinched or mean or stunted in some way and I knew I was no exception. I heard unkindness and jealousy in all the voices that rose around me in supposed merriment.

My aunt moved away. The back of her wedding gown, where she had been sitting, was all wrinkled. The tall bridesmaid came and sat down on the other side of Karen.

"I'm glad I'm not marrying into that family," she said in a low voice. "What a bitch his sister is."

"You'd think it was her wedding," Karen whispered back. "You know, she told me I ought to have gone on a diet. She said my dress was too tight."

"What a nerve!"

"Bitch."

I got up, and went to sit beside Father Pat, who was staring at the empty shot glass in front of him.

"What happened to your shoes?" he asked. He spoke slowly, his words faintly slurred.

"My feet hurt," I said, flushing and looking away from him. I knew I would never tell anyone what had happened as long as I lived but I would never be able to forget it.

"Somebody said you were upstairs."

"I was looking around the hotel."

"It's a grand place." He slid his empty glass back and forth along the tablecloth.

"They're going to tear it down," I said before I could stop myself. I knew I was speaking out of meanness.

"Are they, now? I read something in the paper, but that was a long time ago. I thought it had blown over." He picked up the shot glass, and looked at it curiously. "They tear everything down. By the time you're my age, everything you used to like will be gone."

I looked at the tablecloth, which was covered with bread crumbs and specks of frosting.

"When I went back to Ireland two summers ago," Father Pat continued, "they'd even torn down the church where I said my first Mass. De-consecrated the building and torn it down." He sighed. He reached across the table for the whiskey bottle and poured himself another shot.

I looked at his profile as he put the glass to his lips. His hair was thinning over his temples, and I could see bluish veins through his fine, pale skin. The veins ran deep into his brain, where all the evil things he had heard in confession over the years must still be lodged, fresh and sharp as a packet of straight pins. Inside everyone's head, just below their pretty or bored or wandering eyes, the strangest and most frightening pictures must be permanently etched; yet the real world around them shifted and changed and disappeared.

I wanted to get up and go away somewhere and hide my face but there was nowhere to go.

"Excuse me. You lost your shoe, didn't you?"

I looked up to see the cheerful bellboy with the crewcut who had taken me up to the cupola. He held my high heel in one hand.

"I found this in the hall," he said, blushing until his ears turned red. "I thought it must be yours, so I came down here on my break."

"Oh, thank you," I said, taking the shoe from him. I found it hard to smile. He took a step backwards.

"Well, Cinderella, don't just sit there," said Father Pat with a sudden laugh. "Give the boy some cake. He might be a prince indeed."

"Would you like some cake?" I asked.

He hesitated. "Well, sure."

I got up, and led him over to the cake. The top two tiers were gone, and big chunks of the bottom tier had already been eaten.

"Do you like frosting?"

"That's the best part," the boy said, playing nervously with one of his gold uniform buttons. "You know, I thought of Cinderella, too."

"I didn't," I said.

"Didn't you always want to be Cinderella?"

"I'd rather be the fairy godmother," I said, cutting him a large piece of cake with a huge silver rose on the top. "So I could change things."

"I'll just take this back with me," the boy said as I handed him the paper plate. "I've only got ten minutes."

"Thanks a lot," I said. "It was very nice of you to bring my shoe."

He swallowed. "Don't mention it," he said. He looked a little hurt, and glanced around the room. "It looks like a swell party. I'll have to get married someday just for the fun of it. See you later."

"Goodbye," I said. I wished I could have been warmer to him, but my throat ached. My heart was a lump of coal. I went back to join Father Pat, just as my grandfather stood up, waving his arms at the musicians.

"I've got a song to sing," my grandfather cried, his eyes shining. "Do you know 'The Lambs on the Green Hills'?"

"Sure we do," shouted the accordian player, putting down his beer and adjusting his keyboard.

Father Pat whispered in my ear. "He used to sing that when we were boys. We stood on the hill together, looking at the sea. We thought we could see as far as America. Your grandfather always had a fine voice."

My grandfather began to sing. His tenor voice was high and clear, transcending his age in a way that startled me. I leaned forward. I had heard him singing around the house, in the shower and in the car, but never formally like this. He held onto the lapels of his tuxedo, his eyes closed:

The lambs on the green hills stood gazing at me,
And many strawberries grew round the salt sea,
And many strawberries grew round the salt sea,
And many a ship sailed the ocean.

He opened his eyes a moment, and I saw they were wet. The song went on, telling the story of a bride and the man she had not married, who was going to die for love of her, and who wanted her to sprinkle his grave with flowers so sweet. I could tell that my grandfather really saw the strawberries and the salt sea, and everytime the song returned to the refrain, I saw them, too. And for a moment I was up in the cupola again, with the wind on my face, looking at the lake, with no knowledge of the jet-haired man who lurked at the foot of the stairs.

Father Pat had shut his eyes, too. His lips trembled. When the song was over, he shook himself.

"It gives me the shivers," he said. "I'm over seventy, and I thought I was a boy."

I wiped my forehead, which was covered with cold sweat. I looked around the room at the other wedding guests, who were clapping and whistling and stamping their feet, trying to get my grandfather to sing again, which he refused to do. I felt as if a fever had broken. My grandmother touched my grandfather's hand when he sat down beside her. The groom had his arm about my aunt's shoulder, and was whispering something in her ear which made her smile and look at her ring. People were laughing and having second helpings of the big, ruined cake, and it seemed to me that I knew even less about everything than I ever had.

The Body Politic

Theodore Weesner

FIVE-FIVE AND ONE-TWELVE, thirteen years old, out of an obscure elementary school, a complete unknown, Dale Wheeler walked into the boys' locker room to spin the dial of his combination lock. It was Emerson Junior High, a school with a double gym with a floor the color of whiskey upon which street shoes were never allowed.

The occasion: seventh-grade basketball tryouts.

Dale removed items from his gym bag, laid them on the bench. Two pairs of white wool socks, white high-top sneakers, gym shorts, T-shirt, jock. All but the T-shirt were new. He had to remove staple and paper label from a pair of socks, the jock from the box. The new sneakers, a once-a-year event, promised speed, new squeak-grips on the polished wooden floor, sudden turns, spring. This pair, he told himself, he'd keep strictly for indoor use, a promise he had made to himself back in sixth grade, too, only to break it during a sunny February thaw to the more immediate promise of running outdoors with seeming lightning speed.

The gym bag was new, too, his first, navy blue with brown leather handles, a spontaneous gift from his father as they had shopped on Saturday. Except for the sneakers, P. F. Flyers, and the jock, a Bike—a slight necessity, but his first, and thus not so slight an event after all—the items were free of racing stripes or product names, as apparently uncomplicated as other forces at work in the era in which this otherwise unnoticed chapter in sports history was quietly unfolding.

Dale and his father, Curly Wheeler—the two lived alone together

87

in an apartment on Chevrolet Avenue, in the obscure elementary school district, just up the hill from Chevrolet Plant Ten where Curly worked the second shift—had picked out the items at Hubbard's Hardware & Sporting Goods Store downtown. Dale's list from school did not include a gym bag, and he had imagined carrying everything in a paper bag, much as his father always had a bottle or two in paper bags nearby, in glove box, trunk, under the driver's seat. But his father had tipped one of those bags a few times already by midday Saturday, the last a sizeable snort as they parked in the alley behind Hubbard's, and there were the gym bags on a shelf before them.

"How you going to carry all that gear?"

Dale was looking in the same direction. "Don't those cost a lot?" he said.

"Let's do it right," his father said. There was that reddish glow in his cheeks, the film over his eyes, his Mona Lisa grin.

Blue was the wrong color, though, as Dale realized when a string of other boys—the legendary Sonny Joe Dillard among them—filed by in the main aisle of the locker room, each carrying a kelly green gym bag. The school colors were green and white, Dale knew, alas, in this moment, even as he had known it all along. Green and white, fight fight! "Gee!" he said aloud.

"Belly high . . . without a rubber," one of the gang of five sang out as they filed into a nearby aisle.

Dale's plain white T-shirt also identified him as an outsider. It was true that there were other white T-shirts present in the gathering of twenty-five or thirty, but each was worn by a boy who handled a basketball with his elbows out, or one who could not get his feet, in concert with his hands, to comprehend the concept of *steps*. Then two more boys wearing white T-shirts walked in, but the two—they had to be twins—were blubbery with jelly rolls around their middles, with near-breasts, and each wore knee guards, elbow guards, and wire cages over glasses. Otherwise most of the boys—those who knew the score, it was clear—wore kelly green sleeveless basketball jerseys, although no such item had been included on the mimeographed list. One boy wore a flowered bathing suit which he had outgrown, in any case, perhaps a year earlier.

Coach Burke walked into the gym carrying a new ball, blowing his whistle, shouting at them to return the balls to the ball bin, to *never* take a ball from the ball bin unless he said to! Appearing then, making a jogging entrance from the tunnel onto the glossy floor, were the boys of the green gym bags. The five, Dale noticed, wore uniform gray sweatshirts—over green sleeveless jerseys, it would turn out— above white gym shorts and, laced in a military staircase braid into their white sneakers, matching green shoelaces. They were the ones, they seemed to say in so many ways, who already had it made at Emerson Junior High.

The coach, ball under his arm, tweeted his whistle, told them to sit down. He paced to and fro before them, shifted the new ball hand to hand as he talked. He introduced the Locker Room Man, "Slim," who stood at the tunnel entrance at the moment watching. The best players and hardest workers would make the traveling squad of ten, he told them. That was the way it was. This wasn't elementary school anymore and that was the black and blue reality of competitive sports. A list would be posted on the bulletin board outside his office after practice on Friday. *But,* he added, raising a finger. That wasn't all. Any boy—any one of them who had the desire—could continue to attend practices and, from among *those* boys, *two* alternates would be selected to dress for each home game.

Dale Wheeler sat watching and wondering. Two alternates for each home game. It meant everyone had a chance. Sort of. But did the coach mean the same two, or two new ones each time? There were so many students here in junior high. Hundreds more than in the small brick elementary school he had attended. The building and grounds covered acres. And any number of ninth-grade boys actually had mustaches, were over six feet tall. And some girls—The coach blew his whistle again. He said, sharply, "On your feet!" and they jumped, almost as one, as if the process of selection were related to how quickly one could get upright. All but Sonny Joe, Dale noticed. Sonny Joe Dillard—his arms appeared to reach his knees—pushed up from one hand, was the last to stand. Still he was the first to receive a pass, as the coach snapped the new ball to him and told him to lead a line along the wall of folding doors.

Dale followed into the line and performed as instructed. He joined rows of five, backpedaled, sidestepped side to side, started and stopped. However anxious he felt, he did not have the problems of any number of boys who moved left when they should have moved right, crossed their feet when they should have side stepped, stopped when they should have started. He dribbled in and around strategically placed folding chairs. He exchanged passes along a line of others and took his place at the other end. He followed through one line to shoot a lay-up, and another to rebound and pass off. He began to breathe more deeply, to perspire some, to relax a little, and he began to observe the others in their turns as he waited in lines. And, like others, he glanced to the coach now and then, to see if he could see what the man was taking in.

Junior high basketball. For home games the panels would be folded away, bleachers would unfold from either side, and the space and glossy floor would offer a dimension which was at least exciting and possibly magical. Sonny Joe Dillard, Dale heard in one of the moving lines, could play with the senior team if he wanted.

Dale followed along, tried harder, tried to concentrate. However new he was to organized drills and dashes, shouts and whistles, it was becoming increasingly apparent that he was far from the worst. For while the gang of five seemed to know all or most of the moves, any number of others, here and there, now and again, continued to reveal their various shortcomings. And—that most promising sign—going in on a bounce pass down the middle, to go *up!* and lay the ball over the front edge of the rim without crashing into the coach where he was positioned just under the backboard, Dale heard at his back that phrase which shot him through with sudden promise. "Nice shot there."

Friday waited before them as the week moved along, but Dale went about life and school in all his usual ways. He had never *made* anything like a team before, and even as he entertained a degree of hope, he hardly took on any of the possible anxieties of desire or expectation. Good things came home when one did not stand at the door waiting, his father had told him, and he gave little thought to what it would mean if he did or did not make the team. He would probably keep trying, he thought, on the chance of dressing as an alternate.

He began to eat lunch with Norman Van Slyke, who sat near him in homeroom. Dale's father left him a dollar on the kitchen table every morning for lunch and on his own Dale had fallen into a habit of walking three blocks from school to a small corner grocery he had spotted sometime previously. Cold weather had yet to arrive, and at the store—Sam Jobe's Market—he stood inside near the pop case to eat, or he might sit outside in the sun. Lunch was a packaged pie, usually pineapple but sometimes cherry, a Clark bar or two, and, from a glass-bowl machine, five or six pennies' worth of Spanish peanuts to feed into his bottle of Hire's root beer, which salty beetles, as he thought of them—perhaps Japanese, which were popular at the time, although he had never seen one—he popped to death between his teeth as he drank the root beer.

Norman Van Slyke's looks had made Dale smile the first time he saw him in homeroom. Sparse hairs sprouted already from the short thin boy's upper lip, just under his adhesive-tape-hinged glasses, and his extensive nose projected in the midst of this confusion like an animal reaching its head from a hole in the ground. Norman's features twitched; the creature that was his nose seemed to have a neck at times, to glance around, up and down, or to the side.

Dale started to call him Rat Nose, a name which at once brought snickers of pleasure from the other boy. In turn, Rat Nose identified Dale as Weasel and they took on the names and wore them along the street as easily as old sweatshirts.

The days and the after-school practices continued. Each morning, coming out of Civics and turning right, headed for Geometry, Dale discovered that he passed Sonny Joe Dillard going the other way. On Thursday morning, the taller boy nodded, uttered, "Say," in passing, and on Friday, when Dale spoke first, said, "Hi," to the school's legendary athlete, Sonny Joe winked in a natural and friendly way that reminded Dale of his father's winks.

Dale also heard or learned in the days passing that the boys of the kelly green gym bags had all attended the elementary school attached to the very end of Emerson Junior High. So it was that they had used the glossy hardwood double gymnasium all those years, had stopped by after school to see home games and, as it also came out, had played together for two years as teammates in a Saturday morning league. In practices, when teams were identified, and when they scrimmaged, the five boys, Sonny Joe ever the nucleus, moved as one.

Dale's basketball experience had been different. His elementary school, near Chevy Plants Seven and Ten along the city river, had neither gymnasium nor coach. A basement classroom served as a gym, under the guidance of the gym teacher, Mrs. Roland. Painted blackish-brown, its high windows and ceiling light fixtures caged, the room offered a single netless rim fixed flush to the wall, eight or nine feet from the floor, perhaps two feet from the ceiling. There was clearance enough for either lay-ups or line drives.

No matter, Dale always thought, for in gym class they played noth-

ing but little kid games in circles anyway, and only once was basketball ever given a try. Mrs. Roland, whistle around her neck, glasses on
a separate lanyard, demonstrated—to introduce that one game—by
hoisting the cumbersome ball from her side with both hands, kicking
up one ankle as she tossed it at the basket, hitting the *bottom* of the rim.
Then she selected teams—which selections for any real sport, indoors
or out, were always maddening to Dale, as she chose captains and
teams by height rather than ability. And she officiated the year's single
basketball game by calling one jump ball after another, the contest lasting three minutes or less, concluding on a score of 2 to 0.

Tall boys would always be given the breaks, Mrs. Roland seemed
to say. And if your last name started with *W*, your place in line would
be near the end.

Dale did play outdoors. At least a year earlier, as an eleven-year-
old, he had paused on a sidewalk beside a cement driveway at the rear
of a church along Chevrolet Avenue, and discovered not Jesus but
basketball. The church was First Nazarene and the boys playing under
the outdoor hoop were high school age. Dale stood and watched. At
last when a loose ball came his way, he shagged it and walked it back
several steps to throw it to the boy walking toward him.

"Wanna play, come on," the boy said.

Dale had been too thrilled to be able to say. He did walk toward the
action, though, nodding, although he had just a moment ago touched
a basketball for the first time in his life. "You're on my side," the boy
said. "Gives us three on a side."

Anxious, wide-eyed, Dale moved into the general area as instructed. The boy who had invited him—who was pointing out the
sides, treating him as some actual person he had never known himself
to be—turned out to be the seventeen-year-old son of the church's
minister. Dale had never encountered a generous teenager before, and
his wonder was such that he might have been a possible convert to
nearly anything, but no such strings were attached. The seventeen-
year-old boy was merely that rarest of individuals in Dale's life, a
nice kid.

The game—Twenty-one—progressed, and passes were sent Dale's
way as if he knew what to do. He did not. He passed the ball back each
time, another time bounced it once and passed it back, and no one said
anything critical, nor cast any critical glances, and the minister's son,
who was already a memorable figure to Dale, said at last, when Dale
dribbled another time and passed the ball back, "That's the way."

It would seem that Dale was being indulged, but something in the way the game was managed made it no less real as a contest. The minister's son had Dale put the ball in play each time it was his team's turn to do so, and in time he said to him, "Take a shot," and when Dale passed off instead, he said, "Go ahead, take a shot, or you'll never learn." A chance came again, and even as it may not have been the best opportunity, Dale pushed the ball two-handed toward the basket, only to see it fall short by two or three feet.

His teammates recovered the ball, passed and circled, and the boy said to him, "That's okay, good try, try it again." In time there came another opportunity, closer in, and this time the ball hit on the rim, hesitated, then dropped through, and the boy said only, "There you go, that's the way," as if it were just another basket among all those that might pass through such a metal ring and not Dale Wheeler's very first. Dale continued with the game, too, as if nothing out of the ordinary had happened. But as the evening air descended, he had grown so happy there was a glow in his eyes, and for the first time in his life he was in love with something.

He had to be told to go home. When darkness so filled the air that the ball could be spotted only directly overhead, a black moon against the night sky, and three of the other boys had drifted away, the minister's finally said to him that he had better head on home, it was getting late. As Dale started off, though, the boy called after him, said they played every night at that time, to stop by again, and if he wanted to shoot by himself, the ball would be just inside that side door and he was welcome to use it just so he put it back when he was done.

Dale shot baskets, hours on end, entering into any number of imaginary schemes and games, and that summer and fall alone, until snow and ice covered the driveway, he played away a hundred or more evenings with the older boys, game after game, unto full darkness. The games were three-on-three, although there were evenings when enough boys showed up to make three or four teams, and to continue to play, a threesome had to win or go to the end of the line. Dale loved it; he learned most of the moves and absorbed them into his system as one does. And so it was, on Friday after school, when practice ended and he followed along with the others to the bulletin board between gym and locker room, and read the typed list there, read it from the top —*J. Dillard*— down, the tenth name on the list was *D. Wheeler*.

He was invited to lunch. In school on Monday, outside his homeroom, one of the boys of the green gym bags—Keith Klett, also a guard—appeared at Dale's side and told him to meet them out front at lunchtime. His house was only two blocks away, the boy told him; it was where they went to eat.

Seeing Rat Nose later, Dale mentioned that he was going to eat lunch with the basketball team, and he experienced but the slightest twinge of betrayal. When he gathered with the others by the mailbox, though, there were only six of them who crossed the street to walk along the residential side street and Dale realized, for whatever reason, that he had been selected by the gang of five as something of a sixth man. He was being taken in. And he was not so naïve that he did not know the reason; basketball was at the heart of it and some one person or another, or the coach, had to have noted, as the line went, that he was good.

Four of the five—all but Keith Klett—carried home-packed lunches in paper bags, and Dale was asked by Sonny Joe about the whereabouts of his own.

"I always walk to a grocery store to buy something," Dale said, pointing back the other way.

"You can make a sandwich at my house," Keith Klett said. "No charge."

And so Dale did—nutty peanut butter on fluffy Wonder Bread—in a large kitchen and large house which if not elegant was far more middle-class than any house he had ever visited in a similar way. He was impressed by the space; there seemed so many rooms, rooms of such size, a two-car garage outside, a sun porch, a den; then, up a carpeted turning stairway to a second floor, Keith Klett's bedroom was larger than the living room in the four-room walk-up apartment which he and his father had called home for the last couple years.

No less noticeable to Dale's eyes were the possessions, the furnishings and appliances, a boy's bedroom seemingly as filled with sports equipment as Hubbard's Hardware, and also on a counter a globe which lighted and an aquarium with bubbles but no fish—"He peed in the tank and they all croaked," Sonny Joe said—and model planes, trains, ships, tanks, a desk with a lampshade shaped like a basketball, and, in its own bookcase, an *Encyclopaedia Britannica* set just like the set in the junior high Reference Room. And—the reason they could troop through the house at will, the reason to troop here for lunch in the first place—Keith Klett's parents were both at work.

After making a sandwich in the kitchen, following each of Keith Klett's steps, including the pouring of a glass of milk, Dale followed into the den where the others sat around eating. Hardly anything had been said about basketball, and some joke seemed to be in the air, but Dale had yet to figure out what it was. Sandwich packed away in two or three bites, two-thirds of his glass of milk poured in after, Keith Klett, smiling, was soon on his feet, saying to Dale, "There's something—we have to show you," slipping away to run upstairs as Sonny Joe called after him, "Keith, leave that crap alone, it makes me sick."

There was no response.

"What's he doing?" Dale asked.

"God, you'll see—it'll make you toss your cookies."

Reappearing, a grin on his face, holding something behind his back, Keith Klett moved close before Dale where he sat chewing a mouthful of peanut butter sandwich. The others tittered, giggled, offered expressions of sickness, as Keith Klett hung out near Dale's face and sandwich, a white rectangle of gauze blotched at its center with a blackish-red stain. Even as Dale did not know what it was, he pulled his neck back enough, turtle-fashion, not to be touched by the daintily held object.

"What's that?" he said.

"Get out of here, Keith!" Gene Elliot said, adding to Dale, to them all, "Anybody who gets a charge out of that has to be a pervert."

Still not quite certain of the function of the pad of gauze, Dale decided not to ask. As Keith returned upstairs, white object in a pinch of fingertips, Dale finished his sandwich, drank away his milk, and carried the glass to the kitchen sink where he rinsed it out, as he had been taught by his father. Perhaps it had to do with his father working second shift, leaving him to spend his evenings generally alone, or maybe it had to do with his not having brothers or sisters with whom to trade jokes and stories, but Dale had a sense, realized for probably the first time, as he and the others were walking back to school, that either he was shy or perhaps he did not have much that he wished to say. It was a disappointing realization in its way, and he was disappointed, too, in some attic area of thoughts, with this group of five which had decided to take him in. He had not imagined this; he had imagined something else. And he felt bad still about his betrayal of Rat Nose. One thing Dale did seem to see; he was a person. Each of them was a person, and each of them was different, and so was he, which was not anything he had ever quite seen before.

The season's first game would be away, Friday after school. Whittier Junior High.

Thursday, at the end of practice, they were issued green satin trunks and white jerseys with green satin letters and numbers. Dale would always remember that first digital identity, number 5, would feel a kinship with all who ever wore it. Cheerleaders and a busload of students were scheduled to leave at three P.M. the next day, the coach, clipboard in hand, was telling them as they checked the uniforms for size. Team members were to gather at the rear door at exactly two-thirty.

"You have a parent who can drive?" the coach all at once asked Dale.

"No," Dale said, feeling that old rush of being from the wrong side of something.

"You don't—your mother can't drive?"

"I just live with my father," Dale said.

"He can't drive?"

"He works second shift."

The coach made a mark on his clipboard, went on to question others. In a moment, in the midst of assigning rides, he said, "Keep those uniforms clean now, and be sure to bring clean socks and a towel."

Four cars, including the coach's own, would be making the drive, he announced at last. "Two-thirty on the button," he added. "If you're late, you miss the game. And no one will change cars. Everybody will come back in the same car they go in."

The next afternoon, entering the strange school building across town, filing into a strange locker room, they selected lockers to use and the coach came along, giving each of them a new pair of green shoelaces. Dale—he had ridden over in the coach's car with two other all-but-silent second-stringers—continued more or less silent now, sitting on the bench, removing his still-clean white laces, placing them in his gym bag, replacing them with the green laces. He also unstapled his second new pair of wool socks, thinking that later he would remove the new green laces, and save them and the second pair of socks for games only.

At last, dressed in the school uniform—number 5; he loved the number already and tried, unsuccessfully, to glimpse it over his shoulder—and new socks and bright shoelaces, he stood up from the bench to shake things out, to see how he felt. Nervous, he realized.

Perhaps frightened, although of what exactly, he wasn't sure. Goose-bumped in locations—along thighs, under biceps—where he had not known the chilled sensation to visit him before, he noticed that one, and then another and another, all of them, had laced in the green laces in the stairway military pattern, while his made their way in XX's. He felt himself a fool. Was there time to change? Should he say something?

The coach was holding up both hands. "Now I know you all want to play," he said. "Chances are you won't. Depends on how things go. One thing—I want each and every one of you to understand before we go out that door. You will listen to what I say and you will do as I tell you. There will be no debates. There will be no complaints during or after this game. Anyone who complains, about the game, or about teammates, or about anything, will find himself an ex-member of this team. Nor will there be any arguing with officials. No calls will be disputed. Losers complain and argue. Men get the job done. They stand up to adversity. They win.

"Now, we're going to go out there and have a good warm-up. The starting five will be the starting five from practice and Joe Dillard will be our captain for this game. Now: Let it be said of you that you tried your hardest, that you did your best. Now: Everyone pause, take a deep breath.

"Let's go! Green and white!"

Throughout the warm-up, throughout the entire first half, in a continuing state of awe and shock, Dale Wheeler's goose bumps maintained their topography in unusual places. It was the first time he had ever performed or even moved before a group of people purposely assembled to watch and judge and count, and even as this occasioned excitement in him, a roller-coaster thrill, his greater sense, sitting on the bench in the middle of the second-stringers, was one of high-wire anxiety. His eyes felt froglike, his neck had unforeseen difficulty turning in its socket, and chills kept chasing over his arms and legs like agitated sled dogs.

From folded-down bleachers on this side of the gym only—opposite was a wall with high, wire-covered windows—Whittier Junior High students, teachers and parents clapped, cheered and shouted as the game moved along. Dale sat there. He looked around. His neck continued to feel stiff and sluggish. It occurred to him as he glanced to the lighted scoreboard at the far left end of the gym, that he did not know how long the halves were. Six minutes and departing seconds remained in the first half, then, all at once, five minutes and a new supply of seconds began to disappear into some tunnel of time gone by.

To Dale's right, before the narrow width of bleachers next to the door which led to their locker room, the cheerleaders from his school, half a dozen seventh-grade girls in green and white, worked, against all odds, it seemed, to do their job: *"Dillard, Dillard—he's our man! If he can't do it—nobody can! Yayyyy!"*

Dale did not quite look at the cheerleaders; he was so carefully dressed, he felt he had gone to a dance of some kind when he had never danced a step in his life and would have declined the invitation if he had known it would lead to this. The seconds on the clock chased each other away; then, again, another fresh supply. Dale looked to the action out on the floor without knowing quite what was happening. Nor could he entirely grasp what it was he was doing sitting there on the bench. Even as he had gone through the warm-up drills, he had not looked at any of the spectators, had looked rather ahead, or at the floor, or kept his eye on the ball as it moved here and there. How had it come to this? Where was he? His team, he realized, was behind 17 to 11, and he couldn't have told anyone how this had come to pass.

No substitutions. As the first half ended and the coach stood up, Dale stood with the other second-stringers to follow along with the starting five toward the locker room. Dale felt no disappointment that he had spent this time sitting and watching, nor any urge to be put into the game. Sitting on the bench in that costume, getting his neck to swivel—it had seemed contribution enough. As they passed before the group from their school, however, and names and remarks of encouragement were called out, he heard, distinctly, "Go get 'em, Weasel," and he looked over to see Rat Nose's face looking at him, smiling, pleased, although no more pleased, it appeared, than the creature looking out above his smile and beneath his taped-up glasses, and a pleasure of friendship leapt up in Dale's chest.

The coach paced and talked. They were behind 19 to 11. He slapped a fist into an opened palm. Dale continued to feel overwhelmed by all that surrounded him, but on the thought of Rat Nose sitting out there, calling him Weasel, he had to stop himself from giggling or laughing out loud. For one moment, then another, it seemed the craziest thing that had ever happened to him.

"Now we don't have much time," the coach was saying. "We have to get the ball in to Joe Dillard! If we're going to pull this out, we have to get the ball in to Sonny Joe under the basket! Now let's get out there and do it. Green and white, fight—okay?" he asked.

On the floor, going through a confused warm-up, Dale glanced back at the group from his school, looked to see Rat Nose there in particular, but the group was too far away and at such an angle that he couldn't be sure. At once then, they were being herded back to their bench; maybe they weren't supposed to warm up for the second half—no one seemed to know.

Dale sat in the middle of those on the bench and stared at the game as before. Five-on-five, two officials in black-and-white striped shirts. Whistles. The scrambled movement of basketball at ground level. Hands raised. Shouts from the bleachers. Yet again he had forgotten to check the beginning time, he realized. Nine minutes 30 seconds remained as he looked for the first time. The score? His next realization was that he was not keeping score. He was too nervous for math, he thought. Home 25/Visitors 16. The next time he looked, the clock showed 8 minutes 44 seconds. His team, he realized, had scored but five points so far in the half. The other team's lead was increasing. It looked like his team was going to lose. That's what it looked like. There was Keith Klett snapping a pass to the side to Gene Elliot as they moved before the scrambled concentration of players at the far end, and Dale experienced a vague sense that they were somehow progressing in the wrong direction, and he experienced a vague sense, too, of hearing his name called out: "Wheeler—Wheeler!"

It was his name, in fact, and there was the coach's face as he looked, his fingers indicating sharply that he was to move to his side. The next thing Dale seemed to know, as if he had received a jolt of electricity, was that he was crouched, one hand on the floor, next to the coach's knee. In this location the volume of the game, the cheers and spectators, seemed to have increased three times over. "Check in at the table, next whistle, for Klett, get that ball to Dillard!" Dale heard, saw the coach spit out of the side of his mouth, all the time watching the action as it continued at the far end.

Stealing along in the same crouch, Dale reported in over the table top, said, "Wheeler for Klett—I mean number 5 for number 7."

Taking a duck-step or two, to the center line, Dale looked up to the scoreboard. Home 27/Visitors 16. Seven minutes 31 seconds.

A whistle blew out on the floor and at once a horn blasted behind him, giving him so sudden a scare, he seemed to wet his pants by several drops. "Substitute, Emerson," the man called.

Dale moved onto the floor, out into the view of all, seeking Keith Klett, and spotting him, said, "I'm in for you," and believing he was the object of all eyes, went on past him toward the end of the court where the other team was putting the ball in play, not knowing, in the blur of things, if this was the consequence of a basket or not.

Nor did he see Gene Elliot for the moment; there before him an official was handing the ball to a Whittier player, who passed it at once to another player who turned to start dribbling down court, and Dale dashed toward him and the ball, slapped the ball away, chased it, grabbed it in both hands, pivoted, looked to find his fellow guard to get rid of the ball as he was poked in wrist and forearm by someone's fingers, and a whistle blew, sharply, close by.

"Foul! Whittier! Number 13!" the official snapped. "One shot! Number 5!"

The players returned, taking their positions. "That's the way! Way to go!" came from Dale's teammates.

He stood waiting at the free-throw line. The others settled in, leaned, waited. He had done this a thousand times, and never. The ball was handed over. "One shot," the official said. Dale looked to the distant hoop; he found presence of mind enough to call up something of the endless shots in the church driveway, although the message remained elusive. He shot, from the chest, as he had in the driveway, although they had been taught in practice to shoot from between their legs. Hitting the rim with a thud, the ball held, rolled, tried to get away to the side, could not escape, fell through.

"Way to go, Wheeler," a teammate remarked, passing him on the way down the floor. "That's the way," came from another.

Dale moved toward the out-of-bounds line again, toward the other guard, as the ball was about to be put in play. He looked over for Gene Elliot again, but could not spot him as the ball was passed in, and the guard receiving the ball, more alert this time, started to dribble up court as Dale rushed him, exploded over him, somehow hit the ball as the boy swung it in both hands, knocked it loose, chased it, dribbled it once in the chase, looked again for his teammate as the Whittier player was on him, jumped, shot—saw the ball hit the backboard, hit the rim, go through—and heard an explosion of applause from the other end of the gym.

At once he moved back in, pursuing the ball, as a teammate slapped his back, said, "Great shot!" and he heard his coach call out, "Go ahead with that press, that's the way!" and heard the other team's coach, close by, snarl to his guards, "Keep it away from that guy, will you?" and heard Gene Elliot, inches away, say, "Coach says to go ahead with the press."

There he was, poised, ready, so thrilled already that his eyes seemed aflame, as the Whittier players were all back down court and they were taking more time. He glanced to the clock: 7 minutes 20 seconds. In about ten seconds, he realized, he had scored three points, which message kept coming to him, that he had, in about ten seconds scored three points, that it was true, he had, and it was something, it was all things, and anything he had ever known in his life was different now.

The ball was moved along this time. At the other end, in their zone defense, the other team lost possession of the ball near the basket, and players ran and loped past Dale as he circled back, and the ball was passed to him, and he dribbled along, eluded a Whittier player, passed off to Gene Elliot, saw Sonny Joe Dillard ranging to the right of the basket, and when the ball came back to him—it would be his most satisfying play, one which was risky and in no way accidental, no way lucky—he immediately threw a long one-handed pass, more football than basketball, hard and high, and to his amazement Sonny Joe leaped high, arms extended, whipped the ball out of the air with both hands, dribbled at once on a pivot-turn and laid it in neatly off the board, and there came another explosion from behind them. And there was Sonny Joe loping back down court, seeking him out, grabbing his arm, hissing in a wild, feverish whisper, "That's the way to pass! Keep it up! Keep it up! We're going to beat these guys!"

The game progressed. Dale would intercept a pass and go two-thirds of the court to put in a lay-up just over the front edge of the rim, as they had been instructed, and he would score two more free throws, to go three-for-three, bringing his point total to seven, but his most satisfying play would remain the first long high pass, and the most exciting experience of the game would be the fever which infected them all, especially Sonny Joe, who scored any number of added baskets on his high, hard passes, and Gene Elliot, too, as they all became caught up in the fever, including the coach, who was on his feet shouting, clapping, waving, and the group from their school, whose explosions of applause kept becoming louder and wilder, until, suddenly to Dale, both horn and whistle sounded, and there came another explosion of applause, and the coach and players from the bench were on the floor, grabbing, slapping, and shouting, for the game was over and they had won, and they knew things they had not known before, and none could quite get enough, it seemed, of what it was they had not known until that very moment.

As they moved and were being moved toward the locker room, Sonny Joe was being slapped and congratulated, and so was Dale. There was the coach, arm around Dale's shoulders, voice close, calling to him, "That full-court press was the thing to do! You ignited that comeback! You turned it around!"

The celebration continued in the locker room. The final score: Home 29/Visitors 33. Locker doors were slammed, towels were thrown around, there was the coach congratulating Dale again, slapping his shoulder, calling to them all, "That full-court press turned it around!" Dale learned, too, in the melee, that only two players on his team had scored, he and Sonny Joe, 7 points and 26, and everything, all of it, kept occurring over again for him as a surprise, and as a surprise all over again, and he let it go on as it would, a dozen Christmases and birthdays combined, accepted the compliments, knew in some part of himself already that he was changed by what had happened, had been granted something, knew these things, and did not volunteer in any way that at the time he had simply chased the ball because he had been so confused by all that was happening around him and had not known, otherwise, what it was that he was supposed to do.

Monday it was school and lunch hour as usual. After school, though, as practice moved along, as they ran through drills with the dozen or so alternates, there came a time for the coach to name squads of five, and the name, Dale Wheeler, was called to run out and join the first team, in place of Keith Klett, who was left to stand with the others. It was not something Dale had anticipated — it was a small surprise — but as it happened, the logic was not unreasonable to him. Nor was anything unreasonable to the other four, who slapped and congratulated him in small ways as he took his place as a starter.

Keith Klett stood among the others, had retreated in fact, Dale noticed, to the back row. His eyes appeared not to focus on anything in particular as he stood looking ahead, or glancing around.

They came face-to-face for the first time after practice in the locker room. Dale was sitting on the bench to untie his shoes, and he looked over to the end of his aisle to see Keith Klett staring at him. "You suck-ass," the boy said.

Keith Klett walked on. Dale had not said anything. He sat looking that way for a moment and did not know what to say or what to do.

Nor did he see the other boy when, undressed, towel around his waist, he walked along the main aisle to the shower. It occurred to him that perhaps they would fight, out on the playground or behind the school, and this prospect aroused in him little more than faint anxiety. He seemed to feel nothing more than a numbness in response to the remark; at the same time it would be one, and a moment, that he would never forget.

The next morning Dale asked Rat Nose if he still went to the grocery store for lunch, and they agreed to meet again as they had previously. The surprise to Dale, as lunch hour came and the two of them walked away, leaving the building behind, was a call at their backs and turning to see Sonny Joe Dillard running after them, lunch bag in hand. They waited, and when the tall boy had caught up, the three of them walked along in the street, three abreast. There was no mention of a change of any kind, and they walked this way, as if it were merely another day.

The Time-to-Teach-Jane-Eyre-Again Blues

Linda Bamber

NOT *Jane Eyre* again. Other people are moving on in life or going around in circles or failing utterly, but I'm still doing business at the same old stand. Every year a new load of students is dumped like laundry in front of me, needing to know *Jane Eyre*. Sometimes I take comfort in the thought that it's not just me. All over the country, in Cleveland and Galveston and Tacoma as well as better-known places like Miami, in major universities and state teachers' colleges, everyone does his or her share. The new cohort group is divided into thousands of groups like the one I have to face at 11:30 and everyone takes a whack. It's a community effort, like doing the wash in an Indian village. Everyone down to the river! Sometimes I can almost hear a cheerful hum, all of us preparing together. There should be Preparing-*Jane-Eyre* songs, they should be played in supermarkets like Christmas music at the season of the year when *Jane Eyre* is normally taught. It would lessen the sense of shame.

Now it is November again, the season in which I normally teach *Jane Eyre*. The oak tree outside my study window is full of dead leaves. That's the way oak trees are, they hang on and hang on, sometimes right through the winter. Some years we don't get rid of the old oak leaves until the new ones come out in May.

But if you want a description of November, don't turn to me. Open your books to page one of *Jane Eyre*. Ready? Heeeeeeeeeeeere's— Charlotte!

Folds of scarlet drapery shut in my view to the right hand; to the left were clear panes of glass, protecting, but not separating me from the drear November day. At intervals, while turning over the leaves of my book, I studied the aspect of that winter afternoon. Afar, it offered a pale blank of mist and cloud; near, a scene of wet lawn and storm-beat shrub, with ceaseless rain sweeping away wildly before a long and lamentable blast.

That's great, isn't it? I think that's great. The problem is, what can you say about it? Mark always says, "Just say what you said last year. It's all in your notes, isn't it?" It is in my notes, but it's not that simple. Part of the problem is my notes. Sometimes they look like this:

328   St John at Rosamund's feet
261   Jane flooded by love
Class feeling
Feminism—longing for action
279   "I care for myself"

I suppose that meant something once, but what? And even when my notes are good it doesn't help. Sometimes I come across whole eloquent paragraphs that work themselves up to a point, and I think, Lady, what are you hollering? It's like watching someone on TV with the sound turned off. There's someone at the podium waving her arms and rolling her eyes, but that's all you know.

Mark, listen. You have to bring it up in the system. All the way up. It has to come out of core memory all the way to the skin, where it becomes hot and damp and raises the temperature of the surrounding air. This computer metaphor isn't working out, so I'll get to the point. Teaching is a phallic activity. You can't just spread your legs.

And now for a little self-stimulation. I have to leave the house at eleven, I'm still in my bathrobe, it's 10:15, and I have to feed the dog. That leaves about fifty minutes to prepare if I get started this minute, but really I'd rather be dead. Everything I know about the book swims in a stew, nothing is worth separating off from everything else and actually saying. The passages I marked in previous years are all equally important; there are too many of them and they all illustrate the same large, obvious point. I sit here feeding myself *Jane Eyre* like a mother whose child won't eat. For every teaspoonful that goes in the mouth, three land on the cheek, are dropped on the tray, get caught in the hair or go into the bib. Some that go in come out again. Is anything worse than this? "Structure of the book is episodic rather than architectural,"

I read in my notes. Later I read exactly the same sentence. Still later I read, "The plot bumps along. Not patterned, as in *Pride and Prejudice*." Okay, okay, I'll definitely make the point about the plot. That'll take forty seconds. What next?

Charlotte Brontë herself had problems as a teacher. She wrote about them in her diary like this:

> Friday August 11th . . . I had been toiling for nearly an hour with Miss Lister, Miss Marriott, & Ellen Cook striving to teach them the distinction between an article and a substantive. The parsing lesson was completed, a dead silence had succeeded it in the school-room & I sat sinking from irritation & weariness into a kind of lethargy. The thought came over me: am I to spend all the best part of my life in this wretched bondage, forcibly suppressing my rage at the idleness, the apathy, and the hyperbolical & most asinine stupidity of those fat-headed oafs, and on compulsion assuming an air of kindness, patience, & assiduity?

I know what she means. But really, my problem is different. I don't teach articles and substantives, I teach *Jane Eyre*. Moreover, in any given class, 25 percent of the students are brilliant. The fat-headed oafs don't have a chance. After the parsing lesson Charlotte had to take her students for a walk. Then Lister, Marriott & company pestered her with "vulgar familiar trash" at tea. Finally at dusk she

> crept into the bedroom to be alone for the first time that day. Delicious was the separation I experienced as I laid down on the spare bed & resigned myself to the luxury of twilight & solitude. The stream of Thought, checked all day came flowing free & calm along its channel.

Ah, Thought. How wonderful it is to Think. Right now, however, the effort to think about *Jane Eyre* has dried up Thought at the source. What about Jane as a governess? Is Adele a fat-headed oaf? Also I remember there's a very important scene in the silk factory where Mr. Rochester tries to dress Jane like a tart. Maybe if I start writing about it something will come to me. What I'd really like to do, though, is go to sleep. I know I just got up, but maybe a twenty-minute nap would clear my head. The thought is irresistible. I see an image of my bed in the next room, unmade, accessible, warm with memories. But this is instantly succeeded by an image of myself washed and dressed and standing, an hour and fifteen minutes from now, in front of fifty young adults. I will be wearing a wool jacket and good boots, not this smelly nightie. There will be nothing but the force of my will to hold the group together; the edges of the classroom will be restless, like the outlying provinces of Empire. If they go, the whole class could follow. These are beautifully brought up students, they never pick on me or complain, but if they lose interest I'm dead. Other teachers I know just keep talking. Some students listen, some dream; later in the hour some who were napping perk up. I think that's fine; I just can't do it. It's something chromosomal. The lecture gene was left out. If the class doesn't quiver like a dog about to be fed, the heart goes out of me completely. I become dry, desperate, controlling. The subject shrivels up like plastic wrap near a hot plate. Minute by minute I long to go home.

Bed's out. But I still can't face *Jane Eyre*. I wash the oatmeal pot and check the answering machine for messages. Mark's mother, my yoga teacher and someone from The Green Machine sound as if they were calling from Albania. It's only the cassette, but I don't know where to get a new one. The Green Machine thinks we owe them $32.57 and has thought so for several years. The day I came home to find Leslie Middleman's earrings on the table next to my bed there was a notice on the door framed by big yellow daisies. "The Green Machine wants to kill your weeds!" it said. A friendly greenie was choking some bad crabgrass by the throat.

What would Jane Eyre have done if she had come home to Thornfield one day and found Leslie Middleman in bed with Mr. Rochester? I say "in bed with Mr. Rochester" because that makes it more dramatic. I don't think it would be worth fictionalizing the period between my finding Leslie's earrings and Mark's admitting they were having an affair. Now that I think about it, it seems incredible that I didn't actually *know* what was going on until Mark admitted it. Jane wouldn't have been like that. One look at the earrings and she would have heard a voice saying, "Leave Thornfield at once." Eighteen pages later she would have been gone. She wouldn't have hung out with Mr. Rochester for three days, threatening, crying, sulking and fucking. That wasn't her way. She would have stayed just long enough to hear the story of his life, and then she'd be out of the house. "I *do* love you," she would have said before leaving, "but I must not show or indulge the feeling and this is the last time I must express it."

What integrity. Remember, Jane was besotted with Rochester. She had had a horrible, deprived life, burnt porridge, no love, dresses made of crummy material, and here she was on the verge of wealth, sex, love, everything. Inside her was this chaos of desire. She heard it like "a flood loosened in remote mountains." Then she found out about Bertha, Rochester's wife.

> The whole consciousness of my life lorn, my love lost, my hope quenched, my faith death-struck, swayed full and mighty above me in one sullen mass.

"It came," she says. Jane lies faint, sinks in deep waters, feels no standing. As far as I can make out, Jane has an orgasm of grief.

Can I tell them that? Maybe. It depends on the atmosphere. Sometimes eroticizing the text makes me feel overwrought, like a jumped-up TV producer trying to get people INTO the story. The class withdraws, insulted. Mild as cow's breath on a cold day, a mist of contempt settles over the room. But sometimes the right sexual reference skewers the book. The connection is made, the light dawns, the passage is marked in deep transparent yellow. And who's to say that years later, when a student in that class thinks of *Jane Eyre,* her thoughts don't beat to the faint remembered pulse on p.261, where Jane is ravished by grief?

I take a few notes on my notes. The point about the episodic structure of the book makes sense again, so I jot it down. The point is that Charlotte herself led a life of never enough. In each episode there is a scarcity of material, a terrible danger of running out. I can relate to that. It was heroic of her to keep writing when things kept threatening to stop.

If I don't stop now I'll be late. It is suddenly hard to stop; with a margin of minutes I suddenly have a good idea for the class. I churn the pages of the book, focused, awake. If I don't find the page references, how will I make my point? Now the phone rings. Scribbling, I ignore it. It rings again, Mark's signal. Still turning pages in my book, I pick it up.

"Mark, later, please, I've got to go . . . No, I really have to . . . Don't be mad at me, Mark. Are you mad? . . . Shit. Now you've made me mad . . . For God's sake, I've got a class in twenty-five minutes and I'm not even dressed yet . . . So what? . . . You are? . . . Oh, no . . . That's awful, Mark, I'm really sorry . . . Oh, dear. Listen, I really have to go. I'll call you later . . . Take it easy . . . Yes, of course . . . No, I'm not mad . . . You, too."

This is crazy. I wash and dress in record time and tear down the highway at speed. Out of habit I flick on the radio. A female voice sings, "We're living in a material world, and I'm a material girl." It's Madonna, Amy's favorite. Amy is eleven; she dances around her room singing this stupid song and watching me to check the effect. Why can't she like Bruce Springsteen? Or Cindy Lauper, for that matter? What makes Amy think she can base a rebellion on the brilliant idea of Woman as Object? I tried to discuss these issues with her last week, but she didn't want to hear about it. To show her displeasure she turned down her mouth into the scornful/vulnerable expression that has been a reliable early-warning sign since the day she was born. I let it go. But why am I teaching other people's children *Jane Eyre* while my own child watches MTV? I think again of Jane Eyre and Mr. Rochester in the silk warehouse. "The more he bought me," she said, "the more my cheek burned with a sense of annoyance and degradation." In my mind's eye is a video of Madonna whirling around the silk warehouse with a male chorus buying and draping and ogling. "But it's parodic," my friend Jeremy has told me. "Lighten up. It's just a joke."

To focus my mind I think, "*Jane Eyre. Jane Eyre. Jane Eyre,*" but that's as far as I get. Part of my attention is absorbed by the speed with which I am driving. Any cops? No cops. When I drive past the wetlands a cloud of milkweed hits the windshield at eighty. Never mind cops, what if I kill myself? Is it worth taking chances with my life just to be on time for class?

Yes. It is. This is a matter of life and death.

But outside the classroom things are relaxed. Seeing me, people break off their conversations and saunter in. Annie Suyemoto, wearing ripped blue jeans and a thin white camisole top, is in line at the express money machine.

"I'll be right there," she calls.

"Okay," I call, walking fast. A student with a face like a potato stops me outside the door.

"One thing I don't understand," he says. "Are we supposed to like St. John or not? He's very Christian but I think he's a jerk."

I look at the potato-faced student as if I were seeing him for the first time. Blessings on your head, whoever you are! I say, yes, he's a jerk, or no, he isn't a jerk, or interesting question, why don't you bring it up in class. And now there *will* be a class. We have a student, he asked the question; we have a teacher, she gave the answer. These are the necessary preconditions for a class. Having answered this student, I suddenly feel capable of answering any number of students. I have answers to all questions any student anywhere could ask about *Jane Eyre.*

To understand how Brontë feels about St. John we should compare him to Helen Burns, the other figure of Christian goodness. Then there's the question of passion. Is St. John's passion perverse? Topics develop and divide like microscopic life. I am ready for class to begin.

At my desk a student in chains and tight black pants asks for an extension on her paper. She seems upset, and I wonder, could this be Lucy X? I glance at her stomach but it's perfectly flat. I know about Lucy X from Marjorie Marlinsky, who works at a women's counseling center. Lucy's a computer science major and doesn't even need this class for distribution, but Marjorie couldn't convince her to drop it.

"She can't make any decisions," Marjorie told me. "It's terrible, the pressure she's under."

"No problem," I tell the student warmly. "Just let me know when you can have it in." It wouldn't help to ask her name. Marjorie said they use pseudonyms.

Annie Suyemoto sits down in front, puts one leg up on a post. Today it's basketball sneakers, other days it might be penny loafers or flats with sexy little socks. I really like her.

"Okay, listen to this," I say when things are quiet. I read:

> Folds of scarlet drapery shut in my view to the right hand; to the left were clear panes of glass, protecting, but not separating me from the drear November day. At intervals, while turning over the leaves of my book, I studied the aspect of that winter afternoon. Afar, it offered a pale blank of mist and cloud; near, a scene of wet lawn and storm-beat shrub, with ceaseless rain sweeping away wildly before a long and lamentable blast.

When I finish there is a silence. Friendly or dead? Am I the teacher, the Voice, or am I a very foolish woman? I don't know what made me start with that passage; I am stalled after takeoff, engines cut and the sea shining hideously beneath me. I remember reading that the scarlet drapery shutting Jane into her window seat represents the womb or menstruation or something, but I make it a policy never to start a class discussing wombs and menstruation. Rain is a good topic to start off with, if only I could think of something to say about it. Idiotically, I look out the window as if I expected a deluge. A traffic light, pale in the midday sunshine, changes from red to green. A line of cars starts up. I wish I were in one of them, driving away. I am losing my sense of how long this has been going on.

Into the silence, Annie speaks.

"It makes you want to be there," says Annie. "Even though the weather is bad."

"Exactly!" I say. Is Annie brilliant or is she brilliant? Anyway, she makes me feel brilliant. Her true blue response shoots through my system, realigning all the synapses and exciting within me a powerful desire to speak. A door flies open and language pours into the anteroom, ready to come out. Grammatical structures rush forward, bewigged and perfumed, to keep order. Stalling for time, I take a few more comments, and then I go for it. Words come from nowhere in beautiful shapes. Sentences fly out whole, leaping subordinate clauses and arriving flushed but unwinded at the end. I am surfing the long, ever-breaking wave of Thought, and there's nothing like it.

Do you want to know what I said? Would you like to judge for yourself whether or not it was brilliant? No problem. I talked about desire in *Jane Eyre,* how desire is by definition a matter of lack, how Jane wants what she has not got, Rochester, love, and we want it with and for her; but how secretly the book makes us desire the realities of Jane's life even more than the things she hasn't got. Jane is restless, inflamed by scarlet desires; but she is also a clear pane of glass through which we see the world as it is. Through her we can savor the bad weather, the scarce pleasures, the "one delicious but thin piece of toast," the time Bessie let her eat off a special plate, the "clean and quiet street" where a post office has a single letter for Jane Eyre.

Look, for instance, at the famous opening passage of Chapter Twelve. First Jane stands on the battlements of Thornfield and longs for something beyond her quiet, governess life. She tells herself stories full of "all the incident, life, fire, feeling that I desired but had not in my actual existence." She yearns towards "the busy world, towns, regions full of life I had heard of but never seen." Three pages later she meets Mr. Rochester, whose sexual privilege it is to incarnate the busy world itself. The desire calls up its object, and the rest of the book is spent pursuing and evading it. But where does Jane meet Rochester? On a walk. On one of those walks women in Jane Austen and Charlotte Brontë are always taking. They take walks because they haven't got a damn thing else in the world to do. Often they go to the post office. "One must walk somewhere," said Jane Austen, "and the post office gives one an object." So Jane Eyre puts on her bonnet and cloak and walks two miles to town. Here is how it went:

The ground was hard, the air was still, my road was lonely; . . .
the charm of the hour lay in its approaching dimness, in the low-
gliding and pale-beaming sun. I was a mile from Thornfield, in
a lane noted for wild roses in summer, for nuts and blackberries
in autumn, and even now possessing a few coral treasures in hips
and haws, but whose best winter delight lay in its utter solitude
and leafless repose. If a breath of air stirred, it made no sound
here; for there was not a holly, not an evergreen to rustle, and the
stripped hawthorn and hazel bushes were as still as the white,
worn stones which causewayed the middle of the path.

Do you see what I mean? Winter. Utter solitude and leafless repose.
A few coral treasures in hips and haws. Sandwiched in between the
passionate moments on the battlements and the appearance of Mr.
Rochester is a walk. Wouldn't you like to be on that walk? In the next
paragraph is a sheet of ice covering a brook; do you see how the book
is a pattern of fire and ice, scarlet and white?

Sitting in their blue plastic chairs, my students listen to me. The
chairs have one wide, flat arm for taking notes; many of the students
are filling up their notebooks with what I say. Peter Greenberg and
Julie Sobel, however, take no notes. Peter and Julie can't take notes because they need to stare at me while I talk, or else they won't understand a thing. There are a few students like Peter and Julie in every
class. Their eyes have to be turned, like satellite dishes, towards the
source of information, which I have the honor of being. Peter looks
like the astonished fetus at the end of 2001: A SPACE ODYSSEY. Julie
looks more like a whale. Her intake valve is open, she'll strain for
plankton later. This makes it sound as if Julie isn't smart, which is in-
correct. She's pleasant enough to look at, too, with light springy hair,
a round face, dark blue eyes. But her preliminary processing mecha-
nism, like mine, is stupid. It has one switch, on or off. When the interest
level in the classroom rises to a certain level the switch flips to "on,"
and there she is. I say "there she is" because when she's not interested
I don't see her. Only when things get cooking does she burn in.

Other students in this class are: Haskell Springer, who almost
qualified on the U.S. equestrian team during the last Olympics; Barbara Guetti, whose father is so tyrannical and whose mother so deeply
depressed that Barbara has to wear a different tie every day; Gregory
Stern, who voted for Reagan and has the decency to be ashamed of
himself; Janice Urtiaga, who worked in a Kentucky Fried Chicken

store and participated in chicken fights last summer; and Ursula Lang, who was a student of mine in Freshman Composition, where I didn't much like her. Somewhere in the class is Lucy X, pregnant and miserable. There is a woman from Computer Services who comes on her lunch break and a senior who comes in his ROTC uniform. These people discuss the imagery of fire and ice in *Jane Eyre* in a loose associative way, the way Phil Donahue's guests discuss their sex lives. I let them talk, responding when moved to do so and not when not. Haskell Springer points out that Mr. Rochester's horse slips on the ice when Rochester and Jane first meet, but everyone agrees this has no symbolic value whatsoever. I wonder if the other students think it's as funny as I do that Haskell never fails to bring up a scene with a horse in it. As the discussion goes on I jot down notes, intending to set things straight at the end of the hour. In addition to qualifications and corrections of what the students are saying, I have in mind a large general point, something that will sum things up and show us where we have been going. Then it seems the point has been made. I couldn't say when or by whom, but when I look at my notes they don't refer to anything that hasn't already happened. I crumple up the notes and throw them away.

The hour has gone by quickly. I keep them five minutes over to explain the upcoming assignment, after which I listen to individual bulletins of illness, emotional distress, overwork and death in the family. I let everyone who needs one have an extension on his or her paper, and then I'm alone. Styrofoam coffee cups and cans of Sprite are scattered around the classroom, sitting on the arms of the molded blue chairs. My shirt is rather wet. The class is over.

Do I feel a sense of anticlimax or exhilaration? I do not. When I first started teaching it used to take hours to get over it, but now decompression is instant. As soon as the last student finishes her tale of woe, I shove my books and papers into my briefcase, and a happy thought fills my mind. Lunch!

On Wednesdays I generally have lunch with Jeremy and Sophie, sometimes in the faculty dining room but usually in the student cafeteria. Jeremy teaches Renaissance Literature and is writing something about Renaissance travelers' tales and *Othello;* Sophie works with English-as-a-Second-Language students.

"Doritos Chips," says Jeremy when he sees my tray. "Cheese Nacho Flavor or Bar-B-Que?" The joke is that I eat too much junk food and Jeremy is too fastidious and upscale in his food tastes. It wasn't much of a joke to begin with, and with repetition it has become a real force for entropy. The world around me dims with boredom; then I recover and sit down.

"I don't know," says Sophie. "I just keep coming back to the question of IBM compatibility."

"Don't give in to them," says Jeremy. "This is how monopolies take over." Jeremy and Sophie are both in the market for a word processor. They want to buy identical machines, so they can trade software; but they can't settle on what to buy. I comfort myself with an egg salad sandwich while they talk.

"Did you see Doonesbury this morning?" Sophie finally asks me. I did not. Then Sophie tells a funny story about a Japanese student of hers, and Jeremy says he will be spending Christmas break in New York.

"I haven't been to New York in months," I say. I think about New York for a while, trying to work out where we would stay if we went, and then I tell Sophie and Jeremy something that happened in New York last winter.

"I was walking through the lobby of an apartment building on Central Park West," I tell them. "Not super-fancy, but near Lincoln Center, with art deco doors. I was wearing a pink down coat over blue jeans and thinking, really I should do a little better than this when I come to New York. Just then two women went by looking great.

" 'That's the look,' I thought, studying them. Their clothes were witty and post-modern and mismatched, one colorful, the other black-and-white. As I turned to take another look, the colorful one detached herself from the other and hurried back. Before I knew it she was standing in front of me in her houndstooth coat, talking eagerly.

" 'You're Caroline Jacobs,' " she said. 'Do you remember me? You were my teacher. I had you in three classes, including Freshman English. I saw you just now and I had to come tell you. Everyone has someone who really makes a difference, and for me it was you.' "

"You're kidding!" exclaims Sophie, delighted.

"What happened next?" asks Jeremy, curious.

"I don't remember," I say. "I was flabbergasted."

"Did you recognize her?" asks Sophie.

"Not at all," I say. The three of us start adding up how many students we teach per year and multiplying by how many years we have been teaching. In my case it was 70 students per semester, of which about 20 are repeaters. Times 2 minus 20 is 120 per year. Times 10 is

1200 students. Everyone agrees that I am not at fault for not recognizing the student in New York.

"Of course it's different for me," says Sophie. "Because I work with students individually." Sophie has actually visited ex-students of hers in Brazil and India.

"Yes," I say. "That's an advantage."

"Sometimes," says Sophie.

When lunch is over I walk Sophie and Jeremy back to the main campus and head for the library. The weather has degenerated, and it looks like rain. I am still thinking about the woman in New York.

"Oh, thank you!" I remember saying, but after that it was as if I had forgotten my lines. We stood like two animals who had heretofore only made faces at each other from the safety of our cages. Suddenly we were out on the paths with the people. What would happen next? Would we go out for coffee and become friends? She was something to do with the theater and would be going to the Yale Drama School soon. Well, good luck to her. I should have asked her exactly what I had said that was memorable. I never heard from her again.

It is rainy and dark by the time I drive home. We are only a month from the shortest day of the year, and the darkness is becoming oppressive. Worse than the darkness, however, is the immediate danger of a quarrel with Mark. I have agreed over and over that the Leslie Middleman episode is in the past, but whenever something reminds me of it every gesture of Mark's makes me mad. I decide to pay The Green Machine and be done with it. They're wrong about the bill, but it's worth $32.57 to be done with their reminders. You can't hold the line every time.

Mark finds the envelope on the table in the hall after dinner.

"I thought you said we weren't going to pay them," he says. I am in my study reading Elizabeth Gaskell's *Life of Charlotte Brontë*; Mark is in the doorway wearing the kimono his parents brought him from Japan.

"I changed my mind," I say. I am reading the description of Brontë's funeral; rather than think about The Green Machine, I ask Mark if he wants to hear it.

"Few beyond that circle of hills," I read aloud, "knew that she, whom the nations praised far off, lay dead that Easter morning." Her father and her husband, "stunned with their great grief, desired not the sympathy of strangers." Only one member from each family in the parish was allowed to come to the funeral, and "it became an act of self-denial in many a poor household to give up to another the privilege of paying their last homage to her."

"Her husband?" asks Mark. "I thought she was a spinster."

Of course, I think, annoyed. That's the whole point about the Brontës, isn't it. If you know one thing about them it's that they were lonely, frustrated spinsters."

"Well, weren't they?" insists Mark.

"Yes," I say. "They were. But in the end Charlotte married her father's curate. She was thirty-eight."

"That's nice," says Mark, trying to stay out of trouble. I don't know whether it was nice or it wasn't nice. Mrs. Gaskell claims that Charlotte liked the man perfectly well after marrying him; but Mrs. Gaskell isn't to be trusted. In any case the marriage didn't last. Charlotte died the next year of pregnancy toxemia.

When Amy goes to sleep I take a walk. Mark and I didn't fight, but we didn't really relax either. What *did* I get anything out of today? I ask myself. I don't know any more about art or life or *Jane Eyre* than I did this morning. I haven't made any money. I haven't written anything or had any fun. Why did I bother to get out of bed? It is mild and drizzly; my discontent envelops me in the dark like a vaporous exhalation. I'm passing, of all things, the post office. Now a man on a horse should appear in the mist and eroticize the text. But instead of love, I find myself thinking of death. What will remain of me when I'm gone? Amy, of course, thank God, but what will remain in the world of my efforts?

"Nothing," I think, plodding along the sidewalk. Intellectuals are not supposed to care about leaving a physical memorial to their time on earth, but they do. George Orwell, for instance, worried about the physical space his books would take up by the end of his life. A couple of shelves, he thought; whereas a coal miner could fill whole houses with the product of his labor. I think Orwell was too hard on himself. What if you counted every printed copy of Orwell's books, instead of only one of each? I myself, I suddenly think, passing under a streetlight, would be proud to undergo the trial by bulk. Let everyone I've ever taught come to my funeral, and I'll match my output against any coalminer or longshoreman in America. If I teach another twenty years, that's nearly four thousand people. You'd have to hire a football stadium to get them all in! Let Amy, now in her fifties, gather my students from all nations and states! All age groups will be represented and all cultural persuasions. Lucy X's baby will be in the prime of her life. She was never officially enrolled in the British Novel course, but the rights of the fetus will by now be so well established that merely having been present in the classroom will be enough. It occurs to me with the force of a conviction that Lucy X is the girl with the long, punk wing of reddish hair sticking out of her head. What shall I do about that?

I'm walking faster now, warm and loose. Did you know that walking for ten minutes has a more measurable calming effect than a Valium? It has stopped raining, but there's a nice soft mist. I think I'll take the long walk tonight, up the hill to the observatory. There won't be any stars, of course, but perhaps I don't need them. I am expanding into the atmosphere anyway, into the houses and yards of my neighbors, into the air, into the bare, wet trees of this suburban township, muffled and blurred by the mist.

It is time to take the photo at my funeral. From a point at the top of the stadium, the photographer plans his shot. He wants the photograph to resemble an American Airlines ad, with hundreds of airline employees smiling and looking up. What strikes me, as the students pour onto the field, is again this question of age. When I was teaching them, these people were always between eighteen and twenty-two years old, and I alone was an exile from youth. Only for me did the seasons pass; for the students it was always spring. But now I see that I was mistaken. There are people of all ages here, fading and blossoming and falling to earth. Together these people represent the march of time, the staircase of generations. The photographer, however, does not want them lined up according to age. The point of his photo is The Democracy of Literature, so he wants a pluralistic look. When everything is right, the photographer will send word to a stadium technician, who will light up the scoreboard as if for a touchdown. Haskell Springer, also recently dead, watches with me as the moment approaches.

"What you said about the students staying young," he says. "Sportswriters have the same problem. The athletes stay young, too."

"Hah," I say. "I never thought of that."

"Sure," says Haskell. He died from an equestrian accident, but before that he was a sportswriter for *The Washington Post*. It was Haskell's idea to signal the students by lighting the scoreboard, which will happen any minute now. The photographer is nervous and excited.

"NOW!" he shouts into his headset. Floodlights go on all over the field. Across the field is a familiar face.

"Amy!" I cry. "I think that's Amy!"

"Where?" asks Haskell, just to be nice.

"There!" I point. "In the press box." I see Amy as Haskell must see her, a pleasant-looking, completely undistinguished middle-aged lady. But at that moment somebody distracts her, just when she wanted to face forward for the picture; and when her face turns back my way it has a downturned mouth, vulnerable/scornful, just as it did when she was five.

"Amy!" I cry, waving wildly. I am very glad to see her. A band, stationed in the bleachers, plays a military march. People are crying as at a parade. Everyone lifts a copy of *Jane Eyre* and cheers.

Displacement

David Wong Louie

MRS. CHOW HEARD the widow. She tried reading faster but kept stumbling over the same lines. She thought perhaps she was misreading them: "There comes, then, finally, the prospect of atomic war. If the war is ever to be carried to China, common sense tells us only atomic weapons could promise maximum loss with minimum damage."

When she heard the widow's wheelchair she tossed the copy of *Life* down on the couch, afraid she might be found out. The year was 1952.

Outside the kitchen Chow was lathering the windows. He worked a soft brush in a circular motion. Inside, the widow was accusing Mrs. Chow of stealing her cookies. The widow had a handful of them clutched to her chest and brought one down hard against the table. She was counting. Chow waved, but Mrs. Chow only shook her head. He soaped up the last pane and disappeared.

Standing accused, Mrs. Chow wondered if this was what it was like when her parents faced the liberators who had come to reclaim her family's property in the name of the People. She imagined her mother's response to them: What people? All of my servants are clothed and decently fed.

The widow swept the cookies off the table as if they were a canasta trick won. She started counting again. Mrs. Chow and the widow had played out this scene many times before. As on other occasions, she didn't give the old woman the satisfaction of a plea, guilty or otherwise.

Mrs. Chow ignored the widow's busy, blue hands. She fixed her gaze on the other woman's milky eyes instead. Sight resided at the peripheries. Mornings, before she prepared the tub, emptied the piss-pot, or fried the breakfast meat, Mrs. Chow cradled the widow's oily scalp and applied the yellow drops that preserved what vision was left in the cold, heaven-directed eyes.

"Is she watching?" said the widow. She tilted her big gray head side-ways; a few degrees in any direction Mrs. Chow became a blur. In happier days Mrs. Chow might have positioned herself just right or left of center, neatly within a line of sight.

Mrs. Chow was thirty-five years old. After a decade-long separation from her husband she finally had entered the United States in 1950 un-der the joint auspices of the War Brides and Refugee Relief Acts. She would agree she was a bride, but not a refugee, even though the Red Army had confiscated her home and turned it into a technical school. During the trouble she was away, safely studying in Hong Kong. Her parents, with all their wealth, could've easily escaped, but they were confident a few well-placed bribes among the Red hooligans would put an end to the foolishness. Mrs. Chow assumed her parents now were dead. She had seen pictures in *Life* of minor landlords tried and executed for lesser crimes against the People.

The widow's fondness for calling Mrs. Chow a thief began soon after the old woman broke her hip. At first Mrs. Chow blamed the widow's madness on pain displacement. She had read in a textbook that a malady in one part of the body could show up as a pain in an-other locale—sick kidneys, for instance, might surface as a mouthful of sore gums. The bad hip had weakened the widow's brain function. Mrs. Chow wanted to believe the crazy spells weren't the widow's fault, just as a baby soiling its diapers can't be blamed. But even a mother grows weary of changing them.

"I live with a thief under my roof," the widow said to the kitchen. "I could yell at her, but why waste my breath?"

When the widow was released from the hospital she returned to the house with a live-in nurse. Soon afterward her daughter paid a visit, and the widow told her she didn't want the nurse around anymore. "She can do me," the widow said, pointing in Mrs. Chow's direction. "She won't cost a cent. Besides, I don't like being touched that way by a person who knows what she's touching," she said of the nurse.

Nobody knew, but Mrs. Chow spoke a passable though highly ac-
cented English she had learned in British schools. Her teachers in
Hong Kong always said that if she had the language when she came
to the States she'd be treated better than other immigrants. Chow
couldn't have agreed more. Once she arrived he started to teach her
everything he knew in English. But that amounted to very little, considering he had been here for more than ten years. And what he had
mastered came out crudely and strangely twisted. His phrases, built
from a vocabulary of deference and accommodation, irritated Mrs.
Chow for the way they resembled the obsequious blabber of her servants back home.

The Chows had been hired ostensibly to drive the widow to her
canasta club, to clean the house, to do the shopping, and since the bad
hip, to oversee her personal hygiene. In return they lived rent-free upstairs in the children's rooms, three bedrooms and a large bath. Plenty
of space, it would seem, except the widow wouldn't allow them to remove any of the toys and things from her children's cluttered rooms.

On weekends and Tuesday afternoons Chow borrowed the
widow's tools and gardened for spending money. Friday nights, after
they dropped the widow off at the canasta club, the Chows dined at
Ming's and then went to the amusement park at the beach boardwalk.
First and last, they got in line to ride the Milky Way. On the day the
immigration authorities finally let her go, before she even saw her new
home, Chow took his bride to the boardwalk. He wanted to impress
her with her new country. All that machinery, brainwork, and labor
done for the sake of fun. He never tried the roller coaster before she
arrived; he saved it for her. After that very first time he realized he was
much happier with his feet set on the ground. But not Mrs. Chow:
Oh, this speed, this thrust at the sky this UP! Oh, this raging, clattering, pushy country! So big! And since that first ride she looked forward to Friday nights and the wind whipping through her hair,
stinging her eyes, blowing away the top layers of dailiness. On the
longest, most dangerous descent her dry mouth would open to a silent
O and she would thrust up her arms, as if she could fly away.

Some nights as they waited in line a gang of toughs out on a strut,
trussed in denim and combs, would stop and visit: MacArthur, they
said, will drain the Pacific; the H-bomb will wipe Korea clean of
Commies; the Chows were to blame for Pearl Harbor; the Chows,
they claimed, were Red Chinese spies. On occasion, overextending his
skimpy English, Chow mounted a defense: he had served in the U.S.

Army, his citizenship was blessed by the Department of War, he was a member of the American Legion. The toughs would laugh at the way he talked. Mrs. Chow cringed at his habit of addressing them as "sirs."

"Get out, get out," the widow hissed. She brought her fist down on the table. Cookies broke, fell to the floor.

"Yes, Missus," said Mrs. Chow, thinking how she'd have to clean up the mess.

The widow, whose great-great-great-grandfather had been a central figure within the faction advocating Washington's coronation, was eighty-six years old. Each day Mrs. Chow dispensed medications that kept her alive. At times, though, Mrs. Chow wondered if the widow would notice if she were handed an extra blue pill or one less red.

Mrs. Chow filled an enamel-coated washbasin with warm water from the tap. "What's she doing?" said the widow. "Stealing my water now, is she?" Since Mrs. Chow first came into her service, the widow, with the exception of her hip, had avoided serious illness. But how she had aged: her ears were enlarged; the opalescence in her eyes had spread; her hands worked as if they were chipped from glass. Some nights, awake in their twin-size bed, Mrs. Chow would imagine old age as green liquid that seeped into a person's cells, where it coagulated and, with time, crumbled, caving in the cheeks and the breasts it had once supported. In the dark she fretted that fluids from the widow's old body had taken refuge in her youthful cells. On such nights she reached for Chow, touched him through the cool top sheet, and was comforted by the fit of her fingers in the shallows between his ribs.

Mrs. Chow knelt at the foot of the wheelchair and set the washbasin on the floor. The widow laughed. "Where did my little thief go?" She laughed again, her eyes closing, her head dropping to her shoulder. "Now she's after my water. Better see if the tap's still there." Mrs. Chow abruptly swung aside the wheelchair's footrests and slipped off the widow's matted cloth slippers and dunked her puffy blue feet into the water. It was the widow's nap time, and before she could be put to bed, her physician prescribed a warm footbath to stimulate circulation; otherwise, in her sleep, her blood might settle comfortably in her toes.

Chow was talking long distance to the widow's daughter in Texas. Earlier the widow had told the daughter that the Chows were threatening again to leave. She apologized for her mother's latest spell of wildness. "Humor her," the daughter said. "She must've had another one of her little strokes."

Later Mrs. Chow told her husband she wanted to leave the widow. "My fingers," she said, snapping off the rubber gloves the magazine ads claimed would guarantee her beautiful hands into the next century. "I wasn't made for such work."

When she was a girl her parents had sent her to a Christian school for training in Western-style art. The authorities agreed she was talented. As expected she excelled there. Her portrait of the King was chosen to hang in the school cafeteria. When the Colonial Minister of Education on a tour of the school saw her painting he requested a sitting with the gifted young artist.

A date was set. The rumors said a successful sitting would bring her the ultimate fame: a trip to London to paint the royal family. But a month before the great day she refused to do the Minister's portrait. She gave no reason why; in fact, she stopped talking. The school administration was embarrassed, and her parents were furious. It was a great scandal; a mere child from a country at the edge of revolution but medieval in its affection for authority had snubbed the mighty British colonizers. She was sent home. Her parents first appealed to family pride, then they scolded and threatened her. She hid from them in a wardrobe, where her mother found her holding her fingers over lighted matches.

The great day came and went, no more momentous than the hundreds that had preceded it. That night her father apologized to the world for raising such a child. With a bamboo cane he struck her outstretched hand—heaven help her if she let it fall one inch—and as her bones were young and still pliant, they didn't fracture or break, thus multiplying the blows she had to endure.

"Who'd want you now?" her mother said. Her parents sent her to live with a servant family. She could return home when she was invited. On those rare occasions she refused to go. Many years passed before she met Chow, who had come to the estate seeking work. They were married on the condition he take her far away. He left for America, promising to send for her when he had saved enough money for her passage. She returned to Hong Kong and worked as a secretary. Later she studied at the university.

Now as she talked about leaving the widow, it wasn't the chores or the old woman that she gave as the reason, though in the past she had complained the widow was a nuisance, an infantile brat born of an unwelcomed union. This time she said she had a project in mind, a great canvas of a yet undetermined subject. But that would come. Her imagination would return, she said, once she was away from that house.

It was the morning of a late spring day. A silvery light filtered through the wall of eucalyptus and warmed the dew on the widow's roof, striking the plums and acacia, irises and lilies in such a way that, blended with the heavy air and the noise of a thousand birds, one sensed the universe wasn't so vast, so cold, or so angry, and even Mrs. Chow suspected that it was a loving thing.

Mrs. Chow had finished her morning chores. She was in the bathroom rinsing the smell of bacon from her hands. She couldn't wash deep enough, however, to rid her fingertips of perfumes from the widow's lotions and creams, which, over the course of months, had seeped indelibly into the whorls. But today her failure was less maddening. Today she was confident the odors would eventually fade. She could afford to be patient. They were going to interview for an apartment of their very own.

"Is that new?" Chow asked, pointing to the blouse his wife had on. He adjusted his necktie against the starched collar of a white short-sleeved shirt, which billowed out from baggy, pinstriped slacks. His hair was slicked back with fragrant pomade.

"I think it's the daughter's," said Mrs. Chow. "She won't miss it." Mrs. Chow smoothed the silk undershirt against her stomach. She guessed the shirt was as old as she was; the daughter probably had worn it in her teens. Narrow at the hips and the bust, it fit Mrs. Chow nicely. Such a slight figure, she believed, wasn't fit for labor.

Chow saw no reason to leave the estate. He had found his wife what he thought was the ideal home, certainly not as grand as her parents' place, but one she'd feel comfortable in. Why move, he argued, when there were no approaching armies, no floods, no one telling them to go? Mrs. Chow understood. It was just that he was very Chinese, and very peasant. Sometimes she would tease him. If the early Chinese sojourners who came to America were all Chows, she would say, the railroad wouldn't have been constructed, and Ohio would be all we know of California.

The Chows were riding in the widow's green Buick. As they approached the apartment building Mrs. Chow reapplied lipstick to her mouth.

It was a modern two-story stucco building, painted pink, surrounded by asphalt, with aluminum windows and a flat roof that met the sky like an engineer's level. Because their friends lived in the apartment in question, the Chows were already familiar with its layout. They went to the manager's house at the rear of the property. Here the grounds were also asphalt. Very contemporary, no greenery anywhere. The closest things to trees were the clothesline's posts and crossbars.

The manager's house was a tiny replica of the main building. Chow knocked on the screen door. A radio was on and the smell of baking rushed past the wire mesh. A cat came to the door, followed by a girl. "I'm Velvet," she said. "This is High Noon." She gave the cat's orange tail a tug. "She did this to me," said Velvet, throwing a wicked look at the room behind her. She picked at her hair, ragged as tossed salad; someone apparently had cut it while the girl was in motion. She had gray, almost colorless eyes, which, taken with her hair, gave her the appearance of agitated smoke.

A large woman emerged from the back room, carrying a basket of laundry. She wasn't fat, but large in the way horses are large. Her face was round and pink, with fierce little eyes, and hair the color of olive oil and dripping wet. Her arms were thick and white, like soft tusks of ivory.

"It's the people from China," Velvet said.

The big woman nodded. "Open her up," she told the girl. "It's okay."

The front room was a mess, cluttered with evidence of frantic living. This was, perhaps, entropy in its final stages. The Chows sat on the couch. From all around her Mrs. Chow sensed a slow creep: the low ceiling seemed to be sinking, cat hairs clung to clothing, a fine spray from the fish tank moistened her bare arm.

No one said anything. It was as if they were sitting in a hospital waiting room. The girl watched the Chows. The large woman stared at a green radio at her elbow broadcasting news about the war. Every so often she looked suspiciously up at the Chows. "You know me," she said abruptly, "I'm Remora Cass."

On her left, suspended in a swing, was the biggest, ugliest baby Mrs. Chow had ever seen. It was dozing, arms dangling, great melon head flung so far back that it appeared to be all nostrils and chins. "A pig-boy," Mrs. Chow said in Chinese. Velvet jabbed two fingers into the baby's rubbery cheeks. Then she sprang back from the swing and executed a feral dance, all elbows and knees. She seemed incapable of holding her body still.

She caught Mrs. Chow's eye. "This is Ed," she said. "He has no hair."

Mrs. Chow nodded.

"Quit," said Remora Cass, swatting at the girl as if she were a fly. Then the big woman looked Mrs. Chow in the eyes and said: "I know what you're thinking, and you're right. There's not a baby in the state bigger than Ed; eight pounds, twelve ounces at birth and he doubled that inside a month." She stopped, bringing her palms heavily down on her knees, and shook her wet head. "You don't understand me, do you?"

Mrs. Chow was watching Velvet.

"Quit that!" Remora Cass slapped the girl's hand away from the baby's face.

"Times like this I'd say it's a blessing my Aunt Eleanor's deaf," said Remora Cass. "I've gotten pretty good with sign language." From her overstuffed chair she repeated in pantomime what she had said about the baby.

Velvet mimicked her mother's generous, sweeping movements. When Remora Cass caught sight of her she added a left jab to the girl's head to her repertoire of gestures. Velvet slipped the punch with practiced ease. But the blow struck the swingset. Everyone tensed. Ed flapped his arms and went on sleeping. "Leave us alone," said Remora Cass, "before I really get mad."

The girl chased down the cat and skipped toward the door. "I'm bored anyway," she said.

Remora Cass asked the Chows questions, first about jobs and pets. Then she moved on to matters of politics and patriotism. "What's your feeling about the Red Chinese in Korea?"

A standard question. "Terrible," said Chow, giving his standard answer. "I'm sorry. Too much trouble."

Mrs. Chow sat by quietly. She admired Chow's effort. She had studied the language, but he did the talking; she wanted to move, but he had to plead their case; it was his kin back home who benefited from the new regime, but he had to bad-mouth it.

Remora Cass asked about children.

"No, no, no," Chow said, answering as his friend Bok had coached him. His face was slightly flushed from the question. Chow wanted children, many children . But whenever he discussed the matter with his wife, she answered that she already had one, meaning the old woman, of course, and that she was enough.

"Tell your wife later," the manager said, "what I'm about to tell you now. I don't care what jobs you do, just so long as you have them. What I say goes for the landlady. I'm willing to take a risk on you. Be nice to have nice quiet folks up there like Rikki and Bok. Rent paid up, I can live with anyone. Besides, I'm real partial to Chinese take-out. I know we'll do just right."

The baby moaned, rolling its head from side to side. His mother stared at him as if in all the world there were just the two of them.

Velvet came in holding a beachball. She returned to her place beside the swing and started to hop, alternating legs, with the beachball held to her head. "She must be in some kind of pain," Mrs. Chow said to her husband.

The girl mimicked the Chinese she heard. Mrs. Chow glared at Velvet, as if she were the widow during one of her spells. The look froze the girl, standing on one leg. Then she said, "Can Ed come out to play?"

Chow took hold of his wife's hand and squeezed it, as he did to brace himself before the roller coaster's forward plunge. Then in a single well-rehearsed motion Remora Cass swept off her slipper and punched at the girl. Velvet masterfully sidestepped the slipper and let the beachball fly. The slipper caught the swingset, the beachball bounced off Ed's lap.

The collisions released charged particles into the air that seemed to hold everyone in a momentary state of paralysis. The baby's eyes peeled open, and he blinked at the ceiling. Soon his distended belly started rippling. He cried until he turned purple, then devoted his energy to maintaining that hue. Mrs. Chow had never heard anything as harrowing. She visualized his cry as large cubes forcing their way into her ears.

Remora Cass picked Ed up and bounced on the balls of her feet. "You better start running," she said to Velvet, who was already on her way out the door.

Remora Cass half-smiled at the Chows over the baby's shoulder. "He'll quiet down sooner or later," she said.

Growing up Mrs. Chow was the youngest of five girls. She had to endure the mothering of her sisters who, at an early age, were already in training for their future roles. Each married in her teens, plucked in turn by a Portugese, German, Brit, and New Yorker. They had many babies. But Mrs. Chow thought little of her sisters' example. Even when her parents made life unbearable she never indulged in the hope that a man—foreign or domestic—or a child could save her from her unhappiness.

From the kitchen Remora Cass called Mrs. Chow. The big woman was busy with her baking. The baby was slung over her shoulder. "Let's try something," she said as she transferred the screaming Ed into Mrs. Chow's arms.

Ed was a difficult package. Not only was he heavy and hot and sweaty but he spat and squirmed like a sack of kittens. She tried to think of how it was done. She tried to think of how a baby was held. She remembered Romanesque Madonnas cradling their gentlemanly babies in art history textbooks. If she could get his head up by hers, that would be a start.

Remora Cass told Mrs. Chow to try bouncing and showed her what she meant. "Makes him think he's still inside," she said. Ed emitted a long, sustained wail, then settled into a bout of hiccups. "You have a nice touch with him. He won't do that for just anyone."

As the baby quieted, a pain rolled from the heel of Mrs. Chow's brain, down through her pelvis, to a southern terminus at the backs of her knees. She couldn't blame the baby entirely for her discomfort. He wanted only to escape; animal instinct told him to leap from danger.

She was the one better equipped to escape. She imagined invading soldiers murdering livestock and planting flags in the soil of her ancestral estate, as if it were itself a little nation; they make history by the slaughter of generations of her family; they discover her in the wardrobe, striking matches; they ask where she has hidden her children, and she tells them there are none; they say, good, they'll save ammunition, but also too bad, so young and never to know the pleasure of children (even if they'd have to murder them). Perhaps this would be the subject of her painting, a non-representational canvas that hinted at a world without light. Perhaps—

Ed interrupted her thought. He had developed a new trick. "Woop, woop, woop," he went, thrusting his pelvis against her sternum in the manner of an adult male in the act of mating. She called for Chow.

Remora Cass slid a cookie sheet into the oven and then stuck a bottle of baby formula into Ed's mouth. He drained it instantly. "You do have a way with him," said Remora Cass.

They walked into the front room. The baby was sleepy and dripping curds on his mother's shoulder. Under the swing High Noon, the cat, was licking the nipple of an abandoned bottle. "Scat!" she said. "Now where's my wash gone to?" she asked the room. "What's she up to now?" She scanned the little room, big feet planted in the deep, brown shag carpet, hands on her beefy hips, baby slung over her shoulder like a pelt. "Velvet—" she started. That was all. Her jaw locked, her gums gleamed, her eyes rolled into her skull. Her head flopped backwards, as if at the back of her neck there was a great hinge. Then she yawned, and the walls seemed to shake.

Remora Cass rubbed her eyes. "I'm bushed," she said.

Mrs. Chow went over to the screen door. Chow and the girl were at the clothesline. Except for their hands and legs, they were hidden behind a bedsheet. The girl's feet were in constant motion. From the basket her hands picked up pieces of laundry which Chow's hands then clipped to the line.

"Her daddy's hardly ever here," Remora Cass said. "Works all hours, he does. Has to." She patted Ed on the back, then rubbed her eyes again. "Looks like Velvet's found a friend. She won't do that with anyone. You two are naturals with my two. You should get you some of your own." She looked over at Mrs. Chow and laughed. "Maybe it's best you didn't get that. Here." She set the baby on Mrs. Chow's shoulder. "This is what it's like when they're sleeping."

Before leaving the Chows went to look at Rikki and Bok's apartment. They climbed up the stairs. No one was home. Rikki and Bok had barely started to pack. Bok's naked man, surrounded by an assortment of spears and arrows, was still hanging on the living room wall. Bok had paid good money for the photograph: an aboriginal gent stares into the camera, he's smiling, his teeth are good and large, and in his palms he's holding his sex out like a prize eel.

Mrs. Chow looked at the photograph for as long as it was discreetly possible before she averted her eyes and made her usual remark about Bok's tastes. Beyond the building's edge she saw the manager's cottage, bleached white in the sun. Outside the front door Remora Cass sat in a folding chair, her eyes shut, her pie-tin face turned up to catch the rays, while Velvet, her feet anchored to the asphalt, rolled her mother's hair in pink curlers. Between the big woman's legs the baby lay in a wicker basket. He was quietly rocking from side to side. Remora Cass's chest rose and fell in the rhythm of sleep.

Driving home, they passed the boardwalk, and Mrs. Chow asked if they might stop.

Chow refused to ride the roller coaster in the daytime, no matter how much Mrs. Chow teased. It was hard enough at night, when the heights from which the cars fell were lit by a few rows of bulbs. As he handed her an orange ticket, Chow said, "A drunk doesn't look in mirrors."

The Milky Way clattered into the terminus. After she boarded the ride, she watched Chow, who had wandered from the loading platform and was standing beside a popcorn wagon, looking up at a billboard. His hands were deep in the pockets of his trousers, his legs crossed at the shins. That had been his pose, the brim of his hat low on his brow, as he waited for her to finally pass through the gates of Immigration.

"Go on," an old woman said. "You'll be glad you did." The old woman nudged her young charge toward the empty seat in Mrs. Chow's car. "Go on, she won't bite." The girl looked back at the old woman. "Grand-muth-ther!" she said, and then reluctantly climbed in beside Mrs. Chow.

Once the attendant strapped the girl in she turned from her grandmother and stared at her new companion. The machine jerked away from the platform. They were climbing the first ascent when Mrs. Chow snuck a look at the girl. She was met by the clearest eyes she had ever known, eyes that didn't shy from the encounter. The girl's pupils, despite the bright sun, were fully dilated, stretched with fear. Now that she had Mrs. Chow's attention she turned her gaze slowly toward the vertical track ahead. Mrs. Chow looked beyond the summit to the empty blue sky.

Within seconds they tumbled through that plane and plunged downward, the cars flung suddenly left and right, centrifugal force throwing Mrs. Chow against the girl's rigid body. She was surprised by Chow's absence.

It's gravity that makes the stomach fly, that causes the liver to flutter; it's the body catching up with the speed of falling. Until today, she had never known such sensations. Today there was a weightiness at her core, like a hard, concentrated pull inward, as if an incision had been made and a fist-sized magnet imbedded.

Her arms flew up, two weak wings cutting the rush of wind. But it wasn't the old sensation this time, not the familiar embrace of the whole fleeting continent, but a grasp at something once there, now lost.

Chow had moved into position to see the riders' faces as they careened down the steepest stretch of track. Whenever he was up there with her, his eyes were clenched and his scream so wild and his grip on his life so tenuous that he never noticed her expression. At the top of the rise the cars seemed to stop momentarily, but then up and over, tumbling down, at what appeared, from his safe vantage point, a surprisingly slow speed. Arms shot up, the machine whooshed past him, preceded a split second earlier by the riders' collective scream. And for the first time Chow thought he heard her, she who loved this torture so, scream too.

As she was whipped skyward once more her arms were wrapped around the little girl. Not in flight, not soaring, but anchored by another's being, as her parents stood against the liberators to protect their land.

Some curves, a gentle dip, one last sharp bend, and the ride rumbled to rest. The girl's breath was warm against Mrs. Chow's neck. For a moment longer she held onto the girl, whose small ribs were as thin as paintbrushes.

The Chows walked to the edge of the platform. He looked up at the billboard he had noticed earlier. It was a picture of an American woman with bright red hair, large red lips, and a slightly upturned nose; a fur was draped around her neck, pearls cut across her throat.

"What do you suppose they're selling?" he asked.

His wife pointed at the billboard. She read aloud what was printed there: "No other home permanent wave looks, feels, behaves so much like naturally curly hair."

She then gave a quick translation and asked what he thought of her curling her hair.

He made no reply. For some time now he couldn't lift his eyes from her.

"I won't do it," she said, "but what do you say?"

She turned away from him and stared a long time at the face on the billboard and then at the beach on the other side of the boardwalk and at the ocean, the Pacific Ocean, and at the horizon where all lines of sight converge, before she realized the land on the other side wouldn't come into view.

What Happened to Red Deer

Wayne D. Johnson

RED DEER TURNED the ball in his hand.

They were yelling in the bleachers now. "Chief! Go home, Chief!"

The ball fit in his palm like a stone. He caught the stitching with his nails, then raised his eyes to the catcher. The catcher thrust two fingers at the ground.

A slider.

Red Deer nodded, coiled himself back, leg raised, stretching, and hurled the ball. The ball went low, looked like a gutter ball, then rose and smacked into the catcher's mitt. The umpire jerked his hand over his head, thumb up, and the batter shook his head.

"Out!" the umpire shouted.

There was a chorus of booing from the bleachers.

Red Deer watched them out of the corner of his eye.

Since the beginning of the game they had jeered, and when the game had gone into overtime, they began yelling "Chief! Go home, Chief!"

He had ridden on the crest of it, letting it carry him through the game. But something was happening now and he didn't know what it was. It was as if something were dissolving in him, dissolving and going flat.

Darius, the coach, walked to the mound from the dugout.

"How's your arm holding up?" he said.

"Okay," Red Deer offered.

"We'll have her licked if you can hang in there."

Red Deer pulled the bill of his cap down.

"Don't mind those sons-of-bitches. They're just a bunch of drunks. You're pitching like a pro. Just get back in there and kill 'em." Darius slapped Red Deer on the back, then strode past third, up toward the bleachers.

"What the hell are you waiting for, Chief?" the loudest of the drunks yelled from the stands.

A batter stepped up to the plate. He practiced his swing, dipping in mid-stroke and pulling up. He tapped the bat on his shoes and positioned himself. The umpire and catcher squatted; the catcher pointed to the ground with his index finger. Knuckle. Red Deer turned the ball in his hand, found the stitching with his nails again, drew back like the hammer of a gun and hurled the ball. The ball went straight and fast, right down the pipe. The batter uncoiled, the bat scooped down into the ball, there was a loud crack, and the ball went high, up and back into the bleachers, a foul.

"Whooa, Chief!" the drunks yelled.

Red Deer turned to face the bleachers.

He could see the men who were doing the yelling. They were wearing white shirts and colored ties, and they had brought women with them. Attractive women, who laughed and pushed and when the men yelled laughed into their hands.

"Go home, Chief!" the biggest yelled, standing, a beer in his fist. The woman at his side laughed, pulling at his pants leg.

Red Deer shook his head. He turned to the other side of the field. There his father, Osada, sat with the boy, Bear. A few rows up from them a knot of men from the reservation stood. Red Deer had not asked them to come, and when he had run out onto the playing field, he had been startled to see them. Joe Big Otter had waved and Red Deer had felt something in him sad and old and hurtful.

"Hey! Chief! You missing the Lone Ranger?" There was a cackle of laughter.

The men from the reservation glared across the field.

Red Deer turned the ball in his hand.

He wished the ball were a stone.

He took the sign from the catcher, eyed the batter, drew his body and arm back, and hurled the ball again. The batter swung around, connected, and then it was all moving, Red Deer carried across the field, the ball sizzling by his head, his mitt out, the hard break of the ball against his hand, then opening the mitt and lobbing the ball to first, the baseman reaching, throwing to third, the runner coming on

hard, then sliding, the umpire charging, the ball, the baseman, the runner and the umpire all converging there. In the dust, you couldn't see
at all.

"Safe!" the umpire yelled, spreading his arms wide at his waist.
"Safe!"

An organ broke into a frenzy of scales and the scoreboard flashed.
Bottom of the tenth. Six to five, visitor's lead.

Red Deer swung back to the mound.

"Go home, Chief!" the drunks yelled.

The shortstop caught him on the way. The man on third kicked the
base, watching the two men.

"Two outs. Anything goes home, okay?"

Red Deer nodded.

"Just give 'em some of the old Buck stuff," the shortstop said. He
spit through his teeth and slapped Red Deer on the back.

"Buck!" he said.

But Red Deer was staring off over the bleachers.

In grade school, when they ran the races on the playground, he never
pushed himself and still he could beat them all, even the straining,
grunting boys who couldn't stand to lose to an Indian.

It wasn't a hard thing to do.

He loved to run, and he ran to school and back home again and
wherever else it was he went. Somehow rather than tiring him, as it
did the others, it set him free. He loved the feel of the ground under
his feet, the trees flashing by, the pumping of his lungs, the pain he
pushed through into a solid rhythm that carried him away from everything. If he wanted he would change the rhythm, his legs working
harder, the ground beating up with more power, but always the
ground carried him, and he was surprised, when one day at school a
man watched him run the circumference of the football field, a watch
in his hand.

The man stopped Red Deer back of the goalposts, his face swollen
with excitement, his thumb held down on the watch. "Wait! Stop
there!" he said.

Red Deer had looked back to see where the others were. They
weren't around the field yet.

"I can't believe it," the man said.

Red Deer's teacher came over. "Didn't I tell you he was fast?" he said. "Didn't I tell you?"

"Is that as fast as you can run?"

"No," Red Deer said.

"How old are you?"

"Fifteen."

The man held out his hand. "I just can't believe it," he said. "Jim Thorpe couldn't have done that at your age."

The others ran by, breathing hard, and Red Deer stepped into the stream of bodies. Halfway around the field he looked back. The two men were still talking, the man with the watch gesturing with his hands.

Red Deer heaved the ball down the baseline to the catcher.

"No!" the shortstop yelled. "Goddammit! Throw it around the horn."

Red Deer turned to face the shortstop.

"Haven't you ever played baseball?" The shortstop pointed to the second baseman with his mitt, then shook his head. "What the hell is he doing out here?"

Red Deer shrugged his shoulders. They had him on first, and he didn't know what plays to make. He didn't like standing around so much, and they were always yelling at him.

"Hey! Chief!" Joe Fossen, the catcher, yelled. He threw the ball and Red Deer caught it, tossed it to second, and then it went around again.

It was the first time anyone on the team had called him "Chief." It was the first time *anyone* had called him "Chief."

He wasn't sure he liked it.

But he wasn't sure he liked playing baseball either. It hadn't been his idea.

They had called him down to the principal's office not long after the man with the watch had been on the field, and Red Deer had wondered what they had singled him out for now. After the business with his father and the shooting, it seemed the teachers were afraid of him, or afraid that something would happen to them if they had anything to do with him. And the other Indians didn't know what to make of him, either—he was too big for his age, and there was still a general bad feeling on the reservation about the incident. He had gained notoriety without wanting it in any way.

In the office the principal, a short, baldheaded man behind a desk, had asked Red Deer to sit.

"Well, we've got it all fixed," he said.

"Did I do something?" Red Deer said. His heart was pounding. He felt uncomfortable and crossed his legs and uncrossed them, pressing his feet into the floor so his toes curled under.

"We thought you'd want to play baseball," the man said. He adjusted his glasses, then leaned back in his chair.

Red Deer crossed his legs again.

"Joe Bradley's going to be driving up to Kenora just about every day. We thought you'd like to be playing on the team."

Outside the room a typewriter was snapping.

Red Deer didn't know what to say, so he stood. The principal stood with him.

"So what do you think?" he said.

Red Deer pushed his hands into his pockets, then looked over the man's shoulder, through the window. The wind was blowing and the poplars in the schoolyard swayed.

"Okay," he said. "Sure."

The ball came around the horn again.

"Hey! Chief!" Sampson, the shortstop, yelled. "For Christ's sake don't just stand there!"

Red Deer caught the ball and carefully set it beside the base bag. He covered the distance between first and shortstop and there Joe Sampson stood, his fists tight at his sides. Red Deer hadn't realized how big Joe was until he got right up to him; he was the only boy on the team that could stand head to head with Red Deer.

"Hey!" the coach yelled.

"Don't call me that," Red Deer said.

"Make me," the boy said. He leaned toward Red Deer, so that Red Deer could smell his breath.

The coach headed across the field, then was running.

"Make me, *Chief!*" the boy said.

It made Red Deer think of his father, Osada, and how the men he had been a guide for had called him "Chief." Sometimes, when Red Deer had been out in the boat with him, he could see Osada was enraged when it happened, and other times he didn't seem to care at all.

Sometimes, with the men who had had a sense of humor, he even seemed to like it.

"Break it up!" the coach yelled. He was nearly across the field now.

"Tonto," the boy said.

The word worked like a key in Red Deer's brain, and then as with a stone he hammered at the boy's face, and even when the boy was on the ground and bleeding Red Deer couldn't stop hitting him.

They called him "Buck" after that, and they were all a little afraid of him. He got bigger, his shoulders broadening, his legs getting longer. The boy he had beaten didn't come back; his jaw had been broken and one of his eyes damaged. No one said anything about it, but Red Deer felt badly.

Somehow they all seemed to feel bad.

They drank a good deal and had girl friends and every now and then as they got older a boy would disappear from the team.

"Where's Freddie?" Red Deer had asked one afternoon at practice. Freddie had become a friend of his, though a silent one.

"Didn't you hear?"

"No."

"He's not playing anymore. They got him down at the supermarket in Fort Francis."

"What the hell's he doing down there?"

"Gettin' married, I guess," the boy said, a wry grin on his face.

It puzzled Red Deer. And not long after, when he was down in Fort Francis to see Osada, he stopped by the new supermarket to see if Freddie was there. It really was super. Huge. A long, low, cinderblock building with a giant red and blue sign in front. Red Deer stepped through the doors and it was cold inside and smelled of floor wax, like when they had had dances at the old school. The lights were bluish and buzzed and there were three women in yellow dresses at the registers.

"Is there a Fred Levine who works here?"

The women looked at him suspiciously.

"You mean a young guy? Eighteen or so?" the biggest said, tossing her head back.

A door opened off to one side and Freddie came out. He was wearing a green apron and had his hair slicked back.

"Hey! Freddie!" Red Deer said.

Freddie's eye puckered and his eyebrows drew down and then he smiled, too broadly.

"Come on back," he said.

Red Deer went up the aisle. There were all kinds of beans on the shelves, beans he had never even heard of.

"How's it goin'?" Freddie said.

He seemed nervous and stood on one leg and then on the other.

"How's the team? I heard you guys wupped shit out of Fond Du Lac."

"Nine to three," Red Deer said.

"I heard you were pitchin', too. Is that right?"

Red Deer nodded. Something was wrong. Freddie was the one guy who'd gotten the others to lay off the "Chief" stuff, and they had been friends in the way a pitcher and first baseman can be friends if they are both good at it.

"So what's this all about, Freddie?" Red Deer said. He was so tall now his head was even with the top shelf.

Freddie looked up the aisle one way and down it the other.

"You heard, didn't you?" he said.

"You're getting married."

"That's it," he said.

Red Deer braced himself against the aisle divider. "So what about all that other stuff? Chicago and that school down there?"

"I'm just makin' some money now. See? Then I can go later."

He dusted the shelf Red Deer leaned on, rearranging the cans.

"So," Red Deer said.

The girls laughed up at the registers.

Freddie carefully straightened the cans, his hands shaking. He reminded Red Deer of a squirrel caught in a snare, his eyes wild.

"You don't have to get married, you know," Red Deer said.

Freddie looked up the aisle again and back.

"Look, I gotta go, Buck. I can't just stand around here talking . . ."

A heavyset man with shiny black shoes stepped around the end of the aisle.

"Can I help you?" he said.

"Just a minute," Freddie said.

"Freddie," the man said.

Freddie's face had reddened. "Just let me explain," he said. "It's not what you think . . ."

"It's okay," Red Deer said. Though it was not okay.

"Hang on. Just wait a—"

The manager was coming up the aisle now. Red Deer could not stand to see Freddie this way.

"See you around, Freddie," he said.

He didn't toss up the tuft of Freddie's hair the way he always had, and walking across the parking lot in the bright sun, the new gravel sharp under his feet, Red Deer felt a hollow in his chest.

It seemed to Red Deer that they were all liars. And he had become a liar, too, though he lied in a different way. He said nothing, or as little as possible. It wasn't that there wasn't anything to say, but to say it would have torn up the fabric of all the lies and Red Deer knew none of them would stand for it. So he pretended he didn't feel the discomfort of the whites around him, or the hatred and bad feeling of the other Indians. It got so the only place he could escape the lies was playing baseball, and for that reason he came to love the game. On the field the ball moved, and they played. He could walk out onto the field, the mitt snug on his hand, and win or lose, he would pitch his best and whether his teammates hated him or not, they needed him up there on the mound. Slider. Curveball. Greaseball. Knuckleball. Fast pitch. He could get his fingers on the fine stitching of the ball and it fit into his palm like a planet. Or a shooting star. It was all a game and he saw the line he wanted the ball to take, up to and past the batter. He got to know the boys on the other teams, how they batted, how they ran.

There seemed to be no end to it. It happened so fast he could only do a little at a time, test what his hand could do to the line. But he came along fast, and people knew him.

"Let him have it, Buck!" they'd yell from the stands. "Give it to 'im, Buck!"

But after the games he went home. If he was near the reservation he stayed at his mother's, even though he didn't like his stepfather. He liked playing with the boy, though. Bear was like a little animal, only smarter, and faster, and they'd tumble in the dirt in the yard and the boy loved to play catch. On hot summer afternoons they listened to Minnesota Twins games on the radio, drinking root beer—Red Deer would buy cases of it—and when the Hamm's commercials came on, sung as though by Indians, with a drum pounding in the background, Red Deer and Bear burst out laughing.

It was on one of those afternoons that Red Deer and his stepfather, Joe Big Otter, got to fighting. They were sitting outside the house, drinking under the shade of an umbrella Joe had bought at the supermarket in Fort Francis.

"You see a guy there with slicked back hair?" Red Deer said. "Big nose?"

"No," Joe said.

Red Deer looked up into the umbrella. The umbrella had been on sale. On it Huey, Louie, and Dewey marched with sand buckets, pink, yellow, and candy blue.

The Twins were on the radio.

"I want to hear a story," Bear said.

"Shhhh," Martha Blue Feather said. She reached under Bear's armpit and tickled him.

"What kind of story do you want to hear?" Red Deer said.

"I want to hear a story about cowboys," the boy said.

It made Red Deer sad to hear him say this, and he looked up into the umbrella again and took a sip of his beer.

"Why don't you tell him the one about Litani?" Joe said.

Litani had been shot in the altercation with the marshals, when Osada had gotten the men to take their boys out of the new school. Litani had been Joe's younger brother.

Red Deer did not answer. It was hot and he could tell nothing good would come of this. He noticed how whoever it was who had drawn the ducks for the umbrella had put smiles on their bills. They looked funny holding the pails.

"Tell him that one," Joe Big Otter said. "There's a *cowboy* story."

Red Deer looked across the table. Joe smiled. Martha put her hand on Joe's forearm, gripped him around the wrist.

"You see," Joe said, his drunken eyes on the boy, "there was this proud man—"

"Shut up," Red Deer said.

"He should hear it," Joe said.

"Not the way you're telling it," Red Deer said. He set his beer on the table. He was hoping this would just pass.

Martha pulled at the bottle in Joe's hand. "You've had enough," she said.

"Don't," he said.

"You've had too much. Let go."

"Tell it," Joe said.

Red Deer looked away. He didn't want to tell Bear the story, and he didn't want Joe to tell it either.

"Coward," Joe said.

"Not as big a coward as you with your bottle," Red Deer replied.

Joe stood. The boy's eyes widened. The boy could not understand what they were saying, and when they began to yell, he crawled under the table.

Joe punched Red Deer in the mouth and then Red Deer had Joe by his ponytail and slammed his face into the picnic table. Blood ran down Joe's nose and Red Deer, trying to pull away, got hit in the mouth again. He tried to pin Joe down but Joe was hollering now.

"Your goddamned cowboy—"

Red Deer hit him in the mouth. He felt the teeth give way under his knuckles. Martha's eyes were wide and Joe stumbled back from the table. Martha held her hand to her mouth, and Joe ran inside. Bear was crying under the table. Then Joe swung by the kitchen window with his rifle, and Red Deer was over the garden fence, out across the field, and he didn't stop running until he was miles out of the reservation.

He didn't tell them where he was staying. He'd made himself a lean-to down by the fish hatchery, and at night he'd swim and catch brown trout, and bake them in the hillside behind the lean-to. He knew he couldn't do this very long, but he also knew something would come up. They were playing a game down in Fort Francis, against a Toronto team, and some big name scouts were supposed to be there.

"They're waiting for you," the coach had said.

The morning of the game with Toronto Red Deer got up early. He swam in the clean, bitter cold water, then knocked down the lean-to. The fishery people were getting wise to him anyway, and he'd have to find someplace else. He walked into town, spent his last dollar on a plate of eggs and hash browns and coffee. At two he met the others at the school, and then everything was all right.

The basement was cool, and they suited up, the others snapping each other with their towels and joking.

"Hey! Buckeroo!" one of the boys said, thumping him on the back.

Red Deer took his uniform from his locker, set his clothes out as he always did. He dressed quickly, his hands sure, finally pulling the laces of his tennis shoes tight. He reached into his locker for his cleats and swung them over his shoulder. If he could keep it out of his mind, he thought, everything would be fine.

The game went terribly. The new first baseman was slow, and Red Deer wished Freddie were there. He missed him now, though it didn't occur to him why. He pitched badly, and he watched the scouts in the bleachers. The two men wore widebrimmed hats and pointed, nodded, and scribbled on note pads.

It seemed it was all coming to a grinding end.

They forced their way through a miserable third inning and headed for the dugout.

"What the hell is wrong with you?" the coach said. Everyone else in the dugout looked the other way. "Huh? What's going on?"

Red Deer stared out across the field. Meyers was up to bat. He swung in short choppy strokes.

"Are you listening to me?" the coach said.

"I don't know," Red Deer said.

The coach slapped his hand on his knees. "Well, you goddamned well better know. Do you have any idea how important this game is?" He lowered his voice. "It's your goddamned baby. They didn't come out here to see Hodges."

Beside him Hodges stiffened.

Red Deer felt badly that he had heard. He wasn't a good first baseman and he knew it.

There was a crack of a bat, and everyone in the dugout stood. Red Deer sat on the bench.

"Get up," the coach yelled, but Red Deer wasn't about to. Not like that.

On the mound again he couldn't force the ball down the line, and the game had all gone away somewhere. He was tired, dirty, and hungry. He had lost something, and a deep sadness was setting in. It wasn't this damn game, he thought. It was Bear. He'd lost Bear, and he figured he'd lost his mother, too, only now he could see he'd never really had her, and maybe that hurt the worst.

A big kid named Donnelly got up to bat, kicking his cleats into the dirt like a rooster. They were leading nine/five into the sixth inning and now their batters were all getting cocky.

"Come on, Chief, throw me a fast one," he said.

Red Deer looked into the stands, then at the boy.

"Come on, Chief," he said.

Red Deer tightened his grip on the ball.

"Put her right here, Chief," the boy said, tapping the base with his bat.

Red Deer found the stitches on the ball, gripped it in his hand. He got a kind of tunnel vision, and when Steadman, the catcher, signaled for him to throw a curve, he shook his head. He knew what to do with this one. He settled onto his legs, then stretched as if to break himself, and when he threw the ball it hissed out of his hand, went low, then broke into the catcher's mitt with a dusty thud. The batter's mouth dropped open.

"Steeerike!" the umpire called.

Red Deer caught the ball, tossed it around the horn.

No one said anything.

When it was over, and they had won by two runs, Red Deer dropped the ball on the mound and walked to the dugout.

"Jesus Christ!" the coach said. "That was really something."

Red Deer wiped his face with a towel. He never wanted to play another game like that. He had wanted to kill the boy Donnelly, and had prodded himself along with him, remembering his face and what he had said. And when the boy was up to bat again, and he sensed something dangerous in Red Deer, Red Deer imagined him saying the things he had said over again.

He wasn't happy now—he was drained, and felt ugly.

The two scouts came down to the dugout.

"Hell of a game you pitched."

Red Deer nodded.

They had turned the lights off on the field and now the dugout was dark but for the light coming in from the parking lot. The bigger man's glasses shone in the dark.

"Anything you'd like to say?"

All he wanted now was to be alone.

"I've pitched better," he said. It was what he was supposed to say. And it was true, only now he wished they would leave.

"We'll be getting in touch," the bigger of the two men said.

Red Deer watched them cross the parking lot to the car. The lights came on, and the car crackled out of the lot with the others, dust billowing behind them. Red Deer settled down onto the dirt floor, the cement cool against his sides, the dugout just long enough to hold him. It was all he wanted now.

The rest was easy. It was like falling. A small league team picked him up as a relief pitcher, and then he was playing, and had some jack in his pocket. He traveled a lot, and he forgot about what happened. He learned to forget a lot of things, and he learned how to fight too.

"Hey, Chief," someone would say.

It was like a button they pushed.

He learned to hit first, and hit hard, and it wasn't until later that he got into fights with men bigger than he was. He had his nose broken three times and lost a tooth, a canine, so when he smiled it gave him the look of someone who would take the caps off beer bottles with his teeth for fun.

And on the mound he felt it get bigger in him, like a stone, and he held on to it tighter. He learned to focus it, and he thought of it as being like a train or a bulldozer. All he had to think of was that boy, and it started again.

"Chief," he'd think to himself.

He got to love it, and it was precious.

He found it had all kinds of uses.

On nights when things were going badly, when he felt a slagging in his desire to throw the ball, he could pump himself up with it. It got to be such a thing with him he was afraid he would lose it, and then he nursed it when he wasn't on the field, and soon after he was thrown in jail for nearly killing a man in a bar.

"Don't mess with him," they said.

Red Deer thought it was funny. He was just playing the game. But something had happened, and one night, when he came in from a drunk, he had looked in the mirror in the bathroom of his hotel room and had seen somebody he didn't know staring out at him—a big, fierce-looking Indian with a crooked nose and hard eyes. It scared him so badly that he covered all the mirrors in his room with towels and lay on his bed, his arms pulled tight over his chest.

The morning after, Harvey, his first baseman, had spoken to him in the dugout. It was a hot day at the end of August and Red Deer was tying the laces of his cleats.

His hands shook on the laces.

"You'd better slow down on the sauce," Harvey said.

It occurred to Red Deer to knock Harvey's teeth out, but the look on his face was so concerned that he laughed instead.

"Nothing that doesn't grease the old joints," Red Deer said.

Harvey brushed the dirt off his glove. He shook his head. "I'll tell you something," he said. "Just between the two of us."

Red Deer busied himself with his shoes. He didn't want to hear it.

"I got an ulcer the size of a half-dollar in my gut," Harvey said, "and if it gets any worse they say they're gonna have to cut some out and sew me up. Now I thought that was pretty funny, until they said it might kill me, see." He put his face down by Red Deer's. "Do you see what I'm saying?"

Red Deer grunted, double-tying his laces, pulling on them. He could hardly control his hands now.

"Hey, do you hear what—"

"Shut up, Harve," Red Deer said. There was a buzzing in his brain. He shot to his feet and grabbed Harvey by his shirt and twisted it. "Shut up before I knock out your teeth."

The season ended well enough, and Red Deer got himself a job in a meat packing plant in Ohio, where he had played his last game. He hated the noises and smells at first. He hated the gray walls and the fluorescent lights. He hated his foreman and he hated Vinny, the boy he worked with.

But as with everything else, he learned to shut it out.

"Don't you just love it?" Vinny said. They were cutting the heads off pigs. A fine line of blood squirted up Vinny's rubber smock while he cut with the saw.

Vinny smiled.

He had a few teeth missing, and Red Deer saw himself in the mirror for a second.

"Cut that shit out, Vinny," he said.

But then it was baseball season again, the job and the winter shucked off. He took the train down to Tampa and the tryouts started. The weather was warm and there were birds all over and it was hard to pitch at first.

But it always happened.

"Chief," someone said. "Tonto."

And he was throwing hot again. His arm swollen and hard. He built it up slowly, added Vinny to it, but there were so many now it didn't matter. He didn't even have to think of any specific one, it just came to him in a knotted, hard bundle. A bundle he would spit out his arm and over the bag.

"Jesus," they said. "He throws a real killer-ball."

He was throwing like that in his fifth pick-up game. Hurling himself into it, when a scout for the Cleveland Aces spotted him. He'd never been hotter, and like that, a month later he was in Chicago for an exhibition game against the Cubs, and somehow, someone had found out on the reservation and there they were, Osada and Bear, and Joe Big Otter and his friends.

The lights burned.

A brown bottle sailed up over the netting, turning end over end, flashing, and landed on the field. One of the men in the white shirts and colored ties stood.

"Chief! Go home, Chief!" he shouted.

A bat boy ran out to the bottle.

Darius marched to the mound from the dugout, and the umpires came up from the bases.

"What the hell is going on?" Darius said.

Red Deer glanced up into the lights. Everything seemed so bright now, the field an electric green.

"We got a goddamned game goin' on here. You can't just stand the fuck out here and pick your nose. What the hell is wrong with you? Are you on the sauce or what?"

Red Deer kicked at the mound with his cleats.

"Answer me!"

"I don't know," Red Deer said.

"I'm going to put our relief in if you don't get your ass in gear."

Red Deer turned to Darius, looked down into his eyes.

Darius could tell something was wrong.

"I'm not on the sauce," Red Deer lied.

But it didn't matter now. There was no stopping what was opening. It was just a matter of finishing now. He had to finish it.

"I got it," Red Deer said.

"Well, you better have it," Darius said.

He crossed the field to the dugout and climbed down.

Red Deer pushed his mitt on his hand. He remembered what the man with the watch had said:

"Jim Thorpe couldn't have done that at your age."

Red Deer positioned himself on the mound. Now they had done it to him, too.

"Come on, goddammit!" Darius yelled from the dugout.

"Chief! Hey, you! You old lady, Chief!" the man in the stands yelled.

Red Deer felt the anger flare in him.

The batter was holding his hands up and looking into the sky.

The catcher gave him the sign again, and Red Deer jabbed himself with his anger. Now it hardly moved him at all. It was alternately terrifying, and a relief. And when the anger came again, he gripped the ball, stared down the pipe, got his nails on the stitching of the ball, and heaved the ball down the line as hard as he could. The ball floated, dipped, then slammed into the catcher's mitt and the batter coiled around.

"Steeeeerike!" the umpire called.

The crowd roared.

The tribesmen stood, and when the others took their seats again, they remained standing. Someone started the others banging their feet on the stands, and the booming got louder, a harsh, crushing banging.

With the tribesmen standing, Red Deer could not see Osada, and he wondered whether he was sitting back there or if he had gone.

"Go home, Chief!" the drunk yelled.

Red Deer felt the ball in his hand.

The batter swung around, practicing. He stepped up to the plate, and the catcher gave Red Deer two fingers. It pushed out of him now, and he saw the batter grinning there. "Come on, Chief," the batter was saying. "Come on, Chief."

Red Deer gripped the ball, a stone.

In a flash that burned him, Red Deer saw that he might really do it this time. He saw the ball, hurling down the pipe, no curve, no spin, just hurling, the batter's skull shattering. He could kill him now, and he could call it an accident. It had come to this. And he knew, with absolute certainty, when he stepped onto the mound that he was going to kill the batter. He was going to throw the ball through the side of his head. He would crush him with his hatred, and it would be gone, he would be free maybe, and when he got the signal from the catcher the batter said it again, and Red Deer felt everything in him screaming toward that pitch, the crowd roaring, the blood in his head pounding, and sharper than ever, he saw the line the ball would take, the point where the ball would contact the batter's head, above and back of the ear—it was like tunnel vision, and there was only in front of him the ear and the hair over the man's temple, the ball in his hand, the tremendous power that moved his limbs like iron, threatening to burst him, the crowd roaring like steam and the mound pushing up beneath him. He drew his arm back, then farther, the weight of his rage there compressed, and in an explosion the ball arced around, hard, heavy, and as it shot from his hand, Red Deer caught the stitching with his thumb, and the ball, as though it were on a track, swung wide across the field and smacked square into the batter's startled face.

The umpire burst out from behind the catcher.

The field came alive, the crowd roaring, and Darius scrambled from the dugout. The batter kicked on the ground, and the umpire tried to hold him down.

Red Deer turned his back to it, and tugging at his mitt, walked to the mound. He stared up into the bleachers, at the big man with the bright blue tie, the one who had started it all. The man raised his fist, opened his mouth to shout. Something settled home in Red Deer's chest, found bottom, and he held his eyes on the big man until he turned away. He remembered his father's scream when Litani had been shot, and what the officers had said after the commotion died down.

"It was a *terrible mistake*. We're sorry," the man Harris had said.

Red Deer drew back the bill of his cap. Without the cover for his eyes the stadium lights were blinding.

They were coming up behind him now, he could hear their feet on the dry grass.

He remembered his father's face, how when he had screamed it was as though something had shattered in him, and when the noise had stopped and his mouth had closed, something had gone away.

"Buck!" Darius said.

Red Deer turned to face him. He puffed along, swinging his arms, two press men behind him with cameras.

Darius reached out, grasped Red Deer's forearm. "Buck," he said. "Buck, just tell them—"

Red Deer bent low, and as if to confide in Darius, pulled him closer. He could smell the oil in Darius's hair, his aftershave.

"Buck, you gotta—"

"Let go," Red Deer said, his voice quiet and sure as death now. "Let go of my arm, Darie," he said.

Craving

Joy Williams

THEY WERE IN a bar far from home when she realized he was falling to pieces. That's what she'd thought: Why, he's falling to pieces. The place was called Gary's.

"Honey," he said. He took the napkin from his lap and dipped it in his gin. He leaned toward her and started wiping her face, gently at first but then harder. "Oh honey," he said in alarm. His tie rested in his Mignon Gary as he pressed forward. He was overweight and pale but his hair was dark and he wore elegant yellow shoes. Before this, he had whispered something unintelligible to her. No one watched them. Sweat ran down his face. His drink toppled over and fell on them both.

She was wearing a green dress and the next day she left it behind in the hotel along with the clothes he had been wearing, the tan suit and the tie and the yellow shoes. The clothes had let them down. The following night they were in a different hotel. It was near the coast and their room had a balcony from which they could see the distant ocean. A small plane went by towing a banner which read MARCH IS LION'S EYE BANK MONTH. They knew how to drink. They sought out the slippery places, those places which tempted one to have a drink. Every place was a slippery place. The little plane slowly disappeared.

Denise and Steadman watched the moon rising. It grew more quiet as they listened. Denise played the game she did with herself. She transferred all her own convulsive, compulsive associations to Steadman. She gave them all to him. This was not as difficult as it might have been once because all her thoughts concerned Steadman anyway. Her mind became smooth and flat and borderless but she wasn't thinking anything so she wasn't lost. Then a deeper silence began to unfold and she was still all right. It became like a giant hand being mutely offered. When she sensed that giant hand she got up quickly. The giant hand was always too much for her. She went into the other room and made more drinks. They took suites whenever possible. The gin seemed to need a room of its own. She came back out to the balcony.

"Let's drink this and go get something to eat," she said.

They found themselves in the dining room of the hotel. It was claustrophobic and the service was insincere. They sat on a cracked red leather banquette behind which a mirror rose. On a shelf between them and the mirror lay a pair of limp rubber gloves. Denise did not bring the gloves to Steadman's attention. She reasoned that they had been left behind by some maintenance person. They gazed at a table of seven who were telling loud stories about traffic accidents they had witnessed. They seemed to be trying to top one another with rococo descriptions.

The French have spectacular wrecks . . . a man said.

Oh, the French . . . someone said irritably.

I love that thing Jaws of Life, a woman said. Have you ever seen that thing? . . . She had streaked blond hair and a heavily freckled bosom. She was attractive. Steadman would have found her attractive.

I saw an incredible Mexican bus crash once . . . a small man said. But his remarks were immediately dismissed by the group.

. . . a Mexican wreck . . . there's nothing extraordinary about a Mexican wreck . . .

. . . it's true . . . the landscape is in such a void . . . there's not the same effect . . .

Steadman and Denise listened attentively and ate bread. The woman with the freckled bosom smiled at them and Denise frowned. Personally, she didn't have a car crash story and if she ever did she would never tell it, she decided.

The waitress told them that the previous couple at their table had given her a five-dollar tip but had torn the bill in half so that she was faced with the ignominy of taping it together. She said she despised people, present company excepted, and told them not to order the veal. If they ordered the veal, she told them, she would not serve it. They decided to have another drink and finish the bread. It grew late but no darker and they returned to their room.

The room was not welcoming. It had seen too many people come and go. What did it all mean anyway, this coming and going? The room was highly reflective, though it was well aware that no special aptitude was required to be constantly reminded that time passes and everything with it, purposelessly.

Denise watched Steadman place himself on the bed. He lay on his back, his eyes shut. The room surrounded them. For a while, Denise lay on the bed, too, thinking, Where had it gone, it had gone someplace. The way they were. Then she went into the other room where the writing table and television set were. Their glasses were there and an ice bucket and their new traveling bags, big, soft, gray ones. She turned off the lights and lay on the sofa, feeling a little dizzy. She wrung her hands and rubbed her eyes. They should go someplace, she thought. There was tomorrow, something had to be done with it. She picked over the day's events. Her mind was like a raven picking over gravel, a raven with oily luminous feathers and a single bright eye. She could almost hear it moving across the small stones but she couldn't quite, thank God. Then she heard someone passing by in the corridor, laughing. A thin breeze entered the room and she thought of the distant water as they had seen it from the balcony, folded like a package between two enormous buildings. She looked at their bags, heaped in a corner. Night was a bad time. Night would simply give her no rest. Steadman was quiet now but he might get up soon and they would have their conversation. It was a mess, they were in an awful mess. Her eyes ached and her throat was dry, she hated this room. The room was cold, it didn't like them, she could hear it saying, Well there's a pathetic pair, how did they ever find each other? She'd like to set fire to it. There was someone passing in the hall again, laughing, the fools. The room stared at her lidlessly. Perhaps they could leave tonight. They would go down—Denise and Steadman, Steadman and Denise—past the sleepy night clerk trying to read a book—*10,000 Dreams Interpreted,* it had been once, for they had done this before, left in the night and been on their way with the setting moon falling behind the trees just as the sun was rising. She remembered the way the book looked. It was red and falling apart. She didn't like dreams. Dreams made you live alone in the future and she didn't want to, she wanted Steadman, only Steadman. But you had to be detached—if you weren't detached, everything became intolerable. When she dreamt, which wasn't often, it was pills and fishes. It wasn't an optional thing. It was always fishes and pills. To be on their way while the moon was setting, that's what she wanted. That was right, but was the music appropriate, that was the question. Denise giggled softly. There was no music, was the fact of it, she knew. She rolled off the couch and onto the floor. It was so quiet here, this room was not letting them breathe the way they had to, it was shameful that they'd been given this room instead of another. Listening to Steadman breathe, she tried to breathe. She wished it were June. It was June once and they were somewhere and a mockingbird sang from midnight to daybreak or so it seemed, imitating other birds and Steadman had made a list of all the birds he recognized in the mockingbird's song. Steadman learned things and then remembered them, that's just the way he was . . . Denise crept across the carpet toward Steadman's bed and held onto it. His face was turned toward her, his eyes open, looking at her. That was Steadman, he knew everything but he didn't share. He made her feel like a little animal sometimes, a little animal with animal emotions, breathing animal devotion. But the heart *has* animal emotions is what she wanted to tell him, that's what the heart *is* . . . She stared back at him. She would ask him for the list very quietly, very nicely, the little piece of paper, where was it, he was always putting it someplace and she had already gone through their bags, their beautiful bright traveling bags, ready for the larger stage. That's what it all was out there, the larger stage, and they would have to get on it again soon and meet the demands the larger stage would make.

"Steadman," she said reasonably.

But how could he hear her, this annoying room was listening to every word she said. She had never known a room like this, it wasn't decent, it had everything mixed up. It didn't know, what could it know? It couldn't climb from the basement into a life of spiritual sunshine like she was capable of doing, not that she had but she could . . . The individual in the hall howled with laughter at this. There were several of them out there now, a whole gang, the ones from the dinner party probably, the spectacular-wrecks people, drunk, talking about skidding and gleaming, shining really, all light.

At once Denise realized that the gang was herself and it was morning. Her hands hurt terribly. They were pink as though they'd been boiled. They looked like little pies. She had hurt them somehow. Actually they were broken. Incredible.

She stared at them in the car on the way to the hospital. Those hands weren't going to do anything more for Denise for a while. They were through. Denise made them sick. She could think what she wanted but it wouldn't matter to them.

The doctor in the emergency room wrapped them up, the left first, then the right, indifferently. Even so, some things fascinated him.

"We've got a kid on the third floor," he said. "He was born with all the bones in his head broken. Now there's a problem. Are you aware that our heads all along the line are getting smaller? Our skulls are smaller than those of our brothers in the Paleolithic period. Do you know why? I'll tell you why. Nobody leaves this place without a thought for the day. Society is the answer. Society has reduced our awareness skills. Personal direct contact with the natural world required a continual awareness. Now we don't have that awareness. We are aware of dick-all."

Denise looked at her hands being covered with the casts. They were like little dead creatures safely concealed in a snow-covered burrow. Ugly dishes don't break, she thought. But they had.

"Try to stay alert, miss," the doctor said, playfully slapping her hands which were now utterly exempt.

Then they were driving slowly through a town the hotel had not been part of. It was a southern town with little porches, the houses crowded close together. There seemed to be a lot of dogs and they all appeared to be employed in some way. That's the way it seemed to Denise. There was a bare-chested man so dirty he seemed to be wearing a shirt, sitting outside an empty store. The dog beside him had its leg in a cast.

"Look at that!" Denise said, laughing. She pushed her hands out the window and waved at the dog as they drove by.

"I'm tired, Denise," Steadman was saying. "I'm really tired."

"Yes, yes," Denise said. She was thinking of all the nice things she would do for Steadman whom she loved. She was shy with him. She didn't look at him.

"I think we should stay here for a while until your hands are better," Steadman said.

"I agree, I agree, but no more hotels, we'll get a house for a while." She was crazy about him, everything was going to be fine.

He turned off the road at a sign that said *Cafe Reality* and into a parking lot. Actually it said *Cape Realty*. Denise laughed. "And we'll stop drinking," Denise said. "We'll just stop."

"Sure," Steadman said.

"I don't want to see a lot of places though," Denise said. "You choose."

She sat in the car. She had ruined that room back there. Embarrassing, she thought. But the room had fought back. It made one think, really. Her mind was still charging. Then, abruptly, it stopped. Fear filled her. Something was pouring it into her. The raven that was her mind stood on a stone breakwater with the sea around it, crashing around it.

Steadman returned to the car and put several pictures of a house on her lap. It was private enough with a big tree in front and a pool in back and a tall whitewashed wall all around it.

"I'm going to use this month wisely," Denise assured him.

"Good," Steadman said.

The important thing was to stop drinking. If she could get twenty-four hours away from last night, she could start stopping. Maybe they could get rid of all the glasses in the house. Glasses were always calling to you, trying to make you see things their way. Maybe this house wouldn't have glasses.

The house looked fairly good. There was shade and sun. It had everything. But why were they here? Their drinking had brought them. Denise was determined to learn something, to go on from here, to leave this place refreshed. She yawned nervously. Steadman's forehead was beaded with sweat, the back of his jacket was dark with sweat as he lifted their bags from the trunk.

In one of the rooms, a young woman was sweeping the floor. "I'm the cleaning woman," she said. "Are you renting this place? I'll be through in a minute." She wore shorts and red high-top sneakers. "I'll put on a shirt," she said. "I didn't know anyone was coming. I always sweep without a shirt." With her was a small dog with black saucery eyes, thick ears, and double-dew claws.

"What is that?" Denise asked. It was one of the strangest dogs she had ever seen.

"Everyone asks that," the girl said happily. "It's a Lundehund. It's used for hunting puffins in Norway."

"But what's it doing here?"

"He comes with me while I clean. You'll probably ask next how I ended up with a dog like this. I can't remember the ins and outs of it. I started off wanting one of those Welsh corgis, the ones you always see in pictures of the Queen, greeting her on her return from somewhere or bidding her farewell as she departs. I'm not English, of course. I've never been to England. The Lake District, the Cotswolds, the white cliffs of Dover . . . you couldn't prove any of them by me. I was born in this town and I've never been anywhere. I don't have the money to travel but I make sure that everything I have comes from other places. This shirt comes from Nepal and my perfume comes from Paris. I know what you're going to say, that it's wrong to subject caged civet cats to daily genital scrapings just to make perfume, but it was a present. My sneakers were put together in Brazil and I know you're going to say that Brazilian laborers make only pennies an hour, but I did buy them secondhand. See the little stones in these earrings? They come from Arizona. Navajoland."

She was buttoning her shirt as she spoke and Steadman was smiling at her like a blind man.

Denise was not going to allow the cleaning woman to unnerve her. She had always tried to be vigilant and expectant with Steadman and it had brought them nothing but sorrow. Her hands throbbed and itched. She'd try to sleep while it was still light and then she'd drink a lot of water. She rubbed the dog's ears with her casts.

"You shouldn't be here, should you," she said to the Lundehund. "You should be scrambling up and down rocky crevices, carrying birds' eggs in your teeth."

It was disgusting and sad, Denise thought, but a great many things were. One should be *used*.

The Lundehund placed its paws on her leg and looked at her, widening its eyes and then closing them with joy. Denise didn't know what to think. Her mind was perched on stones, oddly inattentive. The woman and the grotesque dog were clearly catastrophes. She was trying to begin and these catastrophes appeared immediately. Though it wasn't what you thought but the way you acted that was important. Or was it the other way around. It could be both probably.

Denise turned her back on them and went into a narrow monochromatic room that overlooked the pool. There were empty bookcases over a single bed and numerous little indentations in the hardwood floor as though a woman wearing high heels in need of repair had moved back and forth, back and forth. Her own shoes were like that, too, run down. She kicked them off. Once she had been a student and then she had graduated and acquired a lot of things and tried to take care of them. She had painted things and cooked things and stuck seeds in the ground. And doing all that was the *summum bonum,* she had thought. But it had certainly not been the *summum bonum.* Then she had thrown herself into drinking and into love. But things were going to be different here. She was going to be better. Habit didn't possess the key to this place.

She sighed and it seemed to be later. The water in the pool was darker and the shadows were different. Her hair smelled of gin, and her skin. There was someone in the pool, a man, but he left quickly, when she got up. It was just the liquor leaving, she thought. She could understand that. The doors in the house were sliding doors and she could move them back and forth with her foot. Her hands in the casts bobbed beside her as she walked. Steadman was where she had left him but he was sitting down. The cleaning woman was holding him in her arms and he was weeping loudly.

Well that's something, Denise thought. She wished that she were the sort who could weep and be held, be held and weep. But whenever she lost it, she only cried. She had never done anything exactly correctly, she thought.

"I just saw your husband," Denise said. "He was swimming in the pool. No one should be using the pool now that we're here, should they? We've rented this place after all. And we don't need a cleaning woman either. We'll keep it clean. This place is clean enough."

"I don't have a husband," the cleaning woman said. "You have a husband." Her shirt was off again, she just couldn't seem to keep that shirt on. She combed Steadman's hair back with her fingers. There was a tattoo running down the inside of her left arm. Denise had noticed something before but it hadn't been a tattoo. She thought it was a long bruise. Or a shadow. Some kind of a shadow that had been cast.

"Is that really a coffee pot tattooed on your arm?" Denise asked. "A coffee pot and a cup of coffee?"

"Yes, it is," the cleaning woman said. "Because coffee makes me really, really happy. Particularly the first couple of cups. Look," she said, "I can make it pour . . . " She made her muscle quiver and the inked flesh moved, something seemed to pass from the representation of one object into another.

"That is so stupid," Denise said. What kind of a woman would have a coffee pot tattooed on herself and go through this egregious display in front of strangers? She bet she did it all the time, too.

The cleaning woman resumed stroking Steadman's hair. His tears had dried and he looked like a boy, washed and fresh. While Denise was musing on this, the Lundehund rose softly up against her side and began chewing on the casts. He seemed to be winking at her as he did. "Get down," the cleaning woman scolded him. "That's a bad boy."

"You should allow dogs their pleasures," Denise said. "They don't live long." She had intended this remark to make the cleaning woman sad, but everyone realized the truth of it apparently. It had no effect because it was something that was known.

"You're in terrible shape," the cleaning woman said. "Both of you. Let me come a few hours each day. I'll make the meals and keep things tidy. I know what you're thinking, that I'll put poisoned mushrooms in your omelette or Succinylcholine in your seltzer and your heart will stop like *that*"—she clapped her hands together—"but that's not what's going to happen. You're trying to kick the bottle and you're trying to make predictions of what it's going to be like, but I'll tell you about predictions. There are seven possibilities. These apply to everything. There's maybe yes, there's maybe no, there's maybe yes and no, there's maybe indescribable and then there's three more combinations of these."

After considering this for a while, Denise decided that the problem lay clearly with the three combinations of the previous four. Drink, drank, drunk, that's how they had conjugated their lives, she and Steadman. But they weren't there anymore, they were here. This was the subjunctive, Denise thought.

"Look," the cleaning woman said. "We're all outsiders here. It's going to be all right."

It's like when someone dies and someone says it's going to be all right, Denise thought. So stupid!

"We are not all outsiders," Denise said. "If we were, we'd be a group, then we wouldn't be outsiders." This person wanted to be Steadman's mistress, she could tell, she was pressing her lips against his temple, her long breasts lay against his shirt. But mistresses mixed cocktails and wore beautiful clothes which they knew how to take off with style. They knew about art. She couldn't be Steadman's mistress, Denise thought triumphantly. She could only be the mistress of some delusion. Then things were better, and finally she persuaded the woman to leave. She didn't know how she actually managed it, but at some point the cleaning woman gathered up her things, the Lundehund's nails clicked across the floor, the door shut, and they were gone.

Denise looked at Steadman. She was crazy about him, she thought, just crazy about him. Though this wasn't easy, this house. It was small and hot in the dark. They hadn't had a drink in hours. She looked at Steadman's watch, sixteen hours exactly. Maybe they shouldn't try to get better here. That was the problem with little houses. They belonged to other people, even if those other people were far away, but a hotel room didn't belong to anybody. Maybe they should find another room or maybe they should just get back in the car. This was the law of maybe, the doctrine of maybe. She believed in this doctrine of maybe and she believed in her love for Steadman and these were her beliefs.

She smiled at him.

"Denise," he said. "Please."

"You're not in love with her, are you? You haven't fallen in love?"

"Denise," he said, "that was a misunderstanding."

"Oh, I know!" she said brightly.

She was standing in the dark and he was still sitting. She wanted a drink badly. She closed her eyes and swallowed. Her mind was trying to be still, trying to be good but it was frightened. You are what you drink, she thought, you are where you drink, but here they were nothing, nowhere. They had fallen to pieces and here they were. Maybe she should say farewell to love, she thought. It gives you more poise. She should have thought of that long ago. And it prepares you, it prepares you . . . She stared doggedly at Steadman in the dark.

At last he said, Groceries.

She looked at him avidly. She had been thinking about the state they were in. They executed people in this state for certain things, but before they could do it the person had to realize the importance of execution. That was the law. So of course you pretended you didn't realize the importance. As long as you could do that they had to leave you alone.

"So," Steadman said, "what do you want?"

It felt a little like February, actually, that forlorn, spiky, short month, but there had always been a lot to drink in February. She hadn't been thinking about food, but groceries meant more than food. They were medicinal in some way and implied a plan of action. They also meant being here for some duration. Denise did not want duration here.

"Don't go now," she said. "Maybe tomorrow. We don't need groceries now. We should rest and let the time go by and then we'll be further along. There's nothing to drink here, it's fantastic, isn't it?" she said. "Let's lie down. Would you hold me? I can't hold you."

She raised her hands, moving them up and down a little in their white casts. She remembered a bar they had been in, was it Gary's? There were framed hunting and fishing pictures all over the walls. A woman was holding two snow geese by their necks. She held them high, in gloved hands, close to her head, as though they were earrings. That was Reality, Denise thought. Back there, the Bitch, reality.

"Where are you going?" Denise asked.

"I'm not going anywhere," Steadman said. He ran his hands across his face.

"You're not going to get a drink, are you?"

"No," Steadman said. "I am not."

Denise wandered back into the bedroom and sat on the bed. They had agreed that if one were left, the other would never come back. But one wasn't left. Everything was still all right.

She looked at the pool and saw the man again, swimming back and forth. He had no grace, Denise decided, though he swam tirelessly. Denise heard herself speaking to him, asking him to leave. She really could not have him here, he and that woman, they were making things so difficult. Be reasonable, she said. We are here. You can't be here while we are. She said this and that, choosing her words carefully, shouting from inside the house. The man pulled himself out of the pool and stood there dripping. He said . . . I work slowly, slowly like a hare building a pyramid . . . Denise was quite aware of what she'd heard but she didn't believe it. She would not believe such a thing. Besides, Denise thought, that would have to be a rough translation at best, of what he'd said, of course. Then he crouched down and she was afraid of this, she had worried that something like this would happen, that he would begin to dismantle the pool in some way, that he would begin by pulling at the light, the big submerged light at the deep end of the pool, rotating it, twisting it out. Water was spilling and buckling everywhere, darkening the concrete, and the light was trailing its cord behind it, it was like a huge white eye on a long stalk.

Denise couldn't stay here a moment longer. She was trembling, she had to get out. They would get in the car, she and Steadman, they would drive away and never come back. They loved driving in the dark and drinking, mixing cocktails in paper cups, driving around. They had done it a lot. They would mix up some drinks and go out and tease cars. That's what they called it, Steadman and Denise. They'd tailgate them, pounce on them out of nowhere. Crazy stuff.

"Steadman," she called. He knew what she wanted, he knew what they would do, that this had been a mistake. He opened the door to their car, their lovely car, and she smelled the liquor. It was in a glass from before, wedged between the seats. She picked it up with difficulty and looked at it hard, then threw it, glass and all, against the grass.

They drove down the street, picking up speed. They passed a house with two garbage cans on the curb and a wrought-iron sign hanging from a post. The design was of a wrought-iron palm tree and a wrought-iron sea. Below it where the custom lettering was supposed to be it said: YOUR NAME. Delightful! Denise thought. They had ordered it just the way it had appeared in some catalogue.

"God, that was funny," Denise said. People could be funny.

"It really was," Steadman said.

They were driving fast now. They were so much alike, they were just alike, Denise thought. Without the drinking there would just be the two of them, it would be wonderful. Nothing could separate them.

"Roll my window down please," she said.

He reached across her and did.

"Oh thank you, Steadman," she said. Warm humid air passed across her face, lovely air.

"Go faster," she said.

He did. She giggled.

"Slow down, speed up, that road there," she said.

Steadman did, he did.

They had left the town behind. "Turn the lights off maybe," she said.

They rocketed down the road in the dark.

"Maybe turn them on again," Denise said. What *had* it all meant, she wondered.

The road ahead was empty but behind them a car was gaining. She turned and saw the two wild lights moving closer. They're going to tease us, she thought. "Faster," she said. But the car, weaving, was almost upon them and then, with a roar was beside them. It was all outside them now, everything. "There it is, Steadman," Denise said earnestly. It was them all right. It all just hung there for an instant, clearly, then the car swerved around them, turned in inches before their front bumper, and slammed on the brakes.

Pitch Memory

Ethan Canin

THE DAY AFTER Thanksgiving my mother was arrested outside the front doors of the J.C. Penney's, Los Angeles, and when I went to get her I considered leaving her at the security desk. I thought I wanted her in jail.

I wasn't surprised—I'd known all along she was a thief. Small things: a bath towel if she stayed in a hotel, maybe a couple of apples in her purse when she returned from Safeway. "Why shouldn't I," she said, "no one else is going to take care of me." She'd been saying this since my father died eleven years ago in a lawn chair in our backyard. Since then there have been restaurant napkins at our dinner table, hotel soaps in our tub. "No one's going to take care of you, either," she says to me.

It's my first day home, two days after Thanksgiving, and already my mother has begun her warnings. "The world's an ugly place," she said at breakfast, "you've got to bait your own hooks." Now it is afternoon and she reads to me from her list of great women: "Susan B. Anthony, Elizabeth Arden," she calls out to the backyard where I'm sweeping the walk, "Anne Boleyn—"

"What?"

"I'm reading you my list of great women," she yells. "Maria Callas, Catherine the Great—would you put that under C or G?"

"C," says my sister Tessa.

Tessa and I are home because my mother thought it would be a good idea for her two daughters to spend Thanksgiving in our house

163

in Pasadena. Tessa is a cardiovascular surgeon in Houston, Texas, and she arranged to visit some conference on the coast in order to be here. I'm a printmaker and a waitress in Hutchings, Vermont, and came to California because there was a plane ticket and forty dollars for taxi-fare in the envelope my mother sent me. It's the first time I have been home in two years. My mother has called me weekly, sent me letters asking when I planned to start my life. "The world won't wait for you," she said. "I can name other examples — Betsy Ross, Amelia Earhart — the world didn't have to wait for them." Over the phone she read me other lists: Virtues, Pitfalls, Courageous Decisions. She wrote me letters with the addresses of my father's old friends — lawyers, insurance brokers — and now and then these men have stopped on their business travels to telephone me from Vermont Holiday Inns. "Your mother," they said, "is concerned about what you're doing with your life."

As soon as I stepped into my old room the first night, I knew she was stealing again. The box of Kleenex on my table said American Airlines, the vase on my dresser held a vinyl rose. I put down my suitcase and stepped into the bathroom where I closed and locked the door: in the cabinet under the sink were stacks of paper towels, still industrially wrapped; dozens of soap bars, sample-sized. I flushed the toilet, ran the tap water, opened the door. My mother was standing there.

"Welcome home."

"Thanks," I said. "The house seems to be well stocked."

Her stealing started after my father died, though he had bought three times his worth in life insurance and had already made the last house payment by the time his coronary artery closed up one Friday evening after work. That day became the meridian of my mother's life. For a year she wept at red lights and at drawers that didn't close. She began to steal, she began to coach my sister and me about the viciousness of the world, and she began to feed us a whole new kind of diet. She filled a cookie jar with vitamins, then exercised their ritual distribution every morning — a bloom of colors, an exploding halo of pills that she set in a circle at our breakfast plates. It was a new series of associations. C, we learned, was for colds — or even cancer, according to the scientists she believed; E was for the elasticity of the skin, though we had heard otherwise, and D for the strength of our bones. B, we knew, was for the disposition — as if a pill would help — and for sleep, so my mother took it double-dose. Still she had problems sleeping. For years I often heard her go downstairs in the middle of the night. In the mornings her face was wax-yellow; her fingers tapped and twittered on the table top. Instead she dozed in the afternoons, in movie theatres or on the front-room sofa where the sunlight made her dreams bad.

My father had been a horn player when he was in the military, and on the bureau there are photos of him with trumpets, bugles, even a clarion. There he is in the photographs, a young man in an army uniform, and in the cellar of our house there are the instruments — maybe the same ones — hanging from a row of nails on a corkboard. My sister and I played them when we were in grammar school. As we were growing up our house was a litany of brass noises. My mother was a musician also, a pianist, and she taught my sister and me to play. Tessa could pick things up right off the radio, Buddy Holly and Chiffons tunes that boys and then men tapped their feet to. When a new song came on the radio she leaned her ear right up against the grill of the speaker and when the song was finished she went to the piano and played it, straight through, both hands. I don't know what she was listening for when she put her ear so close to the radio. I tried it too, even tried going straight to the piano after and letting my fingers run over the keys without thought, imagining that was how Tessa did it. But whatever it was eluded me. Instead I practiced harder than my sister — major scales, minor scales, arpeggios, blues scales, chromatic scales. I could trill notes she barely had time to reach, but whatever subsonic clue emerged from the radio was as insensible to me as a dog-whistle.

We all quit about the same time. Tessa was a sophomore in college and had decided to go to medical school: she didn't have time to practice. I was a sophomore in high school and had drawn a picture of our piano with a couple of my father's ancient horns resting on it that was chosen for the cover of our school calendar. I drew the picture over Thanksgiving vacation and that December my father died. A few nights before it happened a boy named Billy Stetson had climbed the tree outside my window and come into my bedroom while my parents were downstairs watching television. I was fifteen and we had arranged this. He crawled through the window, took off his shirt in the dark room, and sat on the far end of my bed. He had one hand in his pocket and the other on the blankets around my feet when we heard my father on the stairs. My father loved to play tennis and took the stairs two and three in a leap: Billy had time to look at me, stand, and go into the corner of my room. My father came in. He said that the TV downstairs had gone fuzzy and that he thought it was the wind that had knocked the antenna loose from outside my window. He said close my eyes, he was going to turn on the light. I closed my eyes. I heard the click of the light switch.

"Hello, Billy," said my father.

He didn't mention it the next day. That was the first time I thought of him as a person that one day I would probably know. I remember coming into the kitchen on the evening after he died. My drawing, scissored from the school calendar, hung by banana magnets on the refrigerator.

After that my mother had the piano moved to the den, where she closed the lid and moved our TV couch up against the keyboard. This was how she quit. The piano couldn't be played with the couch up against it, and with the lid closed it began to pile up with books and sweaters and old TV guides. I began drawing instead.

Now, the first night we are all together, we sing. It is a tradition — voices only, no instruments. My mother hums a note, my sister comes in a third above it and then they wait for me to find my note, which seems to lie inscrutably between the pitches I can produce. We have always had this problem.

"Higher," my mother says.

I go higher with my note and then my mother and sister join me and suddenly the sounds are a chord as absolute as a piano's. "That's it," Tessa says. "Good."

My mother and sister harmonize in turn and I follow one of them in the melodies. They both have perfect pitch, as did my father, as I do not. When my father was alive the rest of my family played a game in which they identified cars by the pitches of their horns: we took mountain drives on the weekends, and as we went into the steep, blind turns beneath hoods of poplar and elm my father honked the horn of our Cutlass Supreme. That note, I knew, was a B-flat. If there was a car on the other side of the bend it honked too and my mother and father and sister raced to identify it by pitch. I knew what notes came from what cars — the A of a Pontiac LeSabre, our own B-flat, the sharp C of a Cadillac Coupe — but I didn't know the pitches when I heard them.

"Pontiac," I guessed sometimes.

"No," said my father.

"Of course not," said my mother.

My sister tried to teach me. She tried to get me to reproduce the sound of our Cutlass horn in my head. "Then go up or down the scale from there," she said, "until you reach the note you've heard." I guessed at the cars, sometimes correctly, but I couldn't even reproduce our own B-flat.

"Instead of perfect pitch," my sister said, "maybe it would help if you thought of it as something else. Think of it as pitch memory. You've heard all the notes before, so just try to remember them. If you can keep just one melody in your head, you can match whatever pitch you hear to one you remember. It's just remembering old notes."

Sometimes in the mornings she gave me a note. "Hum it," she said, "hum it for me."

I hummed.

"Okay," she said, "now remember it all day."

I lost a certain part of my youth trying to remember notes. If the pitch was in my range I tried to speak in it all day. Otherwise, I kept it running in my skull. My brain produced a background noise like a machine.

"Okay," Tessa said at dinner, "now hum it for me."

I hummed.

"That's a C-sharp, honey," my mother said. "Tessa gave you an E."

Now, nineteen years later, on our first night together, in the living-room of my mother's house, we sing. My mother is between us and we are facing the large plate-glass window that looks onto the bougainvillea bushes and the sidewalk. It is just evening, and as we sing it grows darker outside so that the living room window begins to become a mirror. My mother notices this and puts a hand on each of our shoulders.

The next morning my mother and I drink tea in the kitchen. She wants to go clothes-shopping tomorrow and on the table she has arranged pages torn from fashion magazines. This year the models have short hair and the photographs are taken in the marble entrance foyers of financial plazas. My mother has asked me to peruse. "Just choose anything you like," she said. "It doesn't mean anything."

The shopping is her idea. Yesterday when I opened the covers of my bed there was an envelope on the sheets: inside a hundred-dollar bill, folded once.

"Mother," I called, "I have a job."

"What, honey?"

"I have a job. Already. A job. I earn my own money."

"I just thought you'd like to buy some clothes."

"Would you prefer clothes to attract a better job or to attract a man?"

Last night I left the hundred-dollar bill on the kitchen table. My mother put it back on my bed. I hung it from the banana magnet on the refrigerator. She put it on my dresser. "Please," she said when I pinned it to the corkboard in the kitchen, "it's just to spruce you up a little." This morning talking to Tessa I found it in my purse.

"Mom wants me to buy clothes," I said to Tessa.

"Maybe you should."

"I don't need clothes," I said. "I *have* clothes. I have two hundred skirts, maybe three hundred blouses. My closet is the size of Macy's third floor."

"Be serious. She worries about you."

"She keeps trying to give me a hundred-dollar bill."

"Take it."

"I won't take it."

"The least you can do is let her buy you some clothes. You don't ever have to wear them. Put them on once, get a picture taken and send it to her. Maybe it'll come in handy."

"She's stealing again," I said.

"What?"

"Mom's stealing again."

"How do you know?"

"Look around. The bathroom closet's a supply warehouse."

"She's worried about things running out."

"Why does she give me hundred-dollar bills, then?"

"She's worried about you, too."

In the afternoon I clip the backyard grass while my mother watches from the kitchen. It is bright outside and I can see only her dark shape moving behind the window. When I finish I rake the cuttings, hand-clip the sidewalk borders, then drag a vinyl chair to the northeast corner of the yard where I know a triangle of sun persists until evening.

When I sit down she slides open the kitchen window and begins to read me a list of virtues. "Dedication," she says, "Discipline." It is not early, and already the advancing shadows mark my calves. I lie back on the chair. "Fortitude," she calls, "Honor."

In our family the violence has always been glancing and reflected. One Thanksgiving when my father was alive he dropped the platter he was carrying to the dining room, and the turkey, which my mother had buttered and basted all afternoon, rolled onto the rug and under the table. "You may as well have dropped me," my mother said and the next day she tore the sideview mirror off my father's Cutlass Supreme backing out too close to the garage.

"Joan of Arc, Jacqueline Kennedy," my mother says. It is Thanksgiving Day and she knows of an open store: we are in the car going to buy me some new clothes. The hundred-dollar bill lies on top of the dashboard, where I have placed it, and, fearful of drafts, my mother will not unlock the electric windows.

"I have a list for you," I say. "Catherine Ablett, Sissy Burson."

"Who are they?"

"They're from my high school class," I say. "Now they're street-walkers."

In the store she walks with her hand on her breast, not speaking, and in apology I finger the material of a few blouses, take a shirt into the dressing room. "Look," I tell her when we're outside again, "it's just that I don't need clothes. I'm happy, mother. I don't want another job, I don't need a husband. I'm happy."

"Nothing's as secure as you think," she says. Then she takes the hundred-dollar bill from her purse. "Please," she whispers, "take the money. You don't have to spend it when I'm here. But please, will you take it?"

There is a group of men watching us. She holds the bill out to me. "Will you take it?"

"Yes, mother," I say and put the bill, folded, into my purse.

For Thanksgiving dinner we go to a restaurant where the turkey is served in oval slices. We drink wine. My mother asks the waiter whether he minds working on Thanksgiving Day and he tells her that everybody's got to earn a living.

"That's right," my mother says when the waiter leaves.

"Mom, I *am* earning a living."

"Are you going to be a waitress the rest of your life?"

"I think I will," I say, and this makes my mother start to cry. Tessa stands, goes to my mother's chair and helps her up, then walks her to the bathroom. There are a few other families in the restaurant and I'm sure they're looking at me. I sit alone at the table drinking my glass of wine. I wonder what my sister and mother are saying in the bathroom. I imagine the other diners in the restaurant getting up one by one, slinking away so I don't notice, into the women's room where my mother fills them in. *Yes, the younger one,* my mother says and pauses — *an artist. No,* says the fat man in the gray blazer, *not an artist. Yes, it's true,* says my mother, *and she's not even married.*

"You don't seem very sorry," Tessa says from behind me. She has returned alone.

"I'm not."

When my mother comes back to the table Tessa pours wine in all of our glasses, makes a toast to some aspect of Thanksgiving. We eat. We talk about the smog in Pasadena and about how pleasant it is to get freshly baked rolls at a restaurant. My mother returns to the salad bar three times: her plate is a ruin of lettuce and onions.

The next afternoon, Tessa is at a conference discussing vinyl heart valves and I am alone in the house when the phone rings and a man tells me that my mother has been arrested for petty larceny outside the Los Angeles branch of J.C. Penney's. It is best if I come to the store.

I get my father's old Cutlass Supreme out of the garage and drive to Penney's. I'm not sure how to ask at the desk where they are keeping a middle-aged woman whose Givenchy handbag brims with loot, but I wait in line anyway. There are customers behind me, and I fumble with my purse, pretend I've forgotten something and let them pass in front. I step back. A man asks if he can help and I tell him no. A group of girl scouts surrounds me, laughing in an ugly way, then passes down the aisle, and I am at the escalator wondering where to proceed before I think of looking at the store directory.

The security desk is in the basement, and I take the escalator down. There, a man in something like a policeman's uniform tells me to come back with him. His glasses are black mirrors. We pass through a door, down a hall, into a square yellow room where my mother is sitting at a table. She looks small.

The guard locks the door and offers me a chair. I sit down. "Well," he says.

On the table between my mother and me is a blouse.

"Well," he says again.

"A blouse," I say.

"Look," says my mother, "this is ridiculous."

"Ma'am, nothing at all like ridiculous. The article was in your hand-bag and you were outside Penney's. On your way to your car, I'd say."

"You don't know that," my mother says.

"What are we going to do?" he says. He walks to a corner of the room, leans against the wall, lights a cigarette. If he weren't a security guard I would think he were a thief. He looks at us, then tucks his thumbs into his belt.

"This is ridiculous," says my mother, "arresting me for forgetting to pay for a blouse. At home my daughter has a closetful of blouses that are twice as expensive."

"It was in your purse, ma'am."

"I was going to pay for it, obviously. Obviously I was going to pay for it. Look, ask my daughter. Don't I often forget? Ask her. Don't I often forget, honey?"

The guard looks at me.

"You did have it outside the store," I say.

My mother will not look at me and I will not look at her. In the guard's black sunglasses the room is reflected. Then I imagine my mother in her neat skirt in front of a magistrate; I imagine her arraignment, some sort of trial or perhaps the decision of a judge only, a man her age. He'll send her—for a day or two, perhaps a week or a month—to one of the low-security prisons in the valley north of here. I have seen one of them from the road: low, sand-colored, circled by a metal fence, it stands behind a row of cyprus and a rectangular high-way sign: San Felipe Women's Correctional Facility.

"I'm going to call the police now," the guard says and picks up the telephone—and it is only then, when I do it, that it seems obvious. The guard holds the phone away from him, looks down at my hand half-covered by my purse. He looks at the floor, then at my hand again.

"Who else knows?" I ask.

"Just me," he says. He looks down. He rubs his chin. Then his arm moves and the bill is out of my fingers and into the pocket of his shirt.

We leave my mother's car in the parking lot and drive home in the Cutlass Supreme. We do not talk. The day, somehow past, is already darkening, and when we arrive the house is empty. My mother goes into the kitchen and I go into the television room where I turn on a movie and sit on the couch. I have entered too late to understand. Soldiers have arrived somewhere to save something, although they don't look like soldiers and I'm not sure who is on which side. The music is full of clock-ticking rhythms. After a while my mother comes in. She could sit in the wood desk-chair or my father's old lazy-lounger, but instead she places herself next to me on the couch, leaning against my shoulder. On my arm I feel where the sweat has wet her blouse.

We watch the movie for a while before I realize she is asleep. Her breathing has become slow. She leans heavily against my shoulder, her head tilted back, and as we sit there her weight begins to make my forearm tingle. Tessa once explained this tingling to me: it is not the blood circulation being cut off, but a disturbance of the nerves. The funny throbbing spreads to my elbow and my mother opens her mouth, and, though she is asleep and breathing through her parted lips, she begins to quietly hum. It must be part of her dream. If I lean toward her to listen I'll wake her, so I lie still.

Presently I hear Tessa come into the house. The door thuds, the coat rack jingles. I put my finger to my lips, and when she peeks into the TV room I motion for her to stay quiet. She comes in and leans down next to us to listen. Then she goes over and turns off the TV. My mother's humming pauses, then continues, and Tessa goes out to the kitchen where I hear her begin to cook our dinner. There is the clang of pots being arranged on the stove, the chime of silverware on the wood table. I lie still. My mother's humming is soft, almost inaudible. Despite all science, I think, we will never understand the sadness of certain notes.

Against *Joie de Vivre*

Phillip Lopate

OVER THE YEARS I have developed a distaste for the spectacle of *joie de vivre,* the knack of knowing how to live. Not that I disapprove of all hearty enjoyment of life. A flushed sense of happiness can overtake a person anywhere, and one is no more to blame for it than the Asiatic flu or a sudden benevolent change in the weather (which is often joy's immediate cause). No, what rankles me is the stylization of this private condition into a bullying social ritual.

The French, who have elevated the picnic to their highest civilized rite, are probably most responsible for promoting this smugly upbeat, flaunting style. It took the French genius for formalizing the informal to bring sticky sacramental sanctity to the baguette, wine and cheese. A pure image of sleeveless *joie de vivre* Sundays can also be found in Renoir's paintings. Weekend satyrs dance and wink; leisure takes on a bohemian stripe. A decent writer, Henry Miller, caught the French malady and ran back to tell us of *pissoirs* in the Paris streets (why this should have impressed him so, I've never figured out).

But if you want a double dose of *joie de vivre,* you need to consult a later, hence more stylized version of the French myth of pagan happiness: those *Family of Man* photographs of endlessly kissing lovers, snapped by Doisneau and Boubat, not to mention Cartier-Bresson's icon of the proud tyke carrying bottles of wine. If Cartier-Bresson and his disciples are excellent photographers for all that, it is in spite of their rubbing our noses in a tediously programmatic "affirmation of life."

173

Though it is traditionally the province of the French, the whole Mediterranean is a hotbed of professional *joie de vivrism,* which they have gotten down to a routine like a crack *son et lumière* display. The Italians export *dolce far niente* as aggressively as tomato paste. For the Greeks, a Zorba dance to life has supplanted classical antiquities as their main touristic lure. Hard to imagine anything as stomach-turning as being forced to participate in such an oppressively robust, folknik effusion. Fortunately, the country has its share of thin, nervous, bitter types, but Greeks do exist who would clutch you to their joyfully stout bellies and crush you there. The *joie de vivrist* is an incorrigible missionary, who presumes that everyone wants to express pro-life feelings in the same stereotyped manner.

A warning: since I myself have a large store of nervous discontent (some would say hostility) I am apt to be harsh in my secret judgments of others, seeing them as defective because they are not enough like me. From moment to moment, the person I am with often seems too shrill, too bland, too something-or-other to allow my own expansiveness to swing into stage center. "Feeling no need to drink, you will promptly despise a drunkard" (Kenneth Burke). So it goes with me — which is why I am not a literary critic. I have no faith that my discriminations in taste are anything but the picky awareness of what will keep me stimulated, based on the peculiar family and class circumstances which formed me. But the knowledge that my discriminations are skewed and not always universally desirable doesn't stop me in the least from making them, just as one never gives up a negative first impression, no matter how many times it is contradicted. A believer in astrology (to cite another false system), having guessed that someone is a Sagittarius, and then told he is a Scorpio, says "Scorpio — yes, of course!" without missing a beat, or relinquishing confidence in his ability to tell people's signs, or in his idea that the person is somehow secretly Sagittarian.

1. The Houseboat

I remember the exact year when my dislike for *joie de vivre* began to crystallize. It was 1969. We had gone to visit an old Greek painter on his houseboat in Sausalito. Old Vartas's vitality was legendary and it was considered a spiritual honor to meet him, like getting an audience with the Pope. Each Sunday he had a sort of open house, or open boat.

My "sponsor," Frank, had been many times to the houseboat, furnishing Vartas with record albums, since the old painter had a passion for San Francisco rock bands. Frank told me that Vartas had been a pal of Henry Miller's, and I, being a writer of Russian descent, would love him. I failed to grasp the syllogism, but, putting aside my instinct to dislike anybody I have been assured I will adore, I prepared myself to give the man a chance.

Greeting us on the gangplank was an old man with thick, lush white hair and snowy eyebrows, his face reddened from the sun. As he took us into the houseboat cabin he told me proudly that he was seventy-seven years old, and gestured toward the paintings that were spaced a few feet apart, leaning on the floor against the wall. They were celebrations of the blue Aegean, boats moored in ports, whitewashed houses on a hill, painted in primary colors and decorated with collaged materials: mirrors, burlap, life-saver candies. These sunny little canvases with their talented innocence, third-generation spirit of Montmartre, bore testimony to a love of life so unbending as to leave an impression of rigid narrow-mindedness as extreme as any Savonarola. Their rejection of sorrow was total. They were the sort of festive paintings that sell at high-rent Madison Avenue galleries specializing in European schlock.

Then I became aware of three young, beautiful women, bare-shouldered, wearing white *dhotis,* each with long blond hair falling onto a sky-blue halter—unmistakably suggesting the Three Graces. They lived with him on the houseboat, I was told, giving no one knew what compensation for their lodgings. Perhaps their only payment was to feed his vanity in front of outsiders. The Greek painter smiled with the air of an old fox around the trio. For their part, they obligingly contributed their praises of Vartas's youthful zip, which of course was taken by some guests as double-entendre for undiminished sexual prowess. The Three Graces also gathered the food-offerings of the visitors to make a midday meal.

Then the boat, equipped with a sail, was launched to sea. I must admit it gave me a spoilsport's pleasure when the winds turned becalmed. We could not move. Aboard were several members of the Bay Area's French colony, who dangled their feet over the sides, passed around bunches of grapes and sang what I imagined were Gallic camping songs. The French know boredom, so they would understand how to behave in such a situation. It has been my observation that many

Frenchmen and women stationed in America have the attitude of taking it easy, slumming at a health resort, and nowhere more so than in California. The émigré crew included a securities analyst, an academic sociologist, a museum administrator and his wife, a modiste: on Vartas's boat they all got drunk and carried on like redskins, noble savages off Tahiti.

Joie de vivre requires a *soupçon* of the primitive. But since the illusion of the primitive soon palls and has nowhere to go, it becomes necessary to make new initiates. A good part of the day, in fact, was taken up with regulars interpreting to first-timers like myself certain mores pertaining to the houseboat, as well as offering tidbits about Vartas's Rabelaisian views of life. Here everyone was encouraged to do what he willed. (How much could you do on a becalmed boat surrounded by strangers?) No one had much solid information about their host's past, which only increased the privileged status of those who knew at least one fact. Useless to ask the object of this venerating speculation, since Vartas said next to nothing (adding to his impressiveness) when he was around, and disappeared below for long stretches of time.

In the evening, after a communal dinner, the new Grateful Dead record Frank had brought was put on the phonograph, and Vartas danced, first by himself, then with all three Graces, bending his arms in broad, hooking sweeps. He stomped his foot and looked around scampishly at the guests for appreciation, not unlike an organ-grinder and his monkey. Imagine, if you will, a being whose generous bestowal of self-satisfaction invites and is willing to receive nothing but flattery in return, a person who has managed to make others buy his somewhat senile projection of indestructibility as a Hymn to Life. In no sense could he be called a charlatan; he delivered what he promised, an incarnation of *joie de vivre,* and if it was shallow, it was also effective, managing even to attract an enviable "harem" (which was what really burned me).

A few years passed.

Some Dutch TV crew, ever on the lookout for exotic bits of Americana that would make good short subjects, planned to do a documentary about Vartas as a sort of paean to eternal youth. I later learned from Frank that Vartas died before the shooting could be completed. A pity, in a way. The home movie I've run off in my head of the old man is getting a little tattered, the colors splotchy, and the scenario goes nowhere, lacks point. All I have for sure is the title: The Man Who Gave *Joie De Vivre* a Bad Name.

"Ah, what a twinkle in the eye the old man has! He'll outlive us all." So we speak of old people who bore us, when we wish to honor them. We often see projected onto old people this worship of the life force. It is not the fault of the old if they then turn around and try to exploit our misguided amazement at their longevity as though it were a personal tour de force. The elderly, when they are honest with themselves, realize they have done nothing particularly to be proud of in lasting to a ripe old age, and then carrying themselves through a thousand more days. Yet you still hear an old woman or man telling a bus driver with a chuckle, "Would you believe that I am eighty-four years old!" As though they should be patted on the back for still knowing how to talk, or as though they had pulled a practical joke on the other riders by staying so spry and mobile. Such insecure, wheedling behavior always embarrassed me. I will look away rather than meet the speaker's eyes and be forced to lie with a smile, "Yes, you are remarkable," which seems condescending on my part and humiliating to us both.

Like children forced to play the cute part adults expect of them, some old people must get confused trying to adapt to a social role of indeterminate standards, which is why they seem to whine: "I'm doing all right, aren't I—for my age?" It is interesting that society's two most powerless groups, children and the elderly, have both been made into sentimental symbols. In the child's little hungry hands grasping for life, joined to the old person's frail slipping fingers hanging onto it, you have one of the commonest advertising metaphors for intense appreciation. It is enough to show a young child sleeping in his or her grandparent's lap to procure *joie de vivre* overload.

2. The Dinner Party

I am invited periodically to dinner parties and brunches—and I go, because I like to be with people and oblige them, even if I secretly cannot share their optimism about these events. I go, not believing that I will have fun, but with the intent of observing people who think a *dinner party* a good time. I eat their fancy food, drink the wine, make my share of entertaining conversation, and often leave having had a pleasant evening. Which does not prevent me from anticipating the next invitation with the same bleak lack of hope. To put it in a nutshell, I am an ingrate.

Although I have traveled a long way from my proletarian origins and, like a perfect little bourgeois, talk, dress, act and spend money, I hold onto my poor-boy's outrage at the "decadence" (meaning, dull entertainment style) of the middle and upper-middle classes; or, like a model Soviet moviegoer watching scenes of pre-revolutionary capitalists gorging caviar, I am appalled, but I dig in with the rest.

Perhaps my uneasiness with dinner parties comes from the simple fact that not a single dinner party was given by my solitudinous parents the whole time I was growing up, and I had to wait until my late twenties before learning the ritual. A spy in the enemy camp, I have made myself a patient observer of strange customs. For the benefit of other late-starting social climbers, this is what I have observed:

As everyone should know, the ritual of the dinner party begins away from the table. Usually in the living room, hors d'oeuvres and walnuts are set out, to start the digestive juices flowing. Here introductions between strangers are also made. Most dinner parties contain at least a few guests who have been unknown to each other before that evening, but whom the host and/or hostess envision would enjoy meeting. These novel pairings and their interactions add spice to the *post-mortem:* who got along with whom? The lack of prior acquaintanceship also ensures that the guests will have to rely on and go through the only people known to everyone, the host and hostess, whose absorption of this helplessly dependent attention is one of the main reasons for throwing dinner parties.

Although an after-work "leisure activity," the dinner party is in fact a celebration of professional identity. Each of the guests has been pre-selected as in a floral bouquet; and in certain developed forms of this ritual there is usually a cunning mix of professions. Yet the point is finally not so much diversity as commonality: what remarkably shared attitudes and interests these people from different vocations demonstrate by conversing intelligently, or at least glibly, on the topics that arise. Naturally, a person cannot discourse too technically about their line of work, so he or she picks precisely those themes that invite overlap. The psychiatrist laments the new breed of ego-less, narcissistic patient who keeps turning up in his office—a beach bum who lacks the work ethic; the college professor bemoans the shoddy intellectual backgrounds and self-centered ignorance of his students; and the bookseller parodies the customer who pronounced "Sophocles" to rhyme with "bifocals." The dinner party is thus an exercise in locating ignorance— elsewhere. Whoever is present is *ipso facto* part of that beleaguered remnant of civilized folk fast disappearing from Earth.

Or think of a dinner party as a club of revolutionaries, a technocratic elite whose social interactions that night are a dry run for some future takeover of the State. These are the future cabinet members (now only a shadow cabinet, alas) meeting to practice for the first time. How well they get on! "The time will soon be ripe, my friends . . . " If this is too fanciful for you, then compare the dinner party to a utopian community, a Brook Farm supper club, where only the best and most useful community members are chosen to participate. The smugness begins as soon as one enters the door, since one is already part of the chosen few. And from then on, every mechanical step in dinner-party process is designed to augment the atmosphere of group *amour-propre*. This is not so say that there won't be one or two people in an absolute torment of exclusion, too shy to speak up, or else suspecting that when they do, their contributions fail to carry the same weight as the others'. The group's all-purpose drone of self-contentment ignores these drowning people—cruelly inattentive in one sense, but benign in another: it invites them to join the shared ethos of success any time they are ready.

The group is asked to repair to the table. Once again they find themselves marveling at a shared perception of life. How delicious the fish soup! How cute the stuffed tomatoes! What did you use for this green sauce? Now comes much talk of ingredients, and credit is given where credit is due. It is Jacques who made the salad. It was Mamie who brought the homemade bread. Everyone pleads with the hostess to sit down, not to work so hard—an empty formula whose hypocrisy bothers no one. Who else is going to put the butter dish on the table? For a moment all become quiet, except for the sounds of eating. This corresponds to the part in a church service which calls for silent prayer.

I am saved from such culinary paganism by the fact that food is largely an indifferent matter to me. I rarely think much about what I am putting in my mouth. Though my savage, illiterate palate has inevitably been educated to some degree by the many meals I have shared with people who care enormously about such things, I resist going any further. I am superstitious that the day I send back a dish at a restaurant, or make a complicated journey to somewhere just for a meal, that day I will have sacrificed my freedom and traded in my soul for a lesser god.

I don't expect the reader to agree with me. That's not the point. Unlike the behavior called for at a dinner party, I am not obliged sitting at my typewriter to help procure consensus every moment. So I am at liberty to declare, to the friend who once told me that dinner parties were one of the only opportunities for intelligently convivial conversation to take place in this cold, fragmented city, that she is crazy. The conversation at dinner parties is of a mind-numbing calibre. No discussion of any clarifying rigor—be it political, spiritual, artistic or financial—can take place in a context where fervent conviction of any kind is frowned upon, and the desire to follow through a sequence of ideas must give way every time to the impressionistic, breezy flitting from topic to topic. Talk must be bubbly but not penetrating. Illumination would only slow the flow. Some hit-and-run remark may accidentally jog an idea loose, but in such cases it is better to scribble a few words down on the napkin for later, than attempt to "think" at a dinner party.

What do people talk about at such gatherings? The latest movies, the priciness of things, word processors, restaurants, muggings and burglaries, private versus public schools, the fool in the White House (there have been so many fools in a row that this subject is getting tired), the undeserved reputations of certain better-known professionals in one's field, the fashions in investments, the investments in fashion. What is traded at the dinner-party table is, of course, class information. You will learn whether you are in the avant-garde or rear guard of your social class, or, preferably, right in step.

As for Serious Subjects, dinner-party guests have the latest *New Yorker* in-depth piece to bring up. People who ordinarily would not spare a moment worrying about the treatment of schizophrenics in mental hospitals, the fate of Great Britain in the Common Market, or the disposal of nuclear wastes, suddenly find their consciences orchestrated in unison about these problems, thanks to their favorite periodical—though a month later they have forgotten all about it and are onto something new.

The dinner party is a suburban form of entertainment. Its spread in our big cities represents an insidious Fifth Column suburbanization of the metropolis. In the suburbs it becomes necessary to be able to discourse knowledgeably about the heart of the city, but from the viewpoint of a day shopper. Dinner-party chatter is the communicative equivalent of roaming around shopping malls.

Much thought has gone into the ideal size for a dinner party—usually with the hostess arriving at the figure eight. Six would give each personality too much weight; ten would lead to splintering side-discussions; eight is the largest number still able to force everyone into the same compulsively congenial conversation. My own strength as a conversationalist comes out less in groups of eight than one-to-one, which may explain my resistance to dinner parties. At the table, unfortunately, any engrossing *tête-à-tête* is frowned upon as antisocial. I often find myself in the frustrating situation of being drawn to several engaging people, in among the bores, and wishing I could have a private conversation with each, without being able to do more than signal across the table a wry recognition of that fact. "Some other time, perhaps," we seem to be saying with our eyes, all evening long.

Later, however—to give the devil his due—when guests and hosts retire from the table back to the living room, the strict demands of group participation may be relaxed, and individuals allowed to pair off in some form of conversational intimacy. But one must be ever on the lookout for the group's need to swoop everybody together again for one last demonstration of collective fealty.

The first to leave breaks the communal spell. There is a sudden rush to the coat closet, the bathroom, the bedroom, as others, under the protection of the first defector's original sin, quit the Party apologetically. The utopian dream has collapsed: left behind are a few loyalists and insomniacs, swillers of a last cognac. "Don't leave yet," begs the host, knowing what a sense of letdown, pain and self-recrimination awaits. Dirty dishes are, if anything, a comfort: the faucet's warm gush serves to stave off the moment of anesthetized stock-taking—Was that really necessary?—in the sobering silence which follows a dinner party.

3. *Joie's Doppelgänger*

I have no desire to rail against the Me Generation. We all know that the current epicurean style of the Good Life, from light foods to Nike running shoes, is a result of market research techniques developed to sell "spot" markets, and, as such, a natural outgrowth of consumer capitalism. I may not like it but I can't pretend that my objections are the result of a high-minded Laschian political analysis. Moreover, my own record of activism is not so noticeably impressive that I can lecture the Sunday brunchers to roll up their sleeves and start fighting social injustices instead of indulging themselves.

No, if I try to understand the reasons for my anti-hedonistic biases, they come from somewhere other than idealism. It's odd, because there seems to be a contradiction between this curmudgeonly feeling inside me and my periodically strong appetite for life. I am reminded of my hero, William Hazlitt with his sarcastic grumpy disposition on the one hand, and his capacity for "gusto" (his word, not Schlitz's) on the other. With Hazlitt, one senses a fanatically tenacious defense of his individuality and independence against some unnamed bully stalking him. He had trained himself to be a connoisseur of vitality, and got irritated when life was not filled to the brim. I am far less irritable — before others; I will laugh if there is the merest *anything* to laugh at. But it is a tense, pouncing pleasure, not one which will allow me to sink into undifferentiated relaxation. The prospect of a long day at the beach makes me panic. There is no harder work I can think of than taking myself off to somewhere pleasant, where I am forced to stay for hours and "have fun." Taking it easy, watching my personality's borders loosen and dissolve, arouses an unpleasantly floating giddiness. I don't even like waterbeds. Fear of Freud's "oceanic feeling," I suppose . . . I distrust anything which will make me pause long enough to be put in touch with my helplessness.

The other repugnance I experience around *joie de vivrism* is that I associate its rituals with depression. All these people sitting around a pool, drinking margaritas, they're not really happy, they're depressed. Perhaps I am generalizing too much from my own despair in such situations. Drunk, sunbaked, stretched out in a beach chair, I am unable to ward off the sensation of being utterly alone, unconnected, cut off from the others.

An article on the Science Page of the *Times* about depression (they seem to run one every few months) described the illness as a pattern of "learned helplessness." Dr. Martin Seligman of the University of Pennsylvania described his series of experiments: "At first mild electrical shocks were given to dogs, from which they were unable to escape. In a second set of experiments, dogs were given shocks from which they could escape — but they didn't try. They just lay there, passively accepting the pain. It seemed that the animals' inability to control their experiences had brought them to a state resembling clinical depression in humans."

Keep busy, I always say. At all costs avoid the trough of passivity, which leads to the Slough of Despond. Someone — a girlfriend, who else? — once accused me of being intolerant of the depressed way of looking at the world, which had its own intelligence and moral integrity, both obviously unavailable to me. It's true. I don't like the smell of depression (it has a smell, a very distinct one, something fetid like morning odors), and I stay away from depressed characters whenever possible. Except when they happen to be my closest friends or family members. It goes without saying that I am also, for all my squeamishness, attracted to depressed people, since they seem to know something I don't. I wouldn't rule out the possibility that the brown-gray logic of depression *is* the truth. In another experiment (also reported on the Science Page), pitting "optimists" against clinically diagnosed "depressives" on their self-perceived abilities to effect outcomes according to their wills, researchers tentatively concluded that depressed people may have a more realistic, clear-sighted view of the world.

Nevertheless, what I don't like about depressives sometimes is their chummy I-told-you-so smugness, like Woody Allen fans who treat acedia as a vanguard position.

And for all that, depressives make the most rabid converts to *joie de vivre*. The reason is, *joie de vivre* and depression are not opposites but relatives of the same family, practically twins. When I see *joie de vivre* rituals, I always notice, like a TV ghost, depression right alongside it. I knew a man, dominated by a powerful father, who thought he had come out of a long depression occasioned, in his mind, by his divorce. Whenever I met him he would say that his life was getting better and better. Now he could run long distances, he was putting healthy food in his system, he was more physically fit at forty than he had been at twenty-five, and now he had dates, he was going out with three different women, he had a good therapist, he was looking forward to renting a bungalow in better woods than the previous summer . . . I don't know whether it was his tone of voice when he said this, his sagging shoulders, or what, but I always had an urge to burst into tears. If only he had admitted he was miserable I could have consoled him outright instead of being embarrassed to notice the deep hurt in him, like a swallowed razor cutting him from inside. And his pain still stunk up the room like in the old days, that sour cabbage smell was in his running suit, yet he wouldn't let on, he thought the smell was gone. The therapist had told him to forgive himself, and he had gone ahead and done it, the poor shlemiel. But tell me: why would anyone need such a stylized, disciplined regimen of enjoyment if he were not depressed?

4. In the Here-and-Now

The argument of both the hedonist and the guru is that if we were but to open ourselves to the richness of the moment, to concentrate on the feast before us, we would be filled with bliss. I have lived in the present from time to time, and I can tell you that it is much over-rated. Occasionally, as a holiday from stroking one's memories or brooding about future worries, I grant you, it can be a nice change of pace. But to "be here now" hour after hour would never work. I don't even approve of stories written in the present tense. As for poets who never use a past participle, they deserve the eternity they are striving for.

Besides, the present has a way of intruding whether you like it or not; why should I go out of my way to meet it? Let it splash on me from time to time, like a car going through a puddle, and I, on the side-walk of my solitude, will salute it grimly like any other modern inconvenience.

If I attend a concert, obviously not to listen to the music but to find a brief breathing space in which to meditate on the past and future, I realize that there may be moments when the music invades my ears and I am forced to pay attention to it, note after note. I believe I take such intrusions gracefully. The present is not always an unwelcome guest, so long as it doesn't stay too long and cut into our time for remembering.

Even for survival, it's not necessary to focus one's full attention on the present. The instincts of a pedestrian crossing the street in a reverie will usually suffice. Alertness is all right as long as it is not treated as a promissory note on happiness. Anyone who recommends attention to the moment as a prescription for grateful wonder is only telling half the truth. To be happy one must pay attention, but to be unhappy one must also have paid attention.

Attention, at best, is a form of prayer. Conversely, as Simone Weil said, prayer is a way of focusing attention. All religions recognize this when they ask their worshipers to repeat the name of their God, a devotional practice which draws the practitioner into a trancelike awareness of the present, and the objects around oneself. With a part of the soul one praises God, and with the other part one expresses a hunger, a dissatisfaction, a desire for more spiritual contact. Praise must never stray too far from longing, that longing which takes us implicitly beyond the present.

I was about to say that the very act of attention implies longing, but this is not necessarily true. Attention is not always infused with desire; it can settle on us most placidly once desire has been momentarily satisfied, like after the sex act. There are also periods following overwork, when the exhausted slave body is freed and the eyes dilate to register with awe the lights of the city; one is too tired to desire anything else.

Such moments are rare. They form the basis for a poetic appreciation of the beauty of the world. However, there seems no reliable way to invoke or prolong them. The rest of the time, when we are not being edgy or impatient, we are often simply *disappointed*, which amounts to a confession that the present is not good enough. People often try to hide their disappointment—just as Berryman's mother told him not to let people see that he was bored, because it suggested that he had no "inner resources." But there is something to be said for disappointment.

This least respected form of suffering, downgraded to a kind of petulance, at least accurately measures the distance between hope and reality. And it has its own peculiar satisfactions: Why else do we return years later to places where we had been happy, if not to savor the bittersweet pleasure of disappointment?

Moreover, it is the other side of a strong, predictive feeling for beauty or appropriate civility or decency: only those with a sense of order and harmony can be disappointed.

We are told that to be disappointed is immature, in that it presupposes having unrealistic expectations, whereas the wise man meets each moment head-on without preconceptions, with freshness and detachment, grateful for anything it offers. However, this pernicious teaching ignores everything we know of the world. If we continue to expect what turns out to be not forthcoming, it is not because we are unworldly in our expectations, but because our very worldliness has taught us to demand of an unjust world that it behave a little more fairly. The least we can do, for instance, is to register the expectation that people in a stronger position be kind and not cruel to those in a weaker, knowing all the while that we will probably be disappointed.

The truth is, most wisdom is embittering. The task of the wise person cannot be to pretend with false naiveté that every moment is new and unprecedented, but to bear the burden of bitterness which experience forces on us with as much uncomplaining dignity as strength will allow. Beyond that, all we can ask of ourselves is that bitterness not cancel out our capacity still to be surprised.

5. Making Love

If it is true that I have the tendency to withhold sympathy from those pleasures or experiences which fall outside my capabilities, the opposite is also true: I admire immoderately those things I cannot do. I've always gone out with women who swam better than I did. It's as if I were asking them to teach me how to make love. Though I know how to make love (more or less) I have never fully shaken that adolescent boy's insecurity that there was more to it than I could ever imagine, and that I needed a full-time instructress. For my first sexual experiences in fact, I chose older women. Later, when I slept with women my own age and younger, I still tended to take the stylistic lead from them, adapting myself to each one's rhythm and ardor, not only because I wanted to be "responsive," but because I secretly thought that women — any woman — understood lovemaking in a way that I did not. In bed I came to them as a student; and I have made them pay later, in other ways, for letting them see me thus. Sex has always been so impromptu, so out of my control, so different each time, that even when I became the confident bull in bed I was dismayed by this surprising sudden power, itself a form of powerlessness because so unpredictable.

Something Michel Leiris wrote in his book, *Manhood,* has always stuck with me: "It has been some time, in any case, since I have ceased to consider the sexual act as a simple matter, but rather as a relatively exceptional act, necessitating certain inner accommodations that are either particularly tragic or particularly exalted, but very different, in either case, from what I regard as my usual disposition."

The transformation from a preoccupied urban intellectual to a sexual animal involves, at times, an almost superhuman strain. To find in one's bed a living, undulating woman of God knows what capacities and secret desires, may seem too high, too formal, too ridiculous or blissful an occasion — not to mention the shock to an undernourished heart like mine of an injection of undiluted affection, if the woman proves loving as well.

Most often, I simply do what the flood allows me to, improvising here or there like a man tying a white flag to a raft that is being swiftly swept along, a plea for love or forgiveness. But as for artistry, control, enslavement through my penis, that's someone else. Which is not to say that there weren't women who were perfectly happy with me as a lover. In those cases, there was some love between us outside of bed: the intimacy was much more intense because we had something big to say to each other before we ever took off our clothes, but which could now be said only with our bodies.

With other women, whom I cared less about, I was sometimes a dud. I am not one of those men who can force himself to make love passionately or athletically when his affections are not engaged. From the perplexity of wide variations in my experiences I have been able to tell myself that I am neither a good nor a bad lover, but one who responds differently according to the emotions present. A banal conclusion; maybe a true one.

It does not do away, however, with some need to have my remaining insecurities about sexual ability laid to rest. I begin to suspect that all my fancy distrust of hedonism comes down to a fear of being judged in this one category: Do I make love well? Every brie and wine picnic, every tanned body relaxing on the beach, every celebration of *joie de vivre* carries a sly wink of some missed sexual enlightenment which may be too threatening to me. I am like the prudish old maid who blushes behind her packages when she sees sexy young people kissing.

When I was twenty I married. My wife was the second woman I had ever slept with. Our marriage was the recognition that we suited one another remarkably well as company—could walk and talk and share insights all day, work side by side like Chinese peasants, read silently together like graduate students, tease each other like brother and sister, and when at night we found our bodies tired, pull the covers over ourselves and become lovers. She was two years older than I, but I was good at faking maturity; and I found her so companionable and trustworthy and able to take care of me that I could not let such a gold mine go by.

Our love life was mild and regular. There was a sweetness to sex, as befitted domesticity. Out of the surplus energy of late afternoons I would find myself coming up behind her sometimes as she worked in the kitchen, taking her away from her involvements, leading her by the hand into the bedroom. I would unbutton her blouse. I would stroke her breasts, and she would get a look in her eyes of quiet intermittent hunger, like a German shepherd being petted; she would seem to listen far off; absent-mindedly daydreaming, she would return my petting, stroke my arm with distracted patience like a mother who has something on the stove, trying to calm her weeping child. I would listen too to guess what she might be hearing, bird calls or steam heat. The enlargement of her nipples under my fingers fascinated me. Goose bumps either rose on her skin where I touched or didn't, I noted with scientific interest, a moment before getting carried away by my own eagerness. Then we were undressing, she was doing something in the bathroom, and I was waiting on the bed, with all the consciousness of a sun mote. I was large and ready. The proud husband, waiting to receive my treasure . . .

I remember our favorite position was she on top, I on the bottom, upthrusting and receiving. Distraction, absentmindedness, return, calm exploration marked our sensual life. To be forgetful seemed the highest grace. We often achieved perfection.

Then I became haunted with images of seductive, heartless cunts. It was the era of the miniskirt, girl–women, Rudi Gernreich bikinis and Tiger Morse underwear, see-through blouses, flashes of flesh which invited the hand to go creeping under and into costumes. I wanted my wife to be more glamorous. We would go shopping for dresses together, and she would complain that her legs were wrong for these new fashions. Or she would come home proudly with a bargain pink and blue felt minidress, bought for three dollars at a discount store, which my aching heart would tell me missed the point completely.

She too became dissatisfied with the absence of furtive excitement in our marriage. She wanted to seduce me, like a stranger on a plane. But I was too easy, so we ended up seducing others. Then we turned back to each other and with one last desperate attempt, before the marriage fell to pieces, sought in the other a plasticity of sensual forms, like the statuary in an Indian temple. In our lovemaking I tried to believe that the body of one woman was the body of all women, and all I achieved was a groping to distance lovingly familiar forms into those of anonymous erotic succubi. The height of this insanity, I remember, was one evening in the park when I pounded my wife's lips with kisses in an effort to provoke something between us like "hot passion." My eyes closed, I practiced a repertoire of French tongue-kisses on her. I shall never forget her frightened silent appeal that I stop, because I had turned into someone she no longer recognized.

But we were young. And so, dependent on each other, like orphans. By the time I left, at twenty-five, I knew I had been a fool, and had ruined everything, but I had to continue being a fool because it had been my odd misfortune to have stumbled onto kindness and tranquility too quickly.

I moved to California in search of an earthly sexual paradise, and that year I tried hardest to make my peace with *joie de vivre*. I was sick but didn't know it—a diseased animal, Nietzsche would say. I hung around Berkeley's campus, stared up at the campanile tower, I sat on the grass watching coeds younger than I, and, pretending that I was still going to university (no deeper sense of being a fraud obtainable), I tried to grasp the rhythms of carefree youth; I blended in at rallies, I stood at the fringes of be-ins, watching new rituals of communal love, someone being passed through the air hand to hand. But I never "trusted the group" enough to let myself be the guinea pig; or if I did, it was only with the proud stubborn conviction that nothing could change me—though I also wanted to change. Swearing I would never learn transcendence, I hitchhiked and climbed mountains. I went to wine-tasting festivals, and also accepted the wine jug from hippie gypsies in a circle around a beach campfire, without first wiping off the lip. I registered for a Free School course in human sexual response, just to get laid; and when that worked, I was shocked, and took up with someone else. There were many women in those years who got naked with me. I wish I could remember their names. I smoked grass with them, and as a sign of faith I took psychedelic drugs, and we made love in bushes and beachhouses, as though hacking through jungles with machetes to stay in touch with our ecstatic genitals while our minds soared off into natural marvels. Such experiences taught me, I will admit, how much romantic feeling can transform the body whose nerve tendrils are receptive to it. Technicolor fantasies of one girlfriend as a señorita with flowers in her impossibly wavy hair would suddenly pitch and roll beneath me, and the bliss of touching her naked suntanned breast and the damp black pubic hairs was too unthinkably perfect to elicit anything but abject gratitude. At such moments I have held the world in my hands and *known* it. I was coming home to the body of Woman, those globes and grasses which had launched me. In the childish fantasy accompanying one sexual climax, under LSD, I was hitting a home run, and the Stars and Stripes flying in the background of my mind's eye as I "slid into home" acclaimed the patriotic rightness of my semenal release. For once I had no guilt about how or when I ejaculated.

If afterwards, when we came down, there was often a sour air of disenchantment and mutual prostitution, that does not take away from the legacy, the rapture of those moments. If I no longer use drugs—in fact, have become anti-drug—I think I still owe them something for showing me how to recognize the all-embracing reflex. At first I needed drugs to teach me about the stupendousness of sex. Later, without them, there would be situations—after a lovely talk or coming home from a party in a taxi—when I would be overcome by amorous tropism towards the woman with me. The appetite for flesh which comes over me at such moments, and the pleasure there is in finally satisfying it, seems so just that I always think I have stumbled into a state of blessed grace. That it can never last, that it is a trick of the mind and the blood, are rumors I push out of sight.

To know rapture is to have one's whole life poisoned. If you will forgive a ridiculous analogy, a tincture of rapture is like a red bandana in the laundry that runs and turns all the white wash pink. We should just as soon stay away from any future ecstatic experiences which spoil everyday living by comparison. Not that I have any intention of stopping. Still, if I will have nothing to do with religious mysticism, it is probably because I sense a susceptibility in that direction. Poetry is also dangerous. All quickening awakenings to Being extract a price later.

Are there people who live under such spells all the time? Was this the secret of the idiotic smile on the half-moon face of the painter Vartas? The lovers of life, the robust Cellinis, the Casanovas? Is there a technique to hedonism that will allow the term of rapture to be indefinitely extended? I don't believe it. The hedonist's despair is still that he is forced to make do with the present. Who knows about the success rate of religious mystics? In any case, I could not bring myself to state that what I am waiting for is God. Such a statement would sound too grandiose and presumptuous, and make too great a rupture in my customary thinking. But I can identify with the pre- if not the post-stage of what Simone Weil describes:

"The soul knows for certain only that it is hungry. The important thing is that it announces its hunger by crying. A child does not stop crying if we suggest to it that perhaps there is no bread. It goes on crying just the same. The danger is not lest the soul should doubt whether there is any bread, but lest, by a lie, it should persuade itself that it is not hungry."

So much for *joie de vivre*. It's too compensatory. I don't really know what I'm waiting for. I know only that until I have gained what I want from this life, my expressions of gratitude and joy will be restricted to variations of a hunter's alertness. I give thanks to a nip in the air that clarifies the scent. But I think it hypocritical to pretend satisfaction while I am still hungry.

One Hundred Foreskins

Louis Berney

THE DAY THE SHORTSTOP died, Katie Mays was in the kitchen, arranging a sprig of baby's breath, fresh from the garden, onto her father's breakfast tray. Merely glancing at the front-page headlines, she opened the *Daily Oklahoman* to page five—sports scores and standings—and placed it neatly next to the cut-glass pitcher of orange juice. More important than Churchill and Stalin, that summer of 1941, was the beginning of American Legion play downtown at Sandlot Park: baseball, not a war distant and exotic, was the reason she was waking her father a full hour earlier than usual.

The telephone in the parlor rang just as she started upstairs. Sheltered and shy for her seventeen years, unused to sudden dilemmas (or so the family legend goes), my mother hesitated. The tray, heavy with bone china, trembled between her thin wrists. Before she could decide whether to continue up or sacrifice the eggs to the chilling breath of the air-cooler, the ringing stopped. She heard, above, her father's voice. A moment later the receiver clicked back into its cradle and Lyman Mays loomed up at the head of the stairs.

My grandfather was a big man, not only in height but in construction. Over the past ten years his broad chest had receded as a paunch had advanced, but the flesh had become neither flaccid nor weak. His carriage was still erect, his jaw strong, his reddish-brown brows thick and wild. His silvering hair, pomaded back from the high forehead, reinforced the unmistakable impression of stern dignity, even when he was clad only in his striped crinkle-crepe pajamas, as he was that

192

morning. Padding down the stairs to his private den he ignored his daughter's urgent apologies, his mouth cinched into a pensive frown, his eyes cloudy with worry. He took a gray-and-green ceramic mallard from the mantelpiece, unscrewed its head and poured a shot of whiskey into a coffee mug. Then he squeezed behind his large oak desk and sighed deeply.

The police said the boy, star shortstop for the Lyman Mays Used Auto Cardinals, had been drunk. Stumbling home from a party, he had gone to bed on the tracks of the Classen Boulevard streetcar line, his head pillowed between the wooden ties. It had been after midnight, there was no moon, and the redbud trees that lined the avenue threw deceptive shadows onto the gravel median. Not until the trolley had dragged the boy several yards, one leg bouncing to the side like the tail of a mouse caught in a cat's mouth, did the conductor realize something was wrong.

"Poor fellow," Lyman Mays murmured, thinking of the dead shortstop's father. He remembered the death of his own precious wife many years before and felt in his chest the sharp pain of empathy. "Bring me the phone from the other room, darling," he told his daughter, who waited nervously against one of the dark paneled walls. "There is much to be done."

For even at his most grief-stricken, my grandfather was not a man given to self-pity or reflection. He saw himself descended from a long line of hardy pioneers who, despite the best efforts of nature, the federal government, and the thieving Indian Nations, had hewed out their fortunes from the inhospitable rock-red plains of central Oklahoma — men who did not cash their chips with two strikes, two out, and the future in scoring position.

"Oh my God," sobbed Melvin, horrified by news of the tragedy.

" 'Whatsoever God doeth, it shall be forever,' " Lyman Mays told his assistant sales manager and first-base coach, " 'nothing can be put to it, nothing taken away.' Ecclesiastes. It is we, Melvin, the living, who must persevere and forge onward."

"Oh my God, Mr. Mays," he sobbed.

But Melvin had been hired for his efficiency and in that time of need, steadied by the commanding voice of Lyman Mays, he did not fail. By noon, with barely six hours remaining until game time, he had scouted out the best replacement shortstop in town, a boy who had led the McGrath Meat Packing Sox in batting the previous two seasons.

"He might not want to play for us, Mr. Mays," Melvin warned, "and they're not going to want to let him go."

" 'And He said unto them,' " Lyman Mays answered, smiling, " 'Why are ye so fearful? How is it that ye have no faith?' Mark."

Lyman Mays changed into his best tropical worsted suit, which he wore whenever negotiating an important transaction. From the window he watched Katie. Stooped beneath the clothesline and whacking an Oriental rug with the banjo-shaped wire beater, she looked lovely in the brilliant June sun—blond hair wispy against her long neck, a sheen of sweat on her upper lip, motes of carpet dust netted in her pale eyelashes.

"A girl a mile less prettier than you, sweetheart," Lyman Mays said as he helped her over the running board of the LaSalle, his breath sweet with peppermint tooth powder, "couldn't help but turn the eye of our young shortstop friend."

That day the hot prairie winds swarmed up from the south, so they smelled the yards long before they saw them, a stew of stenches that became more distinct the closer they came to its source—pits of rotting offals, manure seething with trough flies and boiling down to liquid in the heat, tall chimneys coughing out oily clouds of burnt bone meal and tallow. Just when the stink had become almost unbearable, the car crested a lump of a hill and they looked out on acres and acres of holding pens, so teeming with cattle that the entire landscape, from hillside to horizon, seemed cobbled with the wide brown and black backs of Panhandle Shorthorn and Head Angus.

Lyman Mays rolled the LaSalle down into the sprawling snarl of wooden lairages and shifted to a stop next to a long concrete building with a corrugated iron roof, on the side of which sun-faded letters spelled out "McGrath." Inside the huge slaughterhall, amid rough, echoing shouts and the rhythmic cracking of cleaver blades, hundreds of steer carcasses clicked along on overhead track hangers, stripped, as they progressed from skinning cradle to skinning cradle, of head, hide, innards and spine. A sticky residue of blood and sweat settled on Katie's bare face and arms; she tasted on her lips something that, sweet and sickening, reminded her of pineapple juice. She closed her eyes and clutched her father's arm. Lyman Mays pressed a freshly laundered handkerchief, scented with a drop of Old Spice, to his mouth.

"Could you be able to tell me, sir," he asked a man carving a tongue from a steer's head, "where I might find a gentleman by the name of William Eagle?"

The man wiped his knife on his long leather apron and pointed. "That'd be the little Indian," he said, "stickin' down there in number four."

So it was in the killing pens that Lyman Mays found his new short-stop, crouched next to a nine-hundred-pound heifer. The boy was not the dark, tall, muscular Osage brave Lyman Mays had expected; rather, he was pale, short for his nineteen years — barely an inch over five feet — and slightly built. High, sharp cheekbones and black eyes, coiled deep and dark in the hollows beneath his brow, were the legacy of his lone Creek ancestor, a great-grandfather on his father's side, but his light-brown hair and his size came from his mother's people, who were French.

Full-blooded or not, Bill Eagle made quick work of the heifer. He had it shackled to the hoist only a moment after its heavy body dropped beneath the blow from his partner's sledgehammer. The muscles of his bare back straining, he cranked the tackle until the animal's chin swayed a few inches above the sloping concrete floor and then, smoothing the hide and pulling against the cutting stroke with his left hand, he sliced open its neck from dewlap to sternum. There was a whisper of steam and a fine red mist as the tip of his knife found the main throat arteries and split them in half. A powerful, hiccuping stream of blood pooled greasy and rainbow-flecked around the toes of his rubber boots. He pumped the heifer's foreleg to speed the flow down an iron grill and then shoved the carcass along the overhead rail into the main hall, where a man stood ready to chalk the ripping lines.

Impressed by the strength and agility of a boy so small, but unwilling to concede any bargaining advantages, Lyman Mays stepped decorously around a galvanized steel bucket crusted with some foul-looking substance. He held out his hand. "Good afternoon, son," he said, in the reasonable but stern tones he reserved for the poor and desperate people who came to him peddling their broken-down old Model A's. "I wonder if I might have a word with you?"

Suspicion in his dark eyes, Bill Eagle ran a nervous thumb along the spine of his eight-inch blade and looked up at the imposing, well-dressed man. Aware of his own appearance, he pulled a rough canvas shirt, stitched from one-hundred-pound unbleached sugar sacks, over his head. "Yes, sir."

"I have a proposition for you, son," Lyman Mays said.

It was at that moment Katie Mays fainted. The heat, the fumes, the sight of death, squeezed her lungs tight and freckled her vision with brightly colored spots. Standing in the corner behind her father, silent and attentive, she managed to take a step toward the narrow wooden cattle race — where the air was somewhat fresher — before she shuddered and pitched forward.

Bill Eagle, unable to match Lyman Mays's grave scrutiny, saw her fall. After only a moment of surprised hesitation he sprang forward and slid on his knees across the smooth floor, catching Katie in his arms. He held her, her head cradled in the crook of his lap, and was fascinated by the foreign scent of lilac and honeysuckle and soap, by the tiny golden whiskers that grew in soft swirls on her cheeks, by the sleek, graceful throat that pulsed with a single blue vein. When he brushed a strand of hair from her face, feeling the warm skin of her forehead, her eyes fluttered open.

"You are beautiful," Bill Eagle said with wonder.

Those few seconds were all it took for Lyman Mays to secure a new shortstop for his Used Auto Cardinals, thrice-consecutive state champions in the nineteen-and-under division and destined to repeat yet again, if his eye for great ballplayers was as keen as he knew it was. Even in the urgent bustle of carrying Katie to the car and sending the boozy old knocker running for cold water, Lyman Mays marveled at the speed, the fluidity of movement, in the boy's diving save — as if Bill Eagle lived in a medium of air, those around him in water.

All the necessary arrangements went off without a hitch. Griffin McGrath, in the market for a new Ford Tudor, was easily persuaded to loan the boy out for the summer. Lyman Mays insisted that Bill, whose parents were dead, move out of his cramped, filthy room in the boarding house and into the mansion on 16th Street. This way Bill could quit the packing house and concentrate on his game, explained Lyman Mays, anxious, given the boy's shiftless Indian nature, to keep an eye on his new star athlete. Only a few hours after Katie fainted in the sweltering stench of the killing pen, Bill Eagle was installed in one of the spare bedrooms on the third floor, his little bundle of belongings — glove, comb, Sunday shoes, and sticking knife — deposited in an antique armoire made of polished mahogany.

" 'It came to pass,' " Lyman Mays said that first night at supper, following an opening-day victory in which Bill Eagle doubled twice, " 'Laban ran to meet Jacob and he embraced him and he brought him to his house. And Laban said to him, Surely thou art my bone and my flesh.' Genesis."

Katie glanced across the table at Bill Eagle and gave him a timid smile. "Daddy always said he wanted a son."

And like a son Bill Eagle was treated. Together, as a family, the three of them took their meals, attended church (Lyman Mays had Melvin buy Bill a new white cotton shirt) and rocked away the long evenings of summer, sipping iced lemonade on the front porch and listening to the big six-tube Victor—the "Kraft Music Hall," ball games from St. Louis, Fulton Lewis Jr. and his "Top of the News." At first tense and guarded in the calm elegance of his surroundings, Bill began to adjust to his new life. His offer to earn his keep by running errands or washing the lot-cars refused ("Rest and grow strong, son," Lyman Mays said, "keep your eye on the ball"), his days were peaceful and easy. Soon his sticking knife, tied up in a piece of newspaper, lay forgotten.

Mornings he helped Katie with the household chores—weeding the garden, dusting her father's collection of lead car models, polishing with a rag-wrapped brick the mansion's endless parquet floors—but the remainder of the day, before and after the game, they were free to do whatever they wanted. Never before had Bill Eagle been able to afford such a diversity of amusements (Lyman Mays provided him with a cash allowance). They saw matinees downtown at the Bijou and the Criterion, swam at Sandy Lake Beaches and, on Friday and Saturday nights, took the trolley north to the Belle Isle Amusement Park, where they spun across the pine-plank dance floor to the music of the Lloyd Patterson Orchestra. It was on one Saturday night, early in August, when they walked over to the secluded leeward side of the island, from where the canoe boat rides were launched during the day, and kissed under a vast black Oklahoma sky notched with stars.

Katie cherished the life that had, without warning, become hers. For the first time since her mother died, she knew the love and attention of a person other than her father, was allowed to venture out into the bright, colorful world. She suspected her father's motives, of course, but that didn't matter. When she was with Bill she no longer seemed a part of the big, empty, hollow, suffocating house; she felt lighter than air, liberated, hopeful.

"When I'm with you I haven't ever been happier," she said, with sincerity. She was not sure, exactly, if she was in love with this boy, but she knew she loved how she felt when she was with him.

"I like it here," Bill answered, his heart as joyful as the wild south winds that chased across the plains.

For Lyman Mays, too, it was a glorious summer. After a decade ot sluggish sales down at the car lot, business was finally beginning to pick up. The Cardinals, behind the league-leading hitting of their new shortstop, were once again the scourge of the Oklahoma County American Legion, winning eighteen in a row during one stretch of the season. When, in August, the First Methodist of Classen Boulevard, where Lyman Mays served as a lay preacher, was chosen by church headquarters in Dallas to host the annual Bible Prayer Conference, Lyman Mays bowed his head and gave thanks to God.

" 'And the Lord hath given him twice as much as he had before,' " he quoted at the dinner table that night, in a voice shaken with emotion. "Job."

With a certain unease, though, Lyman Mays observed the young romance that blossomed on his metal porch glider. He had no quarrel with the boy, who, despite his background, was clean, polite and quiet; but Bill Eagle was, simply, from the wrong side of the Santa Fe line, the wrong side of the middle-class neighborhoods honest businessmen were sculpting from the Depression's rubbled wake. But Lyman Mays was a patient man and a prudent one, as he told his friends, and so he waited until the morning after the finals of the state championship, a game won in the eighth inning when Bill Eagle tripled and then scored on a passed ball, before he invited Bill into his den for a glass of lemonade.

"Son," he said, sitting on the edge of his desk, "Mr. McGrath informs me he may run short of hands this autumn. So as much as I hate to do it, I'll have to return your services. I'm a man of my word, Bill."

Bill, sunk down in a leather armchair almost twice his size, studied the oil portraits of short-haired pointers that lined the walls. "You mean to say," he said slowly, "I won't be living with you until next summer?"

"Well, Bill." Lyman Mays shook his head and smiled, his thick red brows arching with sympathy. "You turn twenty in January and there's just no way around the age rule. I've called every official in the league." He pressed the palms of his large, pink hands together. "But I want you to know that everything is arranged—your old room at Mrs. Wasper's, your old shift at the packing house. Mr. McGrath will automatically deduct the money you owe me for summer room and board, so you won't have to worry your head about all those figures. And Bill, I hope you'll be able to pay us a visit some time after you get settled."

And that was that. With seven long miles — crossed by no streetcar line — between Colored Town and Mays House, with Katie tucked away in high school from eight o'clock until four every day, with Bill Eagle back on the twelve-hour killing shifts six days a week, Lyman Mays knew the little case of puppy love would inevitably wither and die.

But Bill gauged differently the caliber of his love for Katie. He pawned a gold-veined locket that had been his mother's and bought a secondhand bicycle. Black frame warped from age and rust, it drifted to the left when ridden — he had to stop, dismount, and point the bike back in the proper direction every fifty feet or so — but it was faster than walking. Each weekday at six o'clock, when the quitting whistles at the stockyards barked, Bill carefully washed the blood and death from his face and pedaled the seven miles north.

Rarely speaking, as if frivolous conversation wasted their precious time together, he and Katie sat on the front porch, held hands, and listened to Bing Crosby on "Maxwell House Coffee Time." When that program ended Katie was required to go back inside and do homework. Bill began the long, dark ride back the boarding house.

Lyman Mays waited, betting that Bill Eagle's cycling adventures would end with the first cold, wet rains of September. Autumn, though, remained unseasonably mild and sunny, and Lyman became more and more irritable as the days passed. He slept fitfully at night, lying awake in the dark and straining for some echo of an approaching storm. He spent hours alone in his den, where he stood at the window and pondered the smooth blue sky, stroking his nose with the tips of his fingers.

Finally, on the first day of October, a chilly squall whipped across the lake. Lyman Mays's hopes were lifted to the heavens. But then he heard, through the clamor of shutters smacking in the gale, the familiar creaking and squeaking of Bill Eagle's bicycle, and he thought he would be driven out of his mind with exasperation.

"When a young man shows such attentions to a young lady of marriageable age," Lyman Mays told the boy, whom he invited into the den that night for another discussion, "it is the responsibility of that young lady's father to discern the young man's intentions." Lyman Mays slowly repeated these last words, hoping to emphasize the frightening implications of imminent, legally binding commitment. "The young man's *intentions*."

Bill Eagle sat and thought for a moment, his face guileless and earnest. Then his eyes brightened with comprehension. He nodded eagerly. "Oh, yes, sir," he said, "I plan on marrying your daughter."

Startled, Lyman Mays glared at the soaked, bedraggled Indian boy who sat shivering before him. When he ascertained at last that Bill Eagle had spoken in all seriousness, a grim smile of amusement came to his lips.

"You see, son," he explained, "Katie has been doing just too much socializing and not enough studying."

Banned then from Katie's presence, Bill Eagle nevertheless continued to make the daily journey northward, by wheel and then, when the old bike crumbled, by foot. The October nights came quicker and colder, but still Bill pressed on, head bent against the Canadian winds, leather apron wound around his hands as partial protection against the insidious chill. Every day he delivered Katie a note, a few words carefully scratched onto a scrap of brown packing paper. Often he lingered to gaze up at her cheerful yellow bedroom window.

Katie, who waited for him from behind her muslin curtains, dashed down to the curb the moment she saw him stamp his numbed feet and turn toward home. She held the day's letter to her breast and watched him disappear into the darkness, pretending that she could feel his warm, gentle presence in the recently vacated space next to the mailbox.

Glowering in the dusky solitude of his den, Lyman Mays watched Bill Eagle continue to materialize, without fail, on the front lawn every evening. Although the boy no longer entered the house or even saw Katie, his effect on her was undiminished. In the past such a beautifully meek and restrained creature, she had taken to occasional smiling, blushing and humming ever since Bill Eagle had invaded their lives. One night, late in October, Lyman Mays sat up in bed, logged with sweat and shaken by the terror of a midnight revelation — that Katie's high spirits might be the result of a plot, planted in the fertile soil of her naïve, impressionable mind, to elope. The next evening he intercepted Bill Eagle and steered him into the den.

Lyman Mays had lost several pounds in the past two months — the collar of his shirt, normally tight against his stout neck, hung loose a fraction of an inch, marring his usually impeccable appearance — but an even greater change had come over Bill Eagle. Thin to start with, the long treks to Mays House, coupled with the brutal labor of the stockyards, had sheared his frame of all excess flesh. The sharp knobs of his collarbone protruded alarmingly and the ridges of his cheekbones had grown even more pronounced. His pale, coarse-grained skin, never swarthy, now had the white, luminescent glow of a boiled soup bone. Despite all this, though, despite the tiny crimson and yellow spurs that muddied his eyes with fatigue, his expression was peaceful, content.

"I plan on marrying your daughter," he said.

"These are hard times, son," Lyman Mays answered, clenching his anger in his fists and attempting one last time to drive a stake of enlightenment into the boy's skull. "As much as I hate to confess this, were you and Kate to marry, I would be unable to offer you any monetary assistance at all." He waited for Bill Eagle to absorb the significance of his words. "What I'm saying, son, is you are on your own if you take my daughter away; neither you nor she will receive one penny from me."

When Bill Eagle nodded, quickly, without surprise or concern, Lyman Mays smoothed onto the desktop the title to a 1939 Packard and anchored it there with a set of keys. "If you promise me, if you give me your word as a man that you'll stay forever away from my daughter, this car is yours."

"No, sir," Bill Eagle said. He rose, unsteady from the thick heat and baked Old Spice aroma of the den. "I plan on marrying your daughter."

The snows came in November but still Bill Eagle paid his nightly visits to Mays House. Now, though, there was more than just the bitter cold with which to contend. Lyman Mays gave Katie a dog for her eighteenth birthday, and that big black rottweiler patrolled the grounds from sundown till sunup. Bill Eagle tried to sneak past it the first time, holding to the cover of the holly bushes, but even with the moon hidden by clouds and the sleet blinding, the dog sensed him. Dead leaves crackled on the porch and Bill turned to see the beast emerge from the shadows, blunt ears cocked back on its triangular head like twin rifle bolts.

Bill paused and the dog leapt, snarling, from the porch. Its hot, slashing jaws caught the meat of his calf and sent him tumbling into a snow bank. With one hand he tried to beat away the animal, while with the other he dragged himself over the yard's fence. He lay exhausted on his back for more than an hour, the blood from his torn leg fading into the snow, the dog's bared fangs gouging at the wooden pickets.

For the next three days Bill Eagle went directly back to the boarding house when his shift at the slaughterhall ended. All night he sat alone in the tiny room, thinking, sharpening his knife on a chunk of flat sandstone. His head ached with loathing for Lyman Mays. On the fourth day, lagging behind in the noisy confusion of quitting time, he speared with his knife one of the long, greasy beef tongues that lay drying on a wire-mesh rack. He carried it to Mays House, where he flung it onto the porch with his strong shortstop's arm. Without waiting, he turned for home.

At the end of seven nights and seven tongues, he was able to cross the yard unmolested. The rottweiler attempted an attack but managed only a few half-hearted steps before it retched up a slime of rich, rotten meat and slunk back to the porch. That evening Bill stood beneath Katie's window for an entire, wonderful hour, watching for her shadow against the shade. Just as he was about to leave, frozen but happy, he saw her raise the sash to peer out into the darkness. Softly clapping his raw hands together, he caught her attention.

"Oh, Bill, I've missed you so," she cried, opening the window and leaning over the sill. "And now you're here again."

Bill looked up at the small, pretty face, her cheeks already rosy from the icy air. "I'll always be here, Katie."

"I thought you'd gone away," she said, "because of that terrible dog."

"I'll never go away, Katie," he whispered.

Lyman Mays's joy had bloomed fresh each successive night Bill Eagle had remained absent from his property, so the discovery that the path to his daughter had been laid open—his watchdog poisoned somehow—was especially bitter. A quiet rage built in his heart as he stood at his den window. He gripped the edge of his desk, watching the boy's dark figure ripple away across the snowy yard. When, finally, reason and locomotion returned to him, he bolted the door, took the ceramic mallard down from the shelf and turned to the Word of God.

The next evening Lyman Mays did not have to ask and Bill Eagle did not have to reply. Silently the one led, obediently the other followed. Bill took his familiar place in the leather armchair. Lyman Mays prodded the fire with an iron poker until it sneezed a shower of sparks. He lifted a King James Bible from the desk and fingered its gold-engraved cover.

" 'And David hath said,' " Lyman Mays intoned, his voice even graver than usual, " 'Do you think that marrying the king's daughter is a matter of so little consequence that a poor man, like myself, can do it? They reported what he said, and Saul replied, Tell David this: all the king wants as the bride-price are the foreskins of one hundred Philistines.' " He turned to face Bill Eagle. "Second Samuel."

"Yes, sir," Bill Eagle said, examining the tops of his tattered shoes. "I plan on marrying your daughter."

"For God's sake, son." Lyman Mays brought the head of the poker down hard on the brick hearth. "Haven't you understood a word I've said?" Bill cleared his throat but was motioned to silence. "Saul loved that little shepherd boy named David, he wanted him to marry his daughter. But Saul knew that David had a man's pride. He knew that David wouldn't take the hand of his daughter unless he had earned it. Do you understand that? Saul gave him the *chance,* son, a chance I'm giving you right now."

"Yes, sir?" Bill stared back down at his feet. Outside the wind cackled through the treetops; the eaves of the big house creaked.

"You young folks may scoff at these sorts of traditions, Bill," Lyman Mays said, "but all I'm asking is that you make an old, God-fearing father happy. Let us say that you will bring me one hundred one-dollar bills by sunset Sunday, one week from today. One hundred foreskins and then you and Kate can be married, with my full blessings."

Bill Eagle looked up. "Mr. Mays, hundred dollars is a lot of money."

The intoxicating sap of triumph rising in his veins, Lyman Mays fixed Bill with a look of contempt. "Son," he said, "my daughter is worth many, many times more than one hundred dollars. If you're not willing to provide *that* much for her, perhaps you should think about what kind of husband you'd make." He moved his face close and whispered, "Perhaps you should think about what kind of *man* you are."

"I plan on marrying your daughter," Bill Eagle said, but Lyman Mays just roared with laughter. He had checked with McGrath to be certain: even the best stickers handled only forty or so steers a day, at a nickel a head. Supposing Bill Eagle had a few possessions to pawn, a few dollars stuffed in a sock beneath his cot—it would take him more than a full month of hard work to get the cash. Banks did not loan that sort of money to Indians. If Bill Eagle resorted to criminal means he undoubtedly would be arrested or shot dead through the heart, either of which result would serve Lyman Mays's purposes.

"Sunset," Lyman Mays called across the yard, confident that Bill

Eagle would never again set foot on it. "One hundred foreskins in one week."

But just as David had been much wiser and more stubborn than wily old Saul had imagined, so was Bill Eagle given to neither rashness nor retreat. He made no foolhardy attempt to rob a bank; nor did he surrender and flee. In the morning he reported for work at the slaughterhall, where he calmly asked the foreman to assign him two killing stalls instead of the usual one.

"What is it, boy," the foreman asked, "you needing a little extra jack?"

"One hundred dollars," Bill Eagle said.

The foreman, alerted by the boy's sullen, dangerous eyes, swallowed a laugh. He pointed silently to a pair of pens at the end of the hall. "Be needing six stalls for that," he muttered when the boy had gone.

From sunup until midnight Bill Eagle hacked away at the torrent of cattle that swept over him. His muscles knotted with a furious pain that went unrelieved by a few hours of sleep on the hard floor of the boiler room. In his dreams he continued to kill, steer after steer, waking even more exhausted than before. When, on the third day, the vessels in his eyes burst from fatigue and blocked his vision with a sticky red mucous, he used his fingertips to find the throat arteries of the steers.

"Jesus God," the foreman said on the fourth day, after he took the time to actually count the number of steers Bill Eagle had stuck and bled. "Ain't no way in hell he can keep this up."

On the fifth day, numbed by the constant pressure of lifting, heaving and cranking, Bill Eagle's fingers began to bend and snap against the heavy carcasses. No longer able to close his broken fist, he knotted his knife to his palm with a strip of cloth. Still he kept on, the tip of his knife never puncturing the rib-side of the artery or allowing blood to run back into the cage.

As word of the miraculous events spread, men from every corner of the slaughterhall gathered to watch. By the seventh day, the crowd around the killing pens was so thick that it took the foreman a number of pokes with a butt hammer to force his way to the front. "Say he's killed a thousand just this week," a legging man said, pulling at his chin thoughtfully. "Say he's got the demon in him."

It was no demon, of course, that powered Bill Eagle those last hours, his eyes swollen shut and his nose streaming blood, nor was it his love for Katie Mays. What occupied his mind and his heart solely and completely as the hour of deadline approached — leaving no room for pain or delirium — was the hateful vision of Lyman Mays's face.

At that exact moment Lyman Mays stood by the fireplace in his den, warming his hands and savoring imminent victory. But just as the crimson winter sun began to settle on the horizon's black, bristling treetops, Katie appeared in the doorway, startling him from his exhilarating meditations.

"Why aren't you attending to your guests?" he asked, frowning. "You will, I hope and expect, make your gentlemen callers feel welcome."

"Daddy," Katie said, neither retreating nor glancing away, "I don't want those boys to come courting. I want to know where Bill is."

Lyman Mays flushed with anger. He noticed, though, with a vague sense of alarm, how Katie continued to stand stubbornly before him. "Honey doll," he said, in a voice suddenly sad and kind, "I would sooner be whipped and nailed to the great wooden cross than see a single drop of pain in your gentle blue eyes."

"Where is he, Daddy?" she demanded quietly, blue eyes far from gentle.

"Last Sunday," Lyman Mays said, "I spoke with Bill. As it is my parental obligation, I brought up the question of his intentions toward you." Pulling a reluctant Katie into his arms, he rocked her stiffly back and forth. "Katie, dear heart," he cooed, "a man who isn't willing to join himself to you in holy wedlock isn't a man who deserves your tears."

But there were no tears, then or later, as Katie pulled away from her father's grasp and climbed the stairs to her room. "He'll come," she said.

And he did. Minutes before the afternoon's last light slipped down the steps of the porch, moments after Lyman Mays finished serving mugs of hot chocolate to the two burly young car salesmen he had invited over for Sunday supper, the doorbell chimed.

"I'm here for Katie," Bill Eagle said. He clutched the doorjamb for support, a crust of dark dried blood reaching from the top of his forehead to his bare, bruised-yellow chest. In the fingers of his crippled right hand he held a thick wedge of bills. "I got you your one hundred foreskins."

A full minute Lyman Mays stared at the battered and pathetic apparition. Then he smiled at Bill Eagle. "Son," he said, "I wouldn't sell my daughter to a stinking half-breed for a thousand, a *million* dollars. Now get the hell off my property."

"No," Bill Eagle said. But his resolve, his hate for Lyman Mays, had finally broken apart. The raw pain of his body, held at bay the past week, rushed back over him in a bitter wash of despair. For a moment neither he nor Lyman Mays moved, just as sticker and steer remain motionless in the long, eerie moment between hammer stroke and collapse. Then Lyman Mays nodded to his two men, on hand for just such a situation. They hurried forward and pinioned a sagging Bill Eagle between them.

"Be certain this young gentleman is aware," Lyman Mays said, "that if he ever so much as lays an eye upon my daughter, I will have him put behind bars for the rest of his life." He slammed the door with a flourish.

When Lyman Mays turned, though, to retire to the solace of his ceramic mallard, he encountered his daughter, who looked at him with eyes full of fury and rancor. He took a hesitant step toward her, his arms outstretched, but she lashed out at him, striking the bridge of his nose with such force that a hot fluid came to his eyes. Making a half-fist of his right hand, he clubbed her a blow that shook a thread of blood and saliva from her mouth.

She sank to the floor without a sound. Worried, repentant, Lyman Mays carried her gently up the stairs. He placed her in the canopied, four-poster bed, tucked the cotton-wool blanket up to her chin and kissed her on the cheek. "I am so sorry, honey doll," he whispered. Then he switched off the light, making sure to lock the bedroom door behind him.

That night, for the first time in months, Lyman Mays slept soundly. He dreamed not of the mess that had plagued him since August, but of an endless string of affluent car buyers. "How're you?" he asked, hopping with delight from customer to customer. "What can I interest you in today?" He was awakened by the clear glow of dawn slatting through the big oak tree outside his window, and by a soft but persistent tapping on his forehead.

"Yes?" Lyman Mays asked, fuzzy with the residue of pleasant dreams, puzzled by the bloodshot black eyes glaring down at him. "What can I interest you in today?"

Bill Eagle held up the index finger with which he had tapped Lyman Mays awake. "Just one foreskin," he said.

Enlightenment came quickly to Lyman Mays then, flooding the

landscape of his mind like a fast-breaking sunrise. Then, before he had a chance to wonder why the boy, crouched atop him, was contorted into such an odd position—torso twisted, right arm hidden behind his back as if he were trying to scratch a hard-to-reach place in the hollow at the base of his spine—Lyman Mays felt a tiny pinprick of cool metal through his crinkle-crepe fabric of his pajama pants, at the busy intersection of trunk and legs.

The wedding was set for the Sunday following. Katie brought down from the attic the dress in which her mother had been married—a floor-length gown of white marquisette over taffeta, fashioned with a fitted bodice, high round neckline and a full skirt trimmed with ruffles of Chantilly lace. Lyman Mays, gracious in defeat, had the parlor of Mays House festooned with wicker baskets of poinsettias, hired a pianist to play traditional selections, and even presented Bill Eagle with a hand-engraved 14-karat solid gold ring, set with seven sparkling diamonds, to give to Katie.

The day of the ceremony, however, the groom could not be found. Lyman Mays grieved publicly for his daughter's broken heart and confided privately to friends that, given the boy's heritage, he was not surprised Bill Eagle had run off. Most sensible people in town knew what was what, though, particularly when the newspaper reported that a body, beaten and bloated past recognition, had washed ashore at Belle Isle Lake. Still, Katie, who discovered over the Christmas holidays that she was carrying a child, never wavered from the unshakable belief that Bill was alive, that he would eventually return for her.

Not long after the aborted wedding, during the first spring thaw, Lyman Mays found a piece of brown packing paper in his mailbox. Scrawled in a crude hand were these words:

" 'And they found the stone rolled away from the sepulchre.' Luke."

Almost certain that his daughter was responsible for the note, Lyman Mays nevertheless had the big oak tree outside his bedroom window chopped down and bought a pistol to place on his nightstand. And never again, for the rest of his long life, could he bring himself to sleep on his back.

Waiting for Mr. Kim

Carol Roh-Spaulding

WHEN GRACIE KANG'S elder twin sisters reached the age of eighteen, they went down to the Alameda County Shipyards and got jobs piecing battleships together for the U.S. Navy. This was the place to find a husband in 1945, if a girl was doing her own looking. They were Americans, after all, and they were of age. Her sisters caught the bus down to the waterfront every day and brought home their paychecks every two weeks. At night, they went out with their girlfriends, meeting boys at the cinema or the drugstore, as long as it was outside of Chinatown.

Gracie's parents would never have thought it was husbands they were after. Girls didn't choose what they were given. But the end of the war distracted everybody. While Mr. Kang tried to keep up with the papers and Mrs. Kang tried to keep up with the laundry, Sung-Sook slipped away one day with a black welder enrolled in the police academy and Sung-Ohk took off with a Chinatown nightclub singer from L.A. with a sister in the movies.

Escaped. Gracie had watched from the doorway that morning as Sung-Sook pulled on her good slip in front of the vanity, lifted her hair, breathed in long and slow. Her eyes came open, she saw Gracie's reflection. "Comeer," she said. "You never say good-bye." She kissed Gracie between the eyes. Gracie had only shrugged: "See you." Then Sung-Ohk from the bathroom: "This family runs a laundry, so where's all the goddamn towels?"

When the girls didn't come home, the lipstick and rouge wiped off their faces, to fold the four o'clock sheets, she understood what was what. On the vanity in the girls' room she found a white paper bell with sugar sprinkles. In silver letters, it read:

CALL TODAY!
MARRY TODAY!
YOUR WEDDING! YOUR WAY!
EIGHTEEN OR OVER?
WE WON'T SAY NAY!
(MAY BORROW VEIL AND BOUQUET)

As simple as having your hair done. Gracie sat at the vanity, thinking of the thousand spirits of the household her mother was always ticking off like a grocery list—spirit of the lamp, the clock, the ashtray. Spirit in the seat of your chair. Spirit of the stove, the closet, the broom, the shoes. Spirit of the breeze in the room, the Frigidaire. Gracie had always been willing to believe in them; she only needed something substantial to go on. Now, in her sisters' room, she felt that the spirits had been there, had moved on, to other inhabited rooms.

Those girls had escaped Thursday evenings with the old *chong-gak*s, who waited effortlessly for her father to give the girls away. No more sitting, knees together, in white blouses and circle skirts, with gritted smiles. Now Gracie would sit, the only girl, while her father made chitchat with Mr. Han and Mr. Kim. Number three daughter, much younger, the dutiful one, wouldn't run away. If her mother had had the say, the girls would have given their parents grandchildren by now. But she didn't have the say, and her father smiled his pleasant, slightly anxious smile at the *chong-gak*s and never ever brought up payment.

He was the one paying now. No one got dinner that night. Pots flew, plates rattled in the cabinets, the stove rumbled in the corner, pictures slid, clanked, tinkled. "Now we'll have a nigger for a grandson and a chink for a son-in-law, Mr. Kang!" her mother shouted. She cursed Korean, but had a gift for American slurs, translating the letter found taped to the laundry boiler into the horrors of marrying for love.

Gracie and Little Gene pressed themselves against the wall, squeezed around the Frigidaire, sidled to the staircase. They sat and backed up one step at a time, away from the stabs and swishes of the broom. "Or didn't you want Korean grandchildren, Mr. Kang? You're the one who let them fall into American love. Could I help it there aren't any good *chong-gak*s around? Thought we'd pack the girls off to Hawaii where the young ones are? Ha. I'd like to see the missionaries pay for that!"

Their father came into view below. Hurried, but with his usual dignity, he ducked and swerved as necessary. Silently, solemnly, he made for the closet, opened the door, and stepped in among the coats. The blows from first the bristled then the butted end of the broom came down upon the door.

Little Gene whispered, "I'm going outside."

"Fine," Gracie told him. "If you can make it to the door."

"Think I can't manage the window? I land in the trash bin, pretty soft!"

Gracie told him, "Bring me back a cigarette, then," and he left her there. A year younger than she and not very big for thirteen, he was still number one son. Gracie stuck her fingers in her mouth all the way to the knuckle, clamped down hard.

She chopped cabbage, scrubbed the bathhouses, washed and pressed and folded linen and laundry, dreaming up lives for her sisters. From their talk and their magazines, she knew how it should go. Sung-Sook stretched out by the pool in a leopard-print bathing suit with pointy bra cups and sipped colored drinks from thin glasses, leaving a pink surprise of lips at the rim. Somebody else served them, fetched them, cleaned them. Her husband shot cardboard men through the heart and came home to barbecue T-bones. Every night they held hands at the double feature. Sung-Ohk slipped into a tight Chinese-doll dress and jeweled cat-eyes, sang to smoky crowds of white people from out of town. Her lips grazed the mike as she whispered, "Thank you, kind people, thank you." In the second act, her husband, in a tux, dipped her, spun her, with slant-eyed-Gene-Kelly-opium flair. All the white people craned their necks and saw that Oriental women could have good legs.

They left Gracie and her mother with all the work. At first, her father tried to help out. He locked up the barbershop at lunch, crossed the street, passed through the kitchen, and stepped into Hell, as they called it. But her mother snapped down the pants press when she saw him and from a blur of steam shouted, "Fool for love! I'm warning you to get out of here, Mr. Kang!"

She bowed her head at the market now. She had stopped going to church. Lost face, it was called. And there was the worry of it. No one knew these men who took the girls away. Maybe one was an opium dealer and the other was a pimp. Maybe those girls were in for big disappointment, even danger. Her father twisted his hands, helpless and silent in the evenings. Her mother clanked the dishes into the sink, banged the washers shut, punched the buttons with her fists, helpless, too.

It was true he was a fool for love, as far as Gracie could tell. Her mother slapped at his hands when he came up behind her at the chopping board to kiss her hair—pretty brave, considering that knife. When her mother tried to walk behind him in the street, he stopped and tried to take her hand. Gracie and her mother were always nearly missing buses because she'd say, "Go on, Mr. Kang. We're coming," and they'd stay behind as she cleaned out her purse or took forever with her coat, just to have it the way she had learned it, her husband a few paces ahead, women behind. Maybe the girls would never have gotten away if he'd been firm about marriage, strict about love.

Where her parents were from, shamans could chase out the demon spirits from dogs, cows, rooms, people. Maybe her father had had the fool chased out of him, because when Thursday came around, he sat in the good chair with the Bible open on his knees, and Gracie sat beside him, waiting. Life was going to go on without her sisters. Her life. Gracie watched her father for lingering signs of foolishness. Above the donated piano, the cuckoo in the clock popped out seven times. As always, her father looked up with a satisfied air. He loved that bird. Her mother believed there was a spirit in the wooden box. The spirit was saying it was time.

Little Gene was free in the streets with that gang of Chinese boys. She waited for her cigarette and his stories—right now, he might be breaking into the high school, popping open the Coca-Cola machine, busting up some lockers. There weren't any Jap boys left to beat up on, and they stayed away from the mostly black neighborhoods or they'd get beat up themselves. Gracie sat with her hands clasped at her knees, worrying about him, admiring him a little.

First came the tap-tap of the missionary ladies from the United Methodist Church. Their hats looked like squat birds' nests through the crushed-ice window. Every Thursday, they seemed to have taken such pains with their dresses and hats and shoes, Gracie couldn't think how they had lasted in the mountain villages of Pyongyang province.

She had never been there herself, or been to mountains at all, but she knew there were tigers in Pyongyang.

Her father rose and assumed his visitors smile. "Everyone will be too polite to mention the girls, Gracie," he told her. That was the only thing at all he said about them to her.

The ladies stepped in, chins pecking. One bore a frosted cake, the other thrust forward a box of canned goods. American apologies. As though the girls had died, Gracie thought. Her father stiffened, but kept his smile.

"We think it's wonderful about the war," the cake lady began.

"Praise be to God that we've stopped the Japanese," the Spam lady went on. They looked at one another.

"The *Japanese* Japanese," said the second. She paused. "And we are so sorry about your country, Mr. Kang."

"But this is your country now," said the first.

Her father eased them onto more conversational subjects. They smiled, heads tilted, as Gracie pressed out "Greensleeves," "Colonial Days," "Jesus, We Greet Thee," on the piano. And at half past the hour, they were up and on their way out, accepting jars of *kimch'i* from her mother with wrinkle-nosed smiles.

The barbershop customers did not come by. Mr. Woo from the bakery and Mr. and Mrs. Lim from the Hunan restaurant stayed away. All the Chinese and Koreans knew about saving face. Except the *chonggaks,* who knew better, surely, but arrived like clockwork anyway, a black blur and a white blur at the window. They always shuffled their feet elaborately on the doorstep before knocking, and her father used to say, "That's very Korean," to Sung-Sook and Sung-Ohk, who didn't bother to fluff their hair or straighten their blouses for the visitors. They used to moan, "Here come the old goats. Failure One and Failure Two." Her father only shushed them, saying, "Respect, daughters, respect." Gracie saw that he could have done better than that if he really expected the girls to marry these men, but after all, the girls were right. Probably her father could see that. They were failures. No families, even at their age. Little money, odd jobs, wasted lives. A week before, they had been only a couple of nuisances who brought her sticks of Beechnut gum and seemed never to fathom her sisters' hostility. They were that stupid, and now they were back. One Korean girl was as good as any other.

Gracie could actually tolerate Mr. Han. He had been clean and trim in his black suit, pressed shirt, and straight tie every Thursday evening since her sisters had turned sixteen. He was a tall, hesitant man with most of his hair, surprisingly good teeth, and little wire glasses so tight over his nose that the lenses steamed up when he was nervous. Everyone knew he had preferred Sung-Ohk, whose kindest remark to him ever was that he looked exactly like the Chinese servant in a Hollywood movie. He always perched on the piano bench as though he didn't mean to stay long, and he mopped his brow when Sung-Ohk glared at him. But he never pulled Gracie onto his lap to kiss her and pat her, and he never, as the girls called it, licked with his eyes.

He left that to Mr. Kim. Mr. Kim in the same white suit, white shirt, white tie, and white shoes which had never really been white, but always the color of pale urine. His teeth were brown from too much tea and sugar and opium. This wasn't her hateful imagination. She had washed his shirts ever since she'd started working. She knew the armpit stains that spread like an infection when she tried to soak them. The hairs and smudges of ash and something like pus in his sheets. She could smell his laundry even before she saw the ticket. His breath stank, too, like herring.

Mr. Kim found everything amusing. "It's been too warm, hasn't it, Mr. Kang?" he said by way of greeting. Then he chuckled, "I'm afraid our friend Mr. Han is almost done in by it."

"Yes, let me get you some iced tea," her father announced. "Mrs. Kang!"

Mr. Kim chuckled again at his companion. "Maybe his heart is suffering. Nearly sixty, you know. Poor soul. He's got a few years on me, anyway, haven't you, old man?"

Mr. Han lowered himself on the piano bench. "Yes, it's been too warm, too much for me."

His companion laughed like one above that kind of weakness. Then he said, "And how is Miss Kang? She's looking very well. She seems to be growing."

Gracie hunched her shoulders, looked anywhere but at him.

"Yes, she's growing," her father answered carefully. "She's still a child." The men smiled at each other with a lot of teeth showing, but their eyes were watchful. "Of course, she's a little lonesome nowadays," her father continued. Mr. Kim eyed him, then he seemed to catch on and slapped his knee—good joke. Mr. Han squinted in some sort of pain.

If Mr. Kim hadn't been in America even longer than her father had, with nothing to show for it but a rented room above the barbershop, then he might have been able to say, "What about this one, Mr. Kang? Are you planning to let her get away, too?" But if he'd had something to show for his twenty or so years in America, he wouldn't be sitting in her father's house and she wouldn't be waiting to be his bride.

Then from the piano bench: "Lonesome, Miss Kang?" Everybody looked. Mr. Han blinked, startled at the attention. He quietly repeated, "Have you, too, been lonesome?" Gracie looked down at her hands. Her father was supposed to answer, let him answer. At that moment, her mother entered, head bowed over the tea tray. Gracie could hear the spirit working in the cuckoo clock.

Her father had told her once that he'd picked cotton and grapes with the Mexicans in the Salinas Valley, and it got so hot you could fry meat on the railroad ties. But that was nothing compared to the sticky summers in Pyongyang, where the stench of human manure brought the bile to your throat. That was why he loved Oakland, he said, where the ocean breeze cleaned you out. It reminded him of his childhood visits to Pusan Harbor, when he'd traveled to visit his father who had been forced into the service of the Japanese. And it reminded him of the day he sailed back from America for his bride.

Bright days, fresh wind. Gracie imagined the women who had waited for the husbands who had never returned. Those women lived in fear, her mother had said. They were no good to marry if the men didn't come back, or if they did return but had no property, they had no legal status in America and no prospects in Korea. Plenty of the women did away with themselves, or their families sold them as concubines. "You think I'm lying?" she told Gracie. "I waited ten years for him. People didn't believe the letters he sent after a while. My family started talking about what to do with me, because I had other sisters waiting to marry, only I was the oldest and they had to get rid of me first!"

Gracie imagined those women, their hands tucked neatly in their bright sleeves, their smooth hair and ancient faces looking out over the water from high rooms. And she thought of Mr. Han gazing from his window out over the alley and between skyscrapers and telephone poles to his glimpse of the San Francisco Bay. Where he was, the sky was black, starless in the city. Where she was, the sun rose, a brisk, hopeful morning.

On a morning like that, Gracie took the sheets and laundry across the street and up to the rented rooms. Usually the *chong-gaks* had coffee and a bun at the bakery and then strolled around the lake, but Gracie always knocked and set the boxes down.

Mr. Han's door inched open under her knuckles. The breeze in the bright room, the sterile light of morning in there, the cord rattling at the blinds. Something invisible crept out from the slit in the door and was with her in the hall.

"Mr. Han? Just your laundry, Mr. Han." Spirits of memory—she and Little Gene climbing onto his knees, reaching into his pockets for malted milk balls or sticks of gum. "Where are *your* children?" they'd asked. "Where is your stove? Where is your sink? Where is your mirror?" Mr. Han had always smiled, as though he were only hiding the things they named, could make them appear whenever he wanted.

She pushed the door open, and the spirits of memory mingled with the spirits of longing and desire. The bulb of the bare nightlight buzzed, like a recollection in a head full of ideas. Mr. Han lay half on, half off the bed. One shoe pressed firmly on the floor, as though half of him had had somewhere to go. The glasses dangled from the metal bed frame. That was where his head was, pressed against the bars. His eyes were rolled back, huge and amazed, toward the window. And at his throat, a stripe of beaded red, the thin lips of flesh puckering slightly, like the edges of a rose.

Spirits scuttered along the walls, swirled upwards, twisting in their airy, familiar paths. They pressed against the ceiling. They watched her in the corner. His spirit was near, she felt, in the white field of his pillow. Or in the curtains that puffed and lifted at the sill like a girl's skirt in the wind.

Gracie squatted and peered under the bed. The gleam there was a thing she had known all of her life, a razor from the barbershop. Clean, almost no blood, like his throat. She knew it was loss of air, not loss of blood, that did it. She knew because she'd heard about it before. Two or three of the neighborhood Japs had done the same, when they found that everything they thought they owned they no longer had a right to. They'd had three days to sell what they could and go. She didn't know where. She only knew that her father had been able to buy the barbershop and the bathhouse because of it.

Wind swelled in the hall, with the spirits of car horns, telephone wires, shop signs, traffic lights, and a siren, not for him. They were present at the new death—curious, laughing, implacable. They sucked the door shut. Gracie started. "Leaving now," she announced. "Mr.

Han," she whispered to the *chong-gak*. Then she remembered he'd become part of something else, something weightless, invisible, near. She said it louder. "Mr. Han. I'm sorry for you, Mr. Han."

Mr. Kim ate with the Kangs that afternoon, after the ambulances had gone, and again in the evening. His fingers trembled. He lowered his head to the rice, unable to lift it to his mouth, scraping feebly with his chopsticks. Of the death he had one thing to say, which he couldn't stop saying: "I walked alone this morning. Why did I decide to walk alone, of all mornings?"

Mrs. Kang muttered guesses about what to do next, not about the body itself or the police inquiry or who was responsible for his room and his things, but about how best to give peace to the spirit of the *chong-gak,* who might otherwise torment the rest of their days. He didn't have a family of his own to torment. She'd prepared a plate of meat and rice and *kimch'i,* saying, "Where do I *put* this?"

Little Gene, jealous that Gracie had found the body and he hadn't, offered, "How 'bout on the sill? Then he can float by whenever. Or in his room? I'll stay in there all night and watch for him." Then he patted his stomach. "Or how 'bout right here?"

"Damn," her mother went on. "I wish now I'd paid more attention to the shamans. But we stayed away from those women unless we needed them. My family was afraid I'd get the call because I was sickly and talked in my sleep, and we have particularly restless ancestors. But I didn't have it in me. Was it food every day for a month or every month for a year? What a mystery. Now we'll have spirits till we all die."

"Girls shouldn't be shamans, anyway," Little Gene announced. "Imagine Gracie chasing spirits away."

Asshole, Gracie mouthed. Little Gene flipped her off. None of the adults understood the sign.

"You don't chase them, honey," Gracie's mother said to her. "You feed them and pay them and talk to them."

"Tell *him,*" Gracie answered. "He's the one who brought it up."

"Feed everyone who's here first," Little Gene suggested. Gracie flipped him off in return.

"What's that you're doing with your fingers, Gracie?" he shot back. She put her finger to her lips and pointed at her father. His eyes were closed. He kept them that way, head bowed, lips moving.

"Fine," her mother announced. "Let's do Christian, Mr. Kang. It's simpler, as far as I'm concerned."

Mr. Kim lifted his head from his rice bowl, looking very old.

Her mother eyed him sternly. "Cheaper, too."

That night Gracie lay in her bed by the open window. Where was his spirit now? In heaven, at God's side? Or restlessly feeding on *bulgogi* and turnips in his room? Or somewhere else entirely, or nowhere at all? Please God or Thousand Spirits, she prayed. Let me marry for love. Please say I'm not waiting for Mr. Kim. It's fine with me if I'm a *chun-yo* forever.

They held a small service at the Korean United Methodist Church. Her father stood up and said a little about the hard life of a *chong-gak* in America, the loneliness of these men, the difficulties for Oriental immigrants. Gracie felt proud of him, though he was less convincing about heaven. No one even knew for certain if Mr. Han had converted.

Mr. Kim sat in white beside Gracie. "Thy kingdom come," he murmured, "thy will be done." And he reached out and took her hand, looking straight ahead to her father. His hand was moist. She could smell him.

"And forgive us our trespasses," she prayed.

"As we forgive those who trespass against us," he continued, and he squeezed her hand with the surety of possession, though her fingers slipped in his palm.

Gracie never got to the "amen." Instead, she leaned into his side, tilted her face to his cheek, and brought her lips to his ear. "You dirty old bastard," she whispered. Then she snatched her hand back and kept her head bowed, trembling. She wished she could pray that he would die, too, if it was the only way. From the corner of her eye, she could see Mr. Kim's offended hand held open on his knee. Sweat glistened in the creases of his palm. She would never be able to look into his eyes again. For a moment, pity and disgust swept through her. Then, as the congregation stood, she said her own prayer. It went, Please oh please oh please.

Little Gene stuck his head in the laundry room. "Hey, you! Mrs. Kim!"

Gracie flung a folded pillowcase at him.

"Whew. Step out of that hellhole for a minute. I've got something to show you."

He slid a cigarette from behind his ear and they went out the alley-side steps and shared it by the trash bin. "The day they give you away, I'll have this right under your window, see? I'll even stuff it with newspapers so you'll land easy."

"Nowhere to run," Gracie told him. It was the name of a movie they'd seen.

"Isn't Hollywood someplace? Isn't Mexico someplace?"

Gracie laughed out loud. "You coming?"

" 'Course I am. Mama's spirit crap is getting on my nerves."

Gracie shrugged. "You're too little to run away. Why should I need help from someone as little as you?"

Little Gene stood on tiptoe and sneered into her face. "Because I'm a boy." Then he grinned and exhaled smoke through his nose and the sides of his mouth.

"Dragon-breath," she called him.

"Come on, Mrs. Kim. This way." They scrambled up the steps, took the staircase to the hall, then stepped through the door that led down again to the ground floor through an unlit passage to the old opium den. It was nothing but a storage room for old washers now, a hot box with a ceiling two stories above them. It baked, winter or summer, because it shared a wall with the boiler.

They'd hid there when they were little, playing hide-and-seek or creating stories about the opium dealers and the man who was supposed to have hung himself in there. They could never figure out where he might have hung himself from since the ceiling was so high and the walls so bare. They looked up in awe. Once, Little Gene thought he'd be clever, and he shut himself in the dryer. Gracie couldn't find him for the longest time, but when she came back for a second look, the round window was steamed up and he wasn't making any noise. She pulled him out. He was grinning, eyes vacant. "You stupid dumb stupid stupid kid."

Little Gene felt for the bulb on the wall, pulled the chain. Now the old dryer was somehow on its side. There were two busted washers and a cane chair. The air was secret, heavy with dust and heat. Gracie felt along the walls for loose bricks, pulled one out, felt around inside like they used to do, looking for stray nuggets or anything else that might have been hidden and forgotten by the Chinese who had lived there before.

Little Gene got on his hands and knees. "Lookit." He eased out a brick flush with the floor. "Lookit," he said again.

Gracie crouched. He crawled back to make way for her, then pushed her head down. "Down there, in the basement."

She saw dim, natural light, blackened redwood, steam-stained. The bathhouse. "So what? I clean 'em every day of my life."

"Just wait," he said.

Then the white blade of a man's back rose into view. Little Gene's hand was a spider up and down her side. "See him, Mrs. Kim? Bet you can't wait."

The back lowered, rose, lowered again, unevenly, painfully. She saw hair slicked back in seaweed streaks, tea-colored splotches on his back, the skin damp and speckled like the belly of a fish. Little Gene's hand was a spider again at her neck. Gracie slapped at him, crouched, looked again. "What the hell's he doing? Rocking himself?"

Little Gene only giggled nervously.

The eyes of Mr. Kim stared toward the thousand spirits, his mouth hung open. Then those eyes rolled back in his head, pupil-less, white, and still. "God, is he dying?" Gracie asked. If she moved a muscle, she would burst. "Is he dying?" she asked again. "Don't touch me," she told her brother, who was impatient with spidery hands.

Little Gene rolled his eyes. "That's all we need. He's not dying, stupid. Unless he dies every day." Life in a dim bathhouse, Gracie thought. Deaths in bright rooms.

A door slammed hard on the other side of the wall. Her mother cursed, called her name. Little Gene giggled and did the stroking motion at his crotch, then Gracie scrambled to her knees and pulled him up with her. He grabbed for the chain on the bulb. Dark. "Don't scream," he giggled.

"Gracie! Damn you!" her mother called.

Then his hands flew to her, one at her shoulder, the other, oily and sweet, cupping her open mouth.

A letter arrived the next Thursday. Sung-Sook had used her head and addressed it to the barbershop. Her father brought it up to her in the evening. Gracie was at her window, leaning out, watching the sky begin to gather color. "For 'Miss Gracie Kang,' " he read. " 'Care of Mr. Park A. Kang.' " There was no return address. The paper smelled faintly like roses.

With his eyes, her father pleaded for news of them. He said, "You look like you're waiting for someone."

She shrugged. "It's Thursday." She wanted him to leave her alone until it was time to go downstairs and sit with Mr. Kim. Instead, he came to the window and looked out with her. "Where's your brother?"

"Wherever he feels like being."

He only smiled. Then he told her, "Mr. Kim has given me money. A lot of money."

She drew herself up. She couldn't look at him. "What money?"

"It's for a ticket, Gracie. He wants me to purchase him a ticket to Pusan and arrange some papers for him."

"Alone?" she asked.

"Alone."

She smiled out at the street, but asked again, "What money?"

Her father answered, "He will be happy to have a chance to tell you good-bye." And he left her at the window.

His money, she knew. Her father's. She kept still at the window. With her eyes closed, she saw farther than she had ever seen. "Did you hear that?" she said out loud, in case any spirits, celestial or domestic, were listening.

Then she carefully opened her letter. There was a piece of pale, gauzy paper, and a couple of photographs — a good thing, since the girls had stolen a bunch of family snapshots when they left.

> Dear Gracie,
>
> I hope they let you see this. You're going to be an auntie now. Sung-Ohk's the lucky one, but me and El are really trying. For a baby, you know. That's El in his rookie uniform and I'm in my wedding dress. We're at the Forbidden City, the club in San Francisco. Louie, that's Sung-Ohk's husband, got us in free on our wedding night. The other picture is of Louie and Sung-Ohk at Newport Beach. Isn't he handsome? Like El. We all live near the beach, ten minutes by freeway.
>
> You'd love it here, but I guess you'd love it anywhere but Oakland. How are the old creeps, anyway? Maybe they'll die before Mom and Dad give you away, ha-ha.
>
> Be good. Don't worry. We're going to figure something out. El says you can stay with us. Sung-Ohk sends her love. I do, too.

The letter fluttered in her hand in the window. She pulled open the drawer at her bedside table, folded the paper neatly back in its creases, and set it inside. Then she took out the only thing her sisters had left behind, the sugar-sprinkled, silver-lettered, instant-ceremony marriage advertisement. Gracie breathed in deeply, as her sister had done with the hope of her new life—as, perhaps, Mr. Han had done, with the hope of his release. Somewhere near, Little Gene laughed out loud in the street. Her mother banged dinner into the oven. Her father waited below, his Bible open on his knees, to greet the missionary ladies, to say goodbye to Mr. Kim. Below, a white, slow figure stepped from a door and headed across the street. Again, she breathed in. And what she took in was her own. Not everything had a name.

Bad Company

Tess Gallagher

THE WIDOW DROVE into the cemetery, parked near the mausoleum, and got out with her flowers. The next day was Memorial Day, and the cemetery would be thronged with people. Entire families would arrive to bring flowers to the graves of their loved ones. Tiny American flags would decorate the graves of the veterans. But today the cemetery was still and deserted.

When she reached her husband's grave she saw that someone had been there before her. The little metal vase affixed to the headstone was crammed with daffodils and dandelions. But whoever had put them there hadn't known the difference between a flower and a weed. She put her flowers down on the flat gravestone and stared at the unsightly wad of flowers. Only a man could have thrown together such a bouquet, she thought.

She raised her hand to her brow and looked around. A short distance away she saw a girl stretched out next to a grave. She hadn't seen her at first because the girl had not been standing. The girl lay propped on one elbow so she could look down at the gravestone next to her. When the widow walked toward her, the girl did not lift her head or move. Then the widow saw her pluck a blade of grass and touch it to her lips before she let it fall. The widow's shadow fell across the girl, and the girl looked up.

"Did you happen to see anyone at that grave over yonder?" the widow asked.

The girl raised herself into a sitting position. She looked at the widow, but didn't say anything.

She's crazy, the widow thought, or else she can't talk. She regretted having spoken to the girl at all. Then the girl stood up and touched her hands together.

"There was a man. About an hour ago," the girl said. "He could of been to that grave."

"It's my husband," the widow said. "His grave. But I don't know who could have left those flowers."

The widow noticed that the grave next to the girl had no flowers. She wondered at this, that anyone would come to a grave and then leave nothing behind. At this time of day the shadows of the evergreens at the near end of the graveyard crept gradually across the grass. It sent a chill through her shoulders. She drew her sweater together at the neck and folded her arms.

"He didn't stay long," the girl volunteered. And then she smiled. The widow thought it was a nice thing after all to speak to this stranger and to be answered courteously in this sorrowful place.

"He was over at the mausoleum too," the girl said.

The widow thought hard who it might be. She only knew one person buried in the mausoleum. He had been dead ten years now and only one member of his family still survived.

"It must have been Lloyd Medly," the widow said. "His brother, Homer, is over there in the mausoleum. His ashes, anyway. They grew up with my husband and me, those boys." The widow had spoken to Lloyd just last week on the telephone. He was in the habit of calling up every few weeks to see how she was doing. "Homer's on my mind a lot," he'd said to her when they'd last talked.

"I don't know anybody in the mausoleum," the girl said. The widow looked down and saw a little white cross engraved over the name on the stone. There were some military designations she didn't understand and, below the name, the dates 1914–1967.

"Nineteen fourteen! That's the year I was born," the widow said, as if surprised that anyone born in that year had already passed on. For a moment it seemed as if she and the one lying there in the ground had briefly touched lives.

"I can barely remember him," the girl said. "But when I stay here a while, things come back to me." She was a pretty girl with high Indian cheekbones. The widow noticed the way her hips went straight down from her waist. She had slow, black eyes, and the widow guessed her to be in her late twenties.

"I can't remember what Homer looked like," the widow said. "But he could yodel like nobody's business. Yodeling had just come in." She thought of Lloyd and how he said he and Arby, another brother, had been lucky to get out of California alive after they'd gone there to bring Homer's body back. Homer had been found dead in a fleabag hotel with Lloyd's phone number in his shirt pocket. "They'd as soon knock you in the head in them places as to look at you," Lloyd said afterwards.

"He was a street wino," the widow said to the girl "But he was a beautiful yodeler. And he could play the guitar too."

"I think my dad used to whistle," the girl said. "I think I remember him whistling." She gazed toward the grove of trees, then across the street to the flat-topped elementary school building. No one was coming in or going out of the building. It occurred to the widow that she had been to the cemetery hundreds of times and had never once seen any children coming to or going from the school. But she knew they did, as surely as she knew that the people buried under the ground had once walked the earth, eaten meals, and answered to their names. She knew this as surely as she knew Homer Medly had been a beautiful yodeler.

"If I died tomorrow, I wonder what my little girls would remember," the girl said suddenly. The widow didn't know what to say to this so she didn't say anything. After a moment the girl said, "I'd like to start bringing my girls with me out here, but I hate to see kids run over the graves."

"I know what you mean," the widow said. But then she thought of her own father. Something he had said when he'd refused to be buried in the big county cemetery back home in Arkansas. "I want to be close enough to home that my grandkids can trample on my grave if they want to." But as it turned out, everyone had moved away, and it hadn't mattered where he was buried.

"I always try to walk at the foot of the graves," the girl said. "But sometimes I forget." She put her hands into the hip pockets of her jeans and looked toward the mausoleum. "Those ones that are ashes, they don't have to worry," she said. She took her hands out of her pockets and sat down again on the grass next to the grave. "Nobody walks over them," she said. "I guess they just sit forever in those little cups."

The widow thought of Homer's remains being contained in a little

cup. She was glad she'd never have to see it. Then she remembered that
Lloyd had said he and his brother had wanted to bring Homer's body
back, but there was too much red tape. And then there was the ex-
pense. So they'd had him cremated and, between them, they'd taken
turns on the plane holding the box with his ashes in it until they got
home. Remembering this made the widow want to say a few words
about Homer. She'd met Homer in her girlhood at nearly the same
time she'd met her husband. For a moment, the thought came to her
that Homer could have been her husband. But just as quickly she dismissed the thought. What had happened to Homer had made a deep
unsettling impression on her. She and Lloyd had talked about it once
when they'd spoken in the supermarket. Lloyd had shaken his head
and said, "Homer could of been something. He just fell in with the
wrong company." And then he hadn't said anything else.

The girl brushed at something on the headstone. "My father was
killed in an accident," she said. "We'd all been in swimming and then
we kids went to the cabin to nap. My mother woke us up, crying.
'Your daddy's drowned,' she said. This drunk guy tried to swim the
river and when my father tried to save him, the man pulled him down.
'Your daddy's drowned,' she kept saying. But you don't understand
things when you're a kid," the girl said. "And you don't understand
things later either."

The widow was struck by this. She touched her teeth against her
bottom lip, then ran her tongue over the lip. She didn't know what to
say, so she said: "There's Homer that lived through the Second World
War and then died in California a pure alcoholic." The widow shook
her head. She didn't understand any of it.

The girl stretched out on the ground once more and made herself
comfortable. She looked up at the widow and nodded once. The
widow felt the girl slipping away into a reverie, into some place she
couldn't follow, and she wanted to say something to hold her back.
But all she could think of was Homer Medly. She couldn't feature why
she couldn't get Homer off her mind. She wanted to tell the girl everything that was important to know about Homer Medly. How he had
fallen into bad company in the person of Lester Yates, a boy who had
molested a young girl and been sent to the penitentiary. How Beulah
Looney had gone to the horse races in Santa Rosa, California, in 1935
and brought back word that Homer was married, and to a fine-
looking woman! But the woman didn't live very long with Homer. He

got drunk and hammered the headlights of their car, then threatened to bite off her nose.

But the widow didn't tell the girl any of this. She couldn't. Besides, the girl looked to be half-asleep. The widow looked down at the girl and it seemed the most natural thing in the world for the girl to be lying there alongside her father's grave. Then the girl raised up on one elbow.

"I came out here the day of my divorce," the girl said. "And then I kept coming out here. One time I lay down and fell asleep," she said. "The caretaker came over and asked me was I all right. Sure, I said. I'm all right." The girl laughed softly and tossed her black hair over her shoulder. "Fact is, I don't know if I was all right. I been coming here trying to figure things out. If my dad was alive I'd ask him what was going to become of me and my girls. There's another man ready to step in and take up where my husband left off. But even if a man runs out on you it's no comfort just to pick up with the next one that comes around. I got to do better," the girl said. "I got to think of my girls, but I got to think of me too."

The widow felt she'd listened in on something important, and she wished she knew what to say to the girl for comfort. She and her husband hadn't been able to have children and, like so much of her life, she'd reconciled herself to it and never looked back. But now she could imagine having a daughter to talk with and to advise. Someone she could help in a difficult time. She felt she'd missed something precious and that she had nothing to offer the girl except to stand there and listen. Since her husband's death nearly a year ago it seemed that she seldom did more than exchange a few words with people. And here she was telling a stranger about Homer and listening to the girl tell her things back. Her memory of Homer seemed to insist on being told, and though the widow didn't understand why this should be, she felt she'd had a part in it. She didn't want this meeting to end until she'd said what she had to say.

The shadows from the stand of trees had darkened the portion of the cemetery that lay in front of the school building. The girl tilted her head toward the place her father was lying, and the widow thought she might be praying—or about to pray.

"Well, I've got peonies to put out," the widow said, and she moved back a few steps. But the girl did not acknowledge her leaving. The widow waited a minute, then turned and headed back across the graves. The ground felt softer than it had when she'd approached the girl, and she couldn't help thinking that each time she put her foot down she had stepped on someone.

She felt relieved when she reached her husband's grave. She stood on the grave as if there at least she had a right to do as she pleased. The grave was like a green island in the midst of other green islands. Then she heard a car start up. She turned to look for the girl, but the girl was no longer there. The girl was gone. Just then the widow saw a little red car head out of the cemetery.

The widow took hold of her flowers and began to fit them into a vase next to the flowers she guessed must be from Lloyd. Once, a few weeks earlier, Lloyd had stopped at her house on the way to the cemetery and she'd given him some flowers to take to Homer and some for her husband. "They were roarers, those two," Lloyd had said as she'd made up the two bouquets. She thought of her husband again. He'd been a drinker like Homer and, except for having married her, he might have fallen in with bad company and ended the way Homer had.

She took her watering can and walked toward the spigot that stood near the mausoleum. She bent down and ran water into the can as she rested her eyes on the mausoleum. Bad company, she thought. And it occurred to her that her husband had been *her* bad company for all those years. And when he hadn't been bad company, he'd been no company at all to her. She listened to the water run into the metal can and wondered what had saved her from being pulled down by the likes of such a man, even as Lester Yates had pulled Homer Medly down.

She let herself recall the time her husband had flown into a rage after a drinking bout and accused her of sleeping around, even though every night of their married life she'd slept nowhere but in the same bed with him. He'd taken her set of china cups out onto the sidewalk and smashed them with the whole neighborhood looking on. From then on they'd passed their evenings in silence. She would knit and he would look after the fire and smoke cigarettes. It was a life to be reckoned with, and God knows she'd done the best she could. But the memory of those long, silent evenings struck at her heart now, and she wished she could go back to that time and speak to her husband. She knew there were old couples who lived differently, couples who took walks together or played checkers or cards together in the evenings. And then it came to her that she had been bad company to him, had even denied him her company, going and coming from the house with barely a nod in his direction, putting his meals on the table out of duty alone, keeping house like a jailer. The idea startled and pained her, especially when she remembered how his illness had come on him until, in the last months, he was docile and then finally helpless near the end. What had she given him? What had she done for him? She could answer only that she had been there—like an implement, a shovel or a hoe, maybe. A lifetime of robbery! she thought. Then she understood that it was herself she had robbed as much as her husband. And there was no way now to get it back.

The water was running over the sides of the can, and she turned off the spigot. She picked up the watering can and stood next to the mausoleum and stared at it as if someone had suddenly thrown an obstacle in her pathway. She couldn't feature why anyone would want to be put into such a place when they died. The front was faced with rough stones and one wall was mostly glass so that visitors could peer inside. The widow had tried the door to this place once, but it was locked. She supposed the relatives had keys, or else they were let in by the caretaker. Homer was situated along the wall on the outside of the mausoleum. Thinking of Homer made her glad her husband hadn't ended up on the wall of the mausoleum as a pile of ashes. There was that to be thankful for.

When she reached his grave she poured water into the vase and then stared at the bronze name plate where enough space had been left for her own name and dates.

She remembered the day she and her husband had quarreled about where to buy their burial plots. Her husband had said he wasn't about to be buried any place that was likely to cave into the ocean. He said this because there were two cemeteries in their town—this one just off the main highway near the elementary school, and the other, which was located at the edge of a cliff overlooking the ocean. He did not want to be near the ocean. He said this several times. Then he had gone down and purchased two plots side by side across from the school and close to the mausoleum. She hadn't said much. Then he had shown her the papers with the location of the graves marked with little X's on a map of the cemetery. The more she thought about it though, the more she set her mind on buying her own plot in the cemetery overlooking the ocean. Then one day she arranged to go there, and she paid for a grave site that very day.

She hadn't meant to tell her husband about her purchase, but one night they'd quarreled bitterly, and she'd flung the news at him. She had *two* grave sites she said—one with him and one away from him;

and she would do as she pleased when the time came. "Take your old bones and throw them in the ocean for all I care," he told her.

They'd left it like that. Right up until he died, her husband hadn't known where his wife was going to be buried. But what a thing to have done to him! To have denied him even that much small comfort. She realized now that if anyone had told her about a woman who had done such a thing to a dying husband she would have been shocked and ashamed for her. But this was the story of herself she was considering, and she was the one who'd sent her life's company lonely to the grave. This thought was so painful to her she felt her body go rigid—as if some force had struck her from the outside, and she had to brace herself to bear it.

She'd taken comfort in the idea of the second grave, even when she couldn't make up her mind where she would finally lie. She had prolonged her decision and she saw this clearly now for what it was, a way to deny this man with whom she had spent her life. Even when she came to the cemetery where her husband lay, she would still be thinking, as she was now, about the cemetery near the ocean—how when she went there she could gaze out at the little fishing boats on the water or listen to the gulls as they wheeled over the bluff. An oil tanker or a freighter might appear and slide serenely across the horizon. She loved how slowly the ships passed, and how she could follow them with her eyes until they were lost in the distance.

She gave the watering can a shake. There was water left in it, and she raised the can to her lips and drank deeply and thought again of the ocean. What she loved about that view was the thought too that those who walked in a cemetery, any cemetery, ought to be able to forget the dead for a moment and gaze out at something larger than themselves. Something mysterious. The ocean tantalized her even as she felt a kind of foreboding when she looked on it with her own death in mind. She could imagine children galloping over the graves, then coming to a stop at the sharp edge of the cliff to stare down at the waves far below. Her visits to the cemetery near the ocean gave her much pleasure even after her grave there was no longer a secret. When her husband asked, "Have you been out there?" she knew what he meant. "I have," she said. And that was the extent of it. Then he had died, and some of the pleasure in her visits to the other grave seemed to have gone with him.

As the widow's life alone settled into its own routine, weeks might go by until, with a start, she would realize she hadn't been to either cemetery. The fact of her two graves became a mystery to her. She thought she understood the torment of those who committed adulterous acts and then returned home—unfaithful and unrepentant. Yet she did nothing to change the situation.

The shadows of the evergreens had reached where she was standing. She saw that the school building across the street was entirely in shadow now. She gathered up the containers she'd used to carry flowers to the grave and picked up her garden shears. On her way to the car she turned and looked at the flowers on her husband's grave. They seemed to accuse her of something paltry, of some falsehood. She had decorated his grave, but there was no comfort in it for her. No comfort, she thought, and she knew she had simply been dutiful toward her husband in death as she had been in life. The thought quickened her step away from there. She reached her car and got in. Her breath was coming hard and unevenly and for a moment she could not think where it was she was supposed to go next.

A month had passed since her visit to the cemetery. Daisies and carnations were in bloom, but the widow hadn't been back to her husband's grave. It was early on a Sunday when she decided to go again. She expected the cemetery to be empty at that time of the morning, but no sooner had she arrived than a little red car drove into the narrow roadway through the cemetery and parked near the mausoleum. Then the driver got out. The widow was not surprised to see that it was the young woman she'd met on her last visit. The widow felt glad when the girl raised her hand in greeting as she passed on her way to her father's grave.

The girl stood by the grave with her head down, thinking. She had on a short red coat and a dress this time, like she might be on her way to church. The widow approved of this—that the girl was dressed up and that she might go on to church. This caused another kind of respect to come into the visit. But what the widow felt most of all, was that this was a wonderful coincidence. She had met the girl twice now in the cemetery and she wondered at this. She thought it must mean something, but she couldn't think what.

The widow took the dead flowers from the vases and emptied the acrid water. There was a stench as if the water itself had a body that could be corrupted. She remembered a time in her girlhood when she and Homer and her husband had been driving to a country dance in the next county. The car radiator had boiled over and they'd walked to a farm and asked for water. The farmer had given them some in a big glass jug. "It's fine for your car, but I wouldn't drink it," the man said. But the day was hot and after they'd filled the radiator each of them lifted the jug and took a drink. The water tasted like something had died in it. "Jesus save me from water like that!" Homer had said. "They invented whiskey to cover up water like that." Her husband agreed that the water tasted bad, but he took another drink anyway. "I was thirsty," he said.

The widow straightened and glanced again toward the girl. She seemed deep in thought as she stood beside the grave. The widow saw that once again she had brought no flowers with her.

"Would you like some flowers for your grave?" the widow called to her. The girl looked startled, as if the idea had never occurred to her. She waited a moment and then smiling she nodded. The widow busied herself choosing flowers from her own bunch to make a modest bouquet. Then she stepped carefully over the graves toward the girl. The girl took the flowers and pressed them to her face to smell them, as if these were the first flowers she'd held in a long time.

"I love carnations," she said. Then, before the widow could stop her, the girl began to dig a hole with her fingers at the top of her father's headstone.

"Wait! Just a minute," the widow said. "I'll find something." She walked to her car and found a jar in the trunk. She returned with this and the girl walked with her toward the mausoleum to draw water to fill the container. The water spigot was near the corner of the mausoleum where Homer's ashes lay, and the widow remembered having told the girl about his death.

"There's Homer," the widow said, and pointed to the wall of the mausoleum. There were four name plates to each marble block and near each name a small fluted vase was attached to the stone. Most of the vases had faded plastic flowers in them, but Homer's vase was empty. The girl opened and closed her black eyes, then lifted her flowers and poured a little of the fresh water into the container fastened to Homer's stone. Then she took two carnations and fitted them into the vase. It was the right thing to do and the widow felt as if she'd done it herself.

As they walked back toward the graves the widow had the impulse to tell the girl about her grave site near the ocean. But before she could say anything, the girl said, "I've got what I came for. I been coming here and asking what it is I'm supposed to do with my life. Well, I'm not for sale. That's what he let me know. I'm free now and I'm going to stay free," the girl said. The widow heard the word "free" as if from a great distance. *Free* she thought, but the word was meaningless to her. It came to her that in all her visits to her husband's grave she'd gotten nothing she needed. She'd just as well go and stand in her own backyard for all she got there. But she didn't let on to the girl she was feeling any of this, and when they set the container of carnations on the grave she said only, "That's better, isn't it."

"Yes," the girl said. "Yes, it is." She seemed then to want to be alone, so the widow made her way back to her husband's grave. But after a few minutes she saw that instead of staying around to enjoy the flowers, the girl was leaving. She waved toward the widow and the widow thought. *I'll never see her again.* Before she could bring herself to lift her hand to wave goodbye, the girl got into her car. Then the motor started, and she watched the car drive out of the cemetery.

A week later the widow drove to the cemetery again. She looked around as she got out of the car, half expecting to see the little red car drive up and the girl get out. But she knew this wouldn't happen. At her husband's grave she cleared away the dead flowers from her last visit.

The widow had brought no flowers and didn't quite know what to do with herself. She looked past the mausoleum and saw that a new field was being cleared to make room for additional graves at the far end of the cemetery. The sight brought a feeling of such desolation that she shuddered. She felt more alone that she had ever felt in her life. For the first time she realized she would continue on this way, alone to the end. Her whole body ached with the dull hopelessness of the feeling. She felt that if she had to speak she would have no voice. She was glad that the girl wasn't there, that she would not have to speak to anyone in this place of regret and loneliness. Suddenly the caretaker came out of a shed in the trees, turned on a sprinkler and disappeared back into the shed. Then, once again, there was no one.

She waited a minute, and then lowered herself onto the grave. The water from the sprinkler whirled and looped over the graves, but it did not reach as far as her husband's grave. She looked around her, but there was no one to be seen. She leaned back on the grave and stretched out her legs. She put her head on the ground and closed her eyes. The sun was warm on her face and arms and she began to feel drowsy.

As she lay there she thought she heard children running and laughing somewhere in the cemetery. But she couldn't separate this sound from the sound of the water, and she did not open her eyes to see if there really were children. The sprinkler made a *whit-whit* noise like a scythe going through a field of tall grass.

"I'm going to rest here a moment," she said out loud without opening her eyes. Then she said, "I've decided. You bought a place for me here, and that's what you wanted. And that's what I want too." Her words went into the air and were gone as quickly as she said them.

She opened her eyes then and with an awful certainty she knew that her husband had heard nothing of what she had said. And not in all of time would he hear her. She'd avoided being pulled down by what she'd considered her husband's bad company, all right. And now she knew exactly how she had done it. She'd cut herself off from him as someone too good for him, as someone too proud to do anything but injury to the likes of him. And this was her reward, that it would not matter to anyone on the face of the earth that she had ever lived. This, she thought, was eternity — to be left so utterly alone and to know that even her choice to be buried next to him would never reach her husband. Was she any better than the meanest wino who died in some fleabag hotel and was eventually reduced to ashes? No, she understood, no better. She had been no better than her husband all those years, and if she had saved him from a death like Homer's, it was only to die doomed and disowned at her own hearth. The enormity of this settled on her as she struggled to raise herself up.

A light mist from the sprinkler touched her face, and when she looked around her, she saw a vastness like that of the ocean. Headstones marked off the grass as far as she could see. She saw plainly a silent and fixed company out there, a company she had not chosen.

She looked and saw the caretaker in the doorway of the shed. He drew on his cigarette as he stood watching her. She raised her hand and then brought it down to let him know she had seen him. He inclined his head and went on smoking.

The Island of Ven

Gina Berriault

"ELLIE, LISTEN TO THIS: *In the evening after sunset, when according to my habit I was contemplating the stars in a clear sky, I noticed that a new and unusual star, surpassing all others in brilliancy, was shining almost directly above my head, and since I had, almost from boyhood, known all the stars in the heavens perfectly, it was quite evident to me that there had never before been any star in that place in the sky. I was so astonished at this sight that I was not ashamed to doubt the trustworthiness of my own eyes. A miracle indeed!* Ellie, you know what it was? A colossal stellar explosion, a supernova. But back then they thought the heavens were changeless, and so there's young Brahe gazing up at the new star one calm evening and he figures it's a miracle. No telescopes yet and he didn't need one. Even when the sun came up he could see it."

Noel read quietly, a lodger respectful of the hour of midnight in this foreign city and of the little family who had rented out a room on this night of the tourist season when all hotels were filled and who were asleep somewhere in the dark apartment. Like a tour guide whose memory isn't equal to the task and who reads over salient points each night before sleep, he was sitting up in bed, reading from the concise but colorful book on early European astronomers. A tour guide, but hers alone.

The beds were single, and he had pushed them together so he could take her in his arms and comfort her in the night, though she never asked for comforting. She lay with her hands under her cheek, palms together, watching his profile and loving him almost reverently, yet

234

at an errant distance from him, as if she loved him only in memory; and at a distance from their son beyond the actual miles, wherever he was on his own journey; and at the farthest distance from their daughter, *Nana,* a distance never to be comprehended, even as the child's sixteen years of life had become only a mystification of the mother.

"Listen, sounds like he went around the bend: *The star was at first like Venus and Jupiter, giving pleasing effects, but as it then became like Mars, there will next come a period of wars, seditions, captivity and death of princes, and destruction of cities, together with dryness and fiery meteors in the air, pestilence and venomous snakes. Lastly, the star became like Saturn, and there will finally come a time of want, death, imprisonment and all sorts of sad things.* Sounds like he freaked out. Imagine Einstein writing that in his journal?"

She saw him as he must have been when he was a boy—six, seven—adjusting the telescope an uncle had given him, bringing a star down close to his backyard for the first time, convinced then, he had told her, that the silvery music of crickets all around in the summer night was really the sound the stars were making. On so many nights of their years together, when he sat late over his work and she heard him go out into the garden to gaze at the stars, she wondered if he were seeing all things again as indivisible, or trying to, or not trying. The measuring of vast distances, incredible velocities—it was this that enthralled him. At parties, when the other guests wandered out into a patio, a garden, lifting their faces to a placid moon, he would gently remind them of something they may have neglected to remember, that those far lights and all the galaxies were racing away from the earth and from one another. *The farther the distance from us, the faster they're leaving us behind. Imagine four hundred million miles an hour?* And they would smile obligingly as over a joke on them all.

His face was softened by the lamplight, and she saw again how Nana had resembled him, and felt again the same mute alarm that, back home, drew her up from the bed in the middle of the night, alone as if she had no husband, nor ever had children, nor even parents to begin. She closed her eyes. This journey was his offering of love, a ritual of healing. By visiting together the places where the early astronomers had lived, the narrow Golden Street in Prague where they had strolled, a castle in Italy from where one had viewed the heavens, he hoped to humanize them for her. They, too, had suffered afflictions of the soul, yet despite their earthly trials they had never turned their eyes away from all that marvelous beckoning up there.

The lamp was switched off. Darkness now in this room in a stranger's house. This night and one more night when they returned from their day's trip to the Island. Noel bent over her and kissed her face imperceptibly as you kiss a sleeping person lost in the self. She said "I'm awake" and he took her in his arms. A street of trees. Branches stirred close to the small, high window, and distant sounds from the Tivoli Gardens — fireworks and music — trembled against the glass. She lay very still. Any movement, no matter how small, might wake the little family like incoherent words spoken out from her sleep.

By boat from Copenhagen to the town of Landskrona on the Swedish Coast. Old brick buildings with corby steps, factories blowing out sulphurous smoke. And now by a tough little boat, its yellow smoke-stack the only touch of color on the heavy gray Baltic Sea or a slender finger of that sea but so wide both shores were lost to view. A sea she had never thought about or ever wished to cross. They had climbed up from the hold to stand on deck. She had felt confined, deprived of the sight of the wind-driven swells the boat was striking against. The other passengers, Swedes, Danes, seemed content down there on hard benches in company of their bicycles and cases of beer and fruit. Like a compliant patient wanting to believe in a cure, she kept her gaze straight ahead to see the island the moment it came in sight. She must have glanced away. The island had risen the moment her head was turned.

The iron, stark look of it gave her an imagined view of immense rocks under the water. An island so precariously small, leveled down eons ago by fierce winds and sweeping torrents and monstrous waves, until water and wind calmed down and lay back. The inhabitants now, how did they feel about it? Stay calm. They must tell themselves to stay calm, and if the waters begin to rise again and the winds to stir again, some exquisite instrument, designed by a mind like Noel's, will detect the slightest threat in the depths of the sea, in the atmosphere, and everyone will be warned in ample time to hop onto their bicycles and peddle away to the nearest church, which, since it was four, five hundred years old, was to last forever.

A harbor town for those who trusted in fair weather always. Houses, gardens, low fences, trees, all on the very edge of deep gray water, little sailboats pleasantly rocking as if upon a transparent azure sea. The boat was moored, the passengers walked their bicycles up the rise and rode off past an approaching wagon drawn by two tawny horses and followed by two men walking leisurely. The horses stopped, the passengers climbed down. Except a little boy and his mother, the boy asleep on the blue wooden bench, his head in his mother's lap. The visor of his cap was tipped back, baring his face to the sky. Tiny purple flowers clung to the edge of his jacket pocket. The boy opened his eyes and, surprised by the sky, closed them again, and Ellie, watching, pictured his face growing older, his eyes less surprised day by day, night by night. Carefully the mother and child climbed down.

"Tycho Brahe's museum?" Noel's voice always sharply friendly in a foreign land. The driver, up on his high seat, appeared to nod.

The wagon joggled along the road that must be in the very center of the island, like a spine, and Noel sat very erect. The pale sun was turning his light hair to silver, a swift aging he didn't know about. Some of the gray of the sea was taken up and spread in a high, flat film over the sky, and the shadow of it, or the reflection, crept over the land, over the fields the tawny color of the horses and over the green meadows and the black cattle and over the thatched roofs of barns and cottages. Roofs thick as those in pictures she had painted for a children's book. Nana in her small chair by her mother's chair had watched everything come to life, sooner for her than for all the other children in the world: squat cottages under an indigo sky dotted with white stars, and in the night-green stalks of grass, a cricket. Unlike those cozy roofs, unlike that painting years ago, these thatched roofs they were passing could be overrun by rivers of fire.

The horses were halted, the driver waited for somebody to climb down. Nobody did. "Tycho Brahe," he said to the air.

Noel leaped down, helped her down, and the horses clopped on. No bicycle, no wagon appeared along the road from either horizon. The silence must be the presence of the sea, unseen but all around, a silence not to be trusted. Across the road—a Turistgarten, deserted, white slat tables and chairs under trees, and far back a yellow-brick hotel strung with colored lightbulbs. On their side of the road—a church, red-brick with slate roof, pink roses in the yard; the Tycho Brahe Museet, closed, so small it must contain only a few precious books, a few drawings. Far back, a row of giant mulberry trees, and by the trees a tall stone statue. The Astronomer.

"It's him!"

Noel hurried toward it, as if the statue were the man himself about to flee, and, following, she found him roaming around the statue, gazing up with scholarly respect, gazing down at the indecipherable inscription carved along the sides of the base. Twice as tall as any man on earth, the astronomer wore a cloak that hung down to the soles of his boots, knickers of many stony folds, a ruff around his neck. His head thrown back, he scanned the heavens, his goatee pointing at the great shallow bowl of earth where his observatory had stood. Out in the fields behind him a farmer was burning chaff and the smoke passed close to the ground, a long, long, ribbon, and farther away a tractor started up and a rabbit bounded along before it. A lone seagull was soaring high over all, just under the layer of gray clouds.

They stepped down the slope of the wide grassy bowl, so shallow it was almost imperceptible, and stood within the lost observatory, within the Castle of the Heavens, as fancifully, as airily beautiful as castles that are only imagined. Every stone gone, carted away by the peasants, and all its coveted carvings taken away by a king's mistress to decorate her own small castle. Nothing left, and where the foundation had been now filled with five centuries of earth. A toad at their feet stayed where it was, unafraid of large, slow animals. Up there at the top of his castle in the night, how did the astronomer look to a boy straining his neck to see from a highest branch? Was he plotting an invasion of the heavens? Was he a nocturnal predator on the trail of a celestial creature? The peasants must have lain awake, afraid that each night was the night the avenging angels would swoop down to destroy the island in an unearthly fire.

"Ellie, are you hungry? Are you thirsty?"

They sat down by the toad, and Noel brought up from his knapsack a bottle of mineral water, raisins, cheese, sweet crackers.

"If you eat this raisin, all my wishes will come true." He kissed her temple.

She took the raisin on her lip, swallowed it. All his wishes, she knew, were for her recovery, and hers were not. The tricks, the jokes, the conundrums—he hoped to take them back to that spirited time at the beginning of their future together, a young couple again, picnicking on the spot from where a universe had flowered.

Along the road now in search of the astronomer's underground observatory, Noel consulting a map given him by the tourist office in Copenhagen. His light boots stirred up puffs of dust, her sandals stirred up none. She had got so thin, her legs, though bare and tan, were a warning to her. The winds—Noel was saying—buffeted the castle, interfering with the precision of observations, and so the astronomer had taken his instruments underground. What did they think *then?* she wondered. Up so high and then so deep? What did they think when they saw him walking along this same road at night, wrapped in his cloak, his gleamy, gloomy eyes always upward, at his side a servant with a lantern, cautioning him about his step. That he was hiding from the wrath of God? That everyone else would perish? That when he poked his silver nose out from his underground refuge, the silver nose affixed with wax to replace his own lost in a duel, it would not melt, it would only turn gold, reflecting that unearthly fire.

By the side of the road, a girl and two boys were running about within a fantasy place no larger than their own yard. Strange copper shapes rose up from a carpet of short dry grass. Geometrical shapes, like a dome, a tent, a cone. The little girl slid down the slanting copper roof of the closed-up entrance, like the entrance to a cellar, and the boys followed, all shouting dares, their voices ringing back on the still air to the church and the mulberry trees. Skylights—they were the astronomer's skylights that segment by segment were opened to the night's panorama. Scales of green-blue patina covered them, and hinges hung loose.

"Come look."

Noel opened a section of the dome, and the children came up beside them, the little girl pressing close to her. Almost twelve feet down to rocks and bottles, earth and rainwater. While Noel and the children looked down into the lost interior, waiting for something to come into view, while the children shuffled their black leather sabots and a rooster crowed close by, she gazed down at the girl's blond hair—how silky, how shiningly new under the sun. The little girl was the first to laugh, a mocking titter, and the boys took it up, roughly. They already knew there was nothing down there.

Out on the sea again, the waters darker, films of rain in the distance, the harbor shrinking, its cottages, low walls, trees, masts, all sliding under the sea. It was night when the boat slowed into the harbor at Landskrona. From far in the heavy dusk, she had mistaken the trees of the town for piles of iron ore or coal. They sat in the dimly lit small waiting station, on a bench against the wall, until yellow lights, white lights moved through the murky night with the hushing presence of a large boat bound for Copenhagen.

Noel led her down into the salon, into the rousing noise of drinkers at every table and the portable organ's music, pounded out by a young man in suit and tie. Glasses everywhere on red tablecloths, gliding on spilled beer. An elderly woman danced alone among the few dancing couples, eyes closed, the flesh of her lifted arms swaying. Next to Ellie at the table, a handsome old man in a dark suit. Noel, leaning across her, asked him where the boat was from. An excursion boat, leaving Copenhagen in the morning and returning at night—and the whole day's pleasure was evident on his rosy face, a look that might have been there the first day of his life.

"American?"

"Yes," said Noel.

"Did you come by flying machine?"

Ellie nodded, looking into his face, seeing a boy out in the night, his eyes lifted to a moving light lower than the stars, an amazing machine that flew and filled the dome of the sky with an echoing roar. As much of a miracle, as much of a portent as Brahe's star.

"We went to Tycho Brahe's island," she said.

"Ah. A tourist garden is there. My sister was there for the honeymoon."

"One night," she said, "he saw an immense star that wasn't there before. He said it meant the death of princes, all sorts of sad things. He believed our destiny is in the stars. Yourself, do you believe that?"

She could see he was amused by her. He must hear this kind of talk from strangers in taverns, fellow passengers on excursion boats out for a day of revelry, their need to be intimately serious rising fast like the foam on their beers.

"Ah yes." Agreeable. A kind man, strongly old, how many faces had he gazed into as he was gazing into hers? Beloved faces, the others, each one gone while he lived on and on. A time to be born and a time to die. It was the only way to accept their going, the only way to ease the alarm.

Spaced green lights in the night, out there: the shore of somewhere moving slowly past. In the taxi to their tranquil street of trees, Noel was silent, wondering, she knew, if she had gone over the edge, if she had given up her mind to the astronomer's superstitious one. A lamp was on in the hall, for them. The little family was asleep.

When he lay down in his separate bed he leaned over her and

brushed the wisps of hair from her brow, hoping, she knew, to clear her mind by clearing her brow. She lifted her arms and brought his head down upon her breasts, an embrace alive again, and, holding him, a picture of the astronomer composed itself for her mind's eye, for her hand someday. Out in his garden, the young Brahe, his face lifted to that strange brilliance, to that inescapable portent, its reflection floating in his eyes and in the gems on his plump fingers and on every leaf turned toward the heavens.

Song

Gordon Jackson

LONG BROWN FINGERS on the yellow keys. Fingertips pressed to silent chords, audible only to him. Ivory cool against dry skin. Again, tries; smiles. The click of hammers falling soundlessly. The old man looked up from the piano and grinned.

" 'I am that I am,' the Lord God said."

> Woke up this mornin', blues walking like a man,
> Woke up this mornin', blues walking like a man;
> I said blues, blues, give me your right hand—

Time began, was: the siren erupts among the metal rafters of the tin building, air-beast crooning, heralding their transformation into things, parts of one unending cogline ratcheting menacingly forward, serpentine, continuous, immense, winding from building to building below ground and above to coalesce ultimately and imperfectly into the entity known as the Pontiac automobile: they, the plant, it, complete and one.

Brown fingers soundless on the yellow keys. Press lightly, touch. Silent chords, audible only to him. And the Lord. The man of God nodded, hunched forward at the old piano, hands long and bony in the yellow light. They waited; the occasional tink of ice against glass.

"How old is he?" Henry whispered.

"He a hundred," Irene said. "That's an actual fact." Then louder: "Play something, *Mister* Brown." Mama laughed.

Abruptly the old man began to play.

Outside the wind hissed over crusted snow, raising a ghostly smoke. The smell of wood fires drifted from chimneys. From within, the dim sound of a piano.

Waking that morning in the gray half-light to see the snow-whitened lawn. Even the road, snow covering everything to the horizon, driven into the backs of trees in a broad stripe. He fell back weakly from the glass, sliding beneath the covers in a ball. The place where he had lain was a warm island surrounded by chill; he centered himself carefully in the dark, arms over his head. He had known winter was coming, but it was something you could never prepare for; he remembered when his mother was alive and he was a small boy, lying in bed until the last moment and then hopping out to dress, shivering before the grate, the old house stirring as the heat came up, the light fragrance of coal smoke which he did not mind loved actually standing over the vent warming to the warm smoky air as his mother cooked oatmeal hot and fragrant in the steamy kitchen (bubbling on the stove in a lovely goo, clapped onto his dish by the ladleful), hot brown-sugared milk drunk first off the edges by the white creamy spoonful the milk sweet and hot-cool tinged with brown, the mass of porridge (for that is what it is, his mother said, porridge you know, just like our ancestors back in Scotland, the Scots invented porridge, my son, and never say Scotch, it is a trashy English word), the mass of porridge hot and scalding at the center beneath the cool pool of milk so that if your spoon strayed into the molten center your tongue would sear and your eyes water blinking away tears there is nothing hotter than porridge and milk on a cold winter's morning—

His breath, the very air, grew stale—

sprang back among the living, threw over the bedclothes, pranced on one foot over the icy floor and into the living room hopping as he dressed.

In the kitchen his father sat chewing. A single bulb burned overhead. Henry went to the stove and poured a cup of coffee.

"You going out tonight?" his father said.

"Maybe."

"With those jigs?"

Passing to the sink with his cup he mentally smashed it on his father's bald head, saying nothing, stood at the sink watching the water overflow his cup into his father's greasy breakfast pan, egg yolk slimed under the stream, tendrils of unborn chickens Jesus always the same as long as he had known him bacon and eggs the same unvarying stupid goddamn breakfast—

coffee overflowed his cup, thinned, ran away beneath the clearing stream—

At the door, sliding into his pea coat, pulling the collar up around his ears, he heard his father mutter as he departed: "Jigs."

Brozius Bonds, M.A., economics, Morehouse, class of '42 dropped a quarter in the slot, stooped at the knees, lanky as a whip, cradling a paper sack inside an elbow as he reached past the glass door of the vending machine for his carton and the siren shrieked overhead, sang through the rafters to a crescendo, held, one beat, two, then fell away abruptly, disappearing into the general upsurge of sound all around, whoops of air wrenches the grinding chattering cacophony of machinery, plant sounds flinging him forward in long strides between rows of piled cartons bright trim-pieces yellow pipes painted floor stripes warning signs and down the center of everything a pretty conga line of hoods swaying in time, brightly colored, lurching now by his own station, unmanned, Henry smiling as Brozey slipped out of his long leather coat and into his apron, winked, thumbed open the carton, twirled, tipped from the sack a golden stream: quaffed, paused, farted—

Henry laughed. "Hey, shit, are you doing fenders tonight or what?" in mock complaint feigning double-time dancing in place, fingering his nine-pound air wrench *wee-e-oww.*

A tip of the acorn beret, majestic, donning gloves, about to do battle, a handful of screws, thrusting, triumphant: "My man."

Later—"Going Mama's tonight?" Brozey said.

"I don't know."

"Oh?" Mock-incredulous inflection, followed by a wicked grin. "Does that mean no Irene tonight? Irene good-night?" He waited, tongue balanced slyly against the edge of teeth. "On payday, say-hey?" A nasty cackle.

"You fucker."

Wild laughter bursting hard upon this ejaculation, Brozey sings Huddy-like: "*I-rene, go-od-ni-i-ight, I-rene, go-o—*"

"Stop it, stop it, I'll go," Henry laughed, happy, blushing in spite of himself. Brozey winked, pink-tongued, grinning, jigged a two-step, arms akimbo.

"Quite."

At the break, he crossed the windswept boulevard and into Mickey's tavern, bellying up to down a Molson's, comparing checks with Jimmy from Paint, regular dinnertime Friday-night foe.

"What you got, Jimmy boy." He felt lucky.

Jimmy smirked. "Three nines."

"You lose, fish, fives over aces," flourishing his stub, 1540551, craftily not forgetting to hold his thumb over the hourly rate in the corner.

"Bullshit," Jimmy said, five lighter, trying vainly to peek.

"No way, José," he said, dancing lighthearted now across the frozen moonlit boulevard thinking only of Irene, through those chain-linked heart-breaker gates, greeting merrily the rosy-cheeked plant dick guarding the portal, "Hey!"

"I was a slave," Josiah said.

"A what?" Henry said, liquoring up.

"But now I am free." The old man looked at him. "You are a slave as well."

"Say what?"

"I said you were a slave—to Mammon."

"Not me. I can walk anytime I want."

"But you will not. Mammon holds you in thrall, sir." The old man looked at him, his eyes yellow as a lizard's in the soft lamplight. "Therefore will I howl for Moab."

He had been uncomfortable there until the evening when the sweet Irene walked over and took him by the hand. Took him in hand.

The black-black man came that night. Henry sat on the couch eating popcorn and drinking scotch. Teachers. Black and White. He observed that the popcorn bowl was the same as his mother's, a kind of milky green glass with rounded, scalloped edges, covered all over with little bumps. Nibbling a fistful of popcorn he observed the black-black man and the interesting Blanche depart arm in arm. Mama laughed.

"Gonna take him *on*," Mama said.

"Bring it to me," Irene called out.

"That woman's having something *done* to her," Mama said. "That yellow gal is."

"No whoremonger has any inheritance in the kingdom of God," Josiah said.

Afterward Blanche emerged across the room, dressed in a saffron robe. The woman's cool beauty, pacifying and inciting, shook the ice in his glass. She walked slowly toward him, leaned into the light at his elbow, pouring a drink, looked at him: lips clear and glossy, unguent in the yellow light; skin smooth as oil; a single brown freckle by her mouth. Then gone, departed, from whence she came. He marveled. Sweet Irene said:

"You want to see her?"

"See her?" Henry said.

"Work out."

"You mean watch?" He shook his head no.

Irene laughed. "Come on."

"We all do love to see Blanche bring it home," Mama whispered. "Go ahead."

They watched from a secret place. He saw.

—the woman make a plume of herself, laving the man with gifts, drawing them down, rippling above him, inverting, glistening—

The black man held her in his huge hands, turning, and the yellow gal gleamed in her turning, crooning.

Henry saw. Money on the table.

Love me.

Then the sweet Irene said, "It's free! Mama says. It's free one time, come on, hurry, while we got the room, we can do anything we want."

Anything. We want.

Entering the dim portal he met the rank odor of love.

"Fear, and the pit, and the snare, shall be upon thee," said the man of God.

In the slow uncoiling of time after dinner he settled in losing his cock-hard energy to the work, losing himself, going automatic the way Brozey had taught him, standing blindly in place while the line flowed past, working to empty himself of all thoughts and then seeing himself there once removed, his mind slipping to California and the sweet-bodied girl of his dreams, Rosie-o, white-skinned goddess in moonlight, desert girl, goddess of sand, moon and stars, hot oilwell nights, the nights they went along the sandy trails among the nodding pumpers (donkeys, you called them) rising in moonlight, gigantic, arching, terrible to see, daring him to ride a forty-ton rig, black and yellow girders crossing out sky, giant ironhead beauty rising endlessly, astraddle (come up behind me, you said, and feel the power), and he, fearful, the great beast shuddering, a carnival ride gone mad, the nightmarish climb, rivets as big as his hand, the low trembling beneath his loins as the crossbeam rose and paused and fell, swift descent, huge head gleaming military and immense (I caught you from behind, moonlight girl, your dress in bunches, stripped to the waist, you held my thighs tight against you, arms outspread, falling with a strangling sigh as I clutched your breasts like stars—) the siren bore in on him like a point, remote and insistent, he stared at his hands, the fingerless tattered glove grasping the silent wrench, the tips of his fingers blackened, exposed, a maroon hood swinging unfinished in front of him, stationary, insistent, *there*— He turned to see Brozey slipping away, whistling for him, one arm going into the sleeve of his coat, other men running for the clock, he felt utterly lost—

"The girl is busy tonight," Blanche said. "She is with Mr. Johnson." The black-black man.

"All night?"

The woman nodded. He would never forget the smile on her face, the way she smiled.

Jealous? Of a whore? How could a man be jealous of a whore? A low groan escaped him. The yellow gal leaned toward him, touched him on the stomach, eyes bright.

"I can make you forget." Her scent, the look on her face, the light pressure of her fingertips, carried him forward like a wave.

He that fleeth from the fear shall fall into the pit—

They cruise in Brozey's Cadillac. Up a narrow, dark, broken-down street.

"What's this?"

Brozey pulls up to the curb with his lights on; waits. After a moment he points. "That's my house." Henry looks, sees the curtains moving.

"He'll be going out the back way," Brozey said. "We'll give the wife a few minutes to straighten up." After a moment they leave.

"Aren't we going in?"

"Naw. If we went in now the bed would still be warm. I just wanted to make him run." He looked at Henry and grinned a terrible grin. "Now I just interrupt."

"I am that I am," Josiah said.

"You shit, nigger," Mama said.

"I am a man of God," Josiah said.

"You going to hell like the rest of us," Mama said. Irene laughed.

"Play something, *Mister* Brown." She looked at Henry and winked. The old man rose and moved slowly to the piano, stepping with exaggerated care. He turned back the cover, his hands long and bony in the yellow light.

"Play that thing, reverend," Mama said. "It cost me enough, Lord knows." Laughs loudly, head back.

The old man fell to playing. First he played "Will the Circle Be Unbroken?" singing in a high reedy voice. Then he played "The Minstrel Boy." Next a booming barrelhouse boogie, spilling over the room, making Mama whoop.

"Honey, don't do me this ta way . . ." Josiah sang. And "Gwine down to de river baby, sit down on de groun . . . wash my troubles on down . . . on down . . . to de groun—" Abruptly Josiah ceased and rose from his seat, closing the lid. The sound of general clapping fell away.

"It is the devil's music, I must apologize." He looked around the room. "Only in the music does the devil have me."

"Josiah, what's got *in*-to you?" Mama said.

"The calamity of Moab is near to come, and his affliction hastesth fast," the old man said, slowly raising his hand and pointing to Henry. "The devil is among us."

Henry sat on the bed. Blanche moved slowly toward him, stopping his breath. The saffron robe slipped from her shoulders. The woman licked her lips lightly, standing over him. Pushed him slowly backward on the bed, kissed him, pendulous and ripe, so that he was taken up by her entire.

"Yellow-yellow-yellow-yellow-yellow gal," Brozey sang from the next room, while Blanche cooed in his ear, urgent and precise: *Hen-ry, fuck me, Hen-ry, fuck me, Hen-ry* . . .

Save for the sound of his name, he forgot all.

"The Negro in America is a elephant who is blind," Josiah says. "He can't see around him and so he don't know his own strength. If he could see he could do anything, but he don't see. We've got to open our eyes and together we can *move*."

"Move where?" Henry says, sipping his scotch.

The old man looked away, closed his eyes as if in prayer. "His chosen young men are gone down to the slaughter. Lord, Lord. Come up, ye horses, and rage, ye chariots, and let the mighty men come forth."

For a time the line was empty. It was unexplained. S-hooks passed by, swaying, nothing below. Henry felt extraordinarily free. He looked around at his station, down the aisle. All around him the plant fell silent. The line made a hissing sound as it ratcheted by. Men stood idly, watching nothing, afraid to look up, each in his place. Henry looked down the line as far as he could see, and after a moment the first bright hoods and fenders appeared around a corner and began swaying his way. The sight sent a chill through him. As he looked on each man was drawn back in turn to his work, slowly, inevitably, the distance to the first shining yellow hood growing smaller by the second. Soon the gap in the line had passed evenly over all.

And he that getteth up out of the pit shall be taken in the snare—

"Got you a downtown woman now, young man, that's for sure." Mama kept her money bound to her wrist in a thick roll with a rubber band, flipping his bills under with a deft move, pulling down the sleeve of her robe: pink chiffon.

"But what can a twenty-year-old nigger do with an M.A. in economics in 1942?" Brozey said. "So I joined the Navy." They lay on the bed together in Blanche's room, the bottle between them.

"Twenty," Henry said. "Jesus. Look at me." He took a swallow of scotch and rolled over, shaking his head and staring at the ceiling.

"They made me a steward. I served peaches and cream to white officers. The U.S.S. *Chicago*." Brozey shrugged. "Nobody told me colored boys didn't fight. I heard the Navy took colored boys, but nobody told me that. Only once: it was what they call now the battle of the Philippine Sea. A night encounter. We tangled with a heavy cruiser, took it up the ass. Those Japs were great night fighters, with these big searchlights shuttered tight, they'd clap them open and catch you dead to rights, lay on a salvo quick as a cat, then cut the lamps. You were blinded, bracketed, dead. We were taking heavy fire, and they ordered all us stewards up from below, from our fire stations, to help load the anti-aircraft guns. We were returning fire with everything we had, lots of dead boys laying all about, I helped pass shells half the night. God, what a thrill. The air was thick with shell fire, red and orange tracers, big balls of flame rolling from our eight-inchers, with me out in the air breathing like a man instead of below decks shaking and shitting. We laid our guns right down on the water, we could see our tracers bounce off the water, going right into them. We were giving it to them, but they were good, they out-gunned us, caught us in their searchlights and we were broken. Thrown to the sea, I lived to see my ship go down. Good-bye, sweet home, Chicago. I never fought again."

"Your mother was a whore, did you know that?"

What he knows is that at nineteen he is already smarter than his father will ever be. They are arguing at breakfast. He has just come in from Mama's.

"You didn't know that, did you? And here you are, catting around with jigs and whores. Jesus H. Christ."

He looks at his father, refusing to react.

"She didn't have a red light, not officially. But she had my bed, my house. She screwed every man in the neighborhood."

He will not speak. Will not. Drunk, he is crafty enough to know where his strength lies.

"Right there in our bed, with your crib alongside. Whoring. Do you remember it? You must."

He thinks of killing him, sees it clearly in his mind, the two of them falling together, grappling there on the linoleum; rejects it. Then he *sees* it. How to hurt his father.

"I quit." His words sound blurred to him, remote. His father looks at him for the first time.

"You what?"

"You heard me."

"I don't believe I did."

"You did." He grins.

"No. It can't be. You're not that stupid." Henry nods, grinning, happy, looking his father full in the face. Sees him redden.

"Goddammit, do you know how many asses I had to kiss to get you in here? No, dammit, I say no!"

Staggering to his room he felt good all over. All he had to do now was do it.

Extended full length, Brozey slept on the floor, his head on a cushion. Bits of popcorn clung to his hair. From the doorway of the bedroom, buttoning his shirt, Henry could see that he would have no ride home. From her chair by the fireplace Mama surveyed the scene.

"Josiah, run this boy home. Take the Buick." Mama winked at Henry. "We takes care of our steadies."

Outside the air was clear and bitterly cold. Chimney smoke rose straight into the sky. At the steps Henry took the old man's arm, but Josiah pulled away. Shuffling to the car, his shoes squeaked over the dry snow.

"Walk," the old man said, standing beside the black car.

"What?" Henry looked at him.

"Don't come back here. Not ever, you hear? I told you to walk!" the old man shouted. "White devil." He drew forth from his coat an ancient pistol, a huge long-barreled Navy Colt, and waggled it in the air, pointing him down the road. "Walk."

Henry looked helplessly around, trying to think. "I need a ride, please." Drunk, the bitter air cut remotely at his face.

" 'I am that I am,' the Lord God said." The old slave raised the gun above his head with both hands and fired into the night sky, a bellowing eruption of flame and smoke that sent him toppling backward into the snow. A flurry of paper wadding drifted down, the sound rolling after down the neighborhood like thunder, enormous, and then a porch light went on across the street, and another, the old man thrashing in the drift, struggling to get to his feet, rising on one knee to calmly thumb the hammer back, and Henry turned and found that he was running, the air cutting instantly into his lungs, the voice of the old slave roaring on the night air: "I have made Esau bare, I have uncovered his secret places, and he shall not be able to hide himself! Run, whitey, run!"

At some point in the middle of his shift he just stopped, letting the unfinished hoods run on by him down the line standing fixed in place, his air wrench at his side. He tried to think of California and found he could not. He looked at Brozey watching him, scowling there in his apron as he worked. Holding the big wrench, unmoving, Henry felt a strange sense of trespass and joy as the unfinished hoods flowed past Then above the clamor of the plant he heard the white shirts begin to bellow on the floor below, the sound of voices growing louder, rising, until he could see them on the stairs running toward him and he fell back in horror with the sure knowledge of what was about to happen.

Honey

Ann Beattie

ELIZABETH'S NEXT-DOOR NEIGHBORS were having a barbecue. Though Elizabeth and Henry had lived in the house since his retirement three years before, they had only once eaten dinner next door, and the neighbors had only once visited them. After Henry's car accident, the Newcombs had called several times, but when Henry returned, they again only silently nodded or waved across the wide expanse of lawn when they caught sight of each other through the scrub pines that separated their property. Mrs. Newcomb was said to be an alcoholic. The boys, though, were beautiful and cheerful. When they were not joking with each other, their expressions became dreamy. The way they wore their hair, and their direct gazes, reminded Elizabeth of Clark Gable. She often saw the boys in Bethel. They were inseparable.

Though Elizabeth was re-potting geraniums, her mind was partly on the boys next door, partly on her daughter, Louisa, who lived in Atlanta and who had had a baby the week before, and partly on Z, who had phoned that morning to say that he would stop by for a visit on the weekend. Her thoughts seemed to jump between those people in time with the slap of the softball into the catcher's mitt next door. As they tended the barbecue grill, the brothers were tossing a ball back and forth. The air smelled of charred meat.

The day before, backing out of a parking place next to the market, Elizabeth had hit a trash can and dented the side of Henry's car. Louisa

253

had not wanted her to come to Atlanta to help out. Z's fiancée drank a bit much.

Elizabeth forced herself to smile, so that she would cheer up. Wind chimes tinkled and a squirrel ran across a branch, and then Elizabeth's smile became genuine. It had been a month since Z's last visit, and she knew that he would be enthusiastic about how verdant everything had become.

Verdant? If a dinosaur had a vocabulary, it might come up with the word verdant. She was almost forty-five. Z was twenty-three. After Z's last visit, Henry had accused her of wanting to be that age. She had gotten a speeding ticket, driving Z's convertible.

Henry suspected the extent of her feelings for Z, of course. The attachment was strong—although the two of them talked around it, privately. She often thought of going to see the remake of "Reckless" with Z at a matinee in New Haven. They had shared a tub of popcorn and licked butter off each other's fingers. Another time, they brown-bagged a half-pint of Courvoisier and slugged it down while, on the screen, Paul Newman drove more crazily than Elizabeth would ever dare to drive.

A few days ago, returning from the train station, Elizabeth had come to an intersection in Weston, and as she came to a stop, Paul Newman pulled up. He went first. Rights of the famous, and of who has the newer car. Although convertibles, in this part of the world, were always an exception and went first.

Next door, the boys had stopped playing ball. One probed the meat, and the other changed the station on the radio. Elizabeth had to strain to hear, but it was what she had initially thought: Janis Joplin, singing "Cry, Baby."

The best songs might be the ones that no one could dance to.

On Saturday, sitting in a lawn chair, Elizabeth started to assign her friends and family roles. Henry would be emperor . . . The lawn sprinkler revolved with the quick regularity of a madman pivoting, spraying shots from a machine gun.

Henry would be Neptune, king of the sea.

A squirrel ran, stopped, dug for something. It seemed not to be real, but the creation of some animator. The wind chimes tinkled. The squirrel ran up the tree, as if a bell had summoned it.

Ellen, Z's fiancée, was inside, on the telephone, getting advice about how to handle Monday's follow-up interview. She was leaning against the corner of the bookcase, drinking bourbon and water. Z detoured from the kitchen to the dining room to nuzzle her neck. He had come in to help Elizabeth, when she left the yard to get trays. One tray was oval, painted to look like a cantaloupe. The other was in the shape of a bull. She had bought them years ago in Mexico. Deviled eggs were spread out on the bull. The canteloupe held a bottle of gin and a bottle of tonic. A lime was in Z's breast pocket. A knife was nestled among the eggs.

Elizabeth held the back door open, and Z walked out. Henry's friend and lawyer, Max, was there, and a friend of Max's named Len. Dixie had stopped by for a drink, en route to her new house in Kent. Dixie was in the process of ending an affair with her architect. He had gotten religion during the building of the house. He had put skylights everywhere, so that God's radiance could shine in.

Z and Max were discussing jade. The man who used to deliver seltzer to Max was now smuggling jade into the country. Max was saying that people were fools to swallow prophylactics filled with drugs: look at the number of deaths. If jade spilled into somebody, it would just be like jellybeans that would never be digested.

Ellen came out of the house. She had had several drinks and, chin up, trying to look sober, she looked like a stunned soldier. She called out to Elizabeth that Louisa was on the phone. "The minute I put it back in the cradle, it rang," Ellen said.

Elizabeth thought: the cradle of the phone; the cradle she had ordered for Louisa's child . . . She was smiling when she picked up the phone, so it came as a surprise that Louisa was angry with her.

"I offered to come," Elizabeth said. "You said you had enough people underfoot."

"You *offered*," Louisa said. "You never said you *wanted* to come. I could hear it in your voice."

"I wanted to come," Elizabeth said. "I was quite hurt you didn't want me. Ask your father."

"Ask my father," Louisa said. She snorted. "So who's there today?" she said. "Neighbors? Friends from far and wide?"

In recent years, Elizabeth had begun to realize that Louisa was envious of her knowing so many people. Louisa was shy, and when she was a child, Elizabeth had thought that surrounding her with people might bring her out. When she taught, she did seem to find many interesting people.

"Oh, go ahead and go back to your party," Louisa said.

"Please tell me to come to Atlanta if you want me," Elizabeth said.

"Yes, *do* conclude this foolishness," Louisa said.

Sometimes Louisa was so good at mocking what she thought were her mother's attitudes that Elizabeth actually cringed. As they hung up, Elizabeth said a silent prayer: Please let her have had this baby for the right reason. Please let it not be because she thinks that if someone needs her, he loves her.

Z was in the doorway when she opened her eyes. She looked at him, as startled as if the lights had just come up in the movies.

"Headache?" he said.

She shook her head no.

"Your eyes were closed," he said. "You were standing so still."

"I was talking on the phone," she said.

He nodded and left the room. He opened the refrigerator to get more ice. She heard the cubes cracking as he ran water, then twisted the tray.

Outside, Dixie was volunteering to go into town and get movies. Henry told her to get one serious one and one funny one. Most people did that when they went to Videoville, to allow for the possibility that they might want to be silly, after all. Elizabeth realized that it was harsh of her to judge Henry — it was overreacting to think of his insisting that Dixie get what he called "a comedy and a tragedy" as ambivalence.

"It was right there," Henry was suddenly saying to Max. "Riiiight there, and I tapped it with the cane. Looked at Jim, back in the cart, and he looked away, to let me know he hadn't noticed. Hell, I had done good to land it there, with one leg that wouldn't even swivel. Who's going to criticize somebody who's half crippled? It'd be like taking exception to finding a blind man in the ladies' room."

On Wednesday Len stopped by, having guessed that the bracelet in his car must have been Dixie's, lost when she borrowed his car to go to Videoville. Henry was upstairs, taking his afternoon nap, when Len arrived. Elizabeth invited him in for an iced tea. He countered with an offer of lunch. He was house-sitting for his brother, whose house was about fifteen miles away. She didn't know she would be driving thirty miles when she got in the car. Why take her there, instead of into Bethel, or to Westport, for lunch? she wondered. He probably thought that she was more fun than she was, because they had gotten involved in a drunken game the other night, playing matador in the backyard with the tablecloth and the bull tray.

She had put on Dixie's bracelet for safekeeping: copper strands, intertwined, speckled with shiny blue stone. The stones flashed in the sunlight. Always, when she was in someone else's yard, she missed the music of the wind chimes and wondered why more people did not hang them in trees.

She and Len strolled through the backyard. She waited while Len went inside and got glasses of wine to sip as they surveyed the garden. The flowers were rather chaotic, with sunflowers growing out of the phlox. Scarlet sage bordered the beds. Len said that he had been surprised that she did not have a garden. She said that gardening was Henry's delight, and of course, so soon after the accident, he wasn't able to do it. He looked at her carefully as she spoke. It was clear to her that she was giving him the opportunity to ask something personal, by mentioning her husband. Instead, he asked about the time she had taught in New Haven. He had been accepted there years ago, he told her, but he had gone instead to Duke. As they strolled, she learned that Max and Len had been college roommates. As he spoke, Elizabeth's attention wandered. Was it possible that she was seeing what she thought?

A duck was floating in a washtub of water, with a large fence around it. Phlox was growing just outside the wire. Bees and butterflies flew around the flowers. There was a duck, floating.

Len smiled at her surprise. He said that the pen had been built for a puppy, but his brother had realized that he could not give the puppy enough time, so he had given it away to an admirer. The duck was there in retirement.

"Follow me," Len said, lifting the duck out of the tub and carrying it into the house. The duck kicked, but made no noise. Perhaps it was not kicking, but trying to swim through the air.

Inside, Len went to the basement door, opened it, and started down the steps. "This way," he hollered back.

She followed him. A fluorescent light blinked on. On one corner of a desk piled high with newspapers, there was a rather large cage with MR. MUSIC DUCK stenciled across the top. The cage was divided into two parts. Len put the duck in on the right and closed the door. The duck shook itself. Then Len reached in his pocket and took out a quarter and dropped it into the metal box attached to the front of the cage.

A board rose, and the duck turned and hurried to a small piano with a light on top of it. With its beak, the duck pulled the string, turned on the light, and then began to thump its beak up and down the keyboard. After five or six notes, the duck hurried to a feed dish and ate its reward.

"They were closing some amusement park," Len said. "My brother bought the duck. The guy who lives two houses over bought the dancing chicken." He reached in the cage, removed the duck, and smiled. He continued to smile as he walked past her, duck clasped under his arm, and started to walk upstairs. At the top, he crossed the kitchen, pushed open the back door, and carried the duck out to the pen. She watched through a window. The duck went back to the water silently. Len looked at it a few seconds, then turned back toward the house.

In the kitchen, Len poured more wine and lifted plates out of the refrigerator. There was cheese and a ham butt. He took out a bunch of radishes—bright red, some of them cracked open so that white worms appeared to be twisted around the bulbs. He washed them and cut off the tops and tips with scissors.

They ate standing at the counter. They talked about the sweaty bicycle riders who had been pouring over the hilly highways near Elizabeth's house all summer. She looked out the window and saw the duck swim and turn, swim and turn. She poured a third glass of wine. That finished the bottle, which she left, empty, in the refrigerator. Len reminisced about his days at Duke. He asked then, rather abruptly, if he should drive her home.

In the car, he put on the radio, and she remembered the crashing keys under the duck's bill as it played the piano. Drinking wine had made her think of the brandy in the bag, and of sitting in the matinee with Z.

She wondered what she would say to Henry about how she had spent the afternoon. That she had eaten lunch and watched a duck play the piano? She felt foolish, somehow—as if the day had been her idea, and a silly idea at that. To cover for the way she felt, and in case Len could read her mind, she invited him to Sunday brunch. He must be lonesome, she realized; presiding over someone else's house and someone else's duck was probably not his idea of a perfect day, either. But who was he, and why had he not said? Or: why did she think that everything had to have a subtext?

She shook his hand when he dropped her off. His eyes were bright, and she realized that the ride back had been much faster than the ride to the house. His eyes riveted on the stones in the bracelet. Henry, too, noticed the bracelet the minute she came in, and told her that he was glad she had gone out and bought herself something pretty. He seemed so genuinely pleased that she did not tell him that it was Dixie's bracelet. It hurt her to disappoint him. It would have saddened him if she had admitted that the bracelet was not hers, just as he had been very worried when she told him, some time ago, that the college where she taught in New Haven was no longer using part-time faculty, and that she would not be teaching there after the end of the semester. She had been able to say that, in spite of his sad face, but of course other thoughts remained private.

Z had young hands. That was what had stopped her. Or maybe she thought that because she wanted to think that there had been one thing that stopped her. He had large, fine hands and long, narrow feet. Sometimes it seemed that she had always known him in summer.

She searched her mind for the title of the poem by Robert Browning about the poor servant girl who had only one day off a year.

Here it was Sunday, and she was entertaining again. Z (without Ellen, who was having a snit); Len; Max; Margie and Joe Ferella, who owned the hardware store; Louisa and the baby.

What a week it had been. Phone calls back and forth between Connecticut and Atlanta, between herself and Louisa, between Louisa and Henry, between Louisa's husband and both of them—and finally, through a flood of tears, after Louisa accused Elizabeth of every example of callousness she could think of, she had said that not only did she want to be with Elizabeth and Henry, but that she wanted to be with them *there*. She wanted them to see the baby.

The baby, in a cotton shirt and diapers, slept on Louisa's chest.

Louisa's hand hovered behind the baby's head, as if it might suddenly snap back. Elizabeth was reminded of the duck, held in the crook of Len's arm—how lightly it rode there, going downstairs to play the piano.

Ellen came after all, in a pink sundress that showed off her tan, wearing high-heeled sandals. She went to the baby and lightly touched its shoulder. She said that the baby was miraculous and fawned over him, no doubt embarrassed that she had made a scene with Z earlier.

She did not seem to want to look at Z. He was obviously surprised that she had come.

They were drinking Soave, with a little Cointreau mixed in. A big glass pitcher of golden liquid sat on the center of the table. The food was vegetables that had been sautéed in an olive oil as green as Max's treasured jade; a plate with three kinds of sausages; a wooden tray with bunches of radishes (she had placed scissors on the board, to see if Len would say anything, just as a reminder of the day); strawberries; sourdough bread; cornbread and honey.

Everyone was exclaiming. Several hands reached for the pitcher at once. Beads of sweat streamed down the glasses. Z complimented Elizabeth on the meal, as he poured more of the wine mixture into her glass. It was so easy to please people: to take advantage of a summerday and to bring out attractive food, with trays rimmed with sprigs of mint, studded with daisies. Even Louisa cheered up. She lifted a sausage with her fingers and smiled. She relinquished the baby to Ellen, and soon Ellen's lips were resting on the baby's tiny pink ear. Pretty, pretty, Elizabeth thought—even though she did not like Ellen much. Pretty the way her lips touched the baby's hair. Pretty the way her diamond sparkled.

She looked around the table, and thought silently: Think only about the ways in which they are wonderful. Henry's cheeks, from the long morning in the sun, were pink enough to make his eyes appear more intensely brown. Next to him, Z raised the lid off the honey pot and she looked at those fingers she loved—the ones that, as he gestured to make a point, seemed to probe the air to see if something tangible could be brought forward. Margie and Joe were as attuned to each other as members of a chorus line (he looked at the cornbread, and her hand pulled the tray forward). Max was so complacent, so at ease, that any prankster would have known where to throw the firecracker for best results. Len, sitting next to Louisa, edged his shoulder a little closer and—as Louisa had done earlier—cupped his hand protectively behind the baby's head. And Louisa, though there were dark circles under her eyes, was still the child—half charming, half exasperating —who picked out her favorite vegetables and left the others.

Next door the brothers, again lighting the barbecue, again tossing the softball, shouted insults to each other and then cracked up at their inventiveness. One threw the ball and it rolled away; the other threw it back underhand, so that it arched high.

What happened, then, out on the lawn, was this: Henry swatted at a bee with a roll of paper towels, and suddenly three or four more buzzed low over the table. Hardly had any of them begun to realize what was happening when bees began to appear everywhere, dropping down on the table like a sudden rain, swarming, so that in a few seconds anyone who had not seen the honey pot on the table to begin with would have seen only a cone of bees the size of a pineapple. And then—however wonderful they had been—Max became in an instant the coward, chair tipped back, colliding almost head-on with Margie Ferella; Henry reached for his cane and was stung on the wrist; as a bee flew past Ellen's nose, she screamed, shooting up from the chair, knocking over her glass of wine. Joe Ferella put his hands over his head and urged the others to do the same. Louisa snatched the baby back from Ellen, hate in her eyes because Ellen had only been concerned with her own safety, and it had seemed certain that she would simply drop the baby and run.

When Elizabeth remembered the afternoon, late that night, in bed, it was as if she had not been a part of it. She had the sense that the day, like a very compelling movie, was something half dreamed. That there was something inevitable and romantic about the way she and Z had risen in unison and reached toward each other reflexively.

Later, Henry had told her that her hand and Z's, clasped across the table, had reminded him of the end of a tennis match, when the winner and the loser gripped hands perfunctorily. And then he had stopped himself. What an odd thing to think of, he had said: clearly there had been no competition at all.

What Ernest Says

Sue Miller

THIS IS WHAT Ernest whispers to her. "You ever had a man to go down on you? How you like me to be going down on you? How you like that? You like Ernest to eat you out?

"You ever suck black cock? How you like suckin me off?"

When Miss Foote calls on her, she is sometimes so confused that she just stares back. Her mouth hangs open, and she doesn't answer. The children laugh. They are glad to see her make a mistake. She is too smart, too big for her britches. Miss Foote calls her up after class. Why is she having so much trouble right now? Miss Foote used to be able to count on her. "You were someone I could rely on, Barbara, when I wanted an example for the other children."

Miss Foote's breath smells overripe, sweet, as though she had had cheese with her lunch several hours ago.

She doesn't look at Miss Foote. Just at her desk, the neat heaps of papers graded and stacked up. Barbara always gets S, superior, on her homework.

She tells Miss Foote she is sorry. She says no, she doesn't know what is wrong. Just sometimes now she has trouble concentrating in class. *Move me,* she wants to say, but she knows she mustn't ask to be moved away from the black kids. Her parents would be ashamed, so ashamed.

At recess the black kids gather under the viaduct. The white kids stay closer to the school. The white kids don't like the black kids. They say bad things about them. They call them *nigger, jigaboo.* Barbara's

262

parents have told her they don't really feel these things, that they have
learned them from their parents and don't know any better. Barbara's
parents have told her the black kids are just as smart, just as good and
nice as the white kids, they just need time and encouragement from the
teachers to catch up. They say it is a shame that Miss Foote has all the
black kids sitting together in the back of the room. They are glad Barbara is sitting next to them. They ask her if there is any one black child
she talks to or has gotten to know.

Ernest, she tells them.

"Oh," her mother says brightly. "A boy. How interesting."

When Ernest leans forward his breath is warm and sticky on Barbara's neck. She can feel her hairs stiffen in response, and a queer vibra-
tion passes down her spine, as though a part of that knotted bone had
become, momentarily, gelatinous.

"I see you on 55th this weekend, girl, and I call to you. You din answer me. You din hear me?"

She cannot even shake her head no. She wasn't on 55th this weekend. She stayed home, except for Sunday when she went to church,
the church her parents belong to, where she is in a confirmation class.
Though this church is in a neighborhood where many blacks live, very
few of them come to the church. In Barbara's confirmation class, there
are only white kids, three white girls, and Dr. Wilson, who has a tired
face and a kind, hoarse voice. She stayed home all weekend except for
church and her mother said, "Isn't there somebody from school, some
nice girl you'd like to have over?"

"The wind be blowin your skirt on 55th, and I think I seen your
pussy, girl. Is that right? Did you show me your pussy on 55th? This
was Saturday, I believe." His tone is so friendly, so conversational, that
Barbara sometimes believes she makes up the words, the dirty words
in her own head. But how can she? She didn't know those words before he said them. She didn't know *cock, pussy, suck, eat.* Still she isn't
sure what they mean, or if he really said them. Did he say them? Maybe
he was saying something else. His accent, their accents are so thick
sometimes she isn't sure what he says, what any of them say. When
they talk together, she can understand almost nothing, but the girls'
bright screams of laughter tell her it is all right, what they say to each
other. Then it occurs to her, perhaps they are all laughing at her?

In class, Miss Foote asks a question. She calls on Sterling Cross.
Barbara looks over at him, next to her. His face is blank. It is as though
Miss Foote hadn't called on him. He blinks. The white kids have

turned around to look at him. They wait. He scratches his head. His pale brown fingers make a soft noise Barbara can hear. Miss Foote calls on Ernest. Barbara's chair is attached to Ernest's desk. She feels it move slightly, but that is all. She knows how his face looks. Impassive, black, no one could expect an answer from it. The radiator hisses. To Barbara it seems that minutes have passed. Slowly she raises her hand. Miss Foote won't look at her. She is waiting for one of the black kids to answer. Barbara waves her hand.

Suddenly Miss Foote says in an irritated voice, "Barbara, you will have to learn you can't always be the center of attention."

Barbara is the smartest girl in class. There is one boy who is probably as smart as she is, Jimmy Nakagawa, but he won't talk when he is called on. He laughs to himself and shakes his head, so Miss Foote never calls on him at all anymore. Barbara and Jimmy Nakagawa never speak to each other, and hardly anyone else ever speaks to either of them. Barbara's parents' friends are always surprised when they hear where she goes to school. "She does just beautifully there," Barbara's mother says. "The instruction is really almost as good as in a private school, and we like her to meet all different kinds of children. She even has a special friend among the black children, a little boy named Ernest."

She is the smartest girl in confirmation class too. They are studying the sacraments, communion. Dr. Wilson says communion is the central ritual of Christian life. He reads Christ's words: "Take, eat, this is my Body, which is given for you; do this in remembrance of me." He asks the girls what the sacrament of communion means. No one raises a hand or says anything. He looks at Barbara. Barbara has studied this. She knows the answer, but she cannot remember it. The room is silent. Dr. Wilson looks angry and tired. He begins to answer his own question. The next Sunday Barbara is sick and doesn't have to go to church or confirmation class. She stays in the house all weekend.

"Hey girl. I be waitin for you last Saturday. You told me you meet me under the viaduck and I wait for you maybe three hours." Barbara shakes her head in confusion. "Why you tell me that when you not goin to meet me, why you do that?"

She never looks at Ernest when he talks to her, but she knows how he looks, she can imagine his mouth as she feels his humid whisper. It is as pink as bubble gum inside, his tongue is pink too, his lips slowly turn pink as they curve into his warm mouth.

Sometimes at recess Barbara stands near the viaduct and listens to the black kids. There are three girls who sing together, Norma Jean is one of them, and Barbara likes the way their voices move so close. Their voices almost touch each other but don't. "Red hots, french fries," they sing, and clap! "And chili macs." Ernest is smoking a cigarette. He sees her looking at him and says something to James. They laugh.

Barbara tells her father she doesn't want to be confirmed. She doesn't feel ready to take communion, to drink the blood, to eat the body of Christ. Her father is understanding. She will go to church with them on Sunday still, but not be confirmed, and, for now, stop the confirmation classes. "What's most important," he says to Barbara, "is to listen to your own inner voice."

Sometimes he doesn't speak to her for days. Behind her back, she hears him talking, laughing, with James, with Sterling, with Norma Jean. She waits for the pause, the break, then the softer, moist voice near her head. She listens to the silence behind her when Miss Foote is talking. She stares intently at Miss Foote's moving mouth, the gold teeth in the back flashing occasionally. She listens to Ernest's breath behind her. Miss Foote calls on her and she stares and doesn't answer.

Miss Foote is upset and sends for her mother. Her mother is concerned. Perhaps there is some physiological problem. Barbara goes to the eye doctor, the ear doctor. The ear doctor whispers at the back of her head, "Can you hear this?" His breath is cool, but it stirs the hairs on her neck. "Yes. Yes," she whispers back with her eyes closed, like a lover in the dark. There is nothing wrong with her, they say. It's nothing organic.

Ernest's desk is empty. Barbara leans back in her chair and watches the door as the latecomers straggle in. After the Pledge of Allegiance, Miss Foote calls the roll and then talks about Ernest. His sixteenth birthday was the day before and he won't be back. Miss Foote says this is a Tragedy, that Ernest should have tried to finish eighth grade anyway, that people should always try to finish what they have begun. She talks about how Ernest is hurting his chances forever to be a success, to make something of himself, by quitting now. She hopes everyone in this classroom will finish eighth grade, whatever their age, whatever their background or skin color, and think about high school, and even college.

In her seat, Barbara tries to hide the slow tears starting down her face.

Flames

Stuart Dybek

I MET KAZMIR at Mrs. Malek's. He was a couple years older than I was, though only a grade ahead of me. His blond hair was just growing back from the baldy sour they'd given him after the school nurse found lice, and the deep, white-welted scar commemorating a fall from a second-story window when he was four ran like a crack across his skull. I remembered the day at school when each class was lined against the wall in the corridor before the nurse's office. It felt like a cross between an air-raid drill and going to Confession. We filed, one at a time, into the nurse's office. Her office was dark, a black drape drawn across the window. One after another, we sat at a school desk from an eighth grade classroom with our heads slightly bowed as one of the heavyset, aproned ladies who cleaned the lunchroom sorted through our hair. The nurse stood beside her, holding a special light, following with the beam of a red bulb the trails that the lunchroom lady's fingers wove through our hair. I held my breath as if waiting for the jab of a shot. Some of the girls cried. We'd all heard how, after they'd found lice, Kazmir, struggling and cursing, had to be tied with clothesline and belts to the barber chair in the basement shop on 24th Street where old Mr. Zyunce, who could hardly understand English, gave haircuts for fifty cents. Zyunce cut a hole through the bottom of a shopping bag, fit it over Kazmir's head, and rolled the sides of the bag down to his neck, so that as he shaved Kazmir's head the hair fell into the bag. Then he daubed Kazmir's scalp with kerosene, and took the bag of blond hair into the alley to burn. Kids said you could hear the lice popping in the flames, but that was made up. Later, at Mrs. Malek's, Kazmir told me how he and his older brother, Roman, had sneaked out at night and pushed Zyunce's barber pole down the basement steps. Kazmir was light-complected with blond eyelashes and pale blue eyes, and as he confided in me about knocking off the barber pole, even though he was grinning, anger burned up his neck into his face. He flushed so hotly it startled me, and I think that must have been the first time I'd ever felt the compelling force of anger I was invited to share, rather than anger directed at me.

Mrs. Malek was our baby sitter for the summer, an old Bohemian woman who dressed in black and lived alone since her husband, the railroad man, had died. She may have worn black even before he died. It was a color many of the older, foreign ladies in the neighborhood gravitated to. Mr. Malek's job had been inspecting the boxcars before the freights left the yard on 17th Street, and apparently he'd had a heart attack inside one of the boxcars. Nobody missed him, and they sealed the boxcar door, and didn't find his body until they opened the door again to unload the train in Billings, Montana. By then he was frozen stiff, and had been missing long enough so that the rumor that he'd gone off on a binge and run out on Mrs. Malek had become the generally accepted truth. It was a rumor that Mrs. Malek herself seemed to confirm. When her husband failed to come home from work, she didn't even report his disappearance to the police. So, when it finally became known that Mr. Malek had died on the job, it was as if, without even trying, he had succeeded in leaving behind the feeling that the world owed him an apology. Mrs. Malek remained silent in what might or might not have been mourning, more alone that she would have been had he died in an ordinary way, while everyone else continued to discuss it. Some said that the heart attack itself hadn't killed him, that he'd probably awakened in the speeding boxcar and frozen to death; and some said it wasn't a heart attack at all, that a hobo killed him because Mr. Malek had a reputation for being a son-of-a-bitch to hobos trying to ride on what he always referred to as *his* trains.

They never had any kids. Mrs. Malek kept chickens in the little dirt yard behind her house on 23rd Place, all kinds—white hens with combs the color of liver and scaly yellow legs, speckled hens with black eyes and legs to match, big red hens that seemed to turn bronze as the afternoon shadows settled in the little yard—chickens right in the middle of the city! She told us to stay away from the chickens when we went out to play, that a wild Polish rooster lived in the coop, and that he'd peck our eyes out.

Kazmir and I played in front of her house at first. I'd heard about his hot temper, but we got along from the start. And when he told me about the attack on Zyunce's barber pole, I knew we'd become friends. It was a more serious secret than one might think pushing over a barber pole would be. Zyunce's barbershop also served as a polling place. During elections the aldermen, precinct captains, and other local politicians would hang around in front, shaking hands and passing out cigars. The barber pole had come to seem like a neighborhood landmark. Besides its bold red and white stripes, a thinner blue stripe wound around it, and when it toppled, people were shocked, as if something unpatriotic had happened. They felt bad for Zyunce, who already seemed so defeated by English. "What's a poor DP supposed to think about America after something like this," they asked.

Kazmir had another secret to tell me, a far more serious one, that it was his older brother, Roman, who pushed him out the window, almost killing him when he was four. They'd been home alone—Roman was supposed to have been watching him—and they were fooling around wrestling, and Roman had pinned him on the sill of the open window, like guys in a movie struggling at the edge of a cliff, and then Roman suddenly just let him go.

"Maybe he thought you were holding on," was all I could think of to say.

"I guess. I never asked him," Kazmir said. "I thought he had me."

When he told me that he'd never told anyone else about how he'd fallen out the window, I didn't know what to say in response. I had no secret like that to trade, and said nothing.

"I shouldn't have told *you*," Kazmir said, his face flushing with that quick, scalded-looking anger, and this time I couldn't tell if it was with anger for what he was remembering, or anger at me and my silence.

"Why not?" I asked.

"You might tell somebody."

"Who would I tell?"

Every day we'd meet at Mrs. Malek's and she'd send us out to play along 23rd, a narrow little street lined with two-flats that were set in tiny front yards sunk below sidewalk level, and with three-story apartment buildings separated by gangways only wide enough for cats. Every day we wandered a little farther from her house, widening our boundaries, and then one afternoon, without even discussing it,

we sneaked around the block, down the alley, and through the back
gate into the tar-papered shed she called the coop. It smelled of sour
grain, straw, and feathers. I held my arms ready to shield my eyes in
case the rooster attacked. But there was no Polish rooster, only dark
corners and intense slats of light slanting from gaps in the siding,
beams of daylight that made the chicken droppings gleam the white
of spilled paint.

Hens clucked as if scolding outside the screen door. Kazmir grinned
at me, then struck a match. He usually carried around a pocketful of
matchbooks. Years later, he would found a gang called the Match-
heads dedicated to torching garbage cans and junked cars, to setting
trash fires behind abandoned factories, and pitching pop-bottle Molo-
tov cocktails from overpasses late at night when the expressways were
nearly deserted. All through the summer they staged hit-and-run fo-
rays as if engaged in guerrilla warfare against the city, though all they
were after was to see the flames dance up incinerating the muggy
night. Just as there are girls who, at the onslaught of adolescence, become obsessed with horses, so there are boys at the same age who
worship fire.

Now he was sparking matches, holding them above his head while
they charred down to his fingertips, as if he were leading us with a
torch through total darkness. The shed was a tangle of rusted tools and
buckets, of enormous saws, rakes, hoes, shovels, an axe, a sledge hammer, a cobwebbed sickle—the only one I'd ever seen other than on pictures of the Russian flag. Rusted lanterns hung from rusted railroad
spikes pounded into the beams. A row of orange crates, stuffed with
straw scooped to the shape of roosting chickens, sat along the wall opposite the screen door, looking like a shipment of nests. Kazmir was
flaring off whole books of matches at once. The shed felt baked and
reeked of sulphur. I was afraid he was going to burn it down.

"We'd better get out of here," I whispered.

He was poking around in a corner where he'd been igniting spider
webs.

"Hey, look," he whispered back. He'd pulled a crushed, canvas tarp
away from a wooden washtub and there, squeaking and squirming
among decomposing rags, were bald bodies not much larger than the
top joint of a finger. They looked like miniature piglets with stringy,
gray tails.

"What are they?" I asked.

"Must be baby rats," Kazmir said.

We'd both heard that some people in the neighborhood didn't like Mrs. Malek keeping chickens because they were afraid it attracted rats. Kazmir took a trowel from a coffee can of rusted tools and prodded, careful not to touch them with his fingers. Their eyes were closed and their front paws looked more like miniature hands.

"I wonder if they have rabies," Kazmir said, his eyes darting around the shed.

"Rabies?" I could feel myself suddenly looking around too for anything scurrying among the tools in the dark corners.

"You get rabies from rats," Kazmir said. "If they bite you, you have to get the shots."

"My father had to get the shots," I said, recalling my father's story of how, as a boy, he went every day for fourteen days to St. Anthony's Hospital for rabies shots after his landlady's dog bit him. The landlady had told his mother, my grandmother, that the dog was a watchdog and that my father shouldn't have bothered it, that she didn't want her watchdog locked up in the dog pound, and that if they told the doctors whose dog it was they'd have to move out of the building. My grandmother had come over on the boat from Poland, as my father put it, and didn't know the score yet, but she knew that cheap flats for a woman with six kids weren't that easy to find, and so my father went for the shots, and every day when he came home my grandmother would give him a warm sponge bath to ease the soreness. The worst part, my father said, was that the whole time he knew the landlady's dog didn't have rabies, it was just mean.

"When his butt got sore they gave him the shots in the stomach," I told Kazmir.

"He shouldn't have told them his butt was sore," Kazmir said. He'd pried the lid off an old paint can, and I watched as he carefully troweled the bald bodies into the can. Then, with a long-handled blade for scraping ice from sidewalks, he churned them up. The can tipped when he tried to get the blade out, and he had to step on the can in order to work the scraper loose, then he jammed the blade into the dirt floor of the shed. I didn't try to help him, and he didn't ask. Outside the screen door, the hubbub of chickens that had seemed to vanish into silence while Kazmir was chopping with the scraper, now seemed louder and more hysterical than before. Kazmir went over to the crates, picked out a couple of brown eggs from the straw, cracked them on the rim of the can, and threw them in, shells and all. Then he pissed in the can, and we took the whole mess outside into the yard to see what the chickens would do.

And when he spilled it into the dirt, the only thing I'd ever seen move faster than those chickens was the whoosh of gasoline the summer before when a tramp tried to burn the weeds along the railroad embankment on 25th. The men who worked for the railroad were supposed to keep the weeds cut back from the tracks, but in late summer, when the weeds sprouted tall, they usually burned them in a hot, quick, intense blaze which in moments reduced the jungle of the embankment into a charred stubble that looked like melted plastic. A bunch of us kids always stood around watching the weeds burn, but this time the railroad men gave a hobo whiskey money to do it while they sat drinking beer from sweaty quart bottles. He poured what they told him was kerosene along both sides of the tracks, slopping it over the weeds, then struck a match and tossed it. A balled blast of orange whumped up and hid him where he stood between the rails surrounded by hip-high weeds that were now even taller flames. The railroad men jumped up, both laughing and hollering for him to get the hell out of there, and between the flames the hobo stood enveloped in bright air that wavered as if it were bending or melting in the heat, an astonished look on his face, the shoulders of his suitcoat smoldering, and then suddenly his astonishment turned into a look of pleading terror, he screamed, and throwing his arm across his eyes as if playing blind man's bluff, he ran through the fire, pitching forward and rolling down the embankment so that it was impossible to tell if it was dust or smoke surrounding him as he thrashed. Chickens were all around us, screeching and pecking and gobbling as if they'd gone crazy, and Mrs. Malek in a rush of black skirts was running out with a broom, yelling in Bohemian, while Kazmir and I stood among the beating wings, trying to kick dirt over the guts as if stamping out flames.

Trains at Night

Alberto Alvaro Ríos

MR. LEE, as he transferred chicken feed from the large bin to his everyday pitcher, noticed how the dust rose from the seeds, how steam rises from a landscape, cold, or hot from a white cup of *café con leche,* how smoke rises from a casual backyard fire, how a soul is given up from a sick man. He did not take meaning from this, it was not instruction to him. He simply saw it.

However, when the soldiers came, he had wished possession of that capability, of effecting a rising beyond his own body, of leaving it for them to take, and thereby not feeling what they would do to him, which was unimaginable.

He saw the moment of his imagined escape everywhere, in everything, in the rising of smoke from a cigarette, in a flock of sparrows taking flight. Even, he thought, in the sound of a song let go from the mouth, a whistled aria. That a note of music should take its rightful place with the birds.

He wished it equally for all of them, but his wish did not work very well. The soldiers rounded up all the Chinese they could find, in a day and a night, without warning or manners, without explanation, by neighbor's direction and by rumor and by store sign. Who could have thought this is what would happen, said the townspeople afterward.

But a soldier is a soldier, and who could say *no* to a soldier's voice. A brown suit like that takes a man, and turns him into his parts. He is nobody's son anymore.

They are always there, without birth and without death, these soldiers. Nobody could say where a soldier comes from. Or who his teachers are, or what they must look like. Where are manners such that a loud step, a stiff neck, a salute in place of the rightful shaking of a hand, are marks of grace. Without the hand offered, where is the chance of agreement. Where is the chance of understanding what another has been through by the feeling of roughness in his palm.

Mr. Lee was married with his body and in his heart for a thousand years to Jesusita, married because of, he would shrug his shoulders, who can say. It was like the workings, the intestines, of an opera, he would suggest, and were they not, the two of them, worthy singers in the plot. She would shake her head at him and say she did not understand.

But she did. Not in the way he said it, but she understood in some other way, in the words spoken by his face, clearly what he said.

Mr. Lee was glad that she herself was not Chinese, today. He was glad that she did not look like she needed to be taken away to the trains. He was glad that she did not look like she could profit from a stay in the place where the train would go. Wherever that was, and whatever it meant. To the landscape at the end of the tracks.

And Mr. Lee was glad that his daughters looked like their mother. That he had not given them on their faces a ticket for the train, had not attached it to them so that they would not lose it, the way one might pin a child's mitten to his jacket. In that way, he was happy not to have been able to provide for them. To have been an unfit father, only in this way. Only today.

The twenties were over now and things had seemed to be getting better, the Revolution, the Depression: it was all over. But to climb out of something like that a country has to grab a hold of something else, some foothold to lift itself, something to step on. That is what this new decade was for, and that is what the Chinese were for, said the president.

Like Mr. Lee, he had said this not in regular words, but with some other part of himself. Something equally understandable, equally forceful.

These kinds of nights happen as one would imagine: the president gets indigestion after a meal of bad fish and spoiled butter, a suspect wheel of cheese. He tries to do something, he tries the carbonating powders.

And more. In pain he orders the arrest of all Chinese in the country and their deportation back to China. Who would complain, after all, or who would complain any louder than anyone else, since there were so many voices of complaint for so many things.

It could have been someone else, the Germans, or the Americans, but what was the use. People thought the Chinese were beginning to own everything, and there were just enough of them. In truth, it was that their store signs stood out so much, and their faces. In truth, which everybody knew, there were many other choices, but this one was the quickest.

There were the people in Alamos, for example, who lived next to the great silver mine. The ones who ran the operation, at home they had silver everything, silver broom covers, brooms themselves made of silver, and silver on the pillars holding up their houses. Anything to which silver might be added was fashionable there.

But to get them to give it up, well, it was a different thing.

His four daughters cried when they heard what was happening, and cried when they heard the soldiers getting closer. But Jesusita did what she could.

In those days the family lived in *Los Apóstoles*, twelve row houses, or rather, twelve row rooms, owned by Don Lázaro, who did not worry about things very much, and who when asked said that he most certainly did not rent to the Chinese. With what he charged, he said, one could hardly call it rent.

That there were twelve apartments gave rise to both the humor of the name and the mathematics of a problem. Since they were all built at once and were identical, if one problem arose, there were as if by magic twelve. It was a simple and devastating equation for Don Lázaro, who did not always put much stock in the laws of multiplication.

Through the years, each of these quarters began to take on an individual aspect, as Don Lázaro approached each problem as something different from the one before and the one after. He did not, after all, want to insult anyone by not giving them the consideration of listening to their particular problem. Nor, for that matter, did he wish to offend them by turning down a *café con leche* as he listened. He was a good listener, and sometimes he would offer to boil the milk for the second cup of coffee. And he gave each problem its own solution.

But at very least, twelve similar-looking yards occupied the space behind these apartments, each with a small fence, or some such barrier. And those who knew their own yard knew their neighbor's.

It was night by now, and as the soldiers came and knocked at the first house, Jesusita took her husband into the next yard, and so on down as the soldiers knocked in sequence, as only soldiers with their peculiar efficiency would do.

There were enough garbage cans and compost heaps, enough odd noises by dogs disturbed and grizzled cats, that Jesusita was able to move her husband with some ease. Not the least reason was the irregular rule of geometry, which stated that a small garbage heap was a large mountain to a lazy man. These soldiers were tired already from so much work in the afternoon, and without respite.

The seven soldiers in the vicinity did not equal one mother calling her child to dinner here. A mother knows how to find a child.

When the soldiers reached the last apartment, Jesusita, who had said she was bringing in laundry, brought her husband back to their rooms, and in through the back door.

His four daughters had said when the soldiers knocked that he was not there, and had not been there for some time, and that they did not know where he was or when he would return, and then shrugged their shoulders.

It figures, the lieutenant, or the captain, or whatever he was, had said, these Chinese, after all. He had a deep voice, too loud.

The daughters said nothing and went about their business, and at that cue the soldier harrumphed and did the same, saying something vague, If you see him, well, you know then, call us, and the daughters replied also with something vague, Of course, all right, then.

When they left, Jesusita brought her husband in and they all helped to hide him inside the cabinet of the radio, a Ward's "Airline" model, with the word *Heterodyne* underneath. It was a brown piece of furniture, part Greek columns and part lyre in decoration. Before they moved the radio back against the wall, they all looked at him, with the radio tubes and wires all above his head.

He looked like something from the movies, something from a Saturday morning, and they wanted to laugh and cry at the same time. And they heard him say, This cannot be happening. And as they looked at him, they saw that he was right. This was not like doing the laundry or preparing the evening meal. This was nothing they knew. This was after all something from the movies. But it was as if the manager had locked the doors of the theater, and they had to live with this beast.

No one saw Mr. Lee for many years. He did not live here anymore, his family said. But they were not sad. He lived in between the bed sheets and in the bathroom. He fit into the small spaces of the house, and did not eat much.

The soldiers never came back to look for him, but then again there was nothing to look for. Everyone in the town knew that he had disappeared. A pity, they would say, *qué lástima*. He was such a smart man.

But times changed, and every now and then people saw him, slowly.

They were not surprised. They understood something of how a thing could happen and not happen. There had been nothing in the newspapers or on the radio about that singular night. They understood how Mr. Lee could be gone and still be here. There was no mystery in seeing something that did not exist. The government had taught them well, and they were good citizens. There were, they knew, many kinds of ghosts.

The rounding up of the Chinese lasted only the one night, as long as the president's heartburn. They loaded them, as people later told one another even in public, into boxcars and open cattle and cotton cars. All over the country the soldiers looked, but especially along the border, where they might have been heard, so many voices, such a different language.

Many of the wives who had grown up in this town went with their men, to live in China. They took their children, too, and something or other in their arms. Some of them later came back, and some did not. They were not treated well. But such a thing was not a new life, and they were used to it. Being treated well was not much of a measure for anything anymore.

Not all of the Chinese left, however, and Mr. Lee was not the only one to be hidden. Some men had been dressed like women, and like animals, which was a gypsy trick. And none of them was seen for many years. There was a yipping at the moon some nights during this time, recognizable as coyotes in any other decade, but some townspeople said it was the Chinese. By this they did not mean that they were still in the animal disguises they had worn, but, rather, it was a remark about the quality of voice they heard.

It was a sound reminiscent of the German man, Mr. Luder, whose wife Margarita had died in childbirth along with the child. In the daytime he had a business in clocks, something regular, but every night he slept on the grave of his wife and child, and he wept.

The business later failed, and all he could do was to sleep on that stone and dirt, or walk around the town getting ready to sleep. This walking toward sleep became his job. People, in fact, had sometimes heard Mr. Luder's sobbing, and thought it was coyotes, and later the sounds of the Chinese. It was a sound many animals shared.

Some time later, as many Chinese had made their way up into Arizona, some of them would be mistaken again, this time for Japanese, and taken away once more. But they were returned. Again without the courtesy of manners.

When the government later rounded up the Yaqui Indians, they did it the other way around. They could not capture the men. But the women and children who came down from the mountains to trade goods were easy enough to take.

This time they put the women in trains, the old trick of how to catch the men, and sent them to the Yucatán just like that. Traveling was dangerous then, as the Yaquis took up the attacking of all the trains in the region. The Yaquis, many people said, were vicious.

Mr. Lee, the townspeople remarked regularly, was very smart, but by smart they meant a great deal more, which they could not say. He was rumored not so much to be Chinese, but to have had a gypsy father himself, who had shown him the ways of other worlds, who had given him the singular ability to live well in a radio. By now they had heard the story of that night from Jesusita. In our radio, she said to them, looking like a Martian.

Everyone had laughed when Jesusita told the story, but not too hard. Of course, they thought, with a look each to the other. Of course. He was not, after all, of this place.

When he walked along the path between the black walnut trees lining the streets, it was clear now that he had made his place. That the government had not been able to take him, no matter what the law.

That he, because of his head that lit up with tubes, knew something more than the law.

They laughed, but not too hard, and they called on him for advice when they were in trouble, because he would understand. They were a little scared of him, of course, because he knew something about things. He knew the underbelly and the tomorrow and yesterday of things, he knew their opposites and their half-turns. He knew the radio, after all, from the inside out.

He was like Mr. Luder, they sometimes said. He knew about life. He knew about it as if he had walked the perimeter of a park, and thereby gauged something of the dimensions of a neat lawn and the heights of the eucalyptus trees.

And his pronunciation of words, unlike the laws of the presidents, never changed, a little stilted even after so many years, a little wrong: it showed that he understood their language better than they did, that he spoke correctly. There was something wrong in this place and in these days, and they heard it in Mr. Lee's accent. He would talk, strangelike, and they knew he was right, about anything, about the weather.

The *wedder,* he would say, and they would understand. And when he smoked, they would think they sometimes saw him in the cloud.

Still Life

Marjorie Waters

THE WOMAN STANDING at the right is Alice Fitzsimons Coffey. Those in the portrait with her knew her as Allie, but I think of her as Mama. Her black hair is pulled away from her face and secured at the crown of her head. Her mouth is straight, and her cheeks, even in this old sepia print, are visibly flushed. She is wearing a dark, floor-length dress, with high collar and long sleeves. At the neckline is a small pin, its center a diamond, with tiny pearls set into gold filigree. I know this pin well. Mama gave it to my mother, who gave it to me, still in the velvet-lined box that held it when my grandfather bought it as a gift for his new wife.

I never knew Mama. She grew old and died before I was born. At the time of this portrait she is about the age that I am now and like me she has a new baby, the first, a son.

Mama's brother stands beside her, a young man with a soft, fleshy face and short hair, parted on the side and combed back from his forehead in a loose wave. He is wearing a black suit and vest, a white shirt with a stiff collar. I believe his name is George, and that the young man to his right is Edward, but I am never certain which brother is which. They lived and worked together, bachelors all their lives, and they so often traveled as a pair in my mother's stories that their names are forever linked in my mind. In photographs of them in middle age, they are altogether alike. Georgeandedward. Edwardandgeorge.

But in this old print the brothers are young still, and different from each other. The one I believe to be Edward is far handsomer. Though the two are dressed all but identically in dark suits, Edward's bow tie bears a straightforward white stripe. He wears his thick hair parted in the middle, a style that combines with the strength and symmetry of his features to make him seem perfectly sewn together. Edward looks fully at the camera's lens, the barest hint of a smile on his lips, while George is focused slightly to one side, wistful and distracted. Much as they matched in later life, as young men the two brothers are quiet opposites: candor and avoidance, resolution and doubt.

Sitting in front of Edward is his sister, Anna Fitzsimons, at around the age of thirty. Of all these faces, hers is the strongest, with her eyes locked hard on the camera and her chin raised. She leans forward slightly, as if she were holding steady against an unseen wind. She wears a dark dress that covers all but hands and head. Over her left breast is pinned a gold watch. (Half a century later, when adults thought I was asleep, I often crept to my mother's bureau, to the drawer where she kept old family treasures, and fingered this watch in the darkness. Sometimes I held the cool, round thing pressed in my hands and sat on the floor, watching shadows move across the wallpaper as cars drove by smooth and slow. And sometimes I opened the hinged doors of the watch and stared at the works in the dim light. I wound the watch and shook it, but I never made it tick, not even when I used a pencil point to urge the tiny wheels to life.)

When Anna was nearly forty, she married a man named Horace, who was then over seventy. Her father disapproved, everyone disapproved, first of the marriage, then of the birth of two sons. But Horace was more than ninety when he died, and he saw both boys into manhood. Anna lived another twenty years without him, and it was during this time that I knew her. I was very young and Anna—I knew her as Auntie—was a tiny old woman, pale as chalk. She still lived in the house that she and Horace had shared as newlyweds, and I visited her there frequently with my mother. I would sit on one of Auntie's ancient chairs and listen silently while the women talked and laughed together as if there were nothing to be afraid of in that house. Sometimes I would walk back to the kitchen to stare at the dented tin cup that hung by its handle over the sink. I imagined Auntie's thin lips, drinking, and frail as she was I could never account for the battered condition of that cup.

Yet here is Auntie as she was, as Anna. Beautiful, strong, almost defiant. And it is her face, her remarkable young face, that draws me to the others here.

At the far right, sitting in front of Mama, is her father, Thomas Fitz-simons, a slim, handsome man with a white moustache and a rim of soft white hair around his head. There is among the family photographs only one other of Thomas, taken thirty years earlier: a head-and-shoulders miniature framed in gilded tin. It is one of thousands of such photographs taken of returning Union soldiers. As a young man his hair was full and dark, but the faces in the two photographs are so much alike that it seems that half of his lifetime passed in a blink.

In this group portrait, Thomas sits in a wicker chair that seems too large for him. He looks dry and thin and ready to shatter. To his right is his wife, Rose Clark Fitzsimons. She is the portrait's center and the reason it exists. Her dress is dark over her large frame, her mouth drawn downward, her eyes focused into a distance only she can see. She is dying. This portrait is the last record of her life.

Rose Clark, my great-grandmother, was born in Ireland and was still a small child when famine claimed her parents and orphaned her and her two older brothers. The children were taken in by neighbors, a family named Gilmore, and they came with them to the small town in upstate New York where Rose would spend her life. (And where her children, and her children's children—every generation until my own—would spend theirs.) Rose remained with her adopted family until 1865, when she married a former soldier with a dark moustache. They bought a house, raised four children, and gathered for this farewell portrait when Rose Clark Fitzsimons was not yet sixty.

I was a child when I saw this photograph for the first time. It was one of dozens my mother kept in a box on a shelf. One day she showed them to me, in all their disarray, infants of one generation face to face with their own grandchildren. Everyone, at every age, thrown together in a jumble, like the memories of a lifetime. She spread them out on her bed and we looked at them, one by one. She had stories for all of them; she filled the day with Mama and George and Auntie and the rest.

The photographs are mine now. I keep them in a box on a shelf, all in a jumble. Except for this fine old portrait, nearly a century old, which hangs over my desk where I can see it as I work. I often find myself watching these faces. I can feel their held breath, the warmth of their skin, the softness of the fabric they wear. And I can see them altogether that morning, hear their footsteps in the small clapboard house on the corner. Grown sons and daughters, once again in their childhood rooms, wordlessly dress in dark clothes, brush their hair.

Rose, in a white cotton sleeping gown, takes Thomas's arm as she rises from her bed. Alice and Anna come into the room to help her dress. Downstairs, George and Edward, ready too soon, wait with their hands in their pockets and look out separate windows. The carriage comes. The boys help their mother into the clear morning air. The ride down Bridge Street is slow and easy, the horse kept to a walk.

In the studio, Rose is seated first. She smooths the folds of her skirt as the others take their places around her. They raise their faces to the camera's eye and draw close together, shoulder to shoulder and arm to arm. Anna rests her hand on her mother's knee. They are ready. The shutter moves and holds them in the moment when the family is whole, and woven together by touch.

Geese

Joyce Carol Oates

YEARS AGO on a Sunday afternoon in late October Hetty and her mother's boyfriend Dyan Trumball—the one who played acoustical guitar with a local band—were walking in the lakeside park a few miles from Hetty's mother's house. Hetty was thirteen years old at the time with a narrow face and dark warm watchful eyes—so nervously quick to smile it looked, sometimes, her mother said, as if she was smiling with just her mouth and didn't mean it at all. She was tall too for her age which made her self-conscious in public, particularly self-conscious when she believed she might be watched. At least with Dyan, who always walked fast and tended to forget Hetty was with him, there was no reason to feel she was being watched. Like an eager little dog she trotted on after.

Dyan lived with Hetty's mother now that Hetty's father was gone, as they said, for good—"for good and good riddance" in Hetty's mother's words—working somewhere in Texas, on the Gulf. But there was no ill will between Hetty's father and Dyan—the two men had been friends for years and just last summer, when he'd known, maybe, he was going to leave, Hetty's father asked Dyan and two of Dyan's friends to help him paint the house. Hetty didn't love Dyan the way she loved her father but she'd taught herself not to think about her father the way she'd taught herself not to think about certain things she knew would not make her happy and were beyond her powers of change—death, for instance, and what exactly happens to the body after death, that sort of ugly awful helpless thing. In any case Hetty's father was *there* and Dyan was *here* and, as Hetty's mother liked to say, you sure can't argue with the principle of the bird in the hand and the bird in the bush. Hetty was clever enough to guess what that meant without needing to ask.

That day, it was sunny and bright but so cold their breaths steamed. A mile out on Lake Ontario a freighter passed in the choppy water trailing smoke the color of lead. Back at the house Dyan had been restless, taking up his guitar and putting it down, switching on the television and switching it off, asked as he often did on Sundays did anyone want to go for a ride? — and Hetty said yes, and there was a pause when Hetty's mother might have been going to say yes but didn't. Hetty's mother and Dyan had been quarreling that morning, early, in what was very likely a carry-over from a quarrel of the night before, and Hetty sensed with a shiver of dread and pleasure that they weren't over it yet. She'd learned that when men and women quarreled in a certain way the part of it that was words was just what you could hear; what you couldn't hear was deeper, not talked about, like an underground stream that flowed, in secret, where it wanted. There was something about this fact, or her knowledge of it, that excited her immensely — but also, she supposed, meanly. She liked it that her mother wasn't with them; that, in her mother's absence, she could sit in the front seat of Dyan's flashy car; that, seen together tramping in the park, she and Dyan might be mistaken for father and daughter. There were classmates of Hetty's who had never seen her father, for instance, and who wouldn't have known who Dyan was.

In summer the park would have been crowded on a Sunday afternoon but today it seemed to be deserted. Hetty heard noises from somewhere along the shore but couldn't see anyone. There'd been only one other car in the parking lot, a low-slung fenderless Ford painted robin's-egg blue and striped in mustard yellow like a racing car. "Some friend of yours?" Hetty had asked in her sarcastic drawl but Dyan hadn't risen to the bait. He hadn't troubled to answer her at all.

Dyan's car was a white Corvette he'd bought second- or third-hand from a friend. The fenders were speckled with rust like gunshot and the car wasn't exactly in A-1 condition—it had survived, Dyan said, a pretty serious accident—but still it looked good: stylish, fancy. Parked in the driveway at Hetty's house, or in the asphalt lot at the park, it looked foreign as an exotic bird.

Dyan was walking ahead as if he'd forgotten Hetty was with him. Climbing the hill in his Cuban-heeled leather boots, impatient, nerved-up, hands shoved in the pockets of his sheepskin jacket. He wasn't a tall man though when he performed with his band he looked tall, and imposing. He had narrow shoulders and slender hips, a glide to his walk that Hetty thought snaky, fascinating. (Whereas Hetty's mother, who'd gained fifteen pounds in the past year—no she was *not* pregnant, if it was anyone's business—walked heavily, it seemed angrily, so that you could feel the floorboards in the house vibrate.) In public Dyan always looked good, with his pomaded hair and smooth-shaven jaws and lustrous thick-lashed eyes, but the rest of the time he didn't trouble to dress with much care. He'd go days without shaving or even washing and wore his long graying-black hair fastened at the nape of his neck with a clip belonging to an ex-girlfriend. (Unless he said that to tease Hetty's mother.) No one could be sweeter and nicer than Dyan Trumball most of the time but he was given to brusque, seemingly impulsive moves when distracted by thoughts or by music playing in his head.

Unlike Hetty's father, Dyan didn't have a really bad temper but he nursed hurts and grudges for days at a stretch so if you tried to joke with him during one of these spells he'd turn a cold uncomprehending drop-dead stare on you. He's in a world of his own, Hetty's mother said, sometimes resentful and sometimes admiring: if there was any difference, Hetty thought, between the two. It seemed there was a place men had access to, like a special key to a room, that women didn't, and if they went there you couldn't follow them and when they came back you didn't know where they'd been except you knew that they'd been gone and were ready to go back or in some way still there and there was nothing you could do about it.

The park was the site of a Revolutionary War battle: Hetty had studied it in sixth grade but had forgotten most of the men's names. There was a historical museum, closed today, and there was a row of cannon overlooking the lake, and, here and there in the scrubby, hilly ground, you could see the ruins of the old fort—crumbled stone and concrete overgrown with moss. It was a bright bitter-green, the moss, soft to the touch—Hetty couldn't resist stooping to touch it—as velvet. "This is viridian green, this color," she told Dyan, "this color here." Dyan looked back at her, startled as if she'd interrupted him in the midst of deep ponderous thoughts. He tried not to show the annoyance he probably felt—his girlfriend's teenaged daughter showing off for his benefit.

"It's *what?*" he said.

"Viridian green. This shade of green," Hetty said importantly. "It's a painter's color."

"Is it," Dyan said. He'd taken out a pack of Camels but was having trouble lighting one in the wind. The stubble on his jaws gave him a soiled, gritty look that suited him, Hetty thought; you weren't so apt to notice his receding chin. He smiled at her now, humoring her. "You studying to be a painter?"

Hetty was taking a course in art at the junior high school but for some reason she shook her head quickly, no. "It's just sort of interesting, colors, if you know what they are—their special names. Then you start seeing them. Like those clouds there, that's rose madder. And yellow ocher in the rocks. Ultramarine, that's the color of the lake on clear days." (Though perhaps she meant cobalt blue, not ultramarine. She'd forgotten which was which.) "But it's really just the reflection of the sky," she said. "It isn't the color in itself. Things aren't there in themselves, did you know that?—really weird. They're only reflecting other things."

Dyan looked skeptical. "If one thing's just reflecting some other thing, how the hell does any of it get *started?*"

"There's theories—different kinds of scientific theories. I don't know what all they are." Hetty's voice trailed off in a way that meant, in their household, please don't ask any more questions. All she'd been saying sounded like nonsense in her own ears.

Dyan managed to light his cigarette and began climbing to the top of the hill and Hetty followed thinking, Little dog, little dog, hurry on after. She felt herself suffused with hatred even as her narrow uplifted face radiated love.

They were above the lake on a high windswept embankment edged with scrubby evergreens and trees too attenuated and sickly to have names. In summer this area was overgrown with wildflowers—Hetty had a vague dreamy memory of, years ago, when she was a little girl, helping her mother pick flowers here, buttercups, Queen Anne's lace, chicory that's so tough and fibrous to break by hand. The wildflower bouquet hadn't lasted long even though Hetty's mother put it in water as soon as they got back home.

Hetty said, "It's beautiful here, isn't it!" breathless and smiling but Dyan only shrugged. He was shading his eyes, squinting as if the whitish light hurt. Looking out over the lake toward the Canadian shore but even on a clear day the horizon was vague and fuzzy as cotton batting.

You *are* in a rotten mood, Hetty thought. But Dyan's rotten moods, unlike her mother's, were of interest. He'd only been living with them for a month or so and there were many things about him not yet known to Hetty.

Dyan threw a stone out over the cliff—wound up and threw, it looked to Hetty, as hard as he could—but the stone didn't go very far. The wind was blowing in their faces. He rubbed his arm muscle and made a joke about being out of condition, too much partying, smoking. "Your mother was supposed to reform me, *she* said," he laughed, "but she's doing a hell of a poor job of it." He didn't look at Hetty. He might have been talking to himself by way of her as, sometimes, Hetty's mother did too. Or did they talk to each other by way of her?

They tramped along the path almost side by side. Hetty watched Dyan out of the corner of her eye, wondering was he thinking of leaving them too; and if he did, what then; what would happen to Hetty's mother then. So far as Hetty knew there was nothing so legal as a "divorce" or even a "separation" but her father was not coming back and that, as Hetty's mother said, was that. She worked as a cocktail waitress at a restaurant just off the interstate highway and it wasn't a bad job as such jobs go—that was how she met Dyan Trumball, for instance—but she didn't make much money and never would: it was the kind of job, Hetty's mother said, that you know by looking at the costume you have to wear, it's a dead end. She talked of taking courses at the local community college, bookkeeping, accounting, office management, but months went by, and years, and it was never quite the right time. With Dyan helping to pay the rent she didn't need to think about such things.

They were lucky about their house: a farmhouse rented cheap from a relative of Hetty's mother.

For some time Dyan and Hetty had been hearing noises—shouts, shrieks, laughter—that might have been a radio turned up high in the stillness of the park. That, and the sound of the waves below. The source of the commotion turned out to be a group of teenage boys who were pitching things down into the lake from the top of the embankment. The boys were loud and jeering and excited about something in a way that made Hetty's heart clench: if she'd been alone she would have turned in the opposite direction but Dyan kept right on as if the rowdiness didn't trouble him, or he was curious to see what the noise meant.

It was a small flock of Canada geese at which the boys were throwing things—the nearly tame geese who lived along the lake shore most of the year. What a sight!—the birds were panicked, helpless, flapping their wings and paddling in circles making desperate honking noises as the boys bombarded them. Hetty couldn't understand why the geese didn't fly away; then she saw there were goslings among them, too young to fly. The adults couldn't fly to safety and leave the goslings but they were unable to protect them from the attack. The young geese were about the size of mourning doves but still undeveloped, vulnerable. It looked as if several had been struck by objects, were injured, or dying. Hetty gave a little scream, tugging frantically at Dyan's arm. "Dyan, make them stop," she said, beginning to cry, "please make them stop." Dyan said nothing; just stood there, hesitant, paralyzed; watching.

Hetty recognized two or three of the boys, from town. They were older, about sixteen. They'd been drinking beer; beer cans floated and bobbed in the choppy waves below, amidst the terrified geese. One of the boys, thickset and stocky, with a haircut so brutally short it might have been done by a razor, gave a ludicrous high-pitched yodel as he pitched a clump of dried mud over the side of the embankment. It looked to Hetty that one of the goslings was struck by it—must have been killed instantaneously.

Dyan cupped his hands to his mouth and called out, "You. Hey. What are you doing?" He was about fifty feet from the boys and didn't seem to want to go any closer. When they saw he wasn't a policeman, didn't have any authority, one of them cupped his hands to his mouth and called back something mean and derisive Hetty didn't quite hear. The others laughed quick and harsh and mirthless and Dyan said sharply, "*Stop* what you're doing—you throw another rock and you're in trouble." His voice was weaker than Hetty was used to hearing it and his face was unevenly flushed, as if sunburnt.

The boy with the close-shaved head said, "Fuck you, mister, you and your girlfriend—" and, swaggering, tossed a final rock at the geese. "It's a free country," he said, wiping his hands on his thighs.

"You heard me—" Dyan said. But the wind was blowing his words away.

The boys edged off, though, jeering and insolent, and Hetty felt her heart beat in loathing of them, how she hated them! could have wished *them* dead! The geese kept up their panicked wing-flapping and honking, turning in circles; Hetty could see the body of a dead gosling bobbing in the debris. "Oh look," she cried, "Dyan, just look!" Tears spilled out of her eyes and ran down her face with alarming swiftness.

Dyan stood stone-still staring not after the boys but where they'd been standing. Where the boy with the shaved head had stood, delivering his insult.

"*Don't* look," he said.

He was breathing quickly. His breath steamed in little quick-fading puffs.

Hetty wanted to slide down the embankment—it was about fifteen feet to a narrow rocky beach—to see if there was anything that could be done. Dyan said angrily, "For Christ's sake *no*. Those geese will attack you. Peck your eyes out." He pulled her back roughly. "Anyway, what can you do? There's nothing you can do."

"If there's some babies that are wounded I could take them to the vet," Hetty said. "We could take them—"

"I said no."

"We—"

"*No.*"

Hetty saw that Dyan's face was flushed with embarrassment and shame. He was so rattled he did something she'd never seen him do, and rarely saw anyone do except old men, or derelicts—he bent at the waist and blew his nose between his fingers, shaking the mucus off onto the ground.

They walked on as if not knowing, or caring, where they went. Hetty heard Dyan muttering to himself like a drunken man—"little bastards," "little fuckers"—though to her way of thinking the boys weren't exactly little. The oldest was probably taller than Dyan, and a good deal heavier.

Behind them the geese were still upset. A human noise almost—frightened, furious, baffled. Hetty said, "I don't know how anybody can be so *mean,* even sons of bitches like that," liking the rough crude texture of the profanity which she wouldn't have dared utter in her mother's presence. She said, her voice catching in a small sob, "I wish they'd be arrested—wish somebody would kill *them.*"

Dyan stopped to light another cigarette, taking shelter behind a tree. Without wanting to, Hetty noted that his hands were trembling. She said again, "—wish somebody would kill *them.* Throw rocks on *them.*" It was a child's rage and Dyan didn't respond.

Later he said in a vague speculative voice, "Those geese—I don't think any of them were really hurt. I think we came along in time."

"Some of the babies—"

"I think we came along in time."

Hetty stared at him. "Some of the babies were hurt. The goslings. You saw it."

"They were too far out to be hit," Dyan said. As if they'd been arguing this point for some time he'd become abrupt, impatient. "They were just scared."

Hetty said slowly, "That's a lie. You saw it just like I did."

"Are you calling me a liar?"

"You saw it just like I did."

Dyan said calmly, smiling, "I am not lying, sweetheart. I don't lie." His teeth, bared, were small and even but slightly discolored. "You're mixing me up with somebody else, maybe—your daddy, maybe. I don't lie."

"Some of the babies were hurt and one of them was killed—I saw it," Hetty said fiercely.

"You're making too much of it. There's too many Canada geese anyway—shitting up things so you don't know where to walk."

"You're a liar."

"I told you—I don't lie."

Hetty thought, I will never speak to you again.

When they returned to the parking lot there the boys were standing around the blue jalopy, talking loudly, laughing, finishing up their supply of beer. The pavement was littered with cans. Dyan's Corvette was parked at the far end of the lot and in the raw clear autumn light it looked startlingly white.

The boys had not seen them, yet. Or gave no sign of seeing them.

Dyan hesitated, not knowing what to do—continue on to his car as if nothing was wrong, or hang back waiting for the boys to leave. The jalopy's four doors were all open but it looked as if the boys were in no hurry to get in. Their laughter cut through the park's stillness, sharp-edged as a hacksaw.

Hetty wanted Dyan to wait—what if the boys threw rocks at them? There was no one else around. Dyan stood motionless for what seemed like a long time but was probably no more than a minute. He ignored Hetty's whispers, shook off her hand on his arm. Finally he took his car keys out of his pocket and, with no word to Hetty, walked to his car stiff and quick and with his shoulders slightly hunched as if he hoped to take up as little space as possible.

Hetty hadn't any choice but to follow after him, her heart beating hard. She saw the boys watching them now. Staring openly. That shaved-head boy whose name she halfway knew—some crudely appropriate name like Bullard, Bullit. She didn't want to look at the boys too obviously and she surely didn't want them to look at her.

Dyan unlocked the passenger's door, purse-lipped. "Get in," he said. Hetty climbed in and Dyan slammed the door behind her. As he crossed to unlock the driver's door Hetty saw something flying overhead—a beer can thrown by one of the boys that sailed past the car and landed in the grass a short distance away. It was far enough away not to have been aimed at Dyan, exactly.

Dyan climbed in the driver's seat and jammed the key in the ignition. He was extremely agitated, Hetty saw; *she* was agitated; sitting very still and small, her buttocks contracted, her chilled fingers clasped tight in her lap. She was wearing a corduroy jacket and jeans, old clothes, and paint-splattered running shoes. Her long hair was windblown and snarled. She thought, they weren't looking at me, there is no reason for them to look at me. A second beer can flew past the car, landing in the grass; closer this time. There were raucous yodeling yells. "Filthy cocksucking sons of bitches," Dyan was saying in a low furious frightened voice, "filthy shiteating little *cunts*," which Hetty knew was the worst thing, the nastiest thing, a man could think to say.

A beer can struck the pavement and rolled clattering past the car.

Dyan backed the Corvette around jerkily, breathing so hard Hetty worried something was wrong with him. He sounded like Hetty's mother or like Hetty herself about to burst into tears. She could see the boys looking after them, loutish and jeering. It was like a scene in a movie, or on television: what would happen next? The one with the shaved head took several quick steps forward in a mock-attack, waving his arms and shouting something unintelligible. Hetty was so worked up her teeth had begun to chatter. "I just wish you had a *gun*," she said. "My daddy would have a *gun*."

Dyan pushed her roughly down on the car seat. She wouldn't ever know why—to hide her from the boys? But the boys had already seen her. To punish her for what she'd said? That made no sense either but things were happening so swiftly, Dyan was so rattled, it might have been the reason. As soon as he was out of the park, and safe, Hetty sat up, furious, brushing her hair out of her face. "Damn you, don't you touch me, you," she said. "You *coward*."

Dyan drove for a half-hour or more in no particular direction, turning up country roads, pressing down hard on the accelerator, using the brakes, muttering obscenities under his breath. He might have been alone, he didn't so much as glance at Hetty. She could hear his breath, still, and feel the heat coming off him — the damp tremulous heat of a dog's breath.

She wiped her face with a Kleenex and blew her nose. Said in a low accusing voice, "You *know* they killed those babies. You saw it plain as I did." She paused. Heartbeat about to trip: danger, delicious. *"Coward."*

Dyan was driving now at a normal speed. Heading home. Both hands gripping the steering wheel and the knuckles drained of blood. His face, thin in profile, with the delicate receding chin, was drained of blood too except for the crude flush on his cheeks. Coward, Hetty thought. She *did* hate him now — she knew him, now. And there would always be that knowledge between them.

But when he turned up the road to her mother's house a ramshackle farmhouse, painted a light cheery yellow — he began whistling. Said, "You maybe got the wrong impression of me back there. It's errone- ous, whatever you're thinking." Hetty was sitting as far away from him as she could. As they turned in the drive she squinted to see if her mother was watching at the window. (She wasn't.) "I wouldn't shoot my mouth off if I was you," Dyan said. He was trying to joke — maybe — but the words came out mean and threatening. Hetty had her fingers closed around the door handle waiting for the car to slow just enough for her to make her escape.

But Dyan was too quick. He grabbed her shoulder, gave her a good hard shake. She screamed, protecting her face with her arms, and, as effortlessly as if he were breaking a kitten's neck, he sent her flying against the door — a blow that knocked the breath out of her. "You better not call anyone 'coward' too many times again," he said, "and you better not tell your momma any far-fetched lies. Like about this either — got it?"

Hetty opened the door and ran.

A few days later Hetty returned to the park, alone, on her way home from school. The Canada geese were gone from that stretch of beach but there were geese elsewhere, and goslings, paddling in the cold choppy water. Every year there were geese along the lake shore, hope-

ful of being fed by visitors and tourists, every year more geese. Hetty
squatted on the embankment watching them. By her first count there
were fourteen goslings, by her second count fifteen. Clumsy little
things, bobbing in the water behind their mothers. Were they the same
geese the boys had attacked? Did it matter? The geese were inter-
changeable, and their goslings.

The adults regarded her with some suspicion but did not paddle
away. Handsome birds, so much thicker-bodied than you might
think—nearly the size of swans, with the swan's high-held head and
slender snaky neck. Their heads were black—matte black. And their
necks. But their bodies were a smooth gray the color of pewter. Broad
round-tipped bills, small indistinct eyes. Hetty wondered could they
see very well. Could they see colors. Could they smell danger? In their
world they must be long accustomed to abrupt changes of fortune—
windfalls of bread or seed, or deadly barrages of rocks. If you hope for
one you will have to resign yourself, sometimes, to the other.

She never told her mother, of course. That time or any other.

Biographical Notes

Linda Bamber is an Associate Professor of English at Tufts University. She has published fiction, poetry, journalism, and a book on Shakespeare entitled *Comic Women, Tragic Men*.

Rick Bass is most recently the author of *The Ninemile Wolves*, as well as four other books of natural history and a story collection, *The Watch*. He lives in Montana and is working on a novel.

Ann Beattie's most recent collection of stories is *What Was Mine* (Random House).

Louis Berney is the author of *The Road to Bobby Joe and Other Stories*, published in 1991 by Harcourt Brace Jovanovich. His stories have appeared in *The New Yorker, Story, The Antioch Review, Quarterly West*, and elsewhere. He is currently at work on a novel.

Gina Berriault is under contract to Pantheon Books for a new collection of short stories. Her most recent collection is *The Infinite Passion of Expectation*.

Ethan Canin has published *Emperor of the Air* (short stories) and *Blue River* (novel), and is completing a new collection of stories for Random House. An M.D., he is currently doing an internship and living in California.

Andre Dubus's most recent book is *Broken Vessels* (Godine).

Stuart Dybek's most recent collection of stories is *The Coast of Chicago*. He teaches in the writing program at Western Michigan University.

Tess Gallagher's collection of stories, *The Lover of Horses,* has been reissued in paperback by Graywolf Press.

Gordon Jackson teaches at Moorhead State University and is working on a novel. A graduate of the Iowa Writers' Workshop, he has published stories in *Sudden Fiction, American Fiction 88,* and *Quarterly West,* among others.

Wayne D. Johnson grew up in Minnesota and lived for many years in the west. His stories have appeared in *The Atlantic, Story,* and other magazines. In 1990, his novel *The Snake Game* (Knopf and Bodley Head) was on the *London Times* bestseller list. A portion of the book was awarded an O. Henry prize.

Phillip Lopate is a novelist and essayist whose most recent book is *Against Joie de Vivre: Personal Essays* (Poseidon Press). He lives in Manhattan with his wife and teaches on the faculty at Bennington College.

David Wong Louie's first collection of short stories, *Pangs of Love* (Knopf, 1991), received the Ploughshares/Emerson College John C. Zacharis First Book Award and the Los Angeles Times Book Prize for First Fiction, The Art Seidenbaum Award.

Sue Miller has published three novels, *The Good Mother, Family Pictures,* and *For Love,* and one collection of short stories, *Inventing the Abbots.* She lives in Boston and is editing a fiction issue of *Ploughshares.*

Joyce Carol Oates, who lives in Princeton, New Jersey, is the author most recently of *Black Water,* a novel; and *Where Is Here?,* a story collection.

Alberto Alvaro Ríos's most recent book is *Teodoro Luna's Two Kisses.* He is Director of the Creative Writing Program at Arizona State University and recently edited an issue of *Ploughshares* entitled *West Real.*

Carol Roh-Spaulding is working on a novel inspired by her Korean-American heritage and progressing toward a Ph.D. in English at the University of Iowa. She lives in the countryside with her cats Bodhi and Sattva.

Maura Stanton's book of stories, *The Country I Come From,* was published by Milkweed Editions in 1988. *Tales of the Supernatural,* her third book of poetry, was published by David R. Godine. She teaches at Indiana University in Bloomington.

Christopher Tilghman's first collection of stories is *In a Father's Place* (Farrar, Straus & Giroux, 1990). He lives outside Boston with his wife and two small sons.

Marjorie Waters is a writer of nonfiction for adults and children. She is currently at work on a family memoir.

Joy Williams has written three novels and two collections of short stories as well as essays on the environment and a guide to the Florida Keys. She lives in Tucson and Key West.

Theodore Weesner is the author of four novels and the recent collection of stories, *Children's Hearts* (Summit Books). He is Coordinator of the MFA in Creative Writing Program at Emerson College.